ClikByte # 1

NO FEAR

Also by Tate James

DEVIL'S BACKBONE

Dear Reader

Watch Your Back

You're Next

MADISON KATE

Hate

Liar

Fake

Kate

HADES

7th Circle

Anarchy

Club 22

Timber

NoFear
Noah Fearly

SkyeHigh
Skye Smith

Torasaurus.rex
Torin Mura

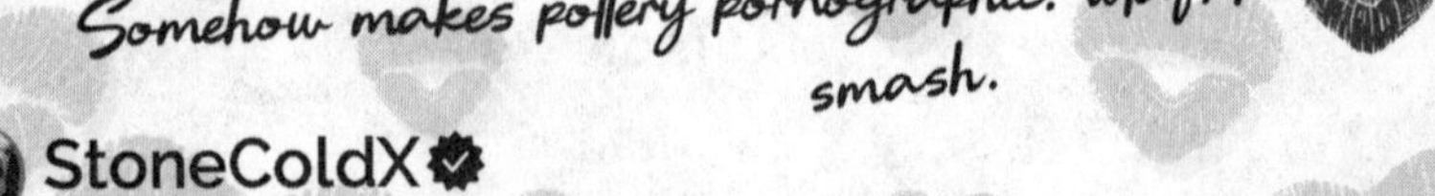

StoneColdX
Xavier Stone

Legit crushed on him since I was 13.
This is going to be so awkward.

July.September
August Gamble

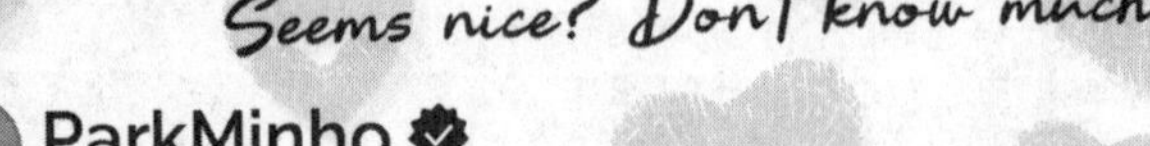

ParkMinho
Minho Park

Double smash.

AceofHarts
Ace Hart

Alpha Daddy
hot but totally intimidating
most likely to figure out my lies

mnizee
Zeth Briggs

Babe. No notes.

This book is dedicated to Steph, who selflessly put her life on hold to join me in a reckless, borderline obsessive, endlessly rewarding deep dive into the glittering world of SKZ. And all the A+ content associated. Looking at you EXchange Island, Kingdom, and SKZ Family 👀

Tate James

The characters and events portrayed in this book are fictitious or are used fictitiously. Any similarity to real persons, living or dead, is purely coincidental and not intended by the author.

Published by Bloom Books, an imprint of Sourcebooks
1935 Brookdale RD, Naperville, IL 60563-2773
(630) 961-3900
sourcebooks.com

Cataloging-in-Publication data is on file with the Library of Congress.

Printed and bound in the United States of America.
LSC 10 9 8 7 6 5 4 3 2 1

ClikByte # 1

NO FEAR

TATE JAMES

Bloom books

ONE

My brother could've died because of me. Might die, actually, because he's been in surgery for hours and we haven't heard a word.

That was the harsh reality on repeat inside my head as I sat in the hospital waiting room, desperately hoping and praying the doctor would return soon and tell me it would all be okay. That my big brother was going to be fine and I hadn't just almost killed him with my stupid, arrogant pursuit of my favorite drug.

Adrenaline.

I trembled as I curled into a ball in the plastic waiting room chair, wrapping my arms around my knees and torturing myself with the memory of the moment of impact.

The split-second look of horror on Miles's face when his foot slipped from that ledge. The suspended moment as he fell through the air. The sickening crunch of breaking bones when his body hit the hard-packed earth some fifty feet below us.

Heck, I didn't even need to imagine it. I'd caught the whole fucking thing on camera. It was supposed to be my latest and greatest stunt, and it ended in a puddle of blood and the piercing scream of ambulance sirens.

"Where's Rich?" I whispered to my manager, Jared, who was slumped in a chair next to me. "He should be here. Where is he?"

Jared blew out a long sigh, scrubbing his hands over his tired face, looking much older than his actual mid-thirties. "I dunno, kid. You're right, though. He should be here."

I nodded, then dropped my head back onto my knees.

Rich should *be here.*

Not only was he Miles's best friend, he was also my boyfriend. He was yesterday, anyway. We'd fought, and things hadn't ended well. But then he'd showed up for today's stunt like nothing had ever happened, like he hadn't told me we were *finished.*

And then Miles slipped.

"I don't understand," I whispered to Jared. "It was an easy climb. Miles can do stunts like that in his fucking sleep. How did this happen?"

It wasn't an exaggeration. Miles and I had been doing parkour since I was six and he was eight. We'd free-climbed even longer than that, if our mom was to be believed. Scaling the side of a construction site without ropes might have seemed insane to most people, but for us it was just a typical Tuesday.

Except Miles had never fallen before. He was better than that. I didn't care for the excuse that all humans were fallible. Miles wasn't. I wasn't. We were the best at what we did; it was why we were both millionaires before Miles even turned twenty.

Well, that and the creation of ClikByte, the social media platform that paid us per click, fueling my relentless pursuit of danger and adventure and paying me well in return. My profile—NoFear—was currently trending as one of the most clicked-on profiles worldwide. I was sitting in the Top Ten Influencers list with close to a hundred million subscribers clicking and watching my videos daily. Hourly.

And the best part? None of them had ever seen my face. Not on my profile, anyway, or Miles's. Rich was a whole other story, but I could only hope no one made the connection that the half-naked girl he was constantly featuring on his channel was really me.

NoFear.

That name perfectly captured the nature of my clips. Miles had always been eager to help me cultivate and satisfy my taste for danger. And now he was broken and in emergency surgery.

Fuck. Mom was going to murder me.

"Hey, how is he?" a familiar voice asked, and I jerked my tear-stained face up to glare at my boyfriend. Ex-boyfriend. Whatever the fuck he was.

"Where the hell have you been?" I demanded, accusing and

angry as hell. He'd fucking *disappeared* the second the ambulances had arrived on the construction site. That was hours ago.

Rich just frowned at me, like it was none of my fucking business where he'd been. "Babe, I had shit to do. How's Miles? Is he okay?"

I stared up at him in outrage. "Are you fucking serious right now?" My voice was just this side of a shriek, and Jared laid a hand on my arm, like that could come anywhere close to tempering my fury. "No, he's not *okay*, you selfish fuck! He just fell from the eighth floor of a building! He's in surgery, and they don't know if he'll make it. But fuck, Rich, if you've got *shit to do,* then by all means, fuck right off."

Rich was Miles's best friend and my first—and only—boyfriend, but he just shrugged like I was making him uncomfortable and scowled. "I didn't fucking push him, Noah," he snapped back at me, "but if you're going to be a bitch about it, I'm not sticking around."

"Rich, what the hell?" Jared exclaimed, giving him the same incredulous expression I was sure I wore. "You're so far out of line right now."

Rich just sneered at Jared, his handsome face twisting into something ugly. "Of course you're here, *Jared*. Taken any lingering glances down my girlfriend's shirt since you got here?" He let out a nasty sort of laugh. "Wait, stupid question. Of course you have."

Jared's jaw clenched, and he rose out of his seat to confront Rich's bullshit. "I get that you're upset about Miles, but insulting

Noah and me isn't going to make things any easier. You need to apologize to her."

Rich recoiled, looking disgusted, and I stifled a sigh. He was predictable as all hell, and he responded terribly to being confronted on *any* subject.

"Fuck you, Jared," he snapped back. I rolled my eyes. *Here we go.* "You don't tell me what to do. You're not *my* manager, remember?" He sneered the words at Jared, and I sighed heavily. It was an old argument between us, but it was the first time Jared was being exposed to it.

"Rich, shut up," I told him, my voice hard as I wrapped my arms tighter around myself. "Shut the fuck up, or go away. I don't need your insecure bullshit while my brother is fighting for his life."

His caramel eyes—the same ones I'd fallen head over heels for when I met him four years ago—turned to me, narrowed in rage. "Screw you, Noah. I deserve better than your drama."

I barked a humorless laugh. "That's ironic. Exit's that way, Rich. Don't bother coming back." I threw a hand in the direction of the sliding doors we'd run through hours ago.

My ex-boyfriend just scowled, and his eyes glittered with a meanness I hadn't fully realized he had within him—until recently, that is. Until my star started shining so much brighter than his, and he let jealousy eat away at his mental health.

"We're done, Noah. Fucking done. She's all yours, *Jared.*" He spat the words out, curling his lip in disgust. "Pro tip, she loves it in the ass."

My face flushed with embarrassment, and I gaped in shock as Rich stormed out of the hospital. *What in the actual, ever-loving fuck just happened?*

"I'm so freaking sorry," I whispered to Jared in a strangled voice. "I have no idea what his fucking problem is, but that was so far out of line, I—"

"Don't even worry about it, Noah," Jared told me with a sigh. "He never should have spoken to you like that. Are you okay?"

My breath hissed out, and I sank back into my seat like a deflated balloon. "Yeah," I replied, folding my arms under my breasts and hugging myself. "Yeah, it's just whatever. Rich has issues, and I'm done with letting him take it all out on me."

Jared sat back down beside me. "Good."

I arched a brow at him. "Good?"

He shrugged, his expression impassive. "Rich is a loose cannon. Toxic. You don't need him in your life, Noah. He's going nowhere fast and dragging you along for the ride."

My first instinct was to argue with him, but he was right. I was better off without Rich...but it didn't make my heart hurt any less. He was my first love, and watching him walk out of those hospital doors was goddamn heartbreaking, no matter how much it needed to happen.

"Fuck him," I mumbled, even as fresh tears poured down my cheeks. "He doesn't deserve me *or* Miles."

Jared sighed and placed his arm around my shoulders, pulling me close. "That's the spirit, kid."

I gave a bitter laugh but didn't argue. I couldn't. The tears were running too fast now. All I could do was sit there and cry. For my brother, for my broken heart, and for my future.

Jared's hug was friendly and caring, not creepy and inappropriate like Rich was always claiming. Rich thought any man that spoke to me did so to get in my pants—he had some serious jealousy issues and insecurity.

We sat like that for ages. My mom was out of the country on a business trip, so she probably wouldn't get my voicemail until she woke up. When she did, I was going to hear it.

Eventually Jared's phone buzzed in his pocket, and he wandered away to answer the call. That meant I was all alone when the doctor finally came out to update me on Miles's status.

My breath froze, and my heart sat in my throat as the doctor walked toward me, his face grim. I was so petrified, I couldn't move. I couldn't even stand up to speak with the doctor, who just crouched in front of my chair with a sympathetic frown.

"Miss Fearly," he said in a gentle tone, "I'm Dr. Smithson. I've been working on your brother since he came in."

I jerked a nod of understanding, since words weren't happening. My eyes stayed glued to the doctor's face, desperately seeking some kind of positive indication. Some kind of *hope*.

"Your brother was in pretty bad shape," the doctor continued, his voice quiet and calm, like he didn't want to risk me turning hysterical. Fuck. That meant it was bad news, right? It meant Miles hadn't made it?

"He's stable now..."

Everything else the doctor was saying faded as my breath whooshed from my lungs and my ears started ringing. He was stable. Miles was stable. That meant he was *alive*. I hadn't killed my big brother.

"...Miss Fearly? Are you okay?" The doctor was watching me carefully, his eyes concerned and sympathetic.

I gave another jerking nod, taking a deep breath and trying to pull my shit together. "Y-yes," I replied, my voice rough with emotion. "Yes, sorry. Carry on."

Dr. Smithson gave me an understanding look, then continued with his update. "It'll be a long road to recovery for Miles. But for now, we've done what we can to get him out of immediate danger. He'll be kept in a medically induced coma until the swelling in his brain comes down, and then he'll need to start an extensive rehabilitation. Miss Fearly, your brother is lucky to be alive, but he may never walk again." Guilt flooded through me, but the doctor was still talking, and I knew I needed to concentrate.

Despite telling myself that, my eyes flickered down the corridor to where Jared was still on his call. He seemed tense and angry, his eyes on me while he spoke to the person on the other line. Whatever he was dealing with, it couldn't be as bad as this.

When I refocused, the doctor was talking about future surgeries Miles was going to need. He'd broken more bones than I could even name, and lots of them would need to be joined with steel pins. My brother was in for a *hard* road ahead, that was for sure. But then Dr. Smithson said something that made my blood run cold.

"What did you say?" I snapped, jerking my gaze back to the middle-aged doctor.

His brows raised slightly. "I asked, is it common for him to pull a stunt like that while under the influence of cocaine? I apologize for asking, but we ran a standard screening panel. We have to for treatment. He tested positive for cocaine and alcohol. Is he a habitual user? My niece is a fan of the ClikByter *NoFear*..." He trailed off, shaking his head. "I'm sorry, that was inappropriate. Let's focus on your brother. "

My hand snapped out, and I grabbed his sleeve before he could walk away. I shook my head in denial. "That can't be right. Miles doesn't do drugs. He would *never* do stunts under the influence of *anything*. We don't need it. The adrenaline is better than any chemical on the market."

The doctor shrugged. "Maybe for you it is, but there's no mistaking cocaine for anything else. He was definitely under the influence at the time of the fall." He left me then, and I needed to drop back into my chair to keep from face-planting on the floor.

Miles had been doing coke? Since when? Why? He wasn't that stupid. Not when we were filming a stunt.

Then, the pieces clicked together in my brain. The shady way Rich had taken off when the ambulances showed up. His sketchy behavior and out-of-control temper. The fight last night. *Fuck.* Fuck! Rich had left our argument and gone partying with my brother. Then they'd both turned up to our stunt still under the influence.

Jesus *Christ.* I hadn't almost killed my brother...*Rich* had.

My fingers curled into fists, and my blood boiled with anger. I'd fucking murder him. Rich was a dead man walking. He goddamn knew better.

"Noah," Jared called out, striding back toward me. "We need to talk about Olympus."

My brows furrowed in a scowl. "What? Now? No, sorry, Jared. No. This isn't the time or the place. Miles was—"

"Yes, Noah," he cut me off. "*Now.*" Jared was tense and anxious, his brow beading with perspiration.

I just shook my head. In order for Olympus to compete in the Clik Games, they needed eight members, but their little brotherhood of dude-bros was only five. They needed three more to round out their team, and they weren't willing to recruit just anyone. They wanted the *best*—which they'd made crystal clear when they offered me one of those places.

A spot I'd already declined several times. It was also the cause of my argument with Rich.

"Jared, I told you: I'm not fucking interested. All Olympus is good for is flexing for the camera and creating thirst traps. I'm better than that, and I'm better than *them.*" My tone was firm, my refusal loaded with disgust. Although each member of Team Olympus was uniquely talented in their own way, they'd opted to cash in on their sex appeal instead. It wasn't good enough to just film a BMX trick jump; they had to do it shirtless, with their rippling abs on display, and throw a flirty wink at the camera as they landed. Total sellouts.

Jared sighed and ran a hand through his hair. "Yeah, well, that was before Miles fell off a construction site owned by Sonny Flickman. Now they have the names behind NoFear, and they're threatening to come after you for the Snake Creek accident."

My jaw fell open. Sonny Flickman was the owner of Team Olympus—told you they were all sellouts—but he also owned most of the locations we chose for our stunts. It was a quiet middle finger to the Olympus Group, and now it was coming back to bite us in the ass.

The incident in question was an innocent cliff dive from the rocks above Snake Creek, into the water below. Miles, Rich, and I had done it for *fun*, not even as a planned stunt. But a couple of weeks later, some kids tried to replicate it, and they died. Their parents sued Olympus Group, because they owned the land and someone needed to be held accountable. The fences around that area of Snake Creek had been damaged, and my video had pointed the kids right to the place they could get through.

In our defense, we had sent an email to Olympus Group *prior* to posting the video, explaining the fence damage and suggesting they get it fixed. Stupidly, we thought we'd done enough, but our email went unanswered, and concerns were apparently unactioned.

"They can't do that," I croaked. "We did nothing wrong. Those kids—"

"It doesn't *matter*, Noah," Jared snapped, exasperated. "They're threatening to sue you *and* Miles for all the break-ins, all the trespassing, *and* for reckless endangerment over Snake Creek. Whether they win or lose, it won't matter. You'll both have your names dragged through the mud."

I could hardly even believe what I was hearing. "Unless I join their fucking team."

Jared nodded. He looked just as furious as I was. "Same offer as they put on the table yesterday," he added quickly, "but with a new condition."

I swallowed heavily. "Do I even want to know?"

He gave me a grim look. "If you break your contract and leave the team before or during the Clik Games, they'll pursue their charges against both you and Miles. What they aren't saying directly but implying heavily is that it will also open you up to personal damage lawsuits. They could bankrupt you, your brother, and your mother. They could go after every dime."

Fuck *me*. I ran my fingers through my long, white-blond hair, trying to wrap my brain around everything that was happening. First Rich, then Miles, now...this.

"Clik Games run for six months," I said quietly. "They want me to help them win, then I'm free to go? Just like that?"

Jared jerked a nod. "Six-ish, depending on challenge stages. I'll ensure the contract is airtight. You compete with Olympus in the Clik Games, then you walk away with an eighth of the winnings, and all charges and liability will be forgotten. I'll get a waiver from them."

"The waiver clears Miles, and we get an NDA that they can't out his identity?"

The last thing I wanted to do was think about all of this, but they weren't leaving me much choice. I didn't care about me so much, but Mom...and Miles...

I could do this for them. The opening ceremony for the Games was in five months. Five months to do my research on *all* my potential competition and make my peace with working on a team of arrogant, narcissistic, egotistical man-whores. Then another six months to win the Clik Games. Based on what Dr. Smithson had said, Miles wouldn't even be finished with his rehab by the time I was released from my Olympus contract.

"What if we don't win?" I asked, picking at a loose thread on my hoodie. "Will I be screwed over by Sonny Dickman and his merry band of crooks?"

Jared sagged in relief. "I'll insist on a contract clause to see that doesn't happen. You'll try your *best* to win, but that's all they can ask."

"Fine," I muttered, feeling a pall settle over my soul, even though both Jared and I knew I'd never let Miles take the blame for my mistakes. "Make the deal. For Miles."

Jared nodded, even though I could tell he wasn't happy about the situation either. "There's one other thing, Noah."

I gave a bitter laugh, swiping at my still-damp cheeks. "Of course there is. Just spit it out. Today can't get much worse."

He gave me a grimace. "You have to move into the house and

participate in their streaming channel content. It's one of the contract points they absolutely wouldn't budge on."

"As *who?*" I stared at Jared. "Norah *freaking* Sparkles? That would cause absolute chaos in a team like that! Their fans are—"

"No," my manager cut me off, shooting me a look of sympathy. "They want NoFear. Their team is all guys, and they want it to stay that way, in line with their brand. You have to be Noah."

"I'm not following you, Jared. Spell it out like I'm an idiot." Because right now I felt like one.

He gave a small grimace. "Noah...it's an all-male team, and I get the impression that they incorrectly assumed *you* were male, thanks to your name. I've since cleared that fact up, but they're insisting."

I stared at him for a long pause, trying to make it make sense. "They...want me to pretend to be a dude? Am I understanding you correctly? And the team is all okay with this?"

Jared shook his head. "Not exactly. But Olympus management is, and they're the ones holding all the cards right now. And you're dead right that Olympus fans would riot if Norah Sparkle suddenly moved into the house."

"For six months? Live as—" I wasn't sure who was more insane, Team Olympus's management for insisting, Jared for bringing it to me, or me for considering it. "So they reveal NoFear as Noah the dude..." Then what he'd just said clicked in my head. "Wait, what? Moving into the house?"

My manager winced and shrugged. "Sorry. It's nonnegotiable."

Oh, look at that. Just when I thought the day couldn't possibly implode any more than it already had, Jared delivered the icing on a shit cake.

I was moving to Mount Olympus.

TWO

"This is never going to work," I muttered with heavy cynicism as our destination drew closer. "No one is going to buy this shit. It's begging for a scandal."

Jared leveled me with a look that said everything words couldn't, and I grimaced. A scandal like *this* was the least of my problems right now. We'd just spent the last month in the slimiest, traumatizing legal nightmare with my piece-of-shit ex-boyfriend, fighting to keep his betrayal under wraps and out of the media. If anything, this Team Olympus ruse would be a good distraction away from what the story *would* have been had he not signed the ironclad NDA my team had forced on him.

"You'll be amazed what people will believe if you lie to their faces," Jared said in response, looking as tired as I felt. "Besides, this is for your protection as much as theirs. You know how fucking unhinged the Acolytes are."

I wrinkled my nose with distaste. The Acolytes were what the fans of Mount Olympus had dubbed themselves, and they took their name *way* too seriously. Hardcore obsession level. As much as I hated to admit it, the female fans were the worst.

"You look good," he assured me when I said nothing. "It's just on you to sell it. Be confident in the act. Besides, the fans will be too feral over NoFear's 'unmasking' to be suspicious over small white lies."

Small white lies was an understatement.

The car began to slow, and the nervous butterflies multiplied inside me. I should have moved into Mount Olympus weeks ago. Should have had plenty of time to get to know my new team and smooth out any personality friction that would undoubtedly arise. But no, I'd been trapped in legal hell with Rich, the dickless wonder, attempting to get the *hundreds* of covert sex tapes removed from the internet.

Bastard.

"The team knows *Noah* is joining them," Jared said, reading my anxiety correctly. "They just don't know Noah is...you know...a girl. And they won't, unless you tell them. Nor do they need to know. So long as you contribute to the best of your abilities as NoFear, then that's all that matters. Right?"

"Right," I muttered with a total lack of confidence, even as I shot a look at the privacy window which had been firmly closed since we got in the car. Not that it mattered—we were already out of time. Team Olympus's car service just slowed to a stop in front of a production stage where a handful of crew stood around looking frustrated and stressed.

I didn't blame them. The decision by Clik Games to live stream the team announcements had been *extremely* last-minute and not something anyone had really prepared for. The fact that I'd be meeting my team for the first time directly before the cameras turned on? Not ideal.

One of the crew waiting for us opened my door before I could voice any more pointless concerns to Jared, and he shot me a sympathetic glance before I stepped out.

"Noah, it's nice to meet you," the guy who'd opened my door said with a quick smile, offering his hand. "I'm Sammy, one of the producers handling your team. They're all waiting in the green room, if you'll follow me?"

"Sure," I murmured, running a hand over my freshly cut hair as Jared got out of the car to join us. I should have gone shorter, maybe, but my stylist assured me shoulder length was *fine*. I was second-guessing freaking everything now.

Jared gave me a small shoulder bump, lowering his head to speak quietly. "Remember, be *confident*. You've got this."

I puffed out my cheeks, shaking my head as we followed the producer inside the building. Confidence, huh? After spending the last two years *masked and anonymous,* it was going to take more than a few words of affirmation to get me through.

Sammy hurried us down the long corridor, glancing at his watch as we passed by other green rooms with team names stuck to the doors. Some I recognized, most I didn't, until we approached the one reading TEAM OLYMPUS.

Before Sammy could knock, the door swung open and the three of us were very nearly mowed down by a stunningly handsome guy with white-blond hair a shade or two lighter than my own—wearing an expression so frosty it could cool the sun.

Ace Hart. Twenty-five. Six foot three. Attended Riverstone Academy for Boys with Miles and Xavier. Team Olympus's leader, multitalented, and one hell of an intimidating man.

"Sammy!" he barked, flicking a dismissive glance my way before locking the terrified producer in his ice-blue glare. "Who the fuck is this, and where the hell is Noah? They're already starting the announcements, which means we have less than five minutes until our team is called."

Sammy drew a shaky breath and shifted his posture to gesture my way. "This *is* Noah," he said with a slight grimace. "Uh, Noah, this is Ace. He's your team captain."

The angry dude snapped his gaze my way, brow pinched with disbelief as he looked me over from head to toe. All the while, I held my breath. This was the real test, right here.

"You're kidding," Ace scoffed. "*You're* NoFear? This is a joke, right?" He turned his attention back to Sammy with an edge of exasperation in his tone and a pinched expression. "What is he, like fifteen?"

I released my breath as discreetly as I could. He wasn't confused because *Noah is a girl*... Nope, he just thought I was a scrawny fifteen-year-old *boy*. Perfect.

"If you don't want me here," I said with as much steel as I could muster up, "I can go. Your management blackmailed me into this agreement in the first fucking place, so by all means, Ace, say the word and I'll dip." My voice was naturally pitched low for a woman, so I didn't need to go putting on a fake one.

His glacial gaze had swung back my way, and I forced myself to hold eye contact without flinching. Jared was right, confidence was the only way to sell this farce, and I wasn't bluffing. Ace had final say over his team, so if he didn't want me, then he could overrule the management's scheming.

Right when I thought he was going to agree and send me home, his lips curled into a cool smile. "All right, I guess you've got balls, even if you haven't hit puberty yet." He appraised me again, then shook his head with a sigh. "Come on inside and meet the team before we get called. This is going to be nuts."

As he turned away to allow us entry into the green room, I met Jared's eyes and gave him a small nod of reassurance. The first test had been passed with Ace, so surely it was smooth sailing from here...*surely*.

The green room was pure chaos. Aside from Ace, there were six more members of Team Olympus, and all of them had managers and publicists, not to mention the hair and makeup crew working diligently to ensure everyone was *flawless* for the camera. For the first time since this stupid fucking ruse had been forced on me, I was kind of glad to be masquerading as a man. Makeup was still expected, sure, but nothing compared to what I was used to.

Ace's sharp whistle silenced the buzz of chatter, and suddenly every eye in the room was focused my way.

Sweat beaded on my spine, and I fought the urge to back out of the room once more. I was no stranger to the spotlight...but this was different.

"This is *him*?" one of the guys asked from where he slouched on a sofa with a guitar in hand. I recognized him as Xavier Stone, a lethally handsome man whom I'd once been utterly infatuated with. Fucking hell, this was going to be harder than I'd imagined, considering how my heart raced when he met my gaze.

Xavier Stone. Twenty-four. Six foot four. Dark brown hair. Hazel eyes. Attended Riverstone Academy for Boys with both Ace and Miles. Also sponsored by Hot Falcon energy drinks for his motocross.

"Where's the rest of him?"

Huh. That fixed that problem. I narrowed my eyes and offered a sarcastic smile. "Hilarious." And honestly, it sort of was. At five foot eight, I'd never been called short in my life...as a girl. But now that I was presenting as a guy? Yeah, I guess I should get used to short jokes.

Xavier just grinned back, no real malice behind his comment. "Just teasing. We're stoked you're here, right?" He smacked the other guy on the sofa with him, who'd been staring at me with a worrying edge of confusion.

Ever so slowly, the staring guy with unnaturally deep-red hair nodded. "Right," he murmured, lips pursed. "Have we met before, Noah? You seem weirdly familiar."

I swallowed hard. Technically, yes. I'd met him—Zeth Briggs—years ago, when he, Xavier, and Ace went to school with Miles. But I was all of eleven or twelve at the time, and there was no way he remembered me from then. Everything I knew of him now came from my research.

Zeth "Z" Briggs. Twenty-two. Six foot two. Brown hair—scratch that, now wine red—and mossy-green eyes. Son of Zeth Briggs Sr., lead singer of Seventeen Daggers and grandson of Atticus Briggs, CEO of Atticus Records. Insanely talented musician and composer but stubbornly refuses to sign a record deal. Instead, seems comfortable with ClikByte fame. Very odd.

Also feels...strangely familiar.

"Nope, I tend to steer clear of..." I trailed off and let my gaze sweep over the room. "All of this."

"We noticed," Ace said with a grunt, then checked the time on his stupidly expensive watch. "How long have we got, Sammy?"

"Uh, couple of minutes. They just started introducing the members of GeeGee now." The producer had a handheld device which showed him the live feed from the production stage. I cringed internally at the mention of GeeGee—an all-women team that was the epitome of girly-girl—since they'd made an offer to recruit me, too. Only *they* had wanted Norah Sparkle, while the boys of Team Olympus wanted NoFear. *Thank fuck.*

"Hi," one of the two Asian guys on the team said, getting up from where he'd been getting his ink-black hair tweaked into the perfectly messy style that artfully hung over one of his pretty green eyes—which I realized were actually contacts when he drew closer. "I'm Torin. We've been dying to meet you, but Xavier's right, dude...you're tiny. And *pretty*. You have really delicate, kind of feminine features."

My brows shot up before I could catch myself, and the small sound that escaped me could *hopefully* be interpreted as irritation rather than panic. Mentally, I recited my notes to calm my nerves.

Torin Mura. Twenty-three years old. Six foot three. Japanese father, Irish mother, raised in Vancouver, Canada. Artist. Best known for overtly sexual, borderline pornographic pottery videos.

"It's not the insult it might seem," someone else drawled, and I needed to look past Torin to find who was talking. "He's just jealous."

Good god. Minho Park was *gorgeous*. He was standing patiently while a stylist messed with the decorative belts looped around his slim waist, but his dark eyes were on me with curiosity.

During the months since I'd agreed to join Team Olympus, I'd done my research on all my teammates, as well as potential competition...but even I could admit I'd watched a whole lot of Minho Park content that was entirely for pleasure and not research.

Minho Park. New recruit. Twenty-three. Six foot two. Born and raised in Los Angeles but spent six years in South Korea as a part of 1-4-3 *before a sex scandal disbanded the group. Now he was a top ClikByter, doing insanely gorgeous dance videos, often with special effects like fire and swords. Drool. Also a global brand ambassador for Portia Levigne Couture.*

"It's true," Torin agreed with an exaggerated sigh, pulling my attention back to him. "Gender neutral fashion is a massive industry right now, and all of this will never snag one of those sweet luxury brand deals." He gestured to his face, and I couldn't help smiling. He was right... Unlike Minho—and me—there was no way in hell Torin Mura would ever pass as even the slightest bit feminine.

Jared had been quietly hovering behind me, letting me take the lead in meeting the team, but when his phone buzzed, he gave my arm a quick squeeze and gestured that he was stepping out of the room.

Torin narrowed his eyes, watching Jared leave. "Your manager?" he asked when the door closed.

I jerked a nod. "Yep." I didn't elaborate. Getting chatty would trip me up. I could just sense it.

"Torin, quit being so needy," another of the team teased, slinging his arm around Torin's shoulders. "You haven't introduced the rest of us. Hi, Short Stack, I'm—"

"August," I cut him off, suddenly nervous and impatient without Jared at my back. "I know. I did my research on all of you."

August Gamble. Also a new recruit. Twenty-two. Six foot one. Brown hair, brown eyes. Born in Sao Paolo, Brazil, but raised in Miami. Trickshot marksman and illusionist on ClikByte.

I glanced over to the one remaining team member who hadn't even tried to introduce himself. "And you must be SkyeHigh...my copycat."

Skye Smith. Twenty years old. Five foot eleven. Blond hair, blue eyes. Australian. Doesn't have a single ounce of originality in his whole body and yet somehow Clikers love him anyway.

The scruffy, sexy blond guy I spoke to just smirked. "No such thing as original ideas these days, *NoFear*, just better ways to do it."

I scoffed, outrage burning in my chest at the sheer audacity of this douchebag and his infuriatingly appealing Australian accent. Insults burned on the tip of my tongue, but Jared stepped back into the green room then and I swallowed it down. Starting fights with my new team less than five minutes after meeting them probably wasn't wise.

"Two-minute warning!" a crew member called out, and one of the makeup artists politely moved Torin and August out of the way so she could dab my face with translucent powder. It gave me a moment to breathe, as everyone became busy ensuring they were ready to go on camera rather than stare at me like an exotic animal in an enclosure.

Ace drifted over while the makeup artist did her thing to ensure I didn't glow under stage lights, but he didn't immediately speak. Instead he just stood there with his arms folded and a thoughtful look on his face.

When the crew started ushering the team out of the green room, I met Ace's eyes and lifted a brow. "Something wrong, boss?"

His head tilted and he ran his tongue over his teeth. "You tell me, Noah." Shit. Had he...somehow figured me out already? How, though? I'd barely said a word and— "Am I going to have problems between you and Skye? We're a *team*, Noah. That means we work together."

Oh. *Ohhhh.* I huffed a small exhale. "No problems here, just don't expect us to be best friends when he's literally built his platform on copying mine. Badly, too, I might add." Ace gave me a hard glare, and Jared subtly poked me in the back. I sighed and rolled my eyes. "I'll behave."

Ace's glare shifted into a smile. "Good. Now, let's go break the internet with your face reveal." He clapped me on the shoulder and steered me out into the hall where the rest of the team were already heading. "Shit, bro, you really are short as fuck."

THREE

Live streaming in general was not something I engaged in with my regular content these days. My entire platform consisted of extreme danger and total anonymity, which really didn't gel with the nature of live streaming, but I hadn't always been NoFear. Back when my whole identity was Norah Sparkle and the ClikByte platform was still fresh, I had frequently used it to speak with followers while curling my hair or learning a new dance routine.

The live stream for the Clik Games introductions was something totally different.

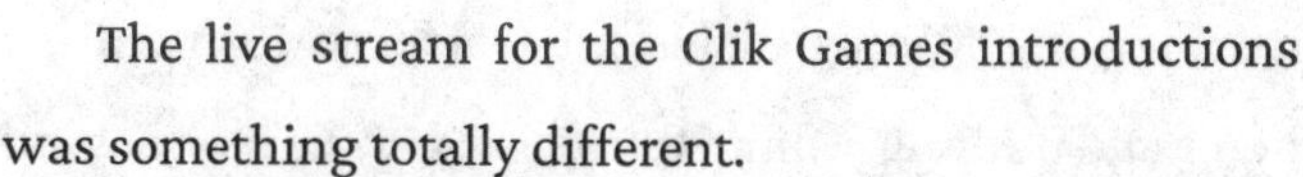

It wasn't a phone on a tripod with a ring light. It was a full-scale production, probably on par with some

movie sets or live televised content. In short, it was overwhelming as hell.

An enthusiastic MC announced our team over the microphone as everyone entered the main stage one by one...with me last. If Jared hadn't been right there waiting with me, I'd have probably run away.

No, that wasn't true. I wasn't doing this whole thing because Jared said I had to. I was doing it to keep Miles safe. So I straightened my spine and channeled my very best *big dick* energy as I strode into the spotlight and smiled tightly at the camera.

Thankfully, it only took a moment, and then I was free to join my team on the tiered seating, sliding into the empty spot between Xavier and Minho.

"You okay?" Xavier asked quietly as the presenter read from his teleprompter with exaggerated excitement for the multiple cameras fixed on him.

I swallowed hard, all too aware of the sweat running down the back of my neck. "Yep, totally fine."

He gave a soft snort. "You don't look fine."

"He's right," Minho murmured, barely even moving his lips as he spoke. "You look like you're about to pass out."

Them saying it was only making it worse, so I gritted my teeth. When I said nothing, Minho turned slightly to look behind us, giving some sort of silent communication, because a moment later someone gave my shoulder a gentle squeeze.

"Listen up, Eight," Ace said in a whisper, leaning down so his head was near my ear. I braced myself for threats or insults, so the gentle nature of his tone surprised me. "This part will be over really quick, then we just have a shitload of waiting around while they do sound bites and interviews. Just hang in there for a few minutes, all right? We've got you."

What was with the supportive, encouraging shit? Everything I'd heard about Ace Hart was negative. Arrogant, conceited, short-tempered...not whatever *this* was. Were the rumors totally wrong about him? Or was this all an act for the cameras?

Whatever it was, it helped. His hand remained on my shoulder as Xavier leaned in to tell me quietly about how the presenter was once photographed with his dick in a jar of peanut butter.

It was such a random fact that a shocked laugh escaped me, and Xavier grinned widely, having achieved what he'd clearly intended. Ace's hand squeezed my shoulder again, like he was reassuring me, and it caused a really odd sensation to build inside me. Like...like I could trust him, which was *wild* when we'd only met ten minutes ago.

He was right, though. The filming ended just a few minutes later, and we were told to return to green rooms for individual team interviews and reactions and God only knew what else. I was painfully uninformed about everything involved with Clik Games, thanks to Rich's bullshit in the months since Miles nearly died. My whole damn focus had been taken up by the fact that I was apparently one of ClikByte: Adults Only's top earners without ever knowing I had a profile...or content. *Bastard.*

"You okay, Noah?" Torin asked, slinging his arm over my shoulders as we filed out of the set stage with all the other teams.

"He's fine," Ace answered for me, which I appreciated since I was internally hyperventilating at the casual contact from Torin Mura. I needed to get my shit under control or these guys would catch me blushing and flirting.

Torin just extended his middle finger at Ace's back as the team leader passed us, then glanced down at me. "Are you, though? You didn't look fine in there."

I swallowed hard, grimacing. "That's not good. I'll be a meme by the end of the day."

Torin barked a laugh. "Nah, you'll have the internet way too feral over your *face* to have anyone noticing how nervous you were. Besides, I think it's to be expected."

"How long have you been doing the anonymous masked-content thing, anyway?" August asked from my other side as we headed toward our green room.

I glanced his way, and my lips curved in a small grin. "As if you don't know. I don't believe for a second that I was the only one doing my research."

"True, but I bet your research turned up a whole lot more useful information than ours did. You're crazy private for someone with such a massive platform, you know?" August seemed genuinely confused about that fact, and my smile widened with amusement.

"Can you blame me? First thing out of Ace's mouth was asking if I was fifteen." I rolled my eyes like I was actually offended by the slight.

Torin chuckled, his arm still comfortably draped over my shoulders. "Fifteen is harsh, but you *are* very pretty for a dude so—"

"Torin!" a girl called out from behind us, making him stiffen ever so slightly before puffing out a short sigh. A glance behind us showed one of the girls from GeeGee making her way toward us with a determined look on her gorgeous face. "Aren't you going to introduce your new member to me, baby?"

Torin's jaw clenched when she called him that, and his smile was so forced it was more of a grimace than anything else. "I hadn't planned to," he admitted with a shrug as we turned to face her.

The girl just rolled her eyes, then aimed a downright sultry smile my way. She was shorter than me, even in chunky platform boots, and her skirt was so short it was more of a belt. If that was their team image, I was more relieved than ever to be blackmailed onto Olympus instead.

"Noah, right? I'm Sakura." She fluttered her long, inky-black lashes and offered her hand.

"Fuck off, Sakura," August snapped, clearly not as patient as Torin when it came to this woman. I knew of her from my competitor research, but everything I'd seen of her was shallow and scripted. She was a dancer...but that term was used very loosely.

She was pretty, had a great body, and could imitate choreography well enough, but other than that I was unclear how she'd amassed such a huge following.

A strong hand gripped the back of my neck, jerking me away from Sakura and making me stumble. "Sakura, why are you eye-fucking my new team member?" Ace asked with an edge of irritation. "I'll save you the energy. He's already signed his contract with Olympus, which means—"

Sakura rolled her heavily lined eyes. "No fucking around. I'm *well* aware. But rules are meant to be broken, Ace, you said—"

"Bye, Sakura!" Ace boomed, all but hauling me into our green room by the scruff of my neck. Torin and August followed quickly behind, closing the door before Ace released me.

"Was that necessary?" I snapped, rubbing the nape of my neck as I glared up at our team leader.

"Yes," he responded with a scowl. "There was a cameraman on his way to catch that little interaction, and I figured you wouldn't want a dating rumor on your first day."

My lips parted, but no sound came out. That hadn't even crossed my mind...

"Look, if you were interested, I'm sure Torin can give you her number, just keep it on the down-low, all right?" Ace patted me on the shoulder with a lot less aggression than he'd just shown the back of my neck.

Jared approached from where he'd been on the phone, casting a worried look between Ace and me. "Everything okay, Noah?"

I jerked a quick nod. "Yeah, of course. Just...not used to this kind of shit."

"Get used to it," Skye said from where he was sprawled on the sofa with his phone in hand. "For the next twelve months, your every waking moment will be on camera for the fans to pick apart and micro-analyze. Hope you don't have any secrets or bad habits you were planning to keep under wraps."

The other guys chuckled, but I locked eyes with Jared as panic tightened my chest. The contracts around their content filming had been so vague it was unclear what exactly I'd signed up for, and our main focus had been all the clauses around keeping Miles out of legal danger...but *every waking moment*? Surely that was just a dramatic exaggeration.

"You'll be fine," Jared reassured me, ignoring the boys. The loaded look he gave me said everything I knew he was thinking. Olympus management knew perfectly well *who* I was, and this whole farce of presenting me as a dude was their idea in the first place. They wouldn't do anything to risk that secret getting out...so long as I didn't do anything to force the issue.

I nodded as convincingly as possible. "Yeah, of course. Totally fine. I've got this. How's Kelly doing?" With impeccable timing, Jared's wife was nine months pregnant and due any day. So that meant I was heading into Mount Olympus without my manager.

His brow drew tight with frustration. "She's fine. She said there's no rush, so if you need me—"

I scoffed, shaking my head. "She's lying. I'm fine here, honestly. Go and be with your wife! Make sure you don't miss your baby's birth."

"You're expecting a baby?" Zeth asked, having clearly been eavesdropping while pretending to browse the minifridge. He was *still* giving me suspicious glances, and I had an uncomfortable feeling he was going to be the one who figured me out first.

Jared nodded. "Yeah, sure am. First one, too, so my wife is... a little anxious."

"Congratulations, man, that's awesome." Zeth clapped Jared on the shoulder in that manly version of a hug that guys did, and Jared grinned with pride. "Don't worry about Noah. We'll look after him."

"Sure will," Ace agreed, offering me a bottle of water. "The company has already assigned an extra manager and stylist anyway."

Jared sighed, giving me yet another worried glance. "Noah's stylist will still be on call, but she's also planned ahead for everything scheduled over the next month." And considering my stylist was one of the few people who knew I was actually a woman, that was a fairly crucial role in the whole silly game.

"Well, then, nothing to worry about," Ace said as I accepted the water from him. "Noah is part of the Olympus family now, regardless of how it came about, and we take care of our own."

His ice-blue eyes locked with mine for the briefest moment, and I sighed internally. I guess Ace was fully aware that I'd been blackmailed into joining their team. Which was disappointing, because it made me think a lot less of him as a leader for allowing that sort of slimy business.

Or maybe I was reading too much into it? I'd told him myself that I was there under duress, but I'd just assumed he didn't register that fact in the midst of processing the new "kid" on his team.

Jared's phone chimed in his hand, and he glanced down at the screen with a tortured expression. He needed to be there for Kelly, but he also didn't want to leave me alone. It was sweet but unnecessary.

"Go home, Jared," I told him firmly. "Despite what Ace thinks, I'm an adult, and I can take care of myself. Besides, you can always call to check in."

Ace chuckled, shooting me a grin as he shrugged. "Calling it how I see it, baby face."

Zeth was squinting at me again, so I quickly ushered Jared out and in the process removed myself from Zeth's scrutiny. Maybe he was just fascinated by how smooth my face was and wanted to swap hair removal tips later? Yeah. Probably that.

Jared made me promise to check in when we eventually returned to the house and assured me that my luggage had already been sent ahead, but it still took everything in me not to drag him back as he exited the green room. Shit. I really was on my own now.

"You good, Noah?" Minho asked as I drifted over to a vacant armchair with my pulse hammering in my throat.

I forced a tight smile to my lips. "Yep." Then, because I was starting to sweat under his beautiful dark gaze, I searched for a distraction. "So, what can you tell me about the team? I figure I should at least pretend I know you all when we have to do team interviews, right?"

His head tilted to the side, such an elegant motion on him. Then again, this was a man who'd started dance training when he was barely three years old, so it stood to reason his every movement was fluid. "Yes, you're right. And us, you. Ace! Noah needs a crash course in all things Olympus."

I nearly choked. My attempt at distraction had just turned into a team meeting with me at the center. Great.

FOUR

The crash course on Team Olympus didn't give me anything I didn't already know, but it was valuable to see the dynamic between the seven of them. While they gave me the facts I already researched, I studied their body language and facial expressions and paid attention to their *tone* instead of their words.

By the time our team interviews were filmed, I had clocked Torin and August as practically inseparable best friends; Xavier, Ace, and Zeth as closer than brothers; Minho as a quiet observer who was more than comfortable letting others speak for him; and—much to my frustration—Skye seemed genuinely likeable.

The interviews took a painful amount of time, but Ace was diligent in making sure everyone had snacks and drinks to keep going until we were eventually told we could leave. Throughout the day my nerves had calmed, and I'd *almost* enjoyed some of the banter as we handled questions from the Clik Games producers, but the moment we were done, I was an anxious wreck.

Jared and Christy—my stylist—had sent all my luggage ahead to the team house, but I'd personally never been there and had no idea what to expect. I only knew that this was where the rest of the team lived full-time. It'd originally been just Ace, Xavier, and Zeth, then Skye and Torin had moved in around a year later. Minho and August were newer recruits to the team, but both had been living in the house at least six months already.

"It's about an hour drive to our place from here," Ace informed me as the team headed out of the production stage with all their staff in tow. It was mind-blowing to see how many *extra* employees they had around them at all times, when I was used to filming content with just me and Miles. And Rich. "Or more if there's traffic. Are you familiar with this area?"

I gave a noncommittal shrug. I'd lived in LA my whole life, because it was closest to the production studios that filmed Dance Babes when I was little. Miles had gone to boarding school—same one as Ace—but I'd been homeschooled to fit into my filming schedules.

"Yeah, somewhat familiar," I replied, walking beside him as we headed toward the waiting cars. There were eight of us, but twice as many staff. How was this going to work? "Your house is in Laguna Beach, right?"

Ace nodded, a gentle touch to my shoulder blade directing me toward the second of the two white vans. "Yeah, we've lived there a couple years already, and it's *home,* so we all agreed to stay there, rather than move into a rental for the duration of the Games."

"Makes sense," I murmured, climbing into the very back row when the doors slid open. I was the smallest, so it made sense to leave leg room for taller people.

Sure enough, it was Skye who climbed into the back with me, and the seats in front of us were claimed by Ace and Xavier. To my relief, it was just the four of us. No managers or publicists, and a privacy screen between us and the driver. Better yet, there were no cameras.

I let out a long breath of relief, letting my spine relax for the first time since arriving on set hours ago.

For a moment I assumed the guys would use the transit time as an opportunity to grill me for information or talk strategy for the competition or...*something*. But Xavier slouched in his seat, put earbuds in, and pulled his black beanie down over his eyes, clearly intending to sleep the whole way.

Ace pulled a laptop out of his bag, then turned in his seat to give me a reassuring smile. "Take a rest if you want, Eight. Cameras will be back on when we get home."

I nodded my understanding, running my fingers through my hair again. It was turning into a nervous habit, especially since I'd never had my hair so short in my whole damn life. I actually liked it, though. Wash day was going to be a breeze.

With a yawn, I tugged my hoodie hood up and pulled out my phone. Jared had already messaged to ask if everything was okay, so I shot off a quick reply, reassuring him before opening the thread from Miles. The *long* thread full of shouty caps and angry face emojis.

Fuck.

My breath hissed out from between my teeth, and a slimy feeling of dread and regret filled my gut as I read his messages. It was what I'd expected, but it still sucked...

I hadn't told him about the Olympus deal. If he'd known, he never would have let me go. Hell, he'd have willingly taken all the legal charges to stop me from joining this team, but keeping that secret meant he just found out...on live stream...along with the rest of the internet.

Miles was *pissed*. Big mad. The worst part, though? He said he was calling Mom.

Sure enough, there was a missed call from our mom several hours earlier. Just one, though, which was...something. She knew I was joining the team and the Clik Games and was supportive, but I *knew* my brother. He'd have gone in ranting about all of Ace's and Xavier's bad reputation points and panicked Mom into thinking I was in danger.

Miles *hated* Ace, for some reason. He never told me why, though, so it couldn't have been over anything that serious.

Right? Besides, from what I'd seen so far, Ace was nothing like the boy Miles had known.

"Hey," Skye murmured, nudging my leg with his knee to pull my attention away from my phone screen. "You're not looking at fan comments, right? That's never a good idea."

I frowned my confusion, shaking my head. "What? No, just... family drama. And I'm not exactly a newbie, SkyeHigh. I'm well aware how brutal comments can be." Although...now he had me wondering what the hell fans were saying of this version of Noah Fearly. Did they like *him*? Or was the feed flooded with comments about how Noah was so *very obviously* a girl, and Norah Sparkle at that.

He studied me a moment, then shrugged. "Okay, if you say so."

Shifting back into his seat, his phone screen tilted my way ever so briefly, and I caught a glimpse of a very familiar backpack in the Byte he was watching. "Are you—" I started to ask, reaching for his phone before he whipped it out of reach.

"No," he replied quickly, but the grin on his lips said he was *lying*.

My jaw dropped. "You're watching my Bytes! Why?"

"Planning my future content, obviously." Skye rolled his eyes dramatically, a smug smile on his face as he shifted his back against the window so I really couldn't see his screen. "Now that I've met you, I don't know how we didn't clock how short you are in these clips. Like...look at this one."

He turned his phone to show me a paused Byte where I'm standing on the open ledge of a construction site. Miles had been filming—as he always was—and Skye had paused on a shot where Miles had jumped out ahead of me. So the Byte showed me—in my full suit and helmet—standing on the ledge, with a mess of construction behind me.

"Either that elevator to your left"—Skye pointed out—"is the biggest elevator door on earth, or you're fucking short. And I guess it wasn't the elevator. Frankly, I'm shocked Ace didn't see this already."

He had a point there. I'd never really made any attempt to "look tall" because why the fuck would I? I didn't particularly care if fans worked out I was a girl. I just didn't want anything tying NoFear to Norah Sparkle.

"I don't see why it's such a big deal," I muttered, resisting the urge to grab for his phone again, because ultimately I couldn't stop him. "You're not exactly a giant yourself, you know?"

Skye's perfect grin spread wide. "I know. But I *am* taller than you, and that's a fucking win in my books. Actually, when's your birthday? If you're the shortest *and* the youngest, you'll totally make my day."

"December fifteenth," I replied, actually engaging with him against my instincts to keep my distance. "When's yours?" Because I already knew he was the same age as me, twenty.

He screwed up his adorable button nose. "You're kidding me. I'm December sixteen! So close to being twins for a minute there, Noah. Sagittarius checks out, though."

I just chuckled because I wasn't a star sign kinda girl; I had no clue what being Sagittarius had to do with fucking anything. Skye being into that was weirdly endearing, though. He definitely gave off new-age hippie sort of vibes.

"Well, I guess that means we can have a fully sick party when we both turn twenty-one, though," he continued, seeming like he was already seeing the benefits of our close birthdays.

"Uh, not to rain on your parade, but last I checked, Clik Games ends before our birthdays," I pointed out. The final results ceremony was scheduled for December fourth, six months from now.

Skye didn't seem put off. "So? You're Team Olympus now, Noah. We're family. Right, boss?"

"Yup," Ace replied, not raising his head from whatever he was doing on his laptop. It made me aware that he'd been listening the whole time, though.

The casual confidence they all had when they spoke like that, as if there was no way I'd *want* to leave their team, was confusing. Because it wasn't said with arrogance, like they were the best of the best and of course I wouldn't leave. More like they believed in fate and the eight of us belonged together. Confusing. Did none of these guys have even an ounce of abandonment issues? Or fear of rejection? Apparently not.

"Hey can I ask you about one of your Bytes?" Skye asked, totally oblivious to my internal puzzlement over their group dynamic. "This one." He showed me his phone again, displaying one of my favorite videos. It was from about a year earlier, when Miles and I had climbed up the side of a hot air balloon in flight to stand on top—before skydiving off.

I licked my lips, nodding. "I guess. What do you want to know?"

The smile that lit up his face was like pure sunshine. "Fuck, where do I even start? What kind of training did you need to do? How'd you find a balloon company that would let you do that? The paperwork must have been insane! And did your camera guy intend to slide down the side like that, or was it an accident? I noticed you have an actual cameraman on most of these stunts, which is so cool, I do everything myself and it really changes the whole vibe of—"

"Skye, take a breath," Ace cut him off, handing over a bottle of water. "Take a drink and let Noah answer your first fifty questions."

Skye actually blushed, accepting the water from his team leader and tossing me a sheepish look. "Sorry."

Fuck. *Fuck.* Why was he *so goddamn likeable?* I came into this team fully prepared to hate his guts for essentially ripping off my whole platform concept, but instead...this? I couldn't hate *this!*

"You're fine," I muttered, somewhat embarrassed myself. "I'm not really used to talking about my content with anyone but...I'll do my best."

Another beaming smile of excitement and I couldn't deny it anymore. Skye wasn't a copycat at all. He was me. Just...without

Miles to share it with. It made me kind of sad for him, and with that in mind I found myself being totally open and honest while answering his dozens of questions during the *long* drive to Laguna Beach.

Eventually we pulled up in front of a staggeringly impressive beachside mansion, and Ace poked Xavier in the shoulder to wake him up.

"All right, cameras will be back on before we get out of the car so if anyone wants to fix their face, do it now." Ace gave a pointed look to Xavier, who'd just tugged off his beanie and caused absolute chaos to his hair. Although it was shaved tight up the sides, it was long and messy on top, and the haphazard way he raked his fingers through it did nothing to help.

"Me? I'm fine," he mumbled, then stifled a yawn with the back of his hand. "This is what sunglasses were made for." He perched a pair of Angry Badger sunglasses—one of his sponsor brands—on his nose and gave Ace a toothy grin.

I stifled my own smile at how vexed Ace looked, but then one of the producers knocked on the window to tell us it was time to get out.

"Ready to see the house, Noah?" Skye asked as we all climbed out, totally unbothered by the half-dozen cameras following our every movement and word. "I made sure to clear out space in our closet for your stuff already."

That made me stumble. "Our...huh?"

Skye wrinkled his cute nose at me again with amusement.

"Ah, Ace didn't tell you? We're roommates. Youngest, shortest, and basically soulmates...kinda makes sense, right?"

Well...*fuck*. This was going to require an urgent call to Jared. Just as soon as the cameras stopped filming.

FIVE

The cameras were on from the moment we got out of the cars right up until it was time to sleep. If it wasn't an actual cameraman, it was the action cameras positioned around the house and production managers *freaking everywhere*. Admittedly, after the filming at the soundstage for so long, it was already dark when we got in, so it was only a few hours I needed to endure. It still sucked having to worry about every word out of my mouth.

"Is it like that all the time?" I asked Skye after changing into my pajamas in our shared bathroom under the excuse of a shower. "With the managers constantly telling you what to do and how to act?" Because as if

it wasn't enough for them to simply film the content, they were actively directing.

Skye yawned, scrubbing his hands through his already messy hair. His was a darker blond than mine, more on the light brown side, but he spent so much time in the sun it'd lightened. "Yeah. I mean, not always. It's just when they're putting together Mount Olympus content, and right now they're frothing over having you in it."

I sighed because, yeah, that made sense. "How often do you put those episodes out?"

"Every two weeks," he replied, getting under his blankets and groaning as he got comfy. "But because of the Games, they'll probably be around more than usual. Just pretend they're not there. You'll get used to it."

I wrinkled my nose because I really didn't think that was going to happen. How the fuck the guys could be so *comfortable* sitting around the table eating Chinese takeout while two cameramen and three managers hovered nearby, blew my damn mind.

"Well, I don't think my presence will do much for ratings," I muttered, getting into my own bed as exhaustion set in. I hadn't managed to call Jared yet to freak out over the shared bedroom situation, and now it was way too late. I'd try him in the morning. Surely I could survive one night without accidentally revealing my vagina, right?

Skye chuckled, punching his pillow into shape. "Yeah, right. I hope you don't snore, dude."

"Likewise," I shot back with a grin. "Night, Skye."

"Night, Noah."

Somehow despite all my reservations around sharing a room, I slept better than I had in *months*. I couldn't remember the last time I'd stayed asleep the whole night without waking, which was even more impressive considering I'd just slept in my chest binder.

A sleepy glance over at Skye's bed told me he was already up, so I took the opportunity to loosen the heavy-duty Velcro of my binder and breathe deeply for a few minutes. Not that I had any *huge* amount of boob to hide in the first place, but I also wasn't so flat-chested I could get away without *something* to deal with my shape.

"Fuck," I whispered aloud as I lay there and imagined my rib-cage expanding with each deep breath. Maybe I didn't need to wear it to bed? It's not like we were sleeping *together,* and as long as I was under blankets, maybe I could get away with it. I sure as hell couldn't sleep in that torture device night after night on top of wearing it all day.

A soft knock on the door made me flip over onto my stomach and drag the blanket up over my head just a second before Skye entered the room.

"Noah?" he whispered. "Are you awake?"

He'd *probably* just seen me hide, so there wasn't a lot of point in faking. "Should I be?" I mumbled from inside my blankets. I needed to get my binder back on, but the fucking Velcro had just stuck to itself.

"Nah, there's no strict schedule. I just wanted to ask if you had thought about who you're hanging out with today?"

I groaned, because...no. Ace had mentioned that I'd have a few days of "settling in," where I could spend time with each of the guys to get to know them all in more *intimate* settings. I'd definitely had a knee-jerk reaction to that before remembering that they thought I was a boy and therefore meant absolutely nothing flirty by that turn of phrase. Simply that it was easier to get to know people when it was one-on-one, rather than in a whole rowdy group.

"You?" I asked, because not only did I feel like I already kinda knew Skye—so it wouldn't be so awkward—but our interests aligned. The last thing I wanted to be stuck doing on Day One was learning how to work clay with a shirtless Torin or testing out my rusty singing voice with Zeth.

"Cool, I can show you the property then." He sounded actually enthusiastic about that, and I decided I'd picked well for a chill intro into Mount Olympus. "So...are you getting up?"

Crap. I popped my head out of the blankets just far enough to squint my sleepy eyes his way. "Uh...yeah. Just give me like ten minutes?"

Skye nodded. "Okay, sure." Then when I made no move to get out of bed, he awkwardly stood up and jerked a thumb over his shoulder. "I'll just...give you some space. You want any coffee?"

"Yes, please." I remembered my manners. "Black, no sugar."

Before he left I took a quick note of what he was wearing so I could match the vibe. Mimicking the guys would be the easiest way to sell my act, for sure.

Alone again, I grabbed my binder, some fresh clothes, and hauled ass into the bathroom to shower. It was a quick process even with washing my hair, and I grinned at myself in the foggy mirror. I put on a tinted moisturizer to keep from looking sick on camera, but I could definitely get used to not having to do a full face of makeup every damn day. My lashes were so short and damaged from recently removing my extensions that I had to admit, I barely looked like myself.

Chest binder back in place, oversized T-shirt, sweatpants, sneakers. Done. If it weren't for the binder, I'd be living my comfortable clothing *dream*. It'd be hard to go back to bodycon dresses and stiletto heels after this, and I was barely twenty-four hours in.

Downstairs in the huge kitchen, Skye had my coffee ready in a travel mug, but my focus was entirely derailed by the sight of Minho and Xavier sitting on stools at the island counter...wearing nothing but their boxer shorts.

Fucking hell. I needed to pop my eyes back into their sockets and stop staring, but it was an effort. A big effort.

"Noah, Skye seems to be under the impression you're hanging out with him today," Xavier said with a scowl, half-eaten bagel in hand as he gestured to my roommate. "But you guys talked non-stop for the whole drive yesterday, so surely you don't need *more* SkyeHigh today?"

I mentally willed my pulse to stop racing as he locked eyes with me over the island. Why weren't they dressed, for fuck's sake? Then again, this was Team Olympus. *Thirst trap* was basically their middle name.

"I thought you were asleep for the whole drive?" I shot back with a wobbly smile. Fuck, was I sweating? A little. Xavier's gaze was painfully disarming, though, especially when I had the *biggest* crush on him as a teenager. Okay, maybe it wasn't so far in my past, because there was no denying how my butterflies were reacting to his proximity.

Xavier shrugged, drawing way too much of my attention to his well-toned and tanned shoulder. He had a tattoo of a thin line running all the way from the back of his neck, wrapping around his arm, and ending in a simple rose on his wrist. I kinda wanted to inspect it closer...maybe trace it with my finger...

"Noah already said he's with me today," Skye said, jerking me out of what was fast turning into a lustful trance as I followed Xavier's tattoo with my eyes. "I'm showing him around the property."

"What if I want to do that?" Minho asked. "I give great tours."

Xavier turned his head to give Minho a confused squint. "Since fucking when?"

The beautiful, former K-pop star just shrugged. "I don't know. Maybe I just need the opportunity. I watched a whole season of *Selling Sunset Springs* last winter."

Xavier snorted a laugh, and Skye snickered.

"I don't know that's a qualification, bro," Skye told Minho with a lopsided smile. "Besides, Ace said we all have to spend one-on-one time with my twin, so just play it cool and maybe he'll pick you next."

Unlikely. I needed to get my hormones in check before doing anything *one on one* with either Xavier or Minho. I'd been lusting after the both of them way too hard while "researching," and it was messing with my head. Skye just felt safer today. Maybe because I did already feel like I knew him?

"We need to be qualified to show the new guy around our own house?" Xavier asked, turning his puzzled squint on Skye. "Where's your diploma, then?"

Skye just rolled his eyes and gave me a push in the direction of the door that led to the rest of the house. "Come on, Noah. If you entertain them, we'll be here all damn day."

"See you later, Noah!" Minho called after us, and my cheeks warmed.

Shit. I severely underestimated how hard it was to maintain this act when I was tied up in knots by their mere presence.

"Don't worry about them," Skye told me as we made our way through the enormous house. "They're just messing around. Everyone is really excited to have you on the team, but I can tell them to tone it down if they're making you uncomfortable."

I shook my head. "No, it's fine. I'm just not used to...all of this."

Skye nodded, like he understood what I was talking about. "You don't usually create content alone, though, right? You have a cameraman that does stunts with you?"

"Yeah," I replied softly, a pang of worry hitting my stomach at the mention of Miles. I'd still not replied to his messages but would have to at some stage. "How do you do it? It's surely not all GoPro footage?"

Skye shrugged. "A lot is. Some is done with tracking drones, too."

My interest piqued at that. "Can you show me? I've always wanted to try them out but never really needed to."

"For sure! Come on. I wanna show you the cliff." He opened a door at the back of the house, leading us out into the expansive yard where a lagoon-style pool was practically taunting me. Not that I was particularly fond of the water these days, but if I was, I'd be shit out of luck. Hard to hide my little secret in a swimsuit.

Wait. What did Skye just say? "Cliff? What—" My question broke off when he led the way down a path beside the pool to reveal a drop-off. The house itself was elevated from the beach, and the guys' clever landscape designer had used that natural height to create an actual cliff, complete with climbing points and... "Is that a trampoline at the bottom?" I asked in surprise.

Skye beamed, turning to face me with his back to the "cliff." "Sure is." Then he fell backward, over the ledge, and dropped out of sight.

Then a moment later, his face reappeared as the trampoline rebounded him back up once more.

"So cool," I breathed, eyes wide as I peered over the edge.

Skye laughed, a staggeringly joyful kind of sound. It was disturbingly relatable...that *rush* of euphoria from doing something dangerous. “Wanna try it out?”

“Fuck yes!” I exclaimed, then took one big step straight off the ledge.

No hesitation, *no fear.*

SiX

We got a whole ten minutes of pure adrenaline on the cliff-trampoline before a half-asleep and scruffy cameraman named Roy came rushing out to film for their episodes. As soon as he started rolling, the mood between Skye and me dampened dramatically. And not just because I was uncomfortable with the constant scrutiny, either—Skye's shine noticeably dimmed, too.

Still, it was the best choice of my first day introductions, camera or not. Skye showed me how the cliff was also rigged for climbing and rappelling, and then let me play with his motion-tracking drone camera. If not for Roy—who smoked, by the way—it'd have been a top-ten core memory kind of day.

"So, Noah," Roy prodded as Skye and I eventually called it quits and made our way back to the house. "How are you settling in so far? Are you excited to start the challenges?"

Skye gave me a shrug and grinned like he also wanted to hear my answer.

"Um, yeah," I awkwardly replied, not stopping to engage in a whole interview now that I had lunch on my mind. "It's going to be an adjustment, for sure."

"Can you elaborate on that?" Roy pushed, puffing as he struggled to keep pace with us up the track to the house.

No...not really? I had gotten way out of the habit of speaking on camera since closing down my Norah Sparkle account, and I was fairly convinced whatever I said could and would be twisted into something awful. So I just gave a tight smile, shrugged, and hurried the fuck up to get inside the house ahead of Roy.

"There he is," Ace announced as we made our way into the enormous open-plan kitchen.

Zeth looked up from his sandwich, his eyes narrowed slightly as he eyed me with confusion. "You survived a morning with Skye, huh? How was it?"

I bit my lip, glancing over my shoulder at Roy, who was panning his camera around the room. "Yeah, it was...cool." My stomach rumbled hard, and I grimaced. We'd skipped breakfast entirely, and I was fucking starving.

"Noah, do you like grilled cheese?" Torin asked from his spot in the kitchen. He wore an apron but seemed like he was shirtless underneath, judging by the naked expanse of his strong, tanned arms. Fucking hell, he was a beautiful man.

I nodded enthusiastically, sliding into one of the vacant barstools, leaving a gap between me and Zeth. The way he watched me was more than a little off-putting—like he knew I was a fraud. "Who doesn't?" I replied with a nervous laugh, hyperaware that the cameras were still rolling.

"You'll get used to it," Minho said quietly, sliding into the empty seat beside me. "The cameras, I mean. And if it reassures you, they literally work for us. If there's anything you don't want making the episode cut, you just say so, and it'll be cut."

That actually hadn't occurred to me, that the team had any creative control over the footage. A small sigh of relief escaped me, and I offered a tight smile his way. "That's good to know."

His answering grin made my stomach flip, and I swallowed hard. He'd tied up his hair in a little ponytail, and it was a *really* good look on him. Having all that inky-black hair pulled back from his face seemed to highlight how delicate his features were and offered no distraction from the intensity of his gaze. It was...overwhelming.

"Any preference for ingredients, Noah?" Torin asked, jerking my attention away from the little trance Minho had just put me under.

"Um, cheese?" I replied with another weak laugh, praying that my face wasn't as pink as it felt. If I didn't stop drooling over my new teammates, they'd work out I was a girl in no time. Or maybe not. Maybe they'd just assume I was gay?

Speaking of...Skye had just sat down in August's lap on one of the sofas, and August was absentmindedly rubbing the younger guy's shoulders while continuing his conversation with Xavier. Was there a sexual relationship between them? The whole team oozed female-gaze sex appeal all over their online presence, but that didn't mean it was the truth. I knew perfectly well how fake it could all be.

I wanted to ask, but it was way too soon.

"Skye took you out to the cliff?" Ace asked, leaning his elbows on the counter opposite where I sat, his gaze intense and far too observant. "How'd you like his setup?"

"It's really cool," I said honestly, nodding. "I live in an apartment, so the space you guys have here is crazy."

"You should see the track." Ace chuckled. "Our land here wasn't big enough for everyone to do everything they want, so we have a second property near Yorba Linda."

By "track" I had to assume it was mostly Xavier's area, since he was the biker. Motocross, BMX, road bikes...anything with two wheels and high energy was Xavier Stone's domain. Fuck, was I drooling again?

Torin rounded the counter and dropped a plate in front of me. "Grilled cheese, extra cheese," he announced with a wink.

"Where's mine?" Minho asked with a pout, staring longingly at my food as the mouthwatering scent of buttery toast wafted to my nose.

Torin reached over me to flick Minho in the forehead. "Use your words like a big boy and ask nicely, Minnie."

Shock held me frozen as I glanced between the two of them. Was this...an argument? Or flirtation? I was so fucking confused.

Minho just smirked back, then turned his eyes all big and round like some kind of adorable woodland creature. "Please, can I have one too, Tor?"

"Of course!" Torin replied, heading back to his stove. "Once I've finished Ace's and Skye's."

"Here, have half of mine," I offered, pushing my plate across after picking up one half. "If I'm still hungry when yours is ready you can return the favor."

Minho gave me a sidelong glance but took the sandwich anyway. "You should eat more," he murmured, taking a bite of the steaming sandwich, "but I'm not one to throw stones in glass houses, so thanks." He gave me an affectionate sort of shoulder bump that made me go all warm and gooey inside, so I took a huge bite to save myself from responding.

"Good, you're all here," someone said a few minutes later, and I looked up to find a sharply suited man in maybe his mid-fifties having just strode into the kitchen area. "Noah, nice to see you here. Are you settling in well?"

I quickly chewed my mouthful and swallowed before answering. "So far, yeah..." I trailed off with confusion, because I had no clue who this man was. None of the guys seemed concerned or surprised by his presence though.

"Good. It occurs to me we never officially met. I'm Mr. Leight, the team manager." He didn't try to offer a smile to seem approachable in any way, and that checked out from what I had learned about him during contract negotiation.

My mood soured, and my eyes narrowed. "I see."

A brief flash of amusement crossed his face, and he tucked his hands into his pockets, shifting his attention to Ace. "Engagement from the introduction stage has been great so far, most clicks and views spiking on Team Olympus announcements as anticipated."

Ace nodded, like this wasn't news to him at all.

"Skye, I understand you spent the morning with Noah, yes?" Mr. Leight arched a brow in Skye's direction, and I noticed that he'd shifted off August's lap and now sat a short distance away.

"Yes, sir," my roommate confirmed.

"Good, the Acolytes are dying to see the two of you working together. This afternoon I want Noah with you, Minho. We need some short-form content uploaded *today,* so can you get some of those trending dance challenges filmed?" Mr. Leight pulled his phone from his pocket as he spoke, barely giving either Minho or me the courtesy of eye contact as he made his demands.

Minho didn't seem bothered, shrugging one tattoo-covered shoulder and tossing me a teasing smile. "Depends if Noah can dance or not. Otherwise all I can promise is a whole lot of blooper reels."

Mr. Leight glanced up from his phone, meeting my panicked eyes, and I nearly choked on my mouthful. He knew damn well who I was and that I'd spent my entire fucking childhood on *Dance Babes*, but I couldn't exactly admit to that here.

"I'm sure you can teach him," the manager muttered dismissively. "Doesn't need to be perfect. Just get it done."

My brow dipped with irritation at his tone, but Minho draping his arm over my shoulders stilled my tongue. "Can do, boss," he said with an edge of sarcasm. His subtle squeeze of my upper arm implied he knew I was about to get mouthy and was warning me not to. But how? He didn't *know* me and had no reason to know how badly my temper had just flared. Mr. Leight was already in my bad books before ever meeting, but now? Now I *really* disliked him.

"Good. Ace, I expect to see your interaction projections and content concepts for the Games in my inbox by Friday. Noah, can I speak with you privately, please? We have some house rules to run through." Mr. Leight turned and strode out of the room without even waiting for me to respond.

My mouth fell open in shock. Was that man serious? Who the fuck did he think he was?

"Just get it over with," Minho murmured with a sigh, dropping his arm off my shoulders, much to my disappointment. "I'll meet you in the practice room when you're done."

I gritted my teeth but bit my tongue. The cameras were still rolling, and I didn't need to go offering up sound bites that could be used against me at a later date. After meeting Mr. Leight, I was less confident that the guys controlled the content after all.

Luckily I didn't have to search all over the house to find the bad-mannered man, as he was waiting in the impressive entry foyer with an irritated look on his face. When he saw me approach, he opened the door and gestured for me to follow him outside onto the porch.

"You could have cut your hair shorter, Noah. You still look like a girl." That was what he said. No pleasantries or even hello? What a dick.

I quirked a brow and folded my arms. "My hair is barely an inch longer than Minho's, and no one thinks he's a girl. Didn't you know? Gender fluidity is very fashionable right now."

Mr. Leight's eyes narrowed, and his jaw flexed. "You seem to be under the impression that you're doing me a favor with this act, Noah. This is for *your* protection. Do you have any concept of what the boys' fans would do if they discovered *Norah Sparkle* living at Mount Olympus? Let alone if they connected you to—"

"Enough," I hissed, cutting him off before he could say *Peaches*. No matter how badly I'd wanted to keep the whole porn thing quiet while my lawyers gagged Rich in iron-clad NDAs, we had needed to come clean with Team Olympus management for several reasons, not the least of which was damage control, in the potential event of a scandal. "I'm doing my part, but it seems like you only want to make things difficult. Why am I sharing a bedroom with Skye? How do you expect me to keep this under wraps when I am literally never alone?"

Mr. Leight's jaw ticked again and his lips tightened. "Changing that now will only raise more questions. You'll figure it out, Noah, or our contract is void." *And Miles would be doing rehab in prison.*

The message was loud and clear. "Is that everything, then? Can I go?"

The sharpness of my tone made him glare daggers. "Just don't fuck it up, Noah. The Acolytes will skin you alive, and you know it."

He wasn't wrong about that. Team Olympus's fandom was toxic as fuck and not known for their compassion or logical thinking when it came to the boys. Parasocial didn't even touch the surface of how some of their fandom behaved.

"Oh, and the fans are already loving your interactions with Minho, so feel free to lean into that harder. As much as they'd rip your spine out for being a girl, they go feral for an implied same-sex relationship. Go figure." With that bomb dropped, Mr. Leight strode down the porch steps and slid into the backseat of his waiting sedan.

Well, fuck. Maybe I didn't need to stop drooling over the guys after all.

SEVEN

It occurred to me after the team manager left that I had no idea where the practice room was that I was meeting Minho in. Eventually—after several minutes of searching and opening doors—I gave up and returned to the kitchen to seek help.

Ace was still there, sitting at the island with Zeth and Xavier, and hopped up quickly to show me the way. Thank fuck, too, because I'd have never found it on my own.

"The house originally had a shitload of guest rooms and useless spaces like formal dining," Ace explained as he led the way upstairs, "but we hated having to drive everywhere for practice, rehearsal, filming...so we converted some spaces. Here." He opened the double doors

at the end of the first-floor hallway, where I'd assumed the master suite was located.

Instead, he revealed a dance studio, complete with a fully mirrored wall and hardwood floor. Minho was already there, sitting on the floor and stretching his hamstrings by grabbing his own toes. In two corners of the room, tripods were set up with cameras, but none of the producers or staff were anywhere to be seen.

"That was quick," Minho commented, looking up at me as we approached. "Did you call him a dick to his face or hold back?"

Ace's brows shot up, and he gave me a puzzled look. "Was that an option?"

I bit back a smile. "It's always an option. Your lovely manager was just offering some words of encouragement. Also, apparently fans think we're cute together." I met Minho's gaze as I said that and tried really hard not to react when he grinned.

"Nice." He extended a hand for me to high-five and I obliged, the smack of our palms echoing through the room. "It's because we're both pretty as fuck, dude."

I snickered, unable to help myself while Ace grumbled something under his breath about *fan service.*

"Ace is just salty because if he gave the Acolytes what they actually wanted in their fan service, he'd be shifting his platform to CB Adults," Minho teased, shooting Ace a smirk before turning his attention back to me. "Fan service is basically giving the fans what they want. It's playing into their rumors and speculations, most of which are wildly inaccurate and almost always involve sex, secret relationships, or kink in some way."

I narrowed my eyes. "I'm well aware what it is and that Team Olympus is basically built off of it with all the casual nudity and flirty camerawork."

"Shirtless isn't nude," Ace corrected, seeming unbothered by my judgmental tone. "We're very good at following the terms and conditions of the platform."

Minho gave me a curious look, then pushed up off the ground and pulled his phone from his pocket. He hummed under his breath while scrolling a folder of what looked like sound samples, all thirty seconds each. Perfect ClikByte short-form length.

"Okay, hmm, let me find something with easy choreography," he murmured, searching the options he'd saved. Ace moved to peer at his screen, and the two of them pondered a couple of possibilities while I twiddled my thumbs and looked around the room. The cameras on the tripods weren't turned on, and my shoulders relaxed dramatically with that realization. Sure, they'd have to film eventually, but maybe my awkward learning phase—where I tried to act like I didn't know what I was doing—could be kept private.

Eventually the guys decided on a clip, and Minho plugged his phone into the sound system to play the thirty-second trending sound.

"I'm guessing your algorithm has you on a different side of ClikByte from me," Minho said with a lazy smile, his head bopping lightly with the tune. "So you probably don't watch a lot of these."

I shrugged, not wanting to make things too hard. "You might be surprised."

"Okay, sick. You staying, Ace?" Minho stretched his shoulders as he shot the question to our white-haired team leader.

Ace cast a curious look my way, then nodded. "Yeah, I'll stay. Noah can't possibly be worse at these dance challenges than me, so it'll make him look better by comparison."

Minho rolled his eyes, and I scoffed. Maybe they weren't constantly flooding my scroll, but I'd dedicated a shitload of time into researching the whole team. Sure, Ace wasn't a natural talent with dance like Minho was... but he was no bumbling fool, either. And what he lacked in skill he made up for with sex appeal by filming nine out of ten Bytes shirtless.

"All right, let's do this. We can do a few practice runs before turning the cameras on." Minho clapped me on the shoulder and gave an encouraging squeeze before moving over to the mirror wall to run through the admittedly very simple dance sequence.

The second he started patiently teaching the kind of choreography I could have learned as a six-year-old, I lost the ability to fake it. When he gestured for me to follow the steps he'd just demonstrated, I executed the full thirty-second sequence with confidence and grinned at the expression on both their faces.

Then instantly regretted it when Minho's eyes narrowed with suspicion and zeroed in on my feet. I wore the men's sneakers that had been added into my boy wardrobe so he couldn't *see* anything damning, right?

"You could have said you knew how to dance sooner," Ace grumbled, raking his fingers through his hair. "Maybe I don't wanna join you two after all."

"No take backs," I replied with a laugh, actually enjoying myself again, just like I had in the morning with Skye on the trampoline, before Roy showed up. "And I could have, yes, but did you ever ask?"

Ace pursed his lips and nodded. "You have a good point, Eight. We made assumptions."

Minho was still squinting at me with curiosity, so I quickly scrambled for a plausible explanation. "My sister was a competitive dancer," I lied with a lopsided shrug, "but she also used to have really bad stage fright and anxiety, so I would practice with her for all the competitions and shit. I guess I picked up a few things along the way." Which was true...if Miles and I swapped positions. He actually had done that for me when we were little. Until I grew into my own confidence and he hit puberty—it was too *embarrassing* to do jazz and ballet with his baby sister.

"Huh, that's kind of adorable," Minho murmured, nodding. "What's her name?"

"Her name?" I repeated, briefly confused. "Oh, my sister. Millie."

"Careful," Ace warned with a smirk. "Minho can't be trusted around sisters. You should have seen the fight when Xavier caught him flirting with his sister, Rachel."

Minho threw his hands in the air with frustration. "I didn't know she was his sister, *and* she lied about her age! Fuck, you guys will never let me live that one down."

He grimaced in my direction. "Mistakes were made. I definitely deserved that black eye."

I laughed, but at the same time my stomach was all in knots again. Right when I'd halfway convinced myself that maybe he wasn't into girls... Wait—was that a good thing or a bad thing, while I was pretending to be a guy? Fuck, I was confusing *myself* now. Then again, that reminded me of the whole scandal that saw Minho removed from his K-pop group after fucking the daughter of his record company's CEO on live stream. Whoops.

As it turned out, Ace was more than an *okay* dancer himself. Even when they turned the cameras on to film our content, it wasn't awkward and uncomfortable like Roy had made it earlier. It was just fun, something I never expected to have while being blackmailed onto this team.

In the end we filmed four different trending dance challenges and saved a whole stack of blooper reels, too. Minho earned my trust in deleting the clip where I gasped and stared open-mouthed as Ace took his shirt off, but when I commented on his dirty delete, he looped an arm around my waist and joked that it would ruin our blossoming romance if I was gaping at Ace.

Fucking hell. Yes, I knew he was joking. Yes, I knew he was referring to Mr. Leight's dumb fucking suggestion about us *leaning into* the fan service. Yes, I knew he didn't actually think I was drooling over Ace's incredible body—even if I was. But...it still got me all fluttery.

When we left the dance studio, I headed straight back to my shared room with Skye and locked the bathroom door securely behind myself. I needed to shower, badly. Actually, what I needed was a nice long shower with my waterproof, battery-operated boyfriend, but my stupid, paranoid ass hadn't even packed it. Because how the fuck would I explain that if it was found?

Besides, I was way too anxious about being caught naked, let alone being caught flicking the lady-bean. Even if I'd been desperate enough to try it, the anxiety would never let me finish.

"This is *fucked,*" I whispered to my foggy reflection after getting out. I stared at my blurred outline for a minute, trying to picture what the guys saw when they looked at me. Whether they genuinely believed Noah was a dude...and what they'd say if they ever found out. Fuck. That thought hit me like a gut punch. *Somehow, I seriously doubt they'd be amused.*

With that sour feeling riding in my chest, I quickly dressed in clean clothes—binder included—and rolled up my sweaty, dirty stuff to place in my hamper. I'd do my own washing, to save any uncomfortable questions, but it'd have to wait until I had a full load or I'd be spending half my life in the laundry room.

Once that was done, I grabbed my phone from beside my bed, where I'd left it charging the night before. Skye had hurried me out of bed when I was half-asleep, and I hadn't thought of it since. It wasn't like I had any friends to text; Rich made damn sure of that a long time ago.

When I saw the list of missed calls and messages, I nearly turned the damn thing off.

As if sensing my thoughts, it lit up in my hand with an incoming call.

Miles.

"Crap," I muttered, then drew a deep breath and answered. Because he was my brother, and I couldn't avoid him forever. "Hey...you." My paranoia that someone might hear me prevented me from saying his name out loud.

"Hey *you*? That's all you have to say? Noah, *what the fuck are you doing?*" My brother yelled down the phone so hard I flinched and moved it away from my ear. Come to think of it, I needed to change his contact info in my phone, too. His voice continued berating me from the speaker as I edited his contact to *Millie.*

"...don't understand what you're doing!" Miles was saying when I put the phone back to my ear.

I sighed heavily, not caring that he could hear me. "You don't need to understand. Last I checked, I'm an adult, capable of making my own choices...both personal and professional. Clik Games is just good business, and you know it."

"Oh, cut the crap, Noah. You've never given two fucks about the Games before. And *Team Olympus*? Are you on drugs?" He meant it as a figure of speech, but it still felt like a slap.

"That's rich, coming from you," I snapped before I could bite my tongue. His instant silence made me wince, and guilt damn near choked me. "I'm sorry, I didn't mean that. How are you doing, anyway? How's rehab?"

Miles gave a frustrated sound followed by a weak laugh. "Shut the fuck up. You're such a brat, you know?" It was said with love, though, no malice or hatred. "Are you doing this because of me, Noah? Because I can't—"

"No," I quickly cut him off, lying my ass off. "It's just a good opportunity, and honestly, I need the distraction right now. I need this...disguise." Okay, that part wasn't a lie. I bit my lip, fighting back the urge to start crying. I'd held it together for so long after finding out that Rich had been uploading sex tapes of me all over the internet, but fuck, it was hard. I was exhausted.

Miles was quiet for a moment, understanding me perfectly, just as he always had. "I'm so sorry, Sparkles. If I'd known..." He blew out a long, agitated breath.

"You'd have probably pushed him off that construction site yourself," I half joked, swallowing back my tears, "and then you'd be on trial for murder, and we'd be a whole lot worse off right now. It's fine. I handled it. And now I'm moving on."

"With Ace and Xavier..." he said with clear disgust. "Noah, you can't trust them. They're not good people."

I bit my lip, glancing at the bedroom door, which remained firmly closed. "I think maybe you're wrong about that, Miles. But if you're right, I guess I'll have to find out for myself. I've got to go, tell Mom I love her."

"Noah," he groaned. "You're such a stubborn shit. Just be safe, okay? And fucking hell, don't let the fans find out you're a girl."

I chuckled. "I won't. Make sure no one else outs me, okay?"

He grumpily agreed, then I ended the call and tucked my phone into my pocket. Weirdly, speaking to Miles had given me a level of clarity I hadn't known I even needed. Blackmail might have been what pushed me into this team, but ultimately they were exactly what I needed right now: a fresh start as someone new. Not Norah, not Peaches...just me. Noah.

EIGHT

It was a weird feeling, having a full team of eight after spending so long preparing for Clik Games and handpicking the perfect members. Noah was a wild card, but I knew that when I decided he would be our final member. It was a risk I'd already accepted, but so far, I felt like *maybe* it was going to work out.

Something about the little dude made me think he was going to fit in perfectly with the rest of us. Also maybe it was a good thing he was so tiny. There hadn't been any of the usual testosterone-flexing shit from Xavier and Torin. Instead everyone just wanted to take care of Noah like a little brother.

"How's the new guy settling in?" Z asked, making himself at home on my office sofa behind me.

I paused the Byte I'd been watching and turned in my swivel chair to glare at his feet up on the arm of the sofa. "You mind?"

A brief moment of indecision crossed his face before he sighed and moved his feet back to the floor. "Sorry."

I just grunted, because he knew full fucking well that'd piss me off, and he did it anyway. "Noah seems to be settling in okay, don't you think?"

Z nodded, his expression thoughtful. "Mm-hmm. He's not happy about the sleeping arrangements, though. What's up with that? Some precious shit needing privacy?"

"Maybe," I murmured, rotating back to my desktop to drum my fingertips on Noah's file, which I'd compiled months earlier. It was thin. Much thinner than the files I had on August and Minho, our other new-ish members, but that was due to a shocking lack of available information on Noah. The guy was private as *fuck*, his digital footprint professionally cleaned, so his reluctance to share a room with Skye shouldn't have been any great surprise.

"At least him and Skye seem to be getting along," Z commented, stretching his arms over his head with a yawn. "I thought for sure that was going to blow up in the green room."

A small smile curved my lips at the memory. Scrappy kid had looked like he was ready to throw punches at Skye during that first interaction. I'd kind of expected it, so I'd shuffled the room assignments around deliberately to force them to interact, but it wasn't necessary. Skye won Noah over before we even arrived home. It'd been three days since then, and they now acted like they'd been friends their whole lives.

"As if anyone can resist Skye's charm," I said with a chuckle. "He's a golden retriever in human form. Are you still trying to work out where you recognize Noah from?"

Z huffed a frustrated sound. "Nah, I gave up. I think maybe he looks like a guy I went to school with. Not really important, I guess. What are you thinking for Team Bonding week?" He nodded to my multiple computer screens featuring various Bytes from our competitors.

We had one week between introductions and the actual start of Clik Games, which was now in four days. The first week for Clik Games was about team bonding, since most teams were not preestablished units. The challenge would be to prepare a Byte that involved *all* eight members but didn't necessarily need to meet any specific genre or niche.

Our problem, though, was how diverse the team specialties were. Again, this was a risk I'd accepted when compiling the team, and although everyone had their distinctly different platforms, they were more versatile than they showed on ClikByte.

"Uh, I'm still undecided," I admitted, running a hand through my hair. "Initially I'd been leaning toward something...safe. Something on brand for Team Olympus, you know?"

Z nodded. "Shirtless shit, minimal risk with maximum thirst factor."

I chuckled again. "Yeah. But after seeing the reactions to Noah from the introduction stages..." I clicked into the statistics spreadsheet I'd compiled with all the public responses to our team announcements. Not just Acolytes—our loyal fan base—but across all social media platforms and all fandoms. They were going feral for Noah's androgynous, almost feminine appearance, and the rumor mill was working overtime with speculations that his NoFear content was all green-screened— that none of it was legit—because he was so pretty. Like that made *any* sense at all.

Z sat forward to read my top highlighted comments with an annoyed twist to his lips. "Fucking keyboard warriors."

"Yeah, but when we rely on public voting, we really need to take the opportunity to squash the doubters, right?" I swapped windows to pull up Noah's ClikByte profile, then pulled up Skye's on my second screen. "Trouble is, that unless you lazy fuckers are hiding a couple hundred skydives under your hats, we can't do any of the aerial shit these two adrenaline junkies get the most Cliks on. So where does that leave us?"

Z didn't take offense to my insult, instead grinning as he reached for my mouse to select a Byte. "Let's watch a few of the top Bytes on both and see what's doable."

For the next few hours, with Xavier joining us some time later, we browsed through both Noah's and Skye's platforms and brainstormed how we could incorporate the whole team into one Byte. It was harder than I'd anticipated...but I saw plenty of great potential for future Bytes, so it wasn't totally wasted time.

"My brain fucking hurts," Xavier admitted eventually, voicing what I'd already been thinking. "Can we break for dinner? Torin and August said they'd cook."

My stomach rumbled at that idea. The two of them were fantastic cooks. "Fuck yes. We still have four days, maybe we just need to marinate on this for a bit."

The three of us left my office and headed for the kitchen, where music was playing *loudly* while Torin and August no doubt created a huge mess. They were excellent cooks, but fucking awful at cleaning up after themselves.

Minho was there with them, sitting on the edge of the island with a beer in hand and being absolutely no help at all in the creation of dinner, while Torin and August tossed ingredients around like they were on a variety show.

"Where are the little dudes?" Xavier asked, glancing around our enormous kitchen.

Minho pointed upstairs. "Noah got a call from his manager and went to take it somewhere quieter. Skye, I'm pretty sure, went to eavesdrop."

My brows rose in surprise. "And you didn't think to tell him that's a bad idea?"

He just shrugged one shoulder and sipped his drink. "Why would I?"

Sometimes I genuinely thought Minho lit fires just for the joy of watching them burn. The guy needed a hobby. I saved my breath trying to explain why we didn't want to start fights with our newest member three days into our arrangement and headed upstairs to find Skye.

Sure enough, I found him outside his and Noah's shared bedroom with his ear against the door. Fucking hell, he wasn't even *attempting* subtlety.

"Skye!" I hissed, keeping my voice low as I approached, but he still flinched so hard he nearly fell flat on his ass. Probably would have if I didn't grab his upper arm to steady his balance.

"Ace, what the *fuck*?" he whispered back, eyes wide with shock. "You nearly gave me a heart attack. What were you thinking, sneaking up on me like that?"

"Me?" I replied, shaking my head in bemusement. "What were *you* thinking?" I gave a pointed look at the closed bedroom door and noted Noah's quiet but clearly irate voice on the other side.

Skye gave a guilty glance at the door, then bit his lip and swiped a hand through his messy gold blond hair. "Uh, I just wanted to get some socks, but Noah's on the phone with his manager. I was just waiting until he's done."

I quirked a brow, glancing down at his feet. At his *socks*, more specifically. "Oh? What's wrong with those?"

Skye looked down at his own feet and hummed. "I don't like the stripes."

"Uh-huh," I drawled, folding my arms over my chest. "So... you weren't trying to hear what Noah was talking to his manager about?"

His big blue eyes narrowed, and his brow furrowed. "I just wanted to know why he seems to have such an issue sharing a room. I thought we were cool but like...maybe he still thought I'm a copycat, like I'm just using him for ideas."

I tilted my head at his phrasing. "Past tense, so I assume you got your answers?"

Skye blushed. Hard. "Yeah, I guess that's not what it was."

Curiosity clawed at me, and I damn near asked *what* he'd heard. But that would make me no better than him for listening in the first place. It'd be a gross invasion of Noah's privacy, and despite whatever strong-arm tactics our company used to make him join the team, I wanted him to feel safe here. I wanted him to trust us.

"Okay. So if you got what you wanted, why are you still listening?" I leveled him with my best disapproving glare, and the adorable little asshole hung his head in shame.

"No good reason," he mumbled.

Just then the door jerked open behind Skye, and I locked gazes with a very flustered Noah, whose eyes widened dramatically when he saw us there.

"What are you guys doing?" he asked in a shaking voice, glancing from me to Skye and back again with a frown. "Were you listening to my conversation?" The edge of panic in that question made me even more desperate to know what'd been said. What had put that odd, shifty look on Skye's face and the brow-sweating kind of stress on Noah as he tried to work out what we'd heard?

Skye said nothing, just glanced up at me with a wince. He'd make a fucking terrible spy.

"No, of course not. Skye wanted to show me something, but we didn't want to interrupt. We didn't hear anything. Right?" I nudged Skye, and he nodded silently.

Why was he acting so strange? Normally when he was trying to lie, he would talk at a million miles an hour, trying to deflect from the main question.

Noah seemed just as confused as me, folding his arms in the oversized hoodie he wore as he squinted at Skye. "Sorry if I shut you out. I just...needed to clear up a few things with my manager."

Skye gave a tight shrug. "You're fine. It's your room too." Again. Weird vibe from him.

"Torin and August are cooking dinner," I said, changing the subject to break the tension. "They're actually good cooks, before you worry. I think I smelled chicken curry when I passed through earlier."

Noah nodded slowly, still seeming uncomfortable. "Uh, are the crew here or...?"

That explained a lot. He was worried about the camera crew that filmed the weekly *Mount Olympus* episodes. Despite what the guys had said at the introduction filming, we weren't being filmed *every minute of every day*. But yeah, there had been a heavy dose of content in the last three days because our producers knew that Noah's arrival would be good for ratings.

Not that it was hard filming. They'd just asked him to spend time with each of the members while working on content, to get to know each other better. I was pretty sure Noah even fell asleep on the floor while Torin was working on a new pottery vase. Weirdly, I was the only one he hadn't spent any one-on-one time with. But that was okay, since I'd managed to find an excuse to drop in on all of the other guys' times for one reason or other.

"Nope, not tonight," I reassured him. "August and Torin probably have the cameras on in the kitchen, but that's because their cooking content is entertaining as shit. Steer clear of the mess and you'll be fine."

Noah's shoulders lowered noticeably with relief, and he flashed me a quick smile. "Okay, good. That I can handle." He started along the hallway, then paused and looked back at us when we didn't follow. "Are you coming?"

I glanced at Skye, confused about the dramatic shift in his mood. His face blushed at the question and he rubbed the back of his neck, avoiding eye contact.

"Yeah, um, yeah..." he mumbled.

I shook my head with a short sigh. "You go ahead, Noah. Skye still needs to show me that thing." I grabbed my youngest team member by the scruff of his neck and directed him into the bedroom before he could act any stranger than he already was.

Noah shrugged and continued as I closed the door between us and leveled Skye with a hard look. "Whatever you overheard—"

"Ace, I think—"

"Nope!" I cut him off, shaking my head firmly. "Whatever you overheard, *you shouldn't have.* I don't want to know, and you have no right to know. Being on our team does not nullify Noah's right to privacy, and you just violated it. That's not okay, Skye, and you know it."

His eyes widened, and his lips twisted in remorse. "You're right."

I studied him for a moment, curiosity clawing at the insides of my skull. "Does what you heard put any of our team in danger?" Because that was the only way I'd accept breaking Noah's privacy.

Indecision tripped across Skye's face as he chewed the corner of his lip, his mind clearly going a million miles an hour. Then he sighed and shook his head. "No. It's nothing like that. It's none of anyone else's business, and I had no right eavesdropping. I'll just..." He trailed off with a pained wince, shrugging.

"You'll pretend this never happened and forget everything you heard Noah discussing with his manager." I said it firmly, not offering any room for debate.

Skye nodded his understanding, his shoulders hunched. "Yes. That."

I frowned at him, debating whether I needed to reprimand him any further. If it were literally any of the others, it'd be an unquestionable yes. But Skye was a good kid. He knew he'd done the wrong thing, and he wouldn't make it worse by gossiping.

"Are you good?" I asked, clapping my hand on his shoulder to give him a little shake. "Do I need to swap roommate assignments?"

Skye vehemently shook his head at that. "No, definitely not. No, we're good. Totally fine. This never happened, and I know nothing." Offering up a lopsided grin, he opened the bedroom door once more. "I'm hungry."

I followed, my stomach also rumbling, but made a mental note to keep an eye on Skye and Noah's relationship. Lovable little dickhead just had to go snooping and make things weird, didn't he?

NINE

My pulse still thumped with adrenaline as I jogged down the stairs toward the kitchen. When I'd opened the door after ending my call with Jared, my whole life had flashed before my eyes. For a hot second I thought *for sure* Ace and Skye had heard everything, despite how low I'd attempted to keep my voice on that call. In fairness, when the frustration got the better of me, I'd let my volume rise somewhat.

But Ace's calm reassured me they'd heard nothing. I had no doubt he was a good actor but not *that* good. He'd have reacted in a big way if he'd heard what I'd been discussing with Jared.

It was a relief, but it also reminded me I needed to be more careful. One good bit of news came out of the conversation: Jared's baby girl had made her grand entrance, and they'd named her Isla.

The commotion coming from the kitchen made me smile, and my nerves relaxed as I followed the noise and my nose. As anticipated, Torin and August were at the center of the action with a half dozen GoPros dotted around the space, and Minho was sitting on the edge of the island counter with a beer in hand, spectating.

When I cautiously made my way closer, eyeing which camera angles would cut me out, Minho gestured for me to join him.

"Blind spot," he assured me, taking my upper arm and pulling me closer so I leaned against the counter between his casually spread legs. He put his beer down and confidently finger combed my hair as though we had known each other for years instead of days. It wasn't the first time he'd done it, though, and I was getting better about not freaking out at the comfortable affection. He was the same with everyone else on the team.

"Do they clean this up afterward?" I joked, my eyes wide as I looked around at the carnage across the huge kitchen.

Minho chuckled, using one of the elastics from his wrist to tie my hair up in a little half-ponytail like he often wore his own. I had enough short layers that he'd never get it all up, but it was a cute style nonetheless. "They would if they had to. But you just wait until Xavier sees it."

I clicked my tongue, nodding as I relaxed my position, resting my elbow on one of his thighs. "Neat freak. Already clocked that one when I accidentally brought mud inside on my sneakers."

"Noah, you wanna cook with us?" August called out, approaching with one of the little handheld cameras running. "Torin keeps burning the rice."

"Whoa, too far!" Torin exclaimed, throwing a stick of celery at the back of August's head. "I'm Japanese, you dickwad! Like I'd ever burn *rice*."

August just snort-laughed. "Half. The Irish in you is confused as fuck about why the potatoes are so small."

I gaped at them, unsure whether to laugh or not, but the decision was made for me when Torin grabbed the retractable sprayer from the huge farm-style sink and squirted it in August's direction. What was more shocking, the fact that he'd done it in the first place or the pressure on that tap for the water spray to actually hit August, was impossible to judge.

"Here we go," Minho groaned, resting one hand on my shoulder as he reached for his beer once more. "Bets on how long it takes Xavier and Ace to break it up?"

August had just retaliated by tossing a whole bowl of flour at Torin, so things were definitely escalating fast. "Someone needs to, or one of them will get hurt," I replied with genuine concern. The floor was both wet *and* floury, so the likeliness of someone slipping was high. I started to move forward to do *something*, but Minho's hand on my shoulder tightened, stopping me.

"Nope, not you, Chicken. You can't risk hurting your back."

Huh? Why would he say that?

I didn't respond, out of both confusion and embarrassment, because he'd just called me *Chicken* as affectionately as someone might say *Sweetheart* or *Babe,* and we weren't even on camera, so it wasn't fan service. Right?

Ace and Skye showed up only a few moments later and our fair leader *thankfully* broke up the food fight between Torin and August, scolding the both of them and ordering them to start cleaning up their mess while he salvaged what was left of the dinner they'd been making.

Skye seemed oddly quiet, frowning at me like he wanted to say something. Maybe about how Minho was toying with my hair again? But I'd seen Skye just as affectionate with August, so I doubted that was an issue. Weird.

Eventually Ace plated up dinner for everyone, and we helped him carry it all over to the enormous wooden dining table adjacent to the kitchen crime scene. He asked Skye to go find Xavier and Zeth, then gestured for us all to take a seat.

As much as Torin and August had been scolded, they were both grinning and relaxed as they joined us at the table.

"Is this a regular cooking experience in Mount Olympus?" I asked in a wry tone, reaching out to brush some flour from Torin's cheek since he'd sat beside me. "I'm shocked you get anything done."

"Not *all* the time," August drawled, accepting a beer from Ace as the team leader handed them out. "But also it's not uncommon. Tor has a real short temper."

Torin rolled his eyes and huffed. “Yeah, because I started that.”

“You literally threw celery at me, bro!” August shot back with mock pearl-clutching. “That’s the definition of starting it.”

Torin glowered playfully. “Because you said—”

“Enough,” Ace snapped, offering Torin a beer. “We are not starting this again now. I’m starving, and seeing this food go to waste will break my heart.”

Xavier and Z—Zeth had told me to call him that—arrived then, and Xavier gave a long, pained groan. “Seriously? What are you guys, rabid racoons or something?”

“Hey, we cleaned up,” Torin protested, glancing over at the kitchen area before wincing. “Sort of.”

“Noah,” Ace said to gain my attention as he offered a beer my way.

I shook my head quickly. “No thanks.” He arched a brow as if curious but didn’t try and change my mind as he handed it to Z instead.

“Do you want something else?” Minho asked, noticing my refusal. “There’s some cider in the fridge, and if you’re into wine we have some—”

“No, no.” I cut him off with an apologetic, slightly embarrassed smile. “I don’t drink. But thanks, that’s thoughtful.”

That admission earned me more than a few puzzled glances, but no one pushed the issue any further, and Ace fetched me a glass of soda instead. He really was attentive to the whole team’s needs; it was admirable.

"So, Eight," Ace said with a teasing smile as he finally sat down at the table, "how was your day with Xavier and Z? Did they play nice?"

I chuckled, glancing at Xavier as he tried to subtly give me a middle finger. He'd very wrongly assumed he could impress me with his motocross tricks over at their other training property and overshot the jump. It was lucky he hadn't been hurt, but his ego was more than bruised enough to make up for it.

"Yeah, it was cool," I said instead of sharing the whole story with the team. They'd see it on the episode footage soon enough anyway. "It was cool seeing Z's songwriting process, even if I was as helpful as a wet sock."

Z grinned and shrugged. "You were more helpful than you realized, Noah."

Ace nodded his agreement. "You'd be surprised how much inspiration Z draws from just being around other people. Especially new people. You'll have inspired a dozen songs by the end of the month, just wait."

That made my brows rise, and I looked down the table at Z in question. He just ruffled his fingers through his unnaturally deep red hair and grinned. "True."

"Okay, well, now that we're all here," Ace redirected the conversation as everyone got stuck in their food, "we should talk plans for the first Games challenge. Technically it begins in four days, and we then have four weeks to film our entry content, but I have an idea of what the challenge will involve already."

Xavier nodded his agreement, smoothly taking over the discussion so Ace could eat his dinner too. "The first stage of Clik Games is always about teamwork. This won't be a shock to anyone competing, least of all the teams with veteran Games players, but we need to decide how we can incorporate all eight of our team into the one Byte."

"Game Bytes can be up to five minutes long," Z added, his fork paused halfway to his mouth, "and don't need to cater to *everyone's* skill set, so long as everyone is included in some way. It'll be judged on Cliks, obviously, but also scored for teamwork."

I had nothing to contribute to this part of the discussion so I focused on my food—which was delicious, mind you—and kept my ears open.

"I have no doubt when they announce the challenge on Monday, they'll add some unexpected criteria which will make too much preplanning irrelevant," Ace continued thoughtfully, "but at this point I'd love to get some ideas of what the eight of us could all do to show *teamwork*."

"And..." Z murmured, his mouth partly full, "the Noah thing."

I stiffened, my gaze darting to Z's with confusion. What *Noah thing*?

"Yes," Ace agreed. "Eight, have you been online much this week?"

I shook my head, dread pooling in my guts. "No. Not since the other day when I accepted the collaboration post from Minho, but I didn't linger. Why? What's happened?"

Fuck. *Fuck.* Had I already been outed? Had someone recognized me from *Dance Babes* or outed me as Norah Sparkle already? Christy and Jared had been so confident that wouldn't happen, but...

"It's not *bad* exactly." August spoke up, flicking flour off the front of his T-shirt. "People are just crazy enamored by your appearance because it's not what they expected."

I blinked at him, trying to make sense of that statement. Why would that be news? I'd built my whole platform as an anonymous character, so of course there would be some sort of reaction, no matter what I looked like.

"There are a few fans who have been speculating that you green-screen your stunts," Ace said, cutting to the point. "It makes zero sense—your appearance makes no difference to the legitimacy of your content—but that's the trending narrative with our haters right now."

My jaw dropped, and if I hadn't already swallowed my food, I'd have choked on it. "They think *what*?"

"It's only a few, and the pushback from Acolytes has been *strong*," Z said with a short sigh, "but those few have been very loud."

My mouth was drier than the Sahara, and the food I'd eaten turned to cement in my stomach. I'd expected hate for my lack of masculinity, my refusal to go shirtless to show off nonexistent abs, or even because I was *small*... but to accuse me of *green screen*? Well, that was just fucked-up.

Did the team think that, too?

"We don't doubt you, Eight," Ace said firmly, like he could read my mind. "Not a single one of us here has any concerns around your content legitimacy. But the reason we bring it up is because this first challenge offers us an opportunity to shut those rumors down. Somehow. I'm not sure how, exactly, but I'll think of something."

I tried to swallow, but it hurt. My throat was tight. After months of worry and planning for every contingency, what was getting me was something I hadn't ever considered as an issue.

"Are you okay, Chicken?" Minho asked quietly, bumping my knee with his under the table. "We'll fix it. Don't stress, all right?"

"He's right," Torin agreed. "None of us have any doubts about how badass you are, Short Stack. We've got your back."

If any of them had offered that sort of reassurance just a few days ago, I'd have laughed at them. But now? I believed them. This wasn't *my* problem to handle alone, because we were a team.

How, though? How the fuck did I prove to the *internet* that my stunts were real and there nothing green-screened about them? That every Byte I filmed contained real danger and real risk of death? It was the internet, for fuck's sake; everything could be edited, therefore everything was suspicious.

The only way to prove the validity of anything was... "Let's do something public," I said out loud, thinking it through as I poked the remainder of my dinner. "Stage something with enough physical eyewitnesses that it can't be denied?"

Silence met my suggestion, and I glanced up at Ace anxiously. Was that a crappy idea? But his expression was thoughtful and sly, like the cogs in his brain were already at work.

"I like it," he finally said. "That has a lot of potential."

"I'm getting seconds," August announced, standing up with his empty plate in hand. "Anyone else?"

Just like that, the conversation shifted away from the Games and the green screen accusations, as if we'd only been discussing the weather. Minho bumped my knee again with his, giving me a small smile, and Torin squeezed my shoulder. Maybe this team thing wasn't the worst ever after all.

TEN

Over the next few days I spent a huge amount of time in Ace's office, brainstorming ideas of how we could both prove my legitimacy in stunts *and* display teamwork when everyone had such incredibly varied skill sets. Oh, and get enough Cliks to win the first round of the games, of course.

Sometimes Xavier and Z joined us, sometimes one of the other guys, but it was evident they relied on Ace to build out the concepts for their content and looked to him for leadership in all areas. He'd told me a thousand times I didn't need to come up with the ideas myself, but after I read the comments from fans—and haters—I felt responsible. And angry. I was angry and needed to prove myself.

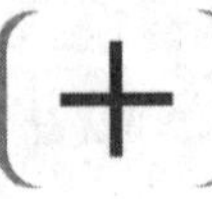

"I feel like some of the other teams took this stage into consideration better than you did," I muttered in frustration after the dozenth discarded idea. "Look at GeeGee... They're basically carbon copies of each other. This challenge will be a fucking breeze for them."

Ace shrugged. "Yeah, but they're all relying on Angela's following to get them the Cliks. The rest of them are barely sitting in the top five hundred creators whereas the eight of *us*..."

I nodded, understanding that part perfectly fine. Technically August was top twenty—currently ranking number sixteen on ClikByte's most followed accounts—but the rest of us sat firmly in the top ten. I was holding second place very smugly after having overtaken Xavier just a few months ago.

Minho was first. I couldn't even dispute that because I was one of his followers myself.

"I have an idea scratching at my brain," I mumbled, raking my fingers through my short hair with a tired groan. "I just can't quite connect the dots. We need it public, right? Really public, lots of eyewitnesses. But we also have to do something that involves the whole team, so it's not good enough to have me and Skye jump off the top of a hotel or some shit." I was just repeating everything we already knew.

"It's late," Ace said, nodding to his clock hanging on the wall above his computer monitors. I glanced at the time and was shocked to see it was past midnight. "Sleep on it. Maybe it'll come to one of us in a dream."

Yawning, I scuffed my feet out of Ace's office and headed back toward my shared room with Skye. To my surprise, he was still awake and scrolling ClikByte on his phone in bed.

"Did you guys come up with something?" he asked, putting his phone down as I hunted for some sleep clothes. Boys—in my experience—didn't wear cute PJs, so I'd had to adjust to wearing baggy boxer shorts and an oversized T-shirt to bed. I desperately wanted to sleep without my chest binder on but couldn't risk taking it off while Skye was awake. Dammit.

I shook my head, yawning again. "No. Maybe the challenge will be something totally different anyway. Maybe they'll give us some unexpected twist like..." My brain hurt too much to think of a silly hypothetical.

"Like doing a synchronized dance in dinosaur suits?" Skye suggested with a lopsided smile. "I'd totally do that. Sounds really easy and funny, too."

I snickered tiredly. "Same. We'd make cute dinosaurs, you and me. Not sure about Xavier, he's more of a Godzilla."

Taking my clothes with me, I slipped into the bathroom to get changed and brush my teeth before returning to my bed. Skye had already turned the main light off, thoughtfully leaving my reading light on so I wouldn't walk into shit getting to the bed, and I groaned as I climbed under my blankets.

For a few minutes, comfortable silence settled across us, and I made another mental note about how glad I was to be sharing with Skye. Literally any of the other guys would have me in a nervous, hormonal mess trying to sleep in the same room as them, but Skye made me feel safe and calm.

"Hey, Noah?" he murmured softly some moments after I flicked off my reading light.

"Mmm?" I replied, already on the edge of sleep, despite how uncomfortable my body was to be trapped in the binder still.

He paused a second before replying. "You shouldn't sleep with that on, you know? Your, um, back brace. It's not good to wear it all the time."

Suddenly I was wide awake. "What?" It came out squeaky with panic.

"Sorry, I wasn't going to say anything because you haven't mentioned it, but Minho told me you might have a back injury that you're supporting, and I noticed you wear a brace under your shirt. You can take it off at night, that's all I meant to say. I won't tell anyone you're injured, if that's what you're worried about."

Words totally failed me. He'd said it in a jumbled rush, like he didn't want to make me uncomfortable but at the same time wanted to reassure me that our room was a safe place. Fuck...he was the best roommate I could have hoped for.

I bit my lip, debating my options. I was wearing a huge T-shirt, and I was under blankets. And I was far from a D cup on the best of days, so really, where was the harm? I'd just been paranoid because the industrial-strength hook-and-loop fastener of the binder itself was loud as hell, and then I'd need to explain it. Which, apparently, I didn't need to anymore.

Back injury. That was why Minho mentioned hurting my back during the kitchen water fight—he'd clearly felt my binder under my shirt and made assumptions.

"Did I make things weird?" Skye asked when I said nothing. "Ignore me. I just...I hope you know that you're totally safe in here. I would never betray your trust, no matter what."

I wet my lips, my breathing shallow and my spine rigid. He was referring to my "back injury" that he seemed to think I was hiding for some reason...but his words meant *so much more* than he fully appreciated.

"Not weird at all," I croaked, forcing the words out before I really made things awkward. Then before I could talk myself out of it, I reached under my shirt to rip the Velcro open. The sigh of relief that gusted out of me couldn't have been stifled if I'd tried. "You're right. It really sucks sleeping in that."

Skye gave a small chuckle in the darkness. "Well, don't do it again. It's bad for your ribs and shit." His blankets rustled as he shifted in his bed, yawning dramatically. "Good night, Noah."

"Night, Skye," I whispered, tucking my binder under my pillow and getting comfier than I'd been the whole time since arriving at Mount Olympus.

When I woke up the next morning, I scurried into the shower while Skye was still sleeping slack-jawed and sprawled across his blankets. By the time he woke, I was fully dressed in my masculine disguise but feeling like a million bucks.

Downstairs, I'd barely finished pouring a coffee when Z found me, rubbing his half-closed eyes with the heel of his hand. "Ace is looking for you, bro. Pretty sure he just woke Skye up."

I frowned over the rim of my cup. "Skye's already awake... sort of." He had mumbled something about caffeine but then dragged his pillow over his head before I'd left the room. "What does Ace need?"

Z shrugged, leaning against the counter and clearly struggling. "Dunno. Aw, is that the last of the coffee?" He glared daggers at the nearly empty pot I'd just poured mine out of.

"Sorry." I winced, trying to avoid eye contact, because proximity with him was *a lot*. Hanging out while he composed music a couple days ago had nearly driven me insane, purely from the magnetic pull he seemed to exude. Weirdly, my brain had already decided that I knew the way he would kiss...what he would taste like...how he'd fuck... "Um, give me a minute, I'll make another."

Z just pouted and eyed the mug in my hand mournfully. "Sure. Want me to hold that for you?"

I was flustered enough that I handed it over without a second thought, only to have him grin smugly and take a huge sip. "You—Z, that's not very nice!" I exclaimed, reaching for the mug and catching nothing but air when he moved it up and out of my reach. "Okay, ha ha, very funny, use my height against me. Here I was feeling bad for you, and you're just using dirty tricks to steal my coffee."

The way he laughed was fucking *mesmerizing*, and I nearly forgot what we were talking about as he met my eyes. His were a dark moss green that worked so damn well with his wine-red hair and lightly tanned skin. My lungs tightened, and I needed to force myself to breathe as I ducked my gaze away.

"I guess I'll make more for *myself* then," I grumbled, turning my back on him and swallowing hard as I tried to pull my shit together. My face was warm, and I was terrified he'd catch me blushing. What the fuck would these guys do if they thought their newest team member was crushing on them all?

Z groaned, moving closer and reaching around to offer my mug back to me. "Shit, bro, you're making me feel like a bully. Here. I only wanted one sip anyway."

I took it, holding my breath when our fingers connected, but then he ruffled my hair and I jabbed him playfully with my elbow. "Asshole."

He laughed. "Guilty. Oh here's Ace. Move. I'll do this." He placed his hands on my hips and physically shifted me away from the coffee machine before I could protest.

"Eight!" Ace called out as he crossed the living area toward the kitchen. "I worked it out!"

My brows shot up, Z's casual contact all but forgotten at the sight of Ace's dark eye circles and familiar T-shirt—the same one he'd been wearing last night. "Did you sleep, Ace?"

He shook his head. "Not yet. But I worked it out. Don't you wanna hear?" Somehow over the course of the last couple days, this had become a joint obsession between Ace and me. Secretly, I loved it. Ace was an insanely hard worker, and everything I'd seen of him in the week since joining the team, I really liked. Which was confusing, with how vehemently my brother hated him. Miles was usually such a good judge of character.

Then again, he had been friends with Rich. So maybe not.

"Go on, then." I nodded, moving out of Z's way as I sipped my coffee. Then my brain tripped over itself, remembering Z just drank from my cup and that meant that—

"High ropes course," Ace announced with a grin, snapping me out of the perverted train of thought I was heading down.

I wrinkled my nose, confused. "Uh...okay. Elaborate."

Ace pulled out his phone, swiping across browser tabs until he displayed an ad for a "corporate team-bonding activity center" which showed a picture of some middle-aged twat in a suit, rigged up with a safety harness, walking across a high-wire while his equally corporate friends cheered him on.

"Okay..." I repeated, scrolling through the description of the *perfect way to bond your corporate team*. "Elaborate *more,* please."

Ace shot me a smirk. "High ropes course, rigged up in the gap between the triangle towers, during the Dazed Dayz festival. Maximum publicity for how many people are there, undeniable that it's legit, fucking loads of danger factor, and displays teamwork. It's perfect, right?"

I blinked a couple of times, looking back at his phone and the grinning idiots in suits and safety harnesses. "No safety net?" I murmured thoughtfully.

Ace's smile dropped, and a small frown creased his brow. "The finer details we can negotiate. But as a concept...?"

I nodded slowly, running it through in my head, actually visualizing how it might play out. “As a concept? It’s perfect. But logistically? I have no idea how we even begin to pull this off.”

Ace’s grin was back, bigger than ever, and it ignited a warmth within me that was almost scary. “Don’t you worry about that, Eight. We have more than enough connections to make this work.”

I believed him, too. Team Olympus was more than just the eight of us, after all. It was a huge fucking company with billions backing it. If Ace wanted something, he got it. My place on the team was proof of that.

ELEVEN

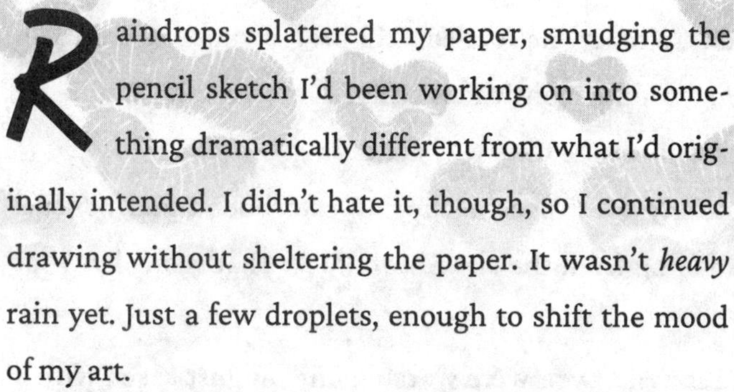

Raindrops splattered my paper, smudging the pencil sketch I'd been working on into something dramatically different from what I'd originally intended. I didn't hate it, though, so I continued drawing without sheltering the paper. It wasn't *heavy* rain yet. Just a few droplets, enough to shift the mood of my art.

Glancing up at my newest muse, I frowned when he wobbled on the suspended cable. Rain wasn't the end of the world for my drawing, but it was dangerous if the wires were slippery.

"Hey, Short Stack!" I called out to the wiry guy cautiously progressing across a tightwire while blindfolded. "It's starting to rain. We should go!"

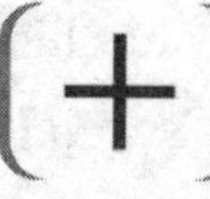

The rest of the guys—except August and me—had returned home hours earlier, but Noah insisted he wanted to stay and practice, so we'd offered to stay with him, which Ace allowed only after delivering a long lecture about being responsible for our newest member's safety and agreeing to drag him home at the first signs of fatigue.

Unfortunately, we all underestimated the scrappy, little dude's endurance. He showed no signs of exhaustion or even boredom after *hours* of walking the wires course we'd rigged up on our forest property in Yorba Linda. In fairness, the twist that'd been thrown at us, along with the first challenge announcement, had us all worried.

"It's not raining," he replied, still progressing one step at a time, his feet sliding along the wire like a dancer's. "I want to get through this one more time without falling."

I rolled my eyes, packing up my sketchbook and pencils. "Water is falling from the sky, Short Stack. That's usually what I call rain."

"Can I see what you were working on?" August asked with a yawn as I headed over to the car, where he'd been editing content on his laptop. Without waiting for my response, he tugged the sketchbook out of my grip and flipped through the pages. He leveled me a hard look with his tawny gaze. "I see... New muse really has his hooks in you, huh?"

If I'd had a fairer complexion, I'd have blushed. "Shut up. He's interesting."

August's grin spread wide, teasing. "I don't disagree. Just pointing out that I haven't seen you fixate on one subject like this in *years*."

I didn't have a response for that. Although he'd only joined Team Olympus six months ago—specifically for the purpose of the Games, same as Minho—we'd been friends a lot longer. Ever since he'd saved me from a nasty case of alcohol poisoning while on vacation in Miami.

"Is he okay with your little obsession?" August murmured, closing his laptop and glancing over toward the muse in question.

I wet my lips and stashed my drawing supplies safely in my bag. "I don't believe it's come up in conversation yet. There's no harm, though. I don't think he would be offended..."

My best friend shifted his focus back to me with a worried frown. "That's not my concern."

I knew what he meant, and I sighed as I rubbed the back of my neck. The last time I'd fixated on a muse, she'd broken my heart so thoroughly I'd nearly destroyed my own career as I spiraled into depression. "It's not the same thing. Noah's just a curiosity."

"If you say so," he replied softly. "I just worry about you."

I forced a teasing smile, giving him a shoulder squeeze. "Aw, Augie, you can just tell me you love me. It won't be weird, I swear."

He scoffed, shaking off my hand. "You're a dickhead, Tor, but you already know I love you. Come on. Let's drag your new *favorite* home before he gets hurt."

I grinned, not even trying to deny the accusation. "Drag is probably not an exaggeration. He'll happily stay here all night if we don't."

As if the weather wanted to help out, the sky rumbled and raindrops started falling faster while I headed back across the grassy clearing to the extensive tightwire setup. Noah hadn't even seemed to flinch at the rain, still gracefully moving along the wires and obstacles—blindfolded—as he committed the course to memory.

"Come on, Short Stack, it's home time," I announced, ducking under a wire to get closer. "If you slip and break a bone, I'll have to go into witness protection, and I'm not cut out for that life."

My little muse just chuckled, shaking his head slightly. His blond hair was tied up in a spiky, little ponytail, but loose bits had escaped all over the place around his blindfold, making him look like an anime character. "Dramatic, much? I've broken bones before; it's not the end of the world."

I rolled my eyes even though he couldn't see. "Yeah, well... try offering that logic to Ace if we have to put you in a cast." I pursed my lips, thinking it over. "Or Minnie, for that matter. You seen that guy with a sword?" I winced and rubbed my throat as I pictured getting it slit open. Minho was *super* attached to Noah already. More than Ace was, even.

Noah's response to that was just a thoughtful hum, then he sighed. "I suppose it is raining now." He wobbled on the wire as he tugged the blindfold off and tucked it into the pocket of his baggy sweatpants.

The twist in the challenge that none of us had really anticipated was a sensory deprivation. Of our team of eight, only two would complete the course unhindered. Two would be gagged and unable to talk, two would be earmuffed and unable to hear, and the remaining two would be blindfolded. On a high ropes course. Ten stories above concrete.

Noah's wobbles didn't seem to faze him at all as he looked down at me. "What time is it, anyway?"

"Almost five," I replied, reaching up toward him. "Jump down. I'll catch you."

The wire course we'd set up to practice on was only ten feet off the ground, but that was high enough to do some damage. Everyone had been practicing with harnesses and safety lines but not stubborn little Noah. Not only had he volunteered for the hardest disadvantage—being blindfolded—he'd also insisted on learning the ropes without a safety line.

He glanced down at me, then stepped off the wire without even the slightest flicker of fear. My heart leaped into my throat for the split-second drop, then I caught his slim frame in my arms and set him safely onto his feet.

"You're a little bit fucked in the head, aren't you?" I commented with a chuckle, making sure he knew it wasn't an insult.

The grin on his face and shine to his eyes couldn't have been doused with *anything*, though. Kid was fucking high as a kite off the adrenaline rush. No wonder he didn't drink or do drugs... substances couldn't compete with his true addiction.

"You're cold," August stated with a frown when we made our way back to the car where he waited. "Here, take my sweater."

I started to disagree—I was fine—but then I realized he was talking to Noah. Which made me pause, because a spark of something unfamiliar burned inside my chest. What the fuck even was that? Noah was visibly cold now that the adrenaline and focus was draining out of him, his skinny arms pebbled with gooseflesh and his pretty face paler than usual, so yeah, he needed a sweater. What was the problem with that?

Frowning, I watched as Noah accepted August's David Blaine hoodie and almost drowned in all the fabric as he pulled it on. Then I wet my lips and mentally cursed. What was the problem? He was wearing *August's* clothes...but I couldn't work out if I was irritated that he wasn't wearing *mine* or because I didn't want anyone wearing Augie's shit.

Yeah, okay. Maybe my best friend had reason to be worried after all. I needed to...keep an eye on myself. Maybe it was a passing fascination. I'd had those before with people I'd found incredibly beautiful. Once I'd drawn them a couple dozen times, I always moved on.

I didn't want to admit to myself that I'd *already* well surpassed that point.

"Thanks, August," Noah said with a warm smile, and I shot my friend a sharp look.

He wasn't paying attention to me, though, as he smiled back at my muse. "No problem, dude. Let's get home and see what Xavier has burned for dinner."

Noah laughed as he climbed into the back seat, and it brought a smile to my own lips. "He really can't cook, can he? Is it because he's never needed to learn?"

August slid into the driver's seat, and I took the passenger beside him. "Oh, he's learned," I replied with a chuckle. "He's just shit at it. No matter how many times we make him try, it always ends in *something* catching fire. Do you have any clue how much takeout the three of them used to order? We're talking six days a week *at least*."

In their defense, both Z and Ace were okay in the kitchen but completely time blind once they got working on a project. So for the most part, they would order takeout because it'd get to be midnight before any of them even thought about a meal. If Ace wasn't sharing a room with Xavier now, he'd probably never sleep either.

"How are you feeling about the obstacle course now?" August asked, glancing in the rearview mirror to give Noah his attention. "We still have loads of time to get it right before we film."

He was right; each challenge gave us a full month to plan, prepare, film, and submit. To keep it fair, all teams would load their entry at the same time on the same day, so there was plenty of time to practice.

"I know," Noah agreed, tugging the elastic out of his little ponytail and ruffling his fingers through the wet, blond strands.

It was only then that I realized I was staring, so I shifted in my seat to face forward once more.

August clocked it—nothing got past him—and he gave me a sidelong glance with his brow creased.

"The sooner I can learn the course, the sooner I can work out how to get the rest of you clumsy fucks across," Noah continued with an edge of teasing. "How are you finding it, August? Are you confident in taking the blindfold disadvantage as well?"

Augie shrugged as he drove. "Better me than anyone else. At least I have good balance."

On the day the challenge twist was announced, we'd all tested out the wires, and aside from Noah, August was the most confident with balance. Shockingly better than Skye, who'd agreed to swap for the earmuff disadvantage. Ace and Xavier would have the responsibility of guiding the team, should they need it.

"Good point," Noah agreed with a sigh. "And so long as you're harnessed, you'll be fine."

"Unlike you," I pointed out. "If you do the real thing without a harness and fall, you'll die." That idea twisted me up inside, burning like acid in my chest. I really didn't like that idea, but I'd be just as upset if any of the team plunged to their death from ten stories up.

Noah didn't seem bothered, giving a light laugh. "At least we'd get a shitload of Cliks for that."

"Jesus," August whispered in shocked disbelief. "That's dark, dude."

He didn't reply, just hummed a thoughtful sound and shifted in his seat. Maybe I wasn't staring at him anymore, but my peripheral vision was on high alert for his every movement. It was fucking concerning how fixated I was becoming.

Still...fixated or not, Noah's attitude toward danger and death had me worried. It was something I needed to raise with Ace sooner rather than later. For all of our sakes, we couldn't let him do this challenge without a harness.

TWELVE

When the teamwork challenge twist was announced, I quite honestly had zero faith in Team Olympus. Except Skye, who I really thought would be fine to do the course blindfolded—and he'd failed spectacularly. August was a surprise, but then when I thought about what kind of body control and focus he needed as a marksman, it checked out.

So after running everyone through the high-wire course, it was decided that August and I—having the best balance while blind—would wear the blindfolds, then Skye and Minho would wear earmuffs, while Torin and Z would be gagged. That left Ace and Xavier with the responsibility of overseeing and guiding the rest of the team through the course.

The guys were right that we had a *heap* of time to practice. A whole month was unexpected, but not unwelcome, except for the fact that we still had a responsibility to maintain or even grow our follower count in anticipation of posting our entry Byte.

For that very reason, I'd let Skye wake me up before dawn so we could go rock climbing with his tracking-drone camera. Surprisingly, Minho and Z had joined us at the last minute and proven they were more than capable of keeping up.

When we arrived home in the early evening, the four of us were all buzzing with energy and joking around as Z read aloud the newest comments on our Byte. He and Skye had done lightning-fast editing on the drive home, and we'd already posted a collaborative Byte between the four of us, with Team Olympus tagged as our contracts demanded.

The new followers were flooding in as our individual audiences crossed over, and the comments were their own form of entertainment.

Every now and then, Z would pause and wrinkle his nose ever so slightly before moving onto a new comment. Undoubtedly, he was skipping the shitty ones.

"Looks like you guys had a nice day," Xavier commented as we entered the kitchen-living area. He was leaning over the counter with a huge, hardcover recipe book open in front of him, which suggested maybe he was planning on cooking dinner. *Yikes.* "Where was my invitation?"

Z scoffed, tucking his phone back in his pocket. "Dude, you and Ace were so deep asleep a tornado wouldn't have woken you. Minnie and I only caught these two sneaking out at five a.m. because Skye tripped over the robo-vac right outside our room and Noah started laughing at him."

"What are you thinking of cooking?" I asked as casually as possible, reaching over the counter to tug the cookbook toward me.

Xavier's eyes narrowed my way, not fooled. "Carbonara. Why?"

I ran my tongue over my teeth, then glanced sideways at Minho, who'd just draped his arm over my shoulders.

"We grabbed tacos on the way home," he smoothly explained. "So none of us are really hungry."

"Yeah, what he said," Skye agreed, never mind that his hand was already buried in a packet of white cheddar PopCorners. "Not hungry at all." Then he stuffed a handful of triangle chips in his mouth.

Xavier rolled his eyes, seeing straight through us even when Z nodded his agreement. "You guys suck. At least I'm trying."

"Trying to give us all food poisoning," Z muttered under his breath but loud enough to be heard by *all* of us, Xavier included, who extended both his middle fingers at us and muttered something about *ungrateful dickheads* before stalking out of the kitchen.

None of the guys seemed worried about hurting Xavier's feelings, all grinning as he stomped his way upstairs. Once Xavier's door slammed shut, Z pulled out his phone once more. "So... tacos? I'll order for delivery."

"Yes," I groaned, rubbing my stomach, "I'm starving. Spicy beef, please."

"You got it, dude." Z's thumbs flew across his screen as he took everyone's orders then wrinkled his nose. "Suppose we better order for everyone. Can someone go ask Ace? He'll be in his office reviewing the final cut of our new episode."

Ah, the *Mount Olympus* episode. My first one. It was all the footage they'd filmed in those first few days in the house. Since then, I'd noticed a huge lack of cameramen and producers in the house. More static mounted cameras, yes, but I'd always rather those than Roy and his friends with their probing questions. I'd been meaning to ask Ace if that was done for any specific reason.

"Yup, I will," I offered, slipping out from under Minho's arm. "Are Tor and Augie home?"

"I'll check their location," Skye offered, pulling out his own phone. The whole team shared their location data with each other for several reasons, not the least of which being for safety in case an extra zealous *fan* decided to cross lines and harm one of us.

It was a sobering thought.

I left them to work out what everyone else wanted and made my way up to Ace's office, tapping lightly on the door before letting myself in without waiting for his response. I'd spent enough time in there planning our teamwork challenge that it was as comfortable as my own room at this stage.

"Hey, Ace," I said, perching my butt on the arm of his sofa.

He glanced back at me, eyes bloodshot and shadowed. "Hey, Eight," he replied with a weak, tired smile. "How's your ankle?"

I frowned, rolling the ankle in question. "How'd you know I hurt it? Did the guys—"

"I saw it on your Byte," he corrected before I could gather outrage at being tattled on. He switched browser windows and brought up the fast-paced climbing and rappelling Byte we'd only posted half an hour ago. Then he clicked through to an exact time stamp and played it at half speed, showing the exact moment I rolled my ankle on a bad foothold about ten feet from the top of the cliff. I caught myself just fine, but he paused the clip, rewound it, played it again slower and zoomed in.

I winced, watching my ankle roll in slow motion. "Nothing gets past you, huh?"

"Nope, I thought you knew that by now," he replied with a worn-out smile, spinning his chair to face me and gesturing for my ankle. "Show me."

Blowing out a sigh, I raised my leg and let him take my foot in his lap as he lifted the leg of my sweatpants and tugged my sock down. He was silent as he inspected the compression bandage that was currently supporting the joint.

"Minho's handiwork?" he guessed, cocking a brow.

I nodded. "Yep. It wasn't even necessary. I was fine to walk on it once we got to the top."

Ace scoffed, his long fingers wrapped around my injured

ankle. "Liar. It was a smart move cutting to the GoPro footage, but I caught your pained little hop as Skye rigged up the ropes, too."

"Damn," I murmured. "Well...it's fine now. I forgot all about it until you asked."

"Regardless, you're not going to the ropes course tomorrow." Ace said it with finality, and I gaped in outrage.

"But I need—"

"To rest your ankle so you don't fall off the high wires when we're ten stories above a crowd of three thousand people," he cut me off with a stern look. "You can have a rest day here while the team practices. Go to the beach or something."

I wrinkled my nose in distaste. "I'm not a fan of water I can drown in," I confessed with an edge of anxiety.

Ace tipped his head, eyeing me with curiosity. "Why not? Have you had a bad experience?"

Fucking hell, didn't I *just* make the comment about nothing getting past him? He was way too damn observant for his own good. I blew out a long sigh, retracting my foot from his lap and fixing my sock. "Something like that, yeah."

Ace said nothing to change the subject or fill the silence. Just stared at me, waiting.

With a frustrated growl, I offered just a little more context. "I was in a car accident a few years ago and crashed into a river. I... drowned, I guess."

His brow creased with confusion or...concern? Something. "But you got out. Clearly."

I shrugged. "Somehow, I must have. I don't remember anything about it or the hours leading up to it, but I was in a coma for a few days and apparently that's normal. I don't *actually* remember the accident, but whenever I'm fully submerged in water..." I shuddered, a full-body quiver. "I guess part of me remembers."

Ace was quiet for a moment, long enough that I could feel he wanted to ask more questions, but it was one of my *least* favorite topics so I quickly stood up again. "Anyway, Z's ordering tacos. I came to see what you wanted."

He gave me another puzzled frown, then sighed. "Yeah, tell him to order my usual. Thanks, Eight. Did you want to review the Mount Olympus episode before I approve it?"

I shook my head, giving a small laugh. "Nope. Pretty sure my contract doesn't give me any kind of veto rights anyway, so what's the point?"

Before he could argue that fact—which was entirely true—I slipped out of his office and headed next door to ask Xavier what he wanted. Sure, we just lied to him, but at the same time it'd be even worse if we excluded him from the order. Except, his door was locked.

"Xavier, do you want tacos? Z's ordering," I called out.

For a moment, there was no response. Then a mumbled, "Yeah, whatever, be down soon." Which was clearly a *please fuck off, I'm busy*.

Shrugging, I left him alone and returned back downstairs to pass along Ace's order. When I mentioned Xavier's door being locked, Z and Minho exchanged a smirk.

"What...does that mean?" I asked suspiciously.

Minho gestured for me to join them on the sofa where they were all sprawled out, watching Skye get his butt kicked by August in *Tekken*. Somehow in the ten days since I'd moved in, they'd all systematically desensitized me to casually affectionate touches to the point my pulse only *slightly* raced when I sat on the carpet and Minho raked his fingers through my messy hair.

"It means he's letting off a little steam," Minnie explained delicately, the amusement undeniable in his voice. "At least he had the grace to lock the door this time."

The other guys all snickered at that, and my face heated. There was no denying the fact I was probably turning bright pink, so I just tried to *ignore it.*

"Xavier has an, um, what would you call it?" Z snapped his fingers, searching for the right phrasing.

"Obsession," August offered.

"Addiction," Skye corrected.

"Infatuation," Z settled on with a wicked grin.

I frowned, not understanding why they were all so entertained. "He's got a girlfriend? Or boyfriend?"

Torin laughed so abruptly while taking a sip of his drink that liquid came out his nose and he spluttered dramatically. August grinned, slapping him on the back helpfully.

"I don't think you can call her a girlfriend when it's a paid subscription," August informed me with a sly grin and a wink. That's when the penny dropped in my head and a cold sweat broke out across my skin, my stomach cramping with dread and disgust.

"ClikByte: Adults Only?" I guessed in a weak voice, desperately hoping they would correct me. Clearly this was a subject of mirth for them all, and their amused smiles gave me chills.

"In his defense," Z replied with a shrug, "it's only one creator he's subscribed to. Or was. Her profile got deleted a couple months ago and he's basically turned into an amateur sleuth trying to track her down again."

Minho snickered. "More like a stalker. Maybe she deleted the profile herself because the so-called fans were getting too creepy."

Fucking hell, I was going to vomit. Surely this was just a coincidence? Right?

"Who..." My voice cracked, and I swallowed past the lump of panic in my throat. "Who was the creator?"

"*Peaches*," both August and Skye replied at the same time, shooting each other a smirk at their accidental jinx.

My whole fucking world tilted, and my pulse roared in my ears. I was past the need to vomit and hurtling straight toward a panic attack. Or passing out. Neither could be easily explained so I needed to *not be here*!

"Chicken, are you okay?" Minho asked with a worried frown, shifting to peer at me more intently. "You're really pale."

No shit. "I'm fine," I lied. "I'm just cold. I'm going to go grab a sweater."

"Take mine," Z offered, already shrugging out of his zip-up hoodie even as I lurched to my feet.

I ignored him, already trying to flee the room with my heart in my throat and my skin crawling with terror and dread and an unbearable load of regret. It was so fucking stupid of me to think I'd left Rich's betrayal in my past, like the internet wasn't forever. Just because I'd gotten the profile deleted and Rich's hands tied up in legal repercussions didn't mean it was gone from people's minds.

"Whoa!" Xavier exclaimed when I ran straight into him as he entered the room. "Watch where you're going, Little Dude." He grasped my upper arms to steady me, but I recoiled from his touch with anger flooding my veins.

A million and one things crowded into my head all at once, and I lost all sense of sanity for a moment, my eyes narrowing at him in disgust. "Leave her alone, Xavier! Did it ever occur to you that Peaches doesn't want you to find her? Fucking hell, what is wrong with you?"

His brows shot up, his expression a mix of confusion and shock for a moment before he connected the dots to presumably guess the guys had filled me in on his *obsession*. "Okay, Little Dude, you legitimately don't know what you're talking about. These dickheads talk a lot of shit, but I bet they totally misrepresented what's actually going on."

Indignation choked me and I made a strangled sort of sound. "I promise you, I know more than you realize."

Xavier's posture relaxed and he folded his arms with a lopsided smile, like I was being *cute*. "Oh yeah? Like what?"

I saw red but retained *just* enough clarity not to completely expose myself as I lost my shit. "Like the fact that Peaches never consented to any of those images or Bytes being uploaded and that the profile was deleted when she sued the sleazebag who'd uploaded it all in the first place!"

Xavier stared back at me for a moment, then chuckled. "As if. The amount of identity clearance on regular ClikByte is insane, there's no way AO is any less strict. Do you know her or something?" His head tilted slightly to the side, curiosity burning in his hazel gaze.

I was so angry my hands shook, so I curled them into balls at my sides to try to hide my intense reaction—as if that were remotely possible at this stage. "Or something," I growled, shoving past him and fleeing upstairs to my room.

Fuck the tacos—my appetite was officially gone.

THIRTEEN

After my blowup at Xavier and subsequent rather dramatic exit, my anxiety spiraled. Hard. I called Jared immediately, while sitting on the floor in the little gap between my bed and the window, but it went to his voicemail. I hung up without leaving a message, then hovered my finger over Miles's contact—*Millie*—before discarding that as an awful idea. He'd only try to use this as an excuse to make me quit.

Fuck. Had I just shown all my cards down there? Did they all *know* now? They must. I was so fucking obvious, but at the same time I kind of felt good for saying what I'd said. Aside from Jared and Miles, no one knew what Rich had done to me. Thankfully, my face had been carefully edited out of all Peaches content, so unless

someone knew my naked body intimately, there was no way to know it was me.

I sat there on the floor, staring blankly at my phone for long enough that my pulse calmed and the tension of anxiety ebbed out of my muscles, leaving me feeling drained. And fuck, now that I thought about it, my ankle actually really hurt. The anti-inflammatories I'd taken at the top of the climb must have worn off.

The bedroom door opened softly, and I sat up enough to peer over my bed and confirm it was just Skye.

"Hey, Noah," he said with a lopsided smile, coming over to join me on the carpet beside the window. "You okay?"

I bit the edge of my lip, putting my phone down. "Yep. So fine. Why wouldn't I be?"

Okay, that could use some work because even I winced at how forced my "okay" voice sounded to my own ears. Skye just smiled and shrugged. "I dunno, you seemed pretty upset downstairs. Do you wanna talk about it?"

I wrinkled my nose. "Guys don't talk about their feelings, Skye." I intended it as a joke, but his smile faded away as a small crease formed in his brow.

"Can I be honest with you, Noah? I feel like...like we're friends, right? And friends should be able to trust each other. Right?" He nervously fidgeted with the carpet, avoiding eye contact while waiting for my response.

Guilt welled up in my chest because he was right. We weren't just roommates and teammates; we were *friends,* and I'd been keeping a major secret from the moment we met. I wet my lips, feeling like shit. "You can always trust me, Skye. We're basically twins, remember? At this point I think I like you more than my own sibling."

A weak smile touched his lips at that comment. "I know. But do you know that you can trust me, too? Being part of Team Olympus doesn't automatically mean we have no secrets or privacy, you know? If you ever needed to *talk*...I'd keep your confidence."

An uneasy feeling curled through me, and I shifted my position to lean closer. "I do trust you, Skye." And I meant it. Three weeks of sharing space had bonded us like I'd never anticipated possible. He was the best friend I'd never had.

He sighed, running a hand through his messy, golden-blond hair. "A couple days after you moved in, I did something...not okay. You had been a bit weird about sharing a room, and I got it in my head that you maybe didn't like me. So when you took a call with your manager, I, um...I listened through the door."

My brow furrowed as I tried to remember the day he was talking about, then it clicked in my brain. I'd opened the door and found him and Ace in the hallway with some weird excuse. Ace had given no reaction at all, so I'd convinced myself they hadn't heard me, but Skye...? Now that I thought about it, Skye had been *weird* all night, and then a few days later he'd told me it was okay to take my "back brace" off at night.

Oh fuck.

I inhaled sharply, panic washing through my whole body, and Skye reacted just as fast, reaching out to grab my hand in his.

"I haven't breathed a word to anyone, Noah, I *swear*. I feel fucking awful for breaching your privacy like that, and then every day that passed without telling you that I knew... I'm an asshole. Noah, I am *so* sorry, but please know that you *can* trust me." His eyes were wide with sincerity and his grasp tight on my hand. "No one else needs to know. I gathered that there are extenuating circumstances, which really are none of my business, but I just need you to understand that this is and will always be a safe space for you, okay? You can be yourself in here."

My lungs were tight, my breathing coming in short and sharp pants, and my throat tightened to the point I couldn't have responded even if I'd had the words. He'd known for three weeks and never said a word. Not to me or anyone else on the team. He hadn't acted differently, except that he'd been sleeping with a blackout mask. He told me it was because he struggled to sleep soundly, but it'd also helped me feel safe without a binder at night.

Fucking hell, that was...incredibly sweet.

"Nothing changes, right?" he asked, his blue eyes wide with worry. "It makes no difference to the Games and the team, so we just pretend I don't know anything. Okay?"

I wet my lips, forcing myself to find *some* response. "Okay," I whispered, my head spinning. "You won't—"

"I *won't*," he insisted, squeezing my hand firmly. "You couldn't waterboard that secret out of me because it's not mine to tell."

I believed him. My breath exhaled in a shaky sigh, and a small measure of tension eased out of my shoulders as I accepted the fact that I believed him. I *trusted* him.

"That stuff with Xavier downstairs..." he said softly, his grip on my hand easing to a gentle hold as I dropped my eyes to the carpet. "It was personal for you, wasn't it? Do you know her?"

It was an echo of what Xavier had asked, but this time I couldn't bury my reaction with anger. My eyeballs heated and my jaw clenched, but it was no use. When I glanced up at Skye, the tears were already overflowing.

His worried expression shifted to shock as he understood exactly what I couldn't ever find the words to say out loud. "Oh. *Oh fuck*... Noah. *Shit.*" He pulled me forward, dragging me into his lap and hugging me like I was an oversized teddy bear he'd just won at a carnival.

I hadn't realized how badly I needed to be hugged until then.

My chest cracked open, and all the months of suppressed emotion came pouring out as I clung to my roommate and just *sobbed*. When I'd first discovered what Rich had done, I'd been full of anger and retribution. Jared hadn't hugged me because I'd never let him see how utterly *broken* I'd been. Miles had been literally in traction, so he couldn't have hugged me even if he'd known I needed it. But Skye? I hadn't even needed to say a damn word and he knew.

He didn't offer any useless platitudes or empty reassurances. He just hugged me tight and let me cry out months—or years—of betrayal, emotional abuse, low self-esteem, and utter heartbreak. When I was done, he dried my face with the sleeve of his hoodie and gave me a firm nod.

"You wanna go watch movies in the theatre room? Everyone else is downstairs playing *Tekken* still. Better yet, it's dark and no one will see how red your eyes are."

A laugh bubbled out of me and I scrubbed a hand through my messy, tangled hair. It was funny, though, because that was how I *expected* him to handle it. I cried, he comforted me, now let's change the subject and move on. Exactly what I needed.

"Yes." I sniffled. "That sounds great. Can we watch something scary?"

"Shit yes, we can." Skye climbed to his feet and offered me a hand to pull me up as well, then started gathering an armful of blankets and pillows off our beds. I liked the way he was thinking.

The theatre was an existing part of the house rather than a converted bedroom, but it was only just big enough for eight plush recliners in two rows of four, facing the full-wall projector screen. Skye and I set up our nest of blankets and pillows in the middle of the front row, then he used the remote to browse through the movie selections on the various streaming services.

"Okay, are we thinking real-life scary, like serial killers or... hmm...religious possession and exorcism?" Skye tipped his head my way, offering me the choice.

"Exorcisms, definitely," I chose quickly. "The messier the better."

He laughed, flicking through the options and settling on one with a clearly demonic nun on the title poster. Perfect.

The opening scene involved a woman screaming so loud it shook us both, and Skye frantically scrambled to turn the volume down as we dissolved into laughter. It wasn't what I'd expected, but it *had* done exactly what I needed: flooded me with sweet adrenaline and chased away the sadness. I could never be sad while my pulse was racing with my very favorite drug.

"What the fuck are you two watching?" Z asked a couple minutes later, coming into the theatre with takeout boxes in hand. "Is this *Sister Demon*? The movie that got banned from commercial cinemas for disturbing content?"

"Yup," I replied, grinning wide and probably looking possessed myself in the darkness of the theatre. The screen itself projected enough light that we could see just fine, and a soft glow from below the seats helped. "Want to join us?"

Z grimaced as the protagonist onscreen slit the throat of a chicken to complete her demon-summoning ritual. "Fuck no. I just came to deliver your tacos."

"Thanks, bro," Skye replied, taking the boxes from Z. "You heading out?"

"Mm-hmm," he nodded, eyes still locked on the screen in horrified fascination. "How the hell do you guys like this shit?"

"What's not to like?" I asked with a laugh, making Z turn to give me a puzzled look.

"Ah. Adrenaline junkies. That checks out."

"Uh-huh, whatever. Have fun with Tessa." Skye flapped a hand like he wanted Z to shut up and leave already, but now I was curious who Tessa was and where Z was going with her.

He just rolled his eyes and left us to our movie, though, so I grabbed the remote to pause our movie. "Explain?" I asked Skye, gesturing to the door where Z just exited. "Tessa?"

Skye shrugged. "His girlfriend."

My jaw dropped. "Z has a girlfriend? Since when? Wait, I thought our contracts stated—"

"Our contracts state we can't *publicly* be involved in any romantic relationships, but what the public doesn't know can't hurt them. Besides, he's been with Tessa for years, on and off. Mostly off, to be fair. She's...a lot. And she hates that he has to hide their relationship."

I was floored. "Is anyone else hiding a secret relationship? I can't believe I didn't know this by now." Also now I was feeling really fucking dumb for all the moments I'd felt like there was some level of *chemistry* with Z when it'd been entirely fabricated in my own mind.

"If they are, I don't know about it either. Although honestly I would not be shocked if there was something more between Torin and August." He said it with a chuckle that implied he was joking...but I *could* kind of see that.

"Are they both...um...into guys?" It was a question I'd been wanting to ask for *weeks,* and Skye was now offering the perfect opportunity.

He just shrugged, though. "No idea. Maybe? I've never asked. Do you have more questions about the team's relationship availability or are we gonna watch this demon summoning go horribly wrong?"

My lips parted and a shocked, indignant sound escaped. "I wasn't— That's not— I don't—"

"Uh-huh, sure," he teased, smirking. "If it's reassuring, I'm pretty sure Z and Xavier are the only ones who are one hundred percent straight, so you could totally have a shot with the others even without revealing your secret."

"Oh my God!" I exclaimed in a strangled voice, smacking him in the face with a pillow. "Not why I was asking *at all!* Fucking hell, Skye, just press play."

His delighted laughter blended seamlessly with the screams from the movie as he started it again, and I shot him a mock-glare as he handed my box of tacos over.

For ten minutes or so we happily ate our tacos in silence, eyes glued to the movie and fully engrossed in the storyline. So much that neither of us noticed Minho and Ace joined us until Minho grabbed my uninjured ankle under the blanket and I screamed.

"Not funny!" I protested, kicking frantically despite how much I was laughing.

Thankfully, they didn't come to chat and were happy to settle in quietly to watch the movie with us. Or, Ace was. Within twenty minutes, Minho was asleep with his head in my lap as I absent-mindedly twisted his silky hair into tiny braids.

Skye glanced over at one stage, meeting my eyes with a pointed look as he dipped his chin to Minnie sleeping peacefully through the screams of the demonic nun. I narrowed my eyes and shot him a middle finger, then continued playing with Minho's hair. Because I liked it. *And him.*

Shit.

FOURTEEN

Noah was avoiding me, and it was starting to get on my fucking nerves. After his totally unhinged blowup about Peaches—which was none of his goddamn business—he'd noticeably gone out of his way to dodge spending time with me.

When I mentioned it to Ace, though, my best friend just shrugged it off. Made some comment about Noah focusing on the challenge, which in itself told me he was full of crap. Me and Ace were the two responsible for guiding the group through the challenges, so we spent the *most* time on our training course. Yet Noah still managed to avoid the crap out of me.

I didn't get it. Why was he so fucking offended on behalf of an anonymous porn star?

Well, he was going to have to get over it because our filming day had officially arrived and we were on our way to inspect the high-wire course rigged up between the triangle towers. It should, theoretically, be the exact same as our training course. Just a hell of a lot higher.

"If you fall from up here, there's no chance of survival," Torin was repeating *again*. "It's not worth the risk, Short Stack. Not even for the Games."

"Why would I fall?" the littlest team member replied with an overconfident smirk, his eyes already sparkling with excitement. "Did you see me fall even once during our practice?"

Torin scowled, glancing over at me for some kind of backup. I just shrugged because it was a pointless discussion with Noah. Everyone had expressed their concerns over the last few weeks, *Skye included*, which said a lot. But nothing would talk Noah out of his stubborn refusal to wear a safety harness during the challenge. So Ace and I had taken precautions without telling the team, and there *should* have been a safety net rigged up. High enough that it could prevent anyone hitting the ground, but low enough that it would still be a *huge* drop from the wires.

If all things went to plan, it wouldn't be used, and it'd basically be invisible to the cameras. But if it was needed...well, then we wouldn't be losing any team members today.

"Fine," Torin huffed, crossing his arms over his chest with a stubborn set to his jaw. "Then I won't wear a harness either."

"Same," Skye added as we climbed out of the minivan.

I blew out a long breath, not bothering to argue with the fucking idiots because they were full of crap. Torin had awful balance and really struggled on the rolling logs obstacle. He was just bluffing to see if that would sway Noah's decision.

It was a wasted effort because Noah also seemed to get that he was only bluffing and completely ignored him.

"Hey." I grabbed our resident daredevil's arm to get his attention while our camera crew piled out of more cars in the underground parking lot we'd arrived in.

Noah frowned and shook his arm out of my grip. "Don't you start, too," he muttered with a scowl. "I've had enough guilt trips to last a lifetime."

My brows rose at his surly attitude when just a minute ago he was basically vibrating with excitement. Was this attitude just reserved for me? That kind of hurt, I had to admit. I *liked* the guy, but it seemed he'd decided I was the worst kind of human for engaging in a perfectly legal transactional relationship on AO.

I swallowed, squashing down that bitter feeling of rejection and disappointment, tucking it away with all the other nasty emotions in a dark cave of trauma within my mind. "I wasn't going to," I replied with a shake of my head. "Only wanted to ask if you're okay with the change of teams. Trust is such a big factor here..."

A couple of days ago, Ace and I had swapped positions in our groupings. As the two without any sensory handicaps, it was our responsibility to guide the others through the course and ensure they didn't fall. After a lot of practice, Ace asked to switch with me because I was more confident completing the course backward, allowing me to keep my eyes on my disadvantaged team. Mainly Noah. I wasn't worried about Torin or Skye; they would both be on safety lines *and* could see full well where to place their feet.

Noah shrugged, dodging eye contact with me *again*. It was fucking infuriating. "Makes no difference to me. You all seem to think the height will have some increased fear factor, but you're forgetting two things, Xavier."

My brow creased, I shook my head with confusion. "What am I forgetting?"

Noah's full lips curled in a smug grin, his eyes finally meeting mine. "I'm blindfolded, dumbass. Twelve feet or two hundred, it makes no difference when you can't see."

Huh. That had never even occurred to me in all the weeks we'd spent practicing. Yes, the degree of danger was a lot higher because a mistake would cost a lot more than falling onto grass. But he'd never fallen on the practice course, so why would this be any different, when he literally couldn't see the drop?

"What's the other thing?" I asked, studying him with interest. Little Dude was *fascinating*, even if he didn't like me much.

He shrugged, smirking. "NoFear isn't my ClikByte name for no reason. Fear quite legitimately isn't a hurdle for me." With a small, somewhat feral laugh, he jogged to catch up with the rest of the team and left me to think about our interaction.

It was a curious way that he'd phrased that. Not that he didn't *feel* fear...just that it wasn't a hurdle. I liked that. Even so, his being blindfolded worked in both our favors because it meant he would have no idea that Ace had arranged for a safety net.

"We good?" Ace asked as I joined the rest of them near the elevators. A few of the film crew had gone ahead to set up already, leaving just two cameramen with us to film our progress. Ace would cut it all together into our entry clip later tonight, so the more footage, the better.

I jerked a nod, forcing a reassuring smile to my lips. "Yep. You?"

Ace nodded. "Safety checks were all completed earlier this morning. Everything is good to go." He shifted his eyes toward Noah, his expression tightening with concern. I hated that our newest team member was causing Ace *more* reasons not to sleep. As if he needed extra stress. Little Dude was probably going to give him a stomach ulcer if he didn't compromise on some of these challenges, but I could also understand that they both seemed to have something to prove here.

Noah needed to prove that he was legit, and doubt from haters online was fueling his determination to one-up all the danger factors. Ace needed to prove that he could pull this odd band of misfits together to create a team. He needed to prove that he'd selected us for more than just our follower count.

"You guys see the leaked footage of Team Kraken's challenge entry?" August asked as we piled into the cargo elevator. He brought it up on his phone and turned it around to show us. They were a mixed team, most consisting of lifestyle vloggers, and their idea of a teamwork challenge was doing a human knot.

"Lame," Z scoffed, shaking his head. "They're not even trying."

"I dunno, the sensory handicaps in that situation could be pretty funny." August shrugged with a grin, putting his phone away. "No one ever said the challenges had to be *successful*, only entertaining."

For the rest of the ride up to the tenth floor, everyone was pretty quiet. Focused. Minho and August seemed the calmest, and that checked out with how quietly confident they both were on the obstacle course. Minho had his arm around Noah's waist while the smaller dude murmured quietly with Skye. They were talking about the obstacle Skye was having the most trouble getting across—the X swing steps—as it was on a downward incline. He was physically more than capable, but he kept messing up his foot placement and making it harder than it needed to be.

I was well aware that our management had encouraged the fan service closeness between Minho and Noah because the fans were frothing over the idea they might be romantically involved. But they weren't limiting that closeness to only in front of cameras, and it was starting to become a concern.

Of course, right now there were two cameras on us, so I said nothing. It was ultimately Ace's responsibility to manage, not mine, but I might need to point it out in case he hadn't noticed.

Fan service was one thing. Actual relationships were against contract simply because if it went wrong, the team would fall to pieces.

"Okay!" one of our producers greeted us as we stepped out of the elevator on the tenth floor. "Boys, are you ready to do this? The high-wire specialists are here to get you geared up, and our tech team will ensure cameras and mics are all operational."

They ushered us into action, and the staff went to work getting everyone ready to go. Noah again insisted that he didn't want or need the safety harness, so then he needed to sign what looked like the longest legal waiver known to man so he or his family couldn't turn around and sue anyone involved for liability. Fair.

"This is new," Little Dude muttered with a sigh as he was about halfway through the pages, initialing every corner.

"What is?" I asked with curiosity, fixing the strap on my chest-mounted camera while peering over his shoulder. "Liability waivers?"

Noah snorted a laugh. "Yeah. Legal paperwork and safety checks."

I hummed my understanding, having done plenty of my own research before NoFear joined our team. Almost every Byte he'd uploaded since starting his platform was a break-and-enter on private land or property.

"I'm surprised you haven't run into any repercussions for the trespassing," I commented thoughtfully. "I bet you pissed off some big corporations along the way."

Noah's shoulders stiffened, and his grip on the pen tightened to the point his knuckles turned white. "Yeah, well, hiding my identity was really working in my favor," he mumbled, sounding irritated as fuck. About what? It's not like we forced him into taking off the mask; his participation on our team was his own choice.

Weird kid.

All too quickly, we were ready to begin, and one of our staff flew a drone camera out the window to capture *all* the angles for content.

Ace went first, clipping his safety line onto the cable running overhead and confidently stepping out across the first precariously swinging steps before ducking through the narrow gap of the hurdle. He paused on the other side of that first obstacle and verbally coached August through exactly where to step, where to place his hands. It was just as we'd practiced, with the added effect of gasps and screams from below us.

It wasn't a quick course for all eight of us to get through, but that was okay. We had so many cameras running that there would be *dozens* of perfect examples to show our teamwork as we worked through the network of challenges rigged up between the three towers, intersecting across a central, suspended platform.

Noah came last, with just me to guide him.

When he stepped out, blindfolded and looking like a strong gust of wind might knock him off the wires, the crowd below went crazy. We were ten stories up, but I'd bet anything there were hundreds of phones using their 20x zoom right now to get a clearer picture.

Ace was right—Noah was adding *huge* appeal to our team. Maybe because he was so small, so delicate. It made everyone want to protect him, despite how capable he was of protecting himself. He was a walking contradiction.

"Take it slow, Little Dude," I coaxed him as he confidently progressed across the wobbly wooden steps and ducked through the obstacle like a fucking ballerina. "There's no time limit on this, just—"

"Shut the fuck up, Xavier," he growled. "I'm trying to concentrate, and you're distracting me."

Oh. Right. I resisted the urge to argue with him and clenched my jaw tight. He was right. He'd memorized the course inside out *without* me talking him through it, so why the hell would he need it now?

But shit. It hurt to keep quiet, watching every wobble and near-miss of his feet. I simply needed to trust. That's what this challenge was really about, after all, wasn't it? Trust. Except it was *me* who needed to trust *him*. Harder than I realized.

FIFTEEN

Regardless of how many times we'd gone through the obstacle course in practice, nothing could have prepared me for the real thing. While I'd never had any issues with heights before, I also had never walked along a fucking tightwire ten stories above the ground before.

Halfway in, we were all struggling. The wind was so much worse than any of us could have anticipated, and the excessive amount of practice both Ace and Noah had guilted us into this past month was the only thing getting us through.

It took *every* ounce of my willpower to focus on my footing and not look for Noah. I had to trust that he could handle himself, just like he had every day that

we'd practiced. I figured out *really* early that my nerves couldn't handle actually watching him on the wires. Not when I knew he wasn't clipped onto a safety line.

This was a hundred times worse than I'd prepared for. My noise-cancelling headphones meant I was alone with my thoughts and the stomach twisting view of the ground far, far, far below us.

I hardly dared to breathe, keeping my eyes on August and Ace ahead of me. Several times already, Ace had grabbed Augie's arm to redirect and save him from missing the steps...but every near miss from August only made me more anxious for Noah.

Fuck. If he fell...

Nope. No, it wasn't an option. He was too good at this shit, and as dangerous as it all seemed to the rest of us, it was on par with a lot of his stunts. He'd free-climbed taller structures than this in the past, so the danger was not new to him.

Our course was nowhere near as complicated as typical tree-top courses, since we only had the three towers to securely tether the wires to. With the addition of a suspended platform in the middle of the triangle, it allowed us to create six obstacle paths. Some we needed to double up to finish back in the tower we'd started from.

Somehow, with my lungs burning and my stomach in knots, I made it to the second-to-last obstacle—a zip line between two towers. One point was just a single story higher to create a decline for gravity, but the nature of the fixed pulley meant it required teamwork to get it back across for the next person to cross.

Ace went first, landing smoothly on the far platform.

He waved dramatically, indicating to me that he was sending the pulley back across, and I gestured back to say I was ready. He pulled it back, then threw it as hard as physically possible, sending the pulley whizzing back up the line. I leaned past August to grab it just as we'd practiced. Because Augie was blindfolded, he couldn't catch it.

"Got it," I said out loud, despite the fact I couldn't hear myself. August could hear me, and that's what counted. "Here." I took one of his hands and placed it on the pulley rope, helping him get a firm grip on the handlebars, and then he was *gone*.

My heart leapt to my throat as I watched my friend flying blindfolded between the two buildings, but then Ace caught him with a strong arm around his waist, and I could breathe again.

Ace threw the pulley back once again, and it was my turn.

Surprisingly, I kind of loved the feeling of zip-lining. It was exhilarating, usually. But today all I could think about was all the ways it could go wrong. It was making me sick. And by the time Ace caught me, I was nearly shaking with anxiety.

"Are you good?" Ace mouthed at me, grasping one of my slightly trembling hands in his.

I swallowed hard, squashing down my nervousness with determination, nodding my head. Freaking out now wouldn't do us any good. It sure as fuck wouldn't help Noah.

As if unable to stop myself, I looked across the course and found him instantly.

Last. He was the last of us, and Xavier stuck to him like glue. That had to give me some level of comfort, that Xavier was with him. He wouldn't let the cute little Chicken fall. Xavier would see that as a failure, and he didn't handle failure well.

Ace poked me in the side to get my attention, giving me a hard look when I met his eyes. "*He's fine.*"

Psychic fuck knew exactly where my head was at. In my defense, I really liked Noah. As a friend. He just...shit, he was just enjoyable to be around. Like he lit up every room he walked into with just a smile. I'd had more fun on Team Olympus in the last month than I'd had in the six months before he joined. Realizing he could dance had only strengthened our bond, too, especially when he was showing off one night and perfectly nailed the full choreography for one of my former group's lesser-known songs. One that I'd written—not that anyone knew.

He told me that his sister, Millie, was a big K-pop fan and she'd forced him to learn the choreo, but I wasn't buying it. Noah was a closet fan, for sure. A small, somewhat perverted part of me wondered if he had any of our albums or posters at home. I was too scared to ask who his bias was, though, just in case it wasn't me. That'd sting.

Ace prodded me again, and I sighed. I needed to focus on the challenge instead of thinking about my favorite human. Waving to Torin in warning, I threw the pulley back across the wire for him. He caught it, but a light smattering of raindrops sent panic flooding through me and I yanked my headphones off. *Fuck the challenge.*

"It's raining!" I exclaimed, spinning to glare at Ace.

He scowled, putting his palm out as if to confirm what was already obvious. Dark gray clouds had formed in the sky, and the droplets were already falling faster. "I can see that."

"It's not supposed to rain today!" I replied, my pulse racing as I looked over to Noah and Xavier. They were halfway through the slightly inclined swing steps toward the zip line platform and had paused there. Xavier's head tipped to the sky in an echo of my own disbelief.

"I'm aware," Ace snapped, clearly frustrated. "Apparently the weather forecast was wrong. Shocker."

Outrage and anger flooded through me, but he shook his head firmly. "We just need to finish."

"Hey, Minnie, did you take your headphones off?" August asked, still blindfolded. "No fair, can I—"

"No!" Ace growled. "Shit, Torin!"

His warning was too late, as Torin came hurtling in on the zip line faster than I could respond, meaning I didn't catch him, and he rebounded along the wire and out of my reach. Fuck. *Double fuck.*

For a moment, Ace and I just stood there, staring and shocked as Torin dangled like a teabag just a fraction farther than we could reach. Close enough for it to be extra frustrating and not at all funny.

"Uh, guys? What's happened?" August asked, and I winced. Torin was gagged, but his eyes conveyed enough expletives that I got the picture. He was *not* happy.

Ace scrubbed a hand over his white-blond hair and groaned. "Nothing. We're fine. Minho, you've got this handled, yes?"

I wrinkled my nose and nodded. "Yep. So fine." Across the course, Noah and Xavier had started moving again, only slightly slower thanks to the rain...but they seemed okay. Cautious, slow, but stable.

Ace murmured for August to continue on with him to make space on the platform, and I whipped my T-shirt over my head before putting my headphones back on. Using my teeth and brute force, I tore my shirt open to create a makeshift rescue rope and tossed it out to Torin. Thank fuck he was close enough that he could catch the fabric between his feet then held on tight as I reeled him in like a giant koi.

"Yeah, yeah," I muttered as he reached the platform and he glared venom at me. "I know. Throw it back over. Skye's waiting." I left him to catch our next team member and hurried across the tightwire that would take me to the ending point. It was a simple one, with a wire at shoulder height to hold for balance, and I made it across before Skye had even caught the pulley for the zip line.

Ducking through the window at the end of the tightwire, I yanked my headphones off and bent double to catch my breath. It was harder than it should have been, since I really hadn't exerted that much energy on the challenge itself.

"Drink some water," Ace ordered, putting a bottle in my face even as he rubbed my back comfortingly. "He'll be pissed if he realizes we had such little faith in his skill, right?"

Fucking hell, Ace always saw straight through me. I didn't even try to deny it, nodding as I took a sip of water and made my way back to the window to watch. We were done, but the rest of the team still needed to make it. "Here comes Tor," I murmured, watching him crossing the tightwire a lot more cautiously than I'd just done it. Fair, though, seeing how fast the rain was now falling.

Beyond him, Skye had just caught Z from the zip line. That meant it was just Xavier and Noah to cross that obstacle...

Torin jumped through the window, unclipping from the safety line and collapsing to the floor with a groan. Several of the Olympus staff rushed over, but he waved them away as he ripped the tape off his mouth with a curse.

"Min, what the *fuck* was that?" he growled, rolling to his knees. "You weren't even paying attention!"

I winced, guilt tightening my chest. "Sorry, Tor. I was distracted." Even as I said it, I gravitated back to the window, waiting eagerly to see the rest of our team finishing the course in the pouring rain.

Skye edged along the tightwire, taking it slow and steady while the rain intensified, and Z threw the zipline pulley back across to Xavier and Noah.

"Yeah, I bet," Torin grumbled, standing beside me. "Quick thinking on the T-shirt thing, though. Fans will just *hate* seeing you shirtless in the rain while saving my dangling ass."

I snorted a laugh, shrugging. "Don't be salty because you didn't think of an excuse to flash your abs." Not that it'd been my intention in any way, but if it got us more Cliks, who was I to complain?

For a few moments the four of us watched in silence until Skye reached us and Ace met him with a towel and bottle of water.

"Holy shit, where did that rain come from?" Skye exclaimed, shaking his head like a wet dog. "That wire is so slippery now. Like...can we somehow get Xavier to call it quits at the end of the zip? Noah could—"

"Do you think he'd listen?" Ace cut him off with a grimace. "Don't worry. Xavier won't let him get hurt."

I hated that he was right, but at the same time... "We have to trust him," I growled, my hands balled into fists at my sides. "He knows his own limits, and we have to trust that."

As we watched, no one daring to speak, Xavier handed Noah the zip line handles and the delicate little dude just launched off the platform without even a moment's hesitation. My heart lodged firmly in my throat as he whizzed down the line at startling speed, but then Z was right there to catch him on the other side.

The air gusted out of me in a huge exhale. "Thank fuck. *Thank fuck.*"

"I feel sick watching this," Torin murmured beside me. "Can our next challenge be something safe, please? Let's do a live drawing class."

"Agreed," August huffed. "We can flip a coin for who needs to be the model."

My lips curled with amusement at that idea, and I locked eyes with Torin. I knew *exactly* what he was thinking...because I was too. Purely on a friendly entertainment level, though, and just because I'd already clocked how quick Noah was to blush when he was uncomfortable. It'd be funny, in a totally platonic way.

Z threw the pulley back across to Xavier, and I watched unblinking as Noah swiped rain off his skinny arms. It was *really* coming down now.

Xavier nailed the zip line, not even needing to be caught as his feet found the platform easily. His balance was impressive. Z started cautiously across the tightwire, balancing by holding onto the top wire as he progressed, and Xavier bent his head to speak with Noah while they waited on the platform. Unless necessary—in the case of someone leading a blindfolded person—it was safer not to have two people on the wire at a time.

Whatever he said, Noah shook his head firmly, water flying from his hair.

"See?" Ace muttered with a sigh. "I'd bet you a hundred bucks he just tried to talk him into calling it quits."

Torin scoffed. "No one is taking that bet."

Z made it to us a moment later and jumped off the wire with a splashy thump. "That was fucked," he announced. "Actually fucked. Who is operating the drone, by the way? They're way too close to the wires."

"Our camera drone?" Ace asked, leaning out the window to search for what Z was talking about.

"It's not us!" the drone operator called out from further along the wall of windows. "I'm over here," she pointed to where her camera drone was battling the weather, "well out of range and using a zoom lens. It's someone else."

"Shit!" August whispered, pressing his hands to the glass as he leaned closer to see Xavier and Noah. "Come on, Noah, you're so close."

My own pulse rushed in my ears as I watched the two last members of our team making their way across the wire. Xavier walked backward, holding on to the guide wire with one hand and keeping his eyes locked on Noah.

Noah... *Fucking hell*, did he actually have a death wish? He wasn't even holding the guide wire at all, just balancing with his arms extended and sliding his little feet along the wet wire like it were nothing more than a painted line on the ground.

Time seemed to stand still. I couldn't blink—couldn't *breathe*—all I could do was watch and wait and hope like fucking hell he would make it safely across. And when he did, I was going to hug him. Really hard. Big hug. I loved hugging Noah.

"Shit, that drone is getting really fucking close," Skye commented. "What the fuck are they doing?"

Right as he said that, a strong gust of wind wobbled both Xavier and Noah on the wire, and my lungs seized. The drone veered out of control, swooping toward our teammates, and I was powerless to do anything other than watch as Xavier yelled and grabbed Noah's arm a split-second before the drone would have hit him in the back of the head.

Regardless of having dodged the drone, his balance was shot. He wobbled, gripping Xavier's hand as he took another step to try to recover. His foot slipped, coming off the wire entirely right as the drone swooped back toward them again. This time Xavier backhanded the flying camera away.

A panicked sound escaped Noah, and it was the kind of sound that kept echoing in my mind as Xavier's movement jerked the smaller guy completely off the wire. All of a sudden, he was dangling over the ten-story drop with nothing but Xavier's grip on his hand to save him from certain death.

"Noah!" Torin exclaimed, one foot back on the wire as though he intended to run back out there and save him. But that movement was enough to make the whole wire wobble, and Xavier flashed a warning look as he barked "Stop!"

We stared in horror as Xavier used his grip on the guide wire to try to haul Noah back up, but whether it was the rain or the lack of balance, it was no use.

"Noah!" I heard him bellow as he looked down at my blindfolded Chicken, our smallest and most fearless member. "I need you to trust me!"

Then he let go.

SIXTEEN

This must be what Miles felt when he fell.

The moment seemed to stretch far longer than physics allowed, but maybe that was the nature of fear. It could play tricks on the mind and seem to stop time. That moment between Xavier telling me to trust him and when he let go of my hand? A lifetime stretched out before and after me.

Then came the drop. The rush of air, and the feeling of utter weightlessness... It was a feeling I was so incredibly used to that it was hard to feel real terror, even when my logical brain reminded me that this time there was no parachute to save me at the last moment. No wingsuit. No counterweight. No safety nets.

I was such an arrogant fool for thinking I could cheat

death for even as long as I had. This had been coming for a long time, but contrary to what I'd convinced myself, I wasn't ready. I didn't want to die. I had people that I cared about now...more than just Miles and Mom. I had the team. All of them. And this would break them, which was insanely selfish on my part.

For the first time since I'd started my adrenaline-fueled stunts, I had to admit that I now had a reason to live.

Then I hit the ground. All the air whooshed out of my lungs and my head rattled, causing everything to go fuzzy. But only for a moment, and then...confusion. Did it hurt? Yes. But not the agonizing pain of breaking every bone in my body and dying.

My head rang and my body ached, but I was alive. How? And why the fuck did it feel like I was at sea?

Groaning, I reached a shaking hand up to pull off the blindfold and blinked up at the sky. Rain pelted down on me, but it was very much real rain...

"What the fuck?" I whispered aloud, swiping a hand over my face to clear some raindrops. Fuck. My arm hurt, my head hurt, my neck and back... Wait, why was I still moving up and down like...

Like I was on a trampoline.

Or a net.

Motherfucker. There was a safety net? Since when? How?

Ugh. Fucking Xavier! *I need you to trust me...* Because the asshole knew about the net. He knew I wouldn't die because he already made sure there was a safety net in place!

Rolling over onto my stomach, a flash of white-hot pain flared through my back and I whimpered pathetically. I might not have died, but I'd still fallen a *long* way. And to make matters worse, there were hundreds of people below me with cameras pointed my way. Fuck. I was going to *murder* Xavier Stone when I got my hands on him.

Then again...would I really rather be dead right now? If not for the safety net, I'd be little more than human ketchup in the middle of that crowd.

"Fuck," I huffed, rolling onto my back once more so I could catch my breath without staring at the people below. They likely already had enough footage to keep me in the media until I was old and gray.

Eventually, I'd have to crawl off the net. But right now I had very little faith that I could do that act gracefully. Not while my back was flashing with pain and my limbs felt like they were made of electric eels. So I closed my eyes and lay there in the pouring rain until the net wobbled and tilted dramatically as my rescue party arrived.

"Noah, are you with us?" a vaguely familiar voice called out, and I peeled my eyes open to see one of the high-wire technicians crawling across the net toward me.

"Hey, Barry," I replied, having spent plenty of time chatting with him during the practice course setup days. "Thanks for the save."

"Don't thank me, kid, that was all Ace." *Ace, too? Traitor.* "Fucking lucky, too. Are you hurt?"

"Maybe," I admitted, knowing it would be stupid to lie after a fall like that. "I'm not paralyzed though."

Barry huffed a coughing laugh. "Well, shit, that's something. You need me to call in a stretcher to get you down?" He was closer now, so we didn't need to speak so loudly.

I wrinkled my nose, shaking my head. "I think I've suffered enough embarrassment for one day. I'll survive getting myself down and just sit in an ice bath when we get home." That seemed like the only viable option, since they didn't make gel ice packs big enough for everything that hurt.

"Maybe it'd be a better idea to—" Barry started to say, but I forced myself to sit up with an agonized wince before he could continue. "Yeah, okay, sure. Just take it slow, Noah. These nets will save you from dying, but that landing would still hurt like a bitch."

"No shit," I growled, starting across the net toward the ladder he'd come up. I needed to get off the net, down the ladder, and out of the fucking public eye so I could fall apart quietly. It was slow going, with my limbs trembling as I crawled. Nearly dying had smacked me with more adrenaline than I'd ever felt, but my body was processing it just as fast, and that left me physically shaking and weak.

Dimly I realized that Olympus security was hard at work to keep random spectators away from the base of the ladder so Barry and I could get down safely. It was kind of nice, knowing we had the support—and staff—that came with a major corporation.

It meant that no one jostled the ladder as I made my cautious way down to the ground, where an Olympus private paramedic waited with a gear bag in hand.

"Noah, hi," the woman greeted me when my feet found the solid ground and I swayed a little. "I'm Samantha. We met this morning. Do you remember?"

I forced a smile at the clearly probing question. "Yeah, I remember. I'm okay, just—"

"*Noah!*" someone bellowed, jerking my attention away from the medic. From across the cleared area—thanks to security—I spotted my team bursting out of the building lobby. Minho was in the lead, sprinting toward me shirtless. Why the fuck was he shirtless? Not that I really minded the view, he looked fucking *incredible* shirtless, but it was confusing nonetheless.

"Don't—" Samantha the paramedic tried to protest as he crashed into me, sweeping me up in a hug that took my feet totally off the ground.

Whatever else she said faded into background noise as my chest tightened and my breath whooshed out of me once more. Words totally fled my brain as he squeezed me against his wet and naked chest.

"I thought you were dead!" he exclaimed, putting me back on my feet but not letting me go. Someone—maybe Barry—handed him an open umbrella, and all of a sudden we were in our own world. The black umbrella canopy blanketed us in privacy, hiding us away and then...

He kissed me.

Or did I kiss him? It was all a blur.

My brain short-circuited and I reacted purely on instinct, returning his kiss with hungry desperation as his fingertips bit into the already aching muscles of my back, pulling me closer until—

"Noah!" someone else yelled, and reality came crashing back down almost as intensely as Minnie's initial embrace.

Shocked, horrified, and overwhelmingly embarrassed, I wrenched myself out of Minho's grip and stumbled backward out of the protection of the umbrella. For one heart-aching moment, we locked eyes, and I saw in painful clarity how bewildered and confused he was.

Shit.

Ace had reached us, though, as had the rest of the team, and chaos erupted. My cheeks burning and my stomach twisted up in absolute knots, I let them fuss for a bit before willingly subjecting myself to Paramedic Samantha's care.

"Are you okay to walk?" she asked me quietly, holding another umbrella over us both. "I'd prefer to take you indoors to check you over."

I nodded, having totally lost my tongue, and let her brush the team aside as she led the way into the building that they'd all just come streaming out of. It had a sterile sort of seating area near the reception desks, and Samantha guided me over to sit before dropping her medical kit to the floor beside me.

"Okay, where do we even begin?" she asked with a heavy exhale, pulling out a penlight and checking my pupil dilation.

"He's got a preexisting back injury," Minho said from behind me, and I stiffened.

What the fuck just happened back there? Did he start that or did I? Everything was so fuzzy.

Samantha raised her eyebrow at me in question, and I gritted my teeth, searching for a plausible explanation. Trouble was, all I could think about was how soft Minho's lips were, and how my whole body had melted in his arms, and how—

"Can I take a look at your back?" Samantha asked, shocking me out of my train of thought.

"N-no," I stuttered, shaking my head and then wincing. Something hurt in my neck, and yeah I really should get it looked at, but not here. Not in front of the team. Not while I was still pretending that I wore a back brace for a previous nonexistent injury rather than a binder to disguise my tits.

Samantha's brow creased at my refusal, confusion etched across her face, but she didn't push the issue. Instead she shifted her focus to checking my neck, getting me to turn my head and check the range of motion and so on, asking me quiet questions about what still hurt and where.

Eventually, she sat back on her heels and gave me a shrug. "I think you're okay. Bruised and sore, definitely. You'll need to take it easy for a few days but...nothing broken, no obvious signs of concussion. I *do* need to look at your back, though. Is it a disc or—"

"Noah, you can probably get that checked with your specialist, right?" Skye interjected, placing a hand on my shoulder to give a light, reassuring squeeze. All seven of them had been hovering behind me the whole time Samantha had been doing her job, and it was starting to suffocate me.

I nodded, wetting my lips. "Yep, I can do that. I really just want a hot shower right now, but I promise to see my specialist tomorrow." Mustering up my most convincing smile, I silently pleaded with the paramedic to just *let it go*.

After a beat, she sighed and shrugged. "It's your call, Noah. But if the pain gets *any* worse, if you have any dizziness, loss of consciousness, or vomiting, I want you to go straight to the emergency room, okay?"

"Yes, absolutely," I agreed. "Understood."

The second Samantha nodded her agreement, I grabbed on to Skye's hand and rose to my feet, letting my roommate pull me into a protective side hug. He didn't need me to tell him how I was feeling, instead just swiftly guiding me across to the elevators where some of the Olympus staff were waiting to head back down to the parking lot.

"You scared the life out of me, Twin," he murmured, leaning down to press a quick kiss on my wet hair. "I'm really glad you're not dead."

A hollow laugh escaped me as I wrapped my arm around his waist to steal some body warmth. "Same, dude. Same."

We stayed like that, linked together, the whole way down to the parking lot and totally ignored the producer who tried asking questions with a camera pointed our way. Fuck that. But as we headed for the waiting vans, Minho grabbed my arm gently.

"Chicken, can we—" he started to ask, and I flexed my fingers on Skye's waist.

"Later, Minnie," Skye interrupted, understanding me perfectly even if he didn't know why. "Noah nearly died today. Let's let him process that, yeah?"

Minho didn't argue that fact, but he did climb into the same van as us, and I was fairly certain he stared at the back of my head the whole way home. It took every ounce of my willpower not to look back, but... *Fucking hell.* Maybe it was me that'd started that kiss, and he was disgusted right now. Horrified. Or worse, maybe he was uncomfortable and felt the need to let me down gently because he wasn't into guys.

I couldn't bear that rejection. Not from him. So I tucked myself into Skye's side and tried to pretend nothing had happened.

Denial was my most faithful best friend.

SEVENTEEN

I fell asleep on the drive back home, which wasn't unexpected in the wake of such an intense adrenaline rush. I was crashing, but that was nothing new. Except I woke up to hear Skye, Minho, and Xavier bickering over whether to wake me up or just carry me inside.

"I'm awake," I mumbled, scrubbing my eyes with the heels of my hands. *Everything hurt.* I stumbled as I climbed out of the van, and Minho caught me with his arm around my waist. "Thanks," I said quietly, still half asleep and groggy.

However, I was not so out of it that I didn't clock the fact that he didn't let go of me as we headed inside, and more than awake enough to notice his fingers had

somehow found the bare skin of my waist beneath my still damp T-shirt.

A shiver of something unrelated to temperature ran through me, and I glanced over at Skye, who was on my other side. He met my eyes with a questioning frown, but I didn't even know what I was trying to say. I liked Minnie touching me...but that was the problem. I *really* liked it. But he was touchy with the whole team, and it meant absolutely nothing. I was making it weird when it shouldn't be.

"Eight, do you want me to call your specialist?" Ace offered as I started up the stairs, my mind fixated on getting a hot shower. Ice would undoubtedly be better for my muscles, but I was cold, and I hated that feeling of bone-deep chills.

It took me a moment to remember what he was talking about, and I shook my head. "No, I can do that," I replied, continuing up more stairs. "You need to start editing, don't you?" We had left the filming of our challenge entry until the last minute possible to avoid the whole thing being leaked by bystanders too early. The deadline to upload was in just six hours, and Ace insisted on cutting the footage together himself even if he did have two of Olympus's producers weighing in with their expertise as well.

Once we made it upstairs, I peeled myself out of Minho's hold and slipped into my shared bedroom with Skye before we could exchange any awkward conversation about that kiss. Shit! Had that been caught on camera by any of the bystanders?

"Hey, do you have my phone?" I asked Skye as he followed me into the room. "I left it in the van this morning."

"Yup, sure do." He pulled it from his pocket, along with his own. "You sure you wanna see it so soon?"

I grimaced, not answering. He assumed I wanted to see the footage of me plummeting from the high wire in the pouring rain after Xavier fucking dropped me. Bastard. But that was unimportant in comparison to what I was actually searching for.

"I'm gonna shower," I mumbled, eyes glued to my phone as I loaded up ClikByte and searched for my creator name. A sickening twist curled through my guts as *hundreds* of videos from today displayed. Not wanting Skye to see what I was searching for, I ducked into the bathroom and locked the door behind me.

Biting my lip, I turned on the shower, then sat on top of the toilet seat as I typed *Noah and Minho* into the search bar. Even more results displayed than I ever could have anticipated and not just from today. There were countless clips of the most innocent moments between the two of us from various Team Olympus content over the past month. Some of them I had no recollection of even happening and others I remembered very clearly...but they hadn't been the intimate flirtation that the Acolytes were implying with their edits and slow-motion zoom screens.

"Fucking hell," I muttered under my breath, trying really hard not to buy into the narrative that fans were pushing between us. Because it wasn't true *at all*. So many out-of-context crops and clever edits painted a totally fictional story of a secret relationship between us. Even worse, the further I scrolled and the deeper into the fan edits I dove, I discovered the relationship fantasies weren't limited to me and Minho. There was a huge faction who were utterly convinced that I was homewrecking the already adorable bond between Torin and August, while others had fabricated a whole storyline about me and Ace engaging in a dom/sub relationship...and that was just the surface.

The ones that made me actually laugh out loud were dating rumors between me and Giselle from GeeGee...which was extra preposterous for the fact that we'd quite literally never met. The only time I knew of that we'd even been in the same location was during the Clik Games introduction filming.

Forcing myself to ignore the absolute insanity of the fan theories, I returned to the footage of today's incident. Had anyone caught me kissing Minho in the rain?

Sitting hunched over my phone on the toilet seat while the bathroom filled with steam, I watched the same scene from dozens of slightly different angles. From me painfully descending the ladder step by step, to Minnie bursting out of the building shirtless and panicked. The way he ran to me and scooped me up in that hug that made my ribs hurt just to watch, but without fail, in *every single clip* that I could find, the black canopy of the umbrella hid us from view until Ace and the guys reached us.

Sure, fans were going crazy for the way he'd hugged me, but they didn't know what'd actually happened. No one did...except the two of us.

Finally satisfied, I let out a long breath of relief and put my phone down. No one knew about the kiss. Assuming Minnie wasn't going to make a whole thing out of it, we could just pretend it'd never happened.

That was good. Really good.

With that band of anxiety eased around my chest, I stripped out of my cold, soggy clothes—hissing in pain as I peeled off my binder—and got into the shower that I so badly needed. The water was hot enough that it hurt, but I bit my lip and suffered because it only *felt* that hot due to how cold I was.

I stayed in there for long enough that Skye knocked on the door to ask if I was okay. That was a sure sign it was time to get out, so no one else got worried enough to come checking on me.

Knowing that I didn't need to hide from Skye, I simply wrapped up in a towel and headed back into the bedroom to find clean clothes, tossing my phone onto the bed so I'd remember where it was.

"You good?" he asked, sitting cross-legged on his own bed and scrolling ClikByte.

I grunted a nothing sort of response because no, I wasn't good. But at the same time, I was alive and relatively uninjured, so I couldn't exactly complain.

"You scared the crap out of everyone," he added, and I glanced over to find him watching me thoughtfully. "What happened out there? Why'd Xavier let you fall?"

I huffed my frustration. "Clearly because he knew there was a net to catch me." I leaned down to fish out some clean sweatpants from my drawer, and a little groan of pain escaped me when my back sang with pain.

"What hurts?" Skye asked, tossing his phone aside.

I retrieved the pants I wanted and tossed him a weak smile. "Fucking *everything*."

He wrinkled his nose in sympathy. "Want me to put some ice rub on your back before you put the Velcro thing on?" He gestured to the clean binder I'd just pulled out.

"Yes," I hissed with a long sigh. "Give me a second." Ducking back into the bathroom, I pulled on underwear and sweatpants, then returned with just my towel covering my boobs. Skye gestured for me to lie down on my stomach and fetched a tube of athletic rub from his dresser.

"Just so we're clear," he said with an edge of teasing as he straddled my hips, keeping his weight on his knees to save tweaking my back any further. "I'm not hitting on you. You're like my *brother*."

I scoffed, tugging a pillow under my face as he started rubbing the strongly scented cream into my back. "Your twin, you mean? The feeling is mutual." Because as objectively attractive as Skye was, he didn't set my heart fluttering like Minnie did. Or Torin, for that matter. Or...shit...way too many of the team. I needed to get that under control fast, or this was going to become a very uncomfortable living situation.

As if summoned by my thoughts, someone knocked on the door, then immediately opened it without waiting for a response.

"Oh, shit," Z exclaimed, freezing one step into our room with a puzzled look on his face.

Well, shit. I was face down, flat against the mattress, so my tits were still hidden but it must look somewhat suspicious with Skye straddling me and my back totally bare.

"Bro, what the fuck?" Skye snapped, his hands easing up on my back as he focused on Z's intrusion. "Ever heard of knocking?"

"I did knock," Z replied defensively, his initial shock seeming to slip away as he clearly recognized the intense smell of athletic rub. "Are you okay, dude? You should have let the paramedic check your back for real."

"I'm fine," I grumbled, careful to stay flatter than a pancake against the quilts. "Just muscle sore and bruised."

Z frowned but gave a small nod of acceptance anyway. "I came to see if you were hungry. We're ordering burgers in for the Olympus staff that are lingering, since Tor refuses to cook for anyone other than our team."

My stomach rumbled, disagreeing with me before I could say no. "Yes, please," I said instead.

Z shot back a lopsided smile. "With pineapple and garlic sriracha, right?"

I gave a small laugh, because they'd all looked at me like I was a psycho when I'd first put in my preferred burger order. What could I say? I liked what I liked. "Yup, perfect. And brown sugar bubble tea, please—not that sugar-free herbal crap Ace keeps buying."

He grinned, nodding. "Got it."

"Uh, do I get food too?" Skye asked as Z started to leave, making the burgundy-haired sex symbol pause with confusion.

"Shit, yeah, sorry, Skye. Your usual, too?" Z ran a hand over the back of his neck, giving an apologetic smile. "Just figured that was a given."

"Uh-huh, sure," Skye murmured, his thumbs working the athletic rub into a particularly sore muscle alongside my spine. I groaned, then clapped a hand over my mouth while hiding my face in the pillow.

Please don't tell me Z just heard that.

"Jesus, Noah," he said with a laugh, confirming that he had definitely heard. I groaned again, this time burying my face in the bed.

Skye laughed. "Chill, Twin, he doesn't suspect anything. Regardless of what you might think, your bare back is gender neutral." He finished rubbing my lower back, then climbed off the bed to go wash his hands.

"Have you seen your notifications, yet?" he called out from the bathroom while I gritted my teeth in pain as I strapped the suffocatingly tight binder over my boobs. Thank *fuck* I'd refused to get the implants Rich had been pressuring me about.

I blew out a heavy breath, pulling a loose T-shirt over my head. "Yeah. Some." I glanced to my phone as it lit up, and I stifled another groan. Miles was calling, which probably meant he had just seen the footage of my fall. Nope. I didn't have the energy for that, so I rejected the call and turned my phone over so I didn't have to see it. I'd call Jared later. After I recovered some. He could deal with Miles for me. Or something.

"All okay?" Skye asked, watching. "Someone harassing you?"

I shook my head with a sigh. "Yes but no. It's my, uh, sister." Because I really didn't need to mess up and say *brother* in front of anyone else. Skye nodded his understanding, though, and didn't push for more information. Eventually, I'd need to call Miles back, but for now I was content to leave my phone behind as we headed downstairs to join the team—and staff—for burgers.

EIGHTEEN

As it turned out, Ace and Xavier had gone to the Olympus head office to cut together all the footage from the dozens of cameras we'd used to film the mission, so it was just the six of us for burgers.

Well...six of us plus four producers, three cameramen, a sound technician, and two hair and makeup artists. Why they were still hanging around when the challenge was done was a mystery to me, and I was too wrung out mentally, physically, and emotionally to ask. They were all sitting around our huge dining table to eat their burgers, though, so I shrugged it off and focused on my food.

I'd become a whole lot less awkward around the staff over the past month, but I was a long way from being

able to pretend they weren't there. Even so, it was a lot easier to ignore the staff than it was to ignore the way Minho kept trying to catch my gaze from across the table.

"You smell like Ice Blue," Torin commented beside me, eating soy and garlic glazed fried chicken pieces. I stole one, because they smelled delicious, and he allowed it. When Z reached over to grab one, though, his hand got smacked.

"Ow, come on, you let Noah have some!" Z complained with a pout, rubbing his knuckles.

Torin shrugged. "I like Noah."

Z scowled. "I thought you liked me, too. Rude."

"You like *me,* though," August said smugly, reaching for a piece of chicken, only to get his hand smacked away as well. "What? Tor! Don't be greedy. You won't eat all that."

Torin shrugged, pulling his container of chicken closer to his chest. "Maybe I will, maybe I won't. What's on the agenda for this evening?" He directed that question down the table to the staff.

One of the producers, a thirty-something guy named Fred, started explaining the footage they wanted to capture for the next *Mount Olympus* episode, which explained why they had so many staff still around.

I zoned out a little bit, the adrenaline crash still fogging my head and the ache in my body crowding what little brain space I had left. Torin's chicken was delicious, though, and I smiled when he pushed the container closer to me in a clear invitation to help myself to more.

"Traitor," August grumbled, and I reached behind Torin to hand him a piece. "Yay! Okay, I see why we all like Noah. Mmm, that's good."

"Noah can't participate in any of that," Skye said, replying to whatever the producers just explained. "He's under medical advice to rest for a couple of days."

Fred the producer frowned. "But he can still be in frame, can he not? I think it's important to ensure Noah is given maximum screen time since he's the newest member."

"Well, I think it's important that he follows doctor's orders and rest his back after a near-fatal accident only a few hours ago," Skye snapped back. "So, no. He will not still be *in frame*, he will be *resting*."

"Seconded," Minho added, flicking me another intense stare, which I dodged by closely inspecting my next bite of burger, just in case it had suddenly morphed into a face-eating spider.

Fred blew out a frustrated breath. "Z, come on, man, back me up here?" Because apparently if Ace and Xavier were both gone, Z was next in charge.

Silly Fred was barking up the wrong tree there because Z just shrugged and shook his head. "Nah, I'm with the team. Noah's sitting this one out. Actually, come to think of it, I've got shit to do this evening as well."

"No, no, no, no," Fred argued, looking stressed. "If we can't film the bubble soccer content with all six of you then I need something else or Leight will have my ass for breakfast."

"Kinky," Torin snickered. "Maybe don't share your personal details so freely, Freddie."

I grinned at that. "As entertaining as bubble soccer sounds, I'm agreeing with Skye and Minnie on this. I need a day." I was struggling to even sit there in the hard dining chair, so the idea of being bounced around in an inflatable ball seemed very painful. "Can we just rain check on it for another day? You wouldn't release the episode for weeks yet, right?"

Fred and one of the other producers, Sally, exchanged a long look, and Sally shrugged. "I don't see why not," she said with a quick smile my way. "We'd be in bigger shit if Noah ended up injured worse than he already is."

Fred gave an exasperated groan, running his hand over his balding head. "Fine, but I want a CB-Live from at least three of you instead. Two hours minimum with fan interaction."

My jaw dropped. *Two hours?* That was a big ask.

"One hour," Skye countered, "but we will find an organic way for Minnie to take his shirt off again."

"Why me?" Minho protested weakly, scowling at Skye. "Why not Z?"

"Because Z wasn't caught running through the rain shirtless like a fucking romance hero this morning, dickhead," Skye replied with a smirk. "And the fans don't give a fuck about seeing *my* abs."

"Bullshit," August accused, "but if it makes you feel better, we'll do the CB-Live with you, too. Noah can chill and Z can go do what he needs to do."

"Deal," Fred agreed, before Minho could protest any further. "Finish eating, then get hair and makeup sorted. I'll let Mr. Leight know about our change of plans. Sally, can you stay to monitor the Live?"

She nodded, wiping her fingers on a napkin. "Yes, sure can."

Rather than get somehow sucked back into joining them on their hour-long Live, I quickly finished my burger, stole another piece of Torin's chicken, then quickly took my trash to the kitchen to toss.

Right when I thought I was in the clear, headed for the stairs, Minho called out my name.

I winced, bracing myself for humiliation as I paused to wait for him. "What's up?" I asked with forced levity in my voice, still refusing to meet his eyes because *fucking hell we'd kissed.* Not a casual friend kiss, either, but a full-on kind of kiss *with tongue.*

"Why are you avoiding me?" he asked, cutting straight to the chase as we made our way up the stairs together. "Is it because—"

"Shh!" I hissed, panic flooding through me at the idea someone might overhear us. "I'm not avoiding you."

"Uh-huh, sure. That's why you've been dodging eye contact since literally the moment we ki—"

"Shh!" I cut him off again, this time spinning to face him and clapping a hand over his mouth, locking eyes with him in the process. "Look, see? Eye contact. We're fine. Nothing happened. People do weird shit when they're drowning in adrenaline, right?"

Minho's brow dipped in a frown as I withdrew my hand. "Oh. I see. Nothing happened." He seemed...puzzled. Did he think I was going to make a big thing out of it? Probably. Holy crap, had he noticed me checking him out these past weeks? He probably knew I had a massive crush and was planning on letting me down easy for the sake of the team, which was *mortifying*.

Swallowing hard, I started to turn away, but he grabbed my arm to pull me back. My breathing hitched and my pulse raced as his grip on my wrist shifted down to interlace our fingers.

"But something *did* happen, Chicken..." he said softly, causing my insides to erupt in fluttery ripples of desire and excitement and anxiety. "If you're worried that—"

"Everything okay here?" someone asked, interrupting whatever Minho was saying and making me jump so hard I jerked my hand from Minnie's grip and bumped my shoulder into the wall. It was Sally, the producer, and she was eyeing the two of us with an uncomfy amount of suspicion. "Minho, you're needed for hair and makeup."

The glare he shot Sally's way was enough to freeze the fucking sun, and I gaped in awe. I'd never seen him anything more than slightly irritated before, but angry was kinda hot on him. Of course, what wasn't?

"I need to speak with Noah," he snapped, reaching for my hand again.

Reluctantly, I evaded his motion and shook my head. "No, I think we're good. He's all yours, Sally." Then before he could disagree, I quickly hurried down the hall to my room and slipped inside.

For a moment, I leaned my shoulders against the door and silently willed my heart to stop fucking racing. But shit, for a moment there I'd thought he was going to tell me he wanted *nothing* to happen again...which was a whole big can of writhing worms that I didn't need to inflict on him *or* the team. I was essentially catfishing them all, which I could justify when it came to simply being on their team, especially since their owners had blackmailed me into it. But a romantic, *sexual* entanglement while pretending to be someone else? That was a line I couldn't cross.

Did I just...come clean? Tell him that I was really a girl, did *not* have a back injury—minus the pain of my crash landing—and *did* have a massive crush on him?

Nope. There was *no way* he would treat me the same if I told him. Then fans would get suspicious, and someone would inevitably connect the dots. It'd be mayhem. The hate and death threats I used to get as Norah Sparkle would be nothing compared to what I'd get if it came out that Noah Fearly was a girl.

Skye was different. Skye had known since almost day one, *and* he didn't want to fuck me.

If Minho knew I was a girl...would he want me? I wasn't sure I wanted to know that answer.

A soft knock on the door saw me nearly swallow my tongue, but to my surprise it was Z standing there, not Minnie.

"Just figured you could use these," he said with a lopsided smile, holding out a little pile of frosty ice packs. "You were moving pretty stiffly downstairs."

"Thanks," I replied, taking them gratefully. "I think I'm just really bruised from the fall."

"Understandable," he murmured, sweeping his fingers through his burgundy hair. The motion drew my attention to a tattoo on his forearm that I'd been meaning to ask about for weeks. There was something incredibly familiar about the design, but I couldn't put my finger on *why*. "Did you know about the safety net?"

I blinked, trying to refocus on what he was saying while my mind was puzzling over his tattoo. "No." I shook my head with a small shrug. "Nope, that was Ace and Xavier's little secret, I guess."

Z nodded thoughtfully. "So you really thought you were going to die today, huh? That's got to leave a mark more serious than just a few bruises. If you ever need to talk to someone..."

I wrinkled my nose, grinning. "Are you offering, Z?"

"Maybe. I'd make a good therapist but couldn't promise not to turn your pain into lyrics after the fact. Anyway, I'm heading out. If you get bored, log into the boys' CB-Live and give them crap." He reached out and ruffled my hair affectionately—brotherly—and something withered inside my chest. He had a girlfriend, and I knew this. So why the fuck did I keep imagining chemistry between us?

Forcing a smile, I gestured to the ice packs. "Thanks for these."

"Anytime, bro," Z shot back, and I closed the door before he could see my smile fall. Something about Z... It was so silly; he was never anything other than *friendly* with me, but I was constantly getting flustered around him. My body couldn't seem to comprehend that we were just bros. Stupid hormones were delusional and really starting to fuck with my friendships.

I needed to get a grip. But first, I was going to watch the boys do their live from the comfort of my own bed.

NiNETEEN

Raised voices and the breaking of glass shocked me out of my sleep sometime far too early in the morning, and I shot out of bed with my heart racing. Confusion fogged my mind, but a quick check of the next bed told me Torin was still soundly asleep, sprawled out like he needed to touch every inch of his mattress all at once.

What just woke me?

The events of the day before came slowly back to mind as I rubbed my eyes with the heel of my hand. The high wires in the rain, Noah's fall. The sheer fucking relief when we realized he'd been caught by a safety net that none of us had even noticed.

Noah was hurting, but he was alive... *Ah, that's what*

it was! Raised voices of an argument downstairs between... Was that Noah and Xavier? Crap. That checked out.

Throwing off my blankets, I quietly slipped out of the bedroom without waking Torin. We'd stayed up pretty late on the CB-Live, which was unlike us. We usually hit the agreed timeframe and ended it, but last night was fun. Maybe because it was four of us and the banter was good, or maybe because Noah was in the comments trolling us all with his sassy remarks.

The fans had been going feral for the interactions, too. They didn't even need Noah on camera; it was enough to see the four of us interacting with his comments. Maybe they had seen the way Tor lit up like a damn Christmas tree when he spotted Noah's profile appear as "watching" our stream. Maybe it was because Sally wasn't micromanaging us as hard as Fred often did. She had her usual whiteboard in hand to guide our answers from behind the camera but barely used it.

"...and I was *right,* too!" Xavier roared as I started down the stairs. "You're just too fucking stubborn to say *thank you* for literally saving your life, Little Dude."

"You weren't right, you arrogant fuck," Noah snarled back, displaying a level of anger I hadn't ever seen from him to date. The most worked up I'd ever seen him was when he confronted Xavier about his Peaches addiction, but that was cold, almost detached disgust. This was something else entirely. "I watched the footage, Xavier, and *you* are the one who knocked me off balance. If you hadn't grabbed my arm and jerked me off my footing,

I never would have fallen. And then you have the fucking audacity to *drop me* after putting me in that position to begin with? So much for *teamwork*!"

Wow.

Reaching the bottom of the stairs, I caught Skye hovering in the foyer looking really guilty. When I arched a brow at him in question, he just shrugged and spread his hands helplessly.

"I'm not eavesdropping," he quickly offered before I could say anything. "I just heard them and was trying to decide if he needed me to intervene or...what."

"I didn't *jerk* you," Xavier yelled back. "I was *protecting you*, and right now I'm starting to seriously wonder why the fuck I bothered!"

I huffed a laugh. "Which one of them do you think needs backup? Sounds like Noah is holding his own against Xav pretty well." Which was no small feat. Xavier had a foul temper when he got a bee in his bonnet and was one of the most stubborn bastards I'd ever met.

Don't get me wrong, I fucking loved him anyway. But shit, I didn't envy Noah for poking that hornets' nest.

"Good point." Skye grimaced. "But Noah... He's not as tough as he acts." He rubbed the back of his neck, eyeing the entryway to the kitchen indecisively, then sighed. "Fuck it, let's see what started this."

He led the way and I followed, making our way through the living area to where Xavier and Noah were locking horns in the kitchen. Confusingly, Noah was sitting cross-legged on the kitchen counter with a petulant scowl on his delicate face and his platinum hair in a frazzled mess around his head.

Xavier was on his hands and knees, cleaning up shards of glass between throwing harsh retorts Noah's way.

"Uh, hey, guys," I said cautiously, eyeing the mess with confusion. I had a heavy dose of trauma associated with violent arguments and needed to ball my hands tightly to get a grip of my own emotions. "What's going on here?"

Xavier shot me a frustrated glare. "The coffeepot broke," he growled, standing up with a careful pile of glass shards in hand. "So just steer clear." He gestured to my bare feet, and I took a cautious step away from the crime scene.

"The coffeepot didn't break itself," Noah scoffed, still comfortably cross-legged on the counter. His feet were also bare, which explained why he was sitting there. No doubt that'd been a factor in their argument at some stage. "Xavier has anger issues."

"Well, that's not news to us," Skye said with a chuckle, pulling up a stool at the island. "We're all decently acquainted with Xavier's temper. But, uh, breaking shit is new. What happened?"

Xavier deposited his pile of glass in the trash, then threw up his hands with frustration. "I didn't do it on purpose!" he yelled, directing that statement at Noah, like it wasn't the first time he'd said it.

"Yes, you did!" Noah barked back, "because it was right after I said I was too fucking tired to play ego games and that I needed to caffeinate in order to clap back properly, and then *blam*! No more coffee."

"Oh right, I deliberately sabotaged your coffee so that you couldn't insult me. Tell me, Little Dude, how's that working out for me? Last I checked, you're doing just fucking fine without the coffee." Xavier grabbed a broom and started aggressively sweeping the floor for the smaller shards of glass, and I watched the two of them in stunned confusion. They were ready to claw each other's eyes out, but...over what?

Noah gave a feral little growl, launching off the counter and clearly intending to leave the room. It all happened lightning fast—Xavier dropping the broom and catching Noah around the waist before his bare feet could reach the glass-covered floor.

"Are you fucking *dense*?" Xav snapped, carrying Noah out of the kitchen and depositing our smallest member safely clear of the broken glass. "Once again, here's the part where you say *thank you*."

"Eat a dick, Xavier." Noah glowered back, extending his middle finger. "And stop fucking calling me *Little Dude*. I'm not that fucking little."

Xavier barked a laugh, returning to pick up his broom. "Yeah, you are. *Little Dude*."

"Jesus, Xavier, let it go," I muttered with disbelief. It was well-known he had a feral temper, but I'd never seen him rise to the bait so easily before. The two of them were both like dogs with a single bone here. "It's not his fault he's short."

"I'm not short!" Noah exclaimed, swinging his glare my way. Crap. "I'm five foot eight, which is literally one inch below the national average for men. It's not my fault that you guys were all apparently crafted for the female gaze by some half-assed romance author or some shit. I'm *average*, which makes Xavier freakishly tall. How about that, huh? How about I start calling you *Godzilla*, huh?"

Well, at least his anger had shifted back to Xavier. Whatever had started this argument, it must have really gotten under Noah's skin in a big way.

"Have at it, Little Dude!" Xavier shot back. "I'll be waiting on that *thank you* when you calm the fuck down."

"Hold your breath while you wait," Noah retorted. "Do us all a fucking favor." Then he stalked out of the kitchen, and a shocked silence fell over the three of us remaining behind.

For a moment, the only sound was the sweep of Xavier's broom collecting up glass shards, then he blew out a long breath and muttered a curse.

"So...wanna talk about it?" Skye asked cautiously.

Xavier glared absolute venom at our little kangaroo, and I reeled back on Skye's behalf. "No, Skye, I do not," he spat angrily.

"Dude, chill," I intervened. "You and Noah clearly have some—"

"He's a stubborn, arrogant, judgmental little fuck, you know that? He plays at being this loveable little puppy, but it's all a front for how much of an *asshole* he really is!"

Skye gave an irritated sound, straightening up to slide off his stool. "Or, wild theory, he actually is a loveable puppy and you're too much of a self-centered dick to appreciate that fact. Maybe, Xavier, *maybe* you're projecting your own shitty personality traits onto Noah because you can't handle the fact that he's a genuinely decent person who doesn't want to put up with your crap simply because you're *Xavier Stone*."

Then Skye was storming out of the kitchen as well, leaving Xavier staring after him with his mouth agape.

"What the fuck was *that* about?" he asked in disbelief, shifting his perplexed gaze my way. "Why is Skye mad at me?"

I shrugged, kinda irritated myself about the lack of coffee pot since I was never usually awake so early. "You insulted Noah, dude. And Skye loves Noah. So essentially, you insulted Skye."

Xavier's eyes widened, and he stared at me like I'd grown another head. Then he groaned and looked to the ceiling like he was seeking help from a higher power...or wishing Ace would swoop in and fix the mess he'd made with Noah *and* Skye.

"Goddammit," he muttered, sweeping up the last of the glass shards into a little pile.

I took pity on him and fetched the vacuum cleaner to help clean up the smallest of the glass fragments so no one would blame him later for an injury.

"So, what started that argument with Noah?" I asked as we finished. The curiosity was getting the better of me, and honestly I was worried. "Seemed pretty heated, and you guys have been at odds for a while."

He nodded, leaning against the counter with a tired look on his face. "Uh, he was upset that I ate the last of the Coco Pops and left the empty box in the pantry." His lips pursed as he met my confused gaze, then he rolled his eyes. "And maybe I also finished the milk and left the empty carton in the fridge."

I snorted a little laugh, shaking my head. "Okay, I probably would have reamed you out for that, too. But that argument was a lot more than milk and cereal..."

"Little Dude doesn't like me," he replied with gritted teeth and a sour expression, "and apparently needed to tell me all the ways I was the worst kind of human for setting up that safety net yesterday. As if it *didn't* save him from becoming a stain on the pavement!"

I nodded slowly, getting a better grasp on their fight. "You do remember that Noah thought he was going to die yesterday, right? Like less than twenty-four hours ago? He felt you let go of his hand, and then free-fell for eight stories before hitting that net. Call me crazy, but I reckon that'd have a little lingering emotion that needed an outlet."

Xavier spread his hands defensively. "So it's okay for him to dump that shit at my door?"

"Well, yeah." I moved closer and clapped him on the shoulder. "Bro...he *felt you let go*. You didn't tell him there was a net. You just *let go*. Regardless of the fact that you knew he'd be okay, *he didn't know*. So yeah, it's kinda okay for him to be a bit worked up about it all. Don't you think? Can't you be the bigger person here and let him process without lashing back?"

Xavier's brows knitted together with bewilderment, and he slowly shook his head. "No, it's not just this. He's been cold toward me ever since that shit about Peaches. This was just—"

"Dude, you're trying to justify being a dickhead, and it's not flying. The kid had a traumatic event yesterday, and we all need to be supportive as he works though the emotional fallout. Not yelling insults and breaking coffeepots." I squeezed his shoulder to show that I wasn't mad or disappointed...just trying to help.

He scowled. "I might see where you're coming from."

I smiled. "I knew you would."

"Fuck, August," he groaned, dropping his head in defeat. "Why does literally everyone else on the team have such an easy time hanging out with him? Every time we speak it's like he's just waiting for me to fuck up so he can call me out."

I laughed at that, releasing his shoulder as I headed for the fridge. "Ah, it's because his pretty face has half the team questioning their sexual orientation, bro. You're just too straight for your own good."

He grunted, not denying that accusation. "You too?" he asked with an edge of disbelief.

I paused at that question, thinking it over. "Jury's out," I finally replied as I grabbed a chocolate protein shake from the fridge. "But I'd be real careful talking shit about him around Tor and Minnie...and you just saw how Skye reacted."

Shit, now that I'd said it out loud, a rush of dread flooded my gut. Noah had real potential to destroy our team, if he chose. And my best friend's heart in the process. Even if their affection for him wasn't *purely platonic* like Tor kept insisting.

I wet my lips, forcing a relaxed smile as I turned back to Xavier. "Guess we have to hope he's as straight as you, huh?"

Xavier blinked at me, looking stricken. "Yeah," he said with a weak smile. "I guess so."

Crap. He'd probably just come to the same realization about Noah's power over our team, but what he'd do about it was what had me more worried than anything. As anxious as I was to not let Noah change things, I also didn't want him to leave. I liked him even more now that I'd seen him rip Xavier to shreds, the little spitfire.

TWENTY

The actual rage that filled my body while arguing with Xavier was shocking even to me. It was suffocating, choking me to the point I thought I was actually going to pass out if I didn't get the fuck away from him and his stupidly inflated ego. Otherwise, I was in serious danger of stabbing him straight in the sexy hazel eyes with a kitchen knife.

"Hey, Noah," Skye called out, running up the stairs to catch up as I stormed back to our room in a blind rage. "Are you okay?"

I clenched my jaw and said nothing until we were back inside the safety of our bedroom with the door shut. "Can you fucking *believe* I used to have a massive

crush on that absolute slug of a human being? What the *fuck* was I thinking?"

Skye blinked at me a couple times, not at all following my train of thought. Which, fair, he wasn't a mind reader. "Seriously? Huh...I sort of thought you were into Minnie or Z. I never would have picked—"

"Not *recently!* Ugh, I meant ages ago. When I was like seventeen or eighteen. Not now. Jesus, Skye, keep up." I grinned, seeing the funny side of this whole mess already. Then I realized what he'd said. "Wait, why would you think I was into Z?"

Skye shrugged. "You legit turn pink anytime he touches you, and the other day when he was drawing on your arm, you asked if anyone was hippopotamus." He stared at me with a pointed look. "You meant hungry. You wanted to know if anyone was *hungry*."

My jaw dropped. "I didn't even notice that." But I *did* remember him drawing little flowers over the palm of my hand while we were watching Torin and August play *Street Fighter* on the living room TV.

Skye grinned. "I notice you didn't deny the allegation about Minnie, though. Interesting. Very interesting."

My face heated and I turned away before I could incriminate myself further, making myself very busy searching for clothes. "I don't know what you're talking about," I grumbled, pulling out my outfit choices. "But seeing as Xavier ruined my chances of coffee this morning, I need to go out and get some. You coming?"

"Coffee? Or bubble tea?" He was the one who'd introduced me to bubble tea in the first fucking place, so it was a genuine question.

I frowned, thinking. "Both? Can we get both?"

"Sold. Give me five minutes to get dressed. Do you wanna ask Ace to drive?"

"Why? He doesn't even like the sweet bubble tea. He gets that low-sugar crap." I wrinkled my nose in disgust and Skye laughed.

"Yeah, but neither of us can drive, and I don't wanna wait for the driver because he'll be *ages* at this time of day."

He had a valid point. Skye and I had both realized about a week after I joined the team that neither of us had actually learned to drive well enough to take our license test. And now, with drivers taking us to all the places for official events, it just didn't seem important.

Skye disappeared into the bathroom, so I quickly got dressed and hauled ass down the hallway to check if Ace was up—ideally before Xavier came back upstairs and reignited our argument all over again.

There was no response when I knocked on their door, though, so I tried Ace's office next. Initially, I thought he wasn't in there either—since his desk chair was empty—but right as I was closing the door I noticed a human-sized lump on the sofa. Was he sleeping? Crap, I shouldn't wake him.

"I'm awake," he mumbled before I could sneak out fully.

"Shit, I'm sorry," I whispered, wincing. "I didn't mean to wake you."

"I wasn't asleep," he replied in a voice that definitely sounded sleepy. "What's up? Who was fighting?"

I bit my lip, moving closer to sit on his office chair. "Uh, that was me and Xavier. I was coming to see if you wanted to get coffee and bubble tea with me and Skye, but I can ask one of the other guys. You go back to sleep, Boss Man."

Ace gave a husky chuckle, pushing himself to sit up. "Coffee *and* bubble tea? Both?"

"Yes," I replied with a playful smile. "Both, please. I want to try more bubble tea flavors, but I also need coffee because Xavier broke our coffeepot before I got any."

Ace groaned, scrubbing his hands over his face and hair. "Fucking Xavier," he mumbled. "Okay, give me a minute and I'll take you guys out. Maybe later we can do some driving lessons."

I hummed a noncommittal sound, because it wasn't the first time he'd mentioned teaching me and Skye how to drive, but neither of us were particularly motivated. Leaving him to wake up, I returned to my room to tell Skye, then headed downstairs. A cautious look into the kitchen told me Xavier was nowhere to be seen, so I let out a breath of relief as I continued through to the garage.

Ace's car was a BMW M3, and I slipped in the back, leaving the front passenger seat for Skye when he came down a minute later.

"What if we can get iced coffee *with* boba in it?" Skye pondered as he buckled himself in.

Before I could tell him that was a fantastic idea, the back door opened and Minho slid into the vacant seat beside me just a moment before Ace got into the driver's seat with a heavy yawn.

"Hi...?" I said by way of greeting to the deadass, half asleep version of Minho slouched beside me.

"Coffee," he mumbled, leaning his messy hair against the headrest and closing his eyes. "I heard we have none."

Fair. "Sorry, that's a little bit my fault."

Minho cracked one eyelid, meeting my gaze as Ace drove us out of the garage. "Nah, that was all Xavier. Bro has anger issues." Quirking one corner of his lips, he reached out and placed his hand palm up between us. An open invitation.

I could have ignored it. Pretended I didn't notice and kept my hands to myself. But I didn't...

The moment I put my hand in his, my heart rate doubled and my breathing shallowed. His fingers curled up, intertwining with mine and holding tight while his lush lips curved into a smile. His eyes were closed again, seemingly going back to sleep while we drove, but his thumb stroked the side of my hand.

It wasn't a wildly scandalous touch by any means. We'd held hands in the exact same way dozens of times before because Minho was an incredibly touchy kind of guy. This time felt so incredibly different, though...since we'd kissed. Like I was hyper-aware of every point of contact between our hands, and my insides twisted up like they were on a roller coaster with no safety harness.

Maybe I did need to clear the air with him. Unless, of course, this was his way of agreeing with my adamant denial? We could just pretend it never happened and continue as we were? That made sense.

I released a long breath, relaxing into my seat a little more while Ace and Skye chatted about the reactions from our Clik Games entry, which had gone live at midnight. I'd still been awake and spent way too long reading the comments before Skye turned the bedroom light off and growled at me to sleep.

"Have you spoken with your sister, Noah?" Ace asked, glancing at me in the mirror. "Your family is probably not thrilled if they saw our Byte upload."

I shrugged, averting my gaze out the window. "Yeah, she's pissed." Which was true, but technically I hadn't *spoken* to Miles directly. He'd just left me a bunch of missed calls and a dozen or so panicked text messages which only stopped when I replied right before the Byte went live.

Admittedly my reply was a curt: *I'm fine, chill, bro*. But it was enough to get an equally curt response telling me that he was never speaking to me again. Which we both knew wasn't true.

Minho gave my fingers a squeeze, arching a curious brow when I glanced over at him, but I just shook my head to let him know I didn't want to elaborate. Skye sensed it, too, smoothly changing the subject to some of our competitors' entry Bytes, but Ace kept glancing at me in the rearview mirror.

"Coffee," Ace announced a few minutes later, pulling up

in front of a cute little French patisserie, "and bubble tea." He pointed across the street, where a grinning cartoon cat drinking boba decorated the front window of a shop. *Boba-Kitty*. Cute.

"You're like a wizard, Ace," I exclaimed in surprise, because I'd definitely figured our double request was asking too much. Excited, I scrambled out of the car and then dithered on the pavement. Which did I want more? Fucking Xavier had to go and break the fucking coffeepot and put me into this impossible situation, didn't he? What an *asshole*.

The memory of my teenage crush on him made me cringe internally. Clearly, I was shallow as hell when I'd put his posters up all over my room because the guy had the personality of an overtired grizzly bear.

Skye made the decision for me, grabbing my hand and dragging me across the road to Boba-Kitty, while Ace and Minnie swaggered their sexy asses into the patisserie. Once inside the bubble tea shop, though, I was delighted to find that Skye wasn't even joking about coffee boba.

We collected our orders, then crossed back over to the patisserie, where Ace and Minho had grabbed an outdoor table. They both wore caps and sunglasses, neither of which I'd remembered to grab on my way out of the house. Damn it.

"What flavor did you get this time, Chicken?" Minho asked when I slid into the seat opposite him.

I grinned, stabbing my cardboard straw through the lid with a satisfying pop. "Coffee, of course. With a mixture of brown sugar and coffee jelly." I took a sip and hummed happily at the sweet concoction.

He watched me over his lowered sunglasses with a bemused smile, then stole the cup from my hand to take a sip himself, holding eye contact with me as he did so. It was downright fucking pornographic, and there was no other way to describe it. My lips parted in shock—and arousal—as he released the straw from his perfect lips and licked a stray droplet from the tip.

What the fuck was that?

"Noah, you good?" Skye asked, jolting me out of the eye-fuck I'd somehow ended up in with Minho. My cheeks must have betrayed me because Skye smirked knowingly. Dickhead.

I cleared my throat, taking my drink back and slouching in my seat. "Yep. Good. It's just really bright out and I forgot my sunglasses." I stuffed my straw back in my mouth and hoped like hell they'd just let it go and change the subject.

"Here." Ace took off his sunglasses and put them on my face with a lopsided grin. "Those suit you, Eight."

Minnie pursed his lush lips thoughtfully, then took off his Portia Levigne Couture cap and settled it on my head. "Probably not a bad idea for you to be incognito, Chicken. We don't need you starting any crazy fangirl riots with that pretty face."

I would have rolled my eyes at him, but thanks to Ace's sunglasses, the gesture would have gone unnoticed, so I just sipped my drink and stole bits of Ace's blueberry muffin whenever I thought he wasn't paying attention. The boys chatted a bit about the upcoming judging panel for Clik Games, and then all of a sudden, a high-pitched shriek startled me so hard I choked on a boba pearl and somehow knocked the dumb cardboard straw clean out of my cup.

"Oh my *God*!" a girl exclaimed, oblivious to my agony. "You're Minho Park! Or is it Park Minho? Um, I'm a huge 1-4-3 fan. Can I get you to sign my photocard?"

I laughed between coughs, clearing the boba from my throat while three young girls in tiny skirts gathered around Minnie, close enough to almost obscure him from view. To his credit, though, he handled the fans with grace and charm, signing their photocards and smiling as they gushed about their favorite songs, and then smoothly deflected when asked about his departure from the group.

Very diplomatic. Extremely sexy. I was falling way too hard.

"I feel bad for taking his hat now," I murmured to Ace as the girls continued to shower Minnie in compliments bordering on the embarrassing. "He was incognito for a reason."

Ace grinned and shrugged. "Nah, no such thing with him. His fans would be able to pick him out of a lineup in a body bag."

"Should we..." I gestured to the girls who were taking what seemed like their tenth selfie with Minho. He seemed to sense my eyes on him, even through my borrowed sunglasses, and shot a grin my way.

"Girls, I'm so sorry, we have to get going," he apologized, pushing back from the table and smoothly dodging around them while the rest of us grabbed our drinks and headed for the car. Thankfully, his fans were polite enough not to follow, but right as I was about to hop in, I paused and pouted down at my drink.

Minho leaned in closer, his hand resting ever so lightly on my lower back. "What's wrong?"

"I dropped my straw," I grumbled with a dramatic sigh, climbing into the backseat of Ace's car with defeat. No point in circling back to the shop for another one now that Minho's photos were probably already being slapped all over fan sites as we spoke.

But still...I'd only had half my drink, and there was no way I could drink it *without* a straw. I wasn't an animal.

Ace must have seen my mental gymnastics, because he disappeared out of the car for a minute, then returned with a whole handful of straws, handing one back to me with a teasing grin. "I'll keep some spares in the glovebox, just in case."

That struck me as almost overwhelmingly sweet...or a commentary on my likeliness to drop my straw again in the future. I'd stick with sweet, because it made me warm and fuzzy inside as Ace smiled at me in the rearview mirror.

Shit, he was pretty...

Why did Miles hate him so much?

TWENTY-ONE

Two days after the broken coffeepot incident, three things had become undeniable.

One: Xavier was still a massive dickwad and seemed to be going out of his way to piss me off any chance he got.

Two: We were going to win the first round of Clik Games by a landslide, largely thanks to my near-death encounter. The Cliks alone were enough that even if all the judges voted us last, we'd still win.

Three: I couldn't keep avoiding Miles. Especially after the fan photos of Minho came out from our bubble-tea trip. Apparently *nothing* got past the Team Olympus fans—the Acolytes—because within a couple of hours

of the photos being posted, the internet was blowing up about my hat.

Minnie's hat.

Apparently it was one he wore a lot, which made sense since he was a global brand ambassador for Portia Levinge. But the fact that it was a hat he wore a lot meant that it was automatically identified as being his hat when I was wearing it.

"Are you sleeping with Minho Park?" Miles asked in a scandalized voice when I finally called him back. "You know he was fired from his K-pop company for live streaming while fucking his boss's daughter, right? Given your recent history with online porn—"

"Shut up," I hissed, not wanting to hear his judgment. "I'm not fucking him. Did you forget that I lack the correct anatomy to keep my identity crisis in place?"

"So they all still think you're a guy?" Miles scoffed with disbelief. "I call bullshit. They have to have worked it out by now, but maybe they don't want to offend you by saying something."

I frowned, considering that possibility. Had they worked me out? No, surely Skye would have told me if that were the case.

"Okay but you're not denying *something* is going on there," Miles pushed. "If Minho knew you were *you*, would this be a thing?"

Would it? Yes...but also no? Minnie isn't attracted to Norah Sparkle or even Noah Fearly the girl. *He's into the shorter than average guy on his team.*

"Irrelevant," I muttered, squashing the sour feelings of rejection those ideas stirred up. "It's not a thing. I just borrowed his hat to hide my identity; it's not a big deal. Why is no one losing their shit about me wearing Ace's sunglasses?"

As soon as I said it, I cringed. Miles *still* hadn't told me what his grudge against Ace was about, but without fail, the mention of the Team Olympus leader got under his skin.

A frustrated sound escaped him, and I had no doubt he was about to launch into a lecture about how I needed to terminate my contract because *no amount of money was worth selling your soul*, so I quickly ended the conversation in the most grown-up way possible.

"Sorry, Miles, my phone is on one percent battery and I can't find my charger so if I cut out—" Then I pressed *end call* and turned my phone off with a grin. He'd done the exact same thing to me dozens of times, so it was just karma.

Stuffing my phone into the pocket of my hoodie, I headed downstairs to join the guys. Staff had been all up in our grills for the last forty-eight hours straight, and we *finally* had a day off. My skin was thanking me for the makeup break. Silly me for thinking the boys just had perfect glass skin naturally.

Approaching the top of the stairs, I slowed my steps as Ace's low, angry voice reached my ears. His office and bedroom were farther along the hall, but Minnie and Z's room was right there and the door was open an inch.

"...knew exactly what you were doing with that hat stunt," Ace was saying, and I froze where I stood. He was talking about me.

Minho scoffed in response. "As if you didn't give him your limited-edition Deity sunglasses first. You can't get mad at me just because no one noticed *that*."

"Oh, fuck off, Min. I was doing something nice for Eight because he was squinting so hard. You were marking your territory. Big difference."

I had officially stopped breathing. What even was air? I sure as fuck didn't need it, not if it might get me caught listening in on a *very* interesting conversation revolving around *me*.

"You're reading way too much into an innocent gesture, Ace," Minho drawled dismissively, and my heart dropped out my ass. "It's just fan service, like Leight told us to do. I'm not even attracted to guys. It's Tor you need to be keeping an eye on. Have you seen his sketchbook lately?"

Wait. What? Hold the fuck up. That was... No, but *fans* didn't see us kiss nor did they see that moment when he cornered me in the hallway. So how could he claim fan service on that? But why the fuck was he dragging Torin's sketchbook into this conversation?

Unless... Did he think the fan service was more believable if one of us was genuinely infatuated? Was he playing me for the Cliks?

My guts twisted, and I decided I didn't want to hear any more. I definitely didn't want to be caught listening, either, so I forced my feet to start moving once again and continued downstairs to seek out Skye. I needed to talk, and he was my only friend. So unfortunately he was going to have to suffer through some girl anxiety.

What I didn't expect was to find a gorgeous girl in lingerie plastered all over the enormous flat-screen TV against the wall.

"Whoa," I exclaimed before I could catch myself. "Um... what?"

Xavier, Skye, August, and Z all snapped their heads my way with varying degrees of guilt and panic, like they'd been caught with their dicks in hand. Then a cold sweat broke out down my spine. Was that what they were doing? Watching porn together and...

"It's a CB-Live," Skye quickly explained, his face pinker than mine when I was caught drooling over Z. "Cat Kay. She's on one of our competitor teams."

I nodded vaguely, studying the girl who seemed to be doing some kind of outfit-of-the-day, but it was just lingerie and various pairs of heels. Now that I was paying more attention, I noticed the stream of live comments scrolling up the left side of the screen and grimaced as I read a few.

"Wow. She's definitely got a type. Is this her usual style of content?" Because I'd done a lot of research on our competitors, and I was sure she usually did cutesy baking shit, not thirst traps bordering on Adults Only content. The comments were going *feral* for it, though.

"No, it's not," August answered, his expression grim and tense. "Sakura tipped us off about this and we wanted to, uh, see for ourselves. Apparently some of the other teams are getting some heavy pressure from their management to step it up."

I wrinkled my nose as the girl on the screen struck another suggestive pose under the guise of showing off her shoes. "And this is what they've gone with? Are those views higher than she normally gets?" I gestured to the view count in the top corner, displaying a constantly changing number somewhere in the ten thousands.

Z shrugged. "Marginally. Read some of the comments, though. She's got some of her usual audience really pissed off. This will harm her overall ranking, for sure."

I watched for a few minutes, mostly reading through the comments and finding Z was totally right. One commenter in particular was offended enough that they were threatening to do horrible things to Cat Kay if she didn't stop her stream.

The girl on-screen browsed through the comments every now and then, answering questions and laughing flirtatiously at the more suggestive ones, but it was easy to see her smile slip when she silently read the hate-filled comments. Fuck, it made me want to reach out and tell her to turn it off or ignore the haters, or... Screw it.

I pulled out my phone and searched the username displayed on the screen, clicking into the CB-Live.

"Uh, what's Little Dude doing?" Xavier asked, gesturing to the big screen, where it showed that NoFear had entered the room. "Bro, we logged in under a burner account so it wouldn't cause shit between the fan groups. You can't go—"

"Shut the fuck up, Xavier," I muttered, already typing out my comment. "I really don't give a rat's ass about your fans."

He made a spluttering sound of outrage. "*My* fans? I'm not worried about *mine*. You should be more concerned with your own, because right now you're very publicly watching a competing ClikByter in her underwear. Your fans will either hate her because they're not her or hate you because you're cheating on Minho. Either way, Little Dude, you're fucked."

"Who's cheating on me?" the gorgeous man himself asked, swaggering into the room without a care in the damn world, Ace following close behind with a fucked-off expression on his handsome face.

Minnie draped an arm over my shoulders, and I resisted the urge to shake him off. No sense in showing him how hurt I was by a conversation I shouldn't have even heard. "Me, apparently," I muttered, hitting send on my message of encouragement to Cat Kay.

"Ignore the haters, Cat. You look beautiful, and it's no one else's business what you choose to do with your platform." August read aloud when my comment appeared on the big screen, then he grimaced and shook his head. "Fuck, bro, you really woke up and chose anarchy today. Mr. Leight is going to castrate you over this."

I rolled my eyes and stuffed my phone back in my pocket. "Whatever, it's not like I commented 'great tits, can I motorboat them?' like some of those viewers have. You guys are so fucking dramatic." Sliding out from under Minho's arm, I turned my back on the TV and made my way over to the kitchen, where I found Torin leaning over the counter, drawing something in his sketchbook.

"Hey, Tor," I said hesitantly, curiosity flooding me as I remembered Minnie's cryptic comment about Torin's sketchbook. "Can I see what you're drawing?"

His gaze jerked up and he slapped the book shut. "Ah, nope. Just absentminded doodling. Are you hungry? I was going to make enchiladas for dinner."

Torin, among his many talents, was a fantastic cook. "Sounds great," I said, edging toward where he'd left his sketchbook as he hunted in the fridge for ingredients.

"Noah!" Z called from the sofa, making me snatch my hand back before I could peek inside the book. "You want proof? Come see the comments now."

Blowing out an irritated sigh, I reluctantly returned while Xavier generously read some out for me.

"'Are you and @NoFear dating or just fucking?'" he read aloud. "'What the fuck is happening? NoFear and CattyKay? Does ParkMinho know?'"

"Aw, this reminds me of the old days in 1-4-3." Minnie laughed, seemingly entertained—unless you knew him well. The tight set to his eyes and the way his hand clenched the arm of the sofa told a different story. "My group literally couldn't speak to another performer about the weather without ending up in a dating scandal."

I frowned at his odd tone but forced my gaze back to the screen, where dozens of commenters seemed to be spiraling out over the one *innocent* comment I'd put up with the hope of saving that poor girl's mental health. And I'd just made it all ten times worse.

"Hey, at least her Cliks are climbing," I pointed out weakly, gesturing to the rapidly increasing viewer count. It was almost triple what it'd been before I commented.

Skye grimaced, ruffling his messy hair with his fingers. "Sure, but so are her threats of violence. Look at that guy, CattyKatsLeftLabia. He's losing his shit about this."

"Nah, he was one of the crazies commenting before Noah dropped a bomb in the comments," Z said with a snort of laughter. "But that definitely pissed him off. Actually, Captain Chaos, if you're still logged into the Live, can you report him for harassment? He's threatening actual harm, which goes against the CB user agreement."

I nodded, pulling out my phone. "For sure. Fucking hell, she looks rattled now. Why doesn't she just end the Live?"

"Because she can *also* see the Cliks climbing, and clearly someone in her management team was leaning pretty hard on the girls to deliver better results," Xavier muttered with a sigh. "This isn't even sexy anymore. It's just kinda sad."

I swung my gaze his way in disgust. "I didn't realize you were trying to get off, Xavier. I thought Peaches was the only online porn you subscribed to?"

"Eat a dick, Little Dude," he sneered back my way. "Oh wait, maybe you'd enjoy that too much."

My jaw dropped, and my brows hitched. "What the fuck is that supposed to mean?"

He smirked, giving me a calculating look. "I think you know exactly what that means. If you wanted to—"

"Oh shit!" Z exclaimed, sitting forward in his seat. He wasn't paying attention to us, though—his eyes were locked on the screen. "Someone is in her house. Dead-ass just saw a shadow figure walk past her doorway!"

What? I abandoned my argument with Xavier and peered at the screen while Cat Kay tried to keep a smile on her face while applying glittery highlighter to her collarbone with a makeup brush. For a minute, we were all silent, watching and waiting to see...something. A shadow figure, whatever that was.

"Z, bro, are you imagining things?" August asked when nothing happened.

Z shook his head, his teeth worrying at the edge of his thumbnail. "No," he muttered, tucking his hands into fists as if to prevent himself from chewing. "Someone is definitely in the house with her. Noah, can you warn her in the comments?"

"No!" Xavier exclaimed, reaching out and physically snatching my phone out of my hand before I could do anything. "Are you kidding? He's done enough damage with that one comment, and you want him to start being all *look behind you* like he's fucking flirting?"

Z threw his hands up, exasperated. "I don't know! But the weirdos in the comments and the shadow in her doorway—" He broke off, eyes on the screen, then gasped. "There!"

"I saw it," Skye confirmed with a grim expression. "Somehow I don't think that's one of her friends or staff."

"Use the burner account to warn her," Xavier suggested, tossing the remote at Z, who flipped it sideways to use the keyboard and rapidly typed out a message.

On the screen, a comment popped up from *AceHarts_Hairy_Nutsack6969,* and I eyed Z with disgust. He just shrugged and shot me a grin.

"Can't say it doesn't blend with all the other usernames. They'd never know it was us." He winked, then typed out another comment warning Cat Kay that she wasn't alone.

I could see the moment she read Z's comment, her smile slipping as she glanced over her shoulder, except the doorway was empty now, so she laughed it off and muttered something about commenters trying to scare her.

We all watched silently, eyes glued to that doorway, until a minute later when something crashed off camera and Cat stiffened up in fear.

"Um, I think maybe you guys were right," she said to the camera, grabbing it off the tripod and taking it with her as she left the room. "Someone is maybe here in the house with me. I need...um... I should call the police."

Then all of a sudden her screen went dark, like the power had just gone out in her house. Or been cut. Because her screen was dark but we could still hear her breathing. It was a short, sharp, panicked sound, accompanied by her footsteps as she tried to hide, maybe? Or get out?

"Someone is in my house," she whimpered, her voice disembodied with the dark screen. Comments were rolling in thick and fast, and her viewers were now in the hundreds of thousands. Then she screamed.

Not just a scream of surprise or shock, either—a *real, blood-curdling scream.* A scream that cut off with a sickening gurgle and a crashing thump like that of a lifeless body being dropped to the floor.

For a minute—a *whole minute*—the screen remained black and comments *flooded* the stream, ranging from people worried about her to irate that they couldn't see what was happening to downright revolting. And then the lights turned back on, and I seriously fucking wished they hadn't.

The CB-Live moderators must have *finally* paid attention because the stream ended abruptly a moment later with a graphic stating, "Content Violates ClikByte User Agreements," but it was too late. We'd all seen what had happened to Cat Kay. I didn't think I'd ever be able to *un*-see it. After all, it was the first time I'd seen someone with their throat slit open so aggressively I could see her spine shining in the glossy, red blood.

"Fuck," Skye breathed, breaking the silence. Then I gagged and took off running for a bathroom before my stomach emptied itself right there on the living room rug.

TWENTY-TWO

No one slept that night. I didn't even bother trying, because the sight of Cat Kay's sliced throat was imprinted so clearly on my brain that I was basically vibrating. After I emptied my stomach, we'd all spent way too long speculating about what we'd just seen.

The stream itself was gone, but dozens of screen recordings had popped up all over ClikByte, and the platform was struggling to get them all taken down quick enough. It was like a fucking hydra; cut one head off and seven more appeared.

Eventually we all hesitantly agreed it was a stunt. Special effects and clever camerawork, designed to drive a flurry of Cliks for Cat's profile. Even so, there was no

sleep coming easy for any of us. We didn't discuss it, but somehow we just ended up sitting around the living room all damn night with a marathon of movies playing with the volume down low.

Sometime the next morning, our doorbell chimed loudly through the house, and I raised my groggy head from where I'd made myself comfy in Skye's lap.

"Who—?" I started to ask, but Ace was already on his way over to the video intercom unit on the wall.

"Crap," he muttered. "Look alive, team. Leight is here to make our day ten times worse."

"Ours?" Xavier replied with a yawn. "Nah, he's here for Little Dude."

I extended my middle finger his way. "Kiss my ass, Godzilla."

He smirked back, not looking anywhere near as rough as I was feeling. "I don't swing that way, no matter how many times you offer it up."

My jaw dropped, and Torin shot me a curious glance. "You fucking *wish*," I spluttered, barely clinging to my dignity while knowing my cheeks were bright pink. "Heard from your faceless porn star recently? Or is that why you're suddenly so invested in my sex life?"

Xavier's smirk slipped, and his eyes darkened with anger. Yeah, I knew perfectly fucking well he hadn't heard from her, but he didn't know *how* I knew. I really should stop bringing *her* up, though. It was playing with fire, and Skye must have thought the same because he gave me a subtle pinch as if to tell me to stop.

"Cut it out, both of you," Z interjected before Xavier could clap back with what would have undoubtedly been a cutting remark. "We're supposed to be a team, remember? Which means none of this petty bullshit."

He was right, but Xavier fucking started it.

Ace returned to the living room with the team manager then, ending our argument for now as we all sat up straighter. The man was intimidating as hell in his Gucci suit and pissed-off expression.

"You all look terrible," he commented by way of greeting. "Did any of you sleep?"

"Ah, not much," Ace admitted, folding his arms but not sitting down. "We weren't expecting you this morning, sir."

Mr. Leight grimaced. "No? After what happened to Cat Kay last night? I know you were watching, thanks to Noah's extremely ill-advised comment on the stream. You didn't think there would be an absolute fucking circus of press to deal with today?"

I inhaled sharply, straightening my spine. "But it was a publicity stunt for her team, right? Special effects and stuff?"

The team manager scowled my way. "No, Mr. Fearly, it was not. Police would like to speak with you about your relationship to Miss Kay, so I'll take you there now. Please get changed and be ready to leave in ten minutes. Ace, we need to speak strategy about how to handle this."

"Handle what?" Ace asked carefully, frowning. "We had nothing to do with her CB-Live, and Noah only—"

"Noah *fucked up big time!*" Mr. Leight exploded, roaring the statement in a rare loss of control. He drew a deep breath, spearing me with an absolute death glare. "Now not only are we dealing with the possibility of his involvement in a murder, but Minho's fans are utterly furious on his behalf and piling hate onto Noah for the perceived slight against their favorite. Do you have any idea how many death threats have come in overnight? No? Well then, perhaps you need to think before you go off making *public comments* on a competitor's account while she's in her underwear."

Speechless, I just sat there, wide-eyed and mouth agape. All I'd wanted to do was build the girl up and reassure her, and now I was being questioned about her murder? Fuck. I really did mess up big time.

"Whatever you two had going"—Mr. Leight gestured between me and Minho—"it's done. I need a fucking crisis management meeting to decide how we repair Noah's popularity out of this."

"Whoa, that's a bit extreme," Minnie protested, shaking his head. "This whole thing will blow over when fans realize that he and Cat have literally *never met*, so us splitting up will only make things ten times worse and make him look more guilty. We should be making a point of *not* letting this change our dynamic because Noah did nothing wrong."

That seemed to make the team manager pause with a thoughtful frown. I also appreciated the fact Minnie was sticking up for me, even if it was just to protect his reputation. Not that he would be suffering from the fallout if he was considered the victim in my theoretical betrayal.

"We can workshop some options with the PR team," Ace said, smoothly stepping in. "But you don't need to escort Noah to the police station. Xavier can take him in so we can get to the office and discuss our next steps."

I grunted a small protest, not wanting to go anywhere with Xavier. But when the alternate option was Mr. Leight? Yeah, I could suck it up.

"Sure," Xavier drawled, pushing to his feet. "I'll go freshen up. You should too, Little Dude. You look like crap."

On second thought, maybe I'd take my chances with Mr. Leight.

"I need a word with you in private before I go, Mr. Fearly," the team manager snapped, gesturing for me to leave the living room with him.

Skye gave my hand a squeeze of reassurance, and I blew out a long sigh as I got up to follow. To my relief, Ace joined us, so I wasn't totally alone with the prickly manager, and Mr. Leight shot Ace a frustrated glance.

"I said *private*," he muttered with frustration.

Ace shrugged. "And I'm team leader, so I need to be privy to all business matters regarding my team. I am assuming you wanted to speak with Noah about the brand deal offer?"

My brows shot up with surprise. "The what?"

Mr. Leight gave a lightning-fast eye roll, but I caught it nonetheless. "Yes. Deity Designs noticed you were wearing a pair of their sunglasses earlier this week and have expressed interest in signing you to their label. They have put forward a good offer, and if you're interested, we can of course negotiate for more."

Shock rendered me speechless. Deity Designs was Ace's brand, and admittedly they had some great clothes, but they were exclusively menswear. Which would work in the short-term, but when my real identity was eventually made public? Nope, that'd be a hugely shitty thing to do to their company.

"That's very flattering, but I'm not interested," I said softly and with genuine regret. I'd never had a luxury designer brand offer before, and it was crazy tempting to just accept it and say *fuck it* to the details. My deal with Hot Falcon energy drinks was totally different, and my only obligation to them was wearing their logos on my helmet and flight suit.

Ace looked like I'd just announced I was secretly a woman and had been catfishing him this whole time. Oh wait. Maybe not *that* shocked, but he was definitely confused.

"Why? Your only existing endorsement is with Hot Falcon, and this wouldn't conflict. They pay *really* well and would supply you a full wardrobe from their upcoming collection, all you—"

"He said no, Ace," Mr. Leight interjected. "Noah made it very clear when we negotiated his team contracts that he wasn't interested in brand deals. It is simply my responsibility to present them nonetheless."

I rolled my eyes, unable to help myself. "Yes, because *you* made it very clear that any deals signed while I'm on the team will be subject to additional agent commissions despite the fact that I do not want or need your representation. So thank you, but no thank you. You've squeezed me into a tight enough position here without me literally paying you for the privilege."

The team manager's eyes narrowed with irritation. "Watch what you're saying, *Mister* Fearly. Our agreement benefited both of us." The underlying threat was crystal clear, and I swallowed hard to get a grip of my emotions.

Everything felt so *raw* this morning.

"Right, well, the answer is no. I'll have my own manager reach out to them directly once the Games are over." Because shit, maybe Jared could come to some kind of androgynous fashion agreement that would allow me to actually be *me* once I was free of Team Olympus.

I gave Ace a small shrug and started to leave because apparently I needed to be questioned about a total stranger's murder this morning. Mr. Leight apparently wasn't content to let me have the last word, though.

"Noah, I plan to work out specifics with Ace, but you should be warned that the company wants to see more *appealing* content in the next team Byte." He said it with an edge of something dark. Threat? Warning? Fuck him, I wasn't biting.

Ace gave a short sigh, sweeping a hand over his hair. "He means thirst traps, Eight. The company wants more thirst traps. Shirtless shit."

Mr. Leight shrugged innocently. "It's what the team is known for, after all."

My jaw dropped as I stared at him in horror. "I can't— That's not going to work for me, and you damn well know it."

"Yeah, he's right," Ace agreed. "Noah has a preexisting back injury that he wears a support brace for. Shirtless is out of the question for him."

"I'm sure you can figure it out, Noah," Mr. Leight said dismissively. "But if you change your mind about the brand deal, you know where to find me."

Mother*fucker*.

Spinning on my heel, I hurried upstairs before he could see how effectively he'd just rattled my cage. And to what fucking end? He didn't want my secret to come out any more than I did, but apparently he wanted the money from this brand deal *more*. No...he was bluffing. He had to be.

"Whoa, dude, chill," Skye exclaimed when I blew into our room like the devil himself was chasing me. Maybe he was...just in a Gucci suit. "What did Leight want?"

Biting my tongue, I grabbed his wrist and dragged him into the bathroom with me and locked the door. Then turned on the shower to ensure we couldn't be overheard as I dumped the whole pitiful conversation into his lap and then whined a little about how panicked I was.

"Yeah..." he said slowly when I finished. "Right. Huh. That's...

hmm. Well, for one thing, congrats on the Deity offer. That's a really big deal, bro."

I stared at him with a pointed look, and he grinned.

"Yeah, yeah, I know why you won't accept it, but the fact they made the offer is fucking awesome. Not that I'm shocked, you're hot shit, even as a dude. Wait, did you have a CB profile as, you know, you? Like as a—"

"Shhh!" I hissed, despite the fact I'd gone to great lengths to ensure no one would listen in the way Skye himself had uncovered my secret. "And yes. But I don't want to tell you what my pseudonym was or you'll never look at me the same way again. There's a reason NoFear was anonymous for so damn long... I have a lot of regrets about the person I used to pretend to be online."

Skye's grin widened, and a teasing glint lit up his eyes. "Well, fuck, now I need to know. Come on, Twin, I'm the best secret keeper *ever*."

I rolled my eyes because yes, he was. But I still wasn't going to show him my Norah Sparkle content because I was fucking embarrassed. Not just for the shallow nature of it all, but also for Rich's involvement. Prick.

"You're missing the point, Twin," I growled. "What the fuck do I do about Mr. Leight's little threat to out me to the team?"

Skye shrugged. "He's bluffing, for sure. Ignore him. He's underestimating how protective this team is of you, and what lengths they'll go to protect your *back injury* if you put your foot down."

I bit my lip, nodding my agreement. He was right, but I also felt like a massive asshole for deceiving them. "Yeah. Or I take the brand deal and let him rip me off."

"Nope, definitely don't do that. Not on the first offer, anyway. You wait. Now that one brand has made a move, they'll all be slobbering for a piece of Noah Fearly. How fucking funny if you get an offer from a predominantly women's label, though, like Minnie's deal with Portia."

I snorted a laugh. "That'd be a hard pass. Minnie somehow still manages to look masculine even in a skirt. I'd look like a woman."

"I should fucking hope so, all things considered," he teased, ruffling my hair with his fingers. "Now, aren't you supposed to be getting interrogated over a murder right now?"

I groaned, dropping my head into my hands. "Damn it. Yes. Okay, fuck off and let me shower." Scooting off the vanity counter, I crossed to the door and yanked it open, yelping when I locked eyes with Xavier standing in the middle of our room.

His eyes narrowed with suspicion as he looked from me to Skye and back again. "What were you two doing in there?"

Words failed me. Skye was unaffected, though, brushing past me with a lazy laugh. "Making out, obviously. Why, you jealous?" Then he kicked the bathroom door shut with his heel, closing me in and cutting off whatever Xavier's snarky response would have been.

Such a shit stirrer...but a funny one.

TWENTY-THREE

Considering how many people on the internet were making up the most unhinged theories about my secret relationship with Cat Kay, it was no wonder the police wanted to speak with me. They'd have been negligent *not* to, but with my entire team able to vouch for my whereabouts *and* the fact that we'd never met, their questions were over pretty quickly.

The most shocking part of the whole experience was that Xavier wasn't a dickhead. We barely spoke on the way there, but he stayed with me the whole time—not budging even when one of the cops tried to intimidate him out of the room. Xavier, and an attorney provided by Team Olympus apparently, kept any possible

intimidation factor to a minimum, and the attorney kept the questioning on point.

"You good?" he asked when we were back in the car. It was Ace's BMW, because apparently Xavier only owned bikes, and I would rather chew glass than be his backpack.

I flicked a curious glance his way, taken aback by his rare display of concern. "Yeah, fine. Shocked that Cat Kay is *actually* dead and it wasn't all a stunt, but otherwise...fine." Then I paused, debating whether to let silence reign supreme or say the thing on my mind.

"What?" Xavier demanded when I held my tongue.

I pursed my lips, turning to meet his suspicious glance. "Hmm?"

"You were going to add something more and then you stopped yourself. What was it?"

"No, I wasn't," I lied, giving a small shrug. "You must be imagining things."

Xavier scoffed. "Bullshit. What were you going to say?"

Blowing out a long breath, I rubbed my eyes with the heels of my hands. "I was going to say, I'm *fine* but desperately need coffee, since we no longer have coffee at home. But then I decided that you'd probably delight in bypassing every possible coffee shop between here and home just to torture me."

He glanced my way again, catching my eye for the briefest moment, but it was enough to show his genuine confusion. He didn't respond, so I let the matter drop and turned my focus out the window instead. But to my surprise, a few minutes later he pulled into a Starbucks drive-thru and ordered for both of us without even needing to ask what I wanted.

"Thanks," I said quietly when he handed mine over.

Xavier huffed. "Don't make a big fucking deal out of it, Little Dude. I also quite like coffee."

"I wasn't going to," I grumbled indignantly, taking a little sip of my coffee. "Just wondering why you know my coffee order."

Xavier, international man of mystery, just grunted and said nothing in response. And technically I hadn't asked a question, so he was under no obligation to provide that information. I, of course, was then too proud to rephrase it as a question and let him know how much I was fixating on the fact he knew how I liked my coffee. So we stayed silent the rest of the way home.

To my disappointment, Skye wasn't there when we got inside. Apparently he'd gone into the Olympus office with Ace to help brainstorm ideas for upcoming content alongside a host of stuffy corporate dicks who'd probably never made a Byte in their lives.

Harsh? A little. Possibly unfair, too, given I'd never met the management team, but if Mr. Leight was any indication, then they could all kiss my ass.

Crap. That reminded me of his attempt to strong-arm me into taking the Deity brand deal, which in turn made sense why Skye had volunteered to help on content ideas. He was looking out for my best interests in vetoing shirtless thirst traps.

"Short Stack, how did things go with the police?" Torin asked when I wandered outside to the porch. He was sitting on the edge of the rock wall with his sketchbook open and a pencil in hand while Z and August played tennis in the background. Shirtless, of course.

"Fucking hell," I murmured under my breath, attempting to subtly wet my lips and ensure I wasn't physically drooling as I headed over to Torin. "As good as can be expected, I guess? They seemed satisfied that I had never met Cat by the time I left, so..." I shrugged, because that was the best I had.

"Did Xavier stop for coffee?" he asked, gesturing with his pencil to my cup in hand. "Did he get some for the rest of us still suffering the aftereffects of his tantrum?"

I winced, giving my coffee a guilty look. "Um..."

"Rude." Torin chuckled, shaking his head.

Curiosity got the better of me, and I stepped closer. "I'll let you have the rest if you show me what you're drawing."

His brows lifted and he gave me a funny look, then shrugged. "It's not great." He turned the sketchbook to show me the *extremely* detailed pencil drawing of a goldfinch sitting on a branch. "He flew away a few minutes ago, so I've been trying to get his eyes right from memory, but something isn't clicking."

Huh. I don't know what I was expecting to find in his sketchbook, but birds hadn't even crossed my mind. Why the fuck had Minho made it sound like he was drawing *me*?

"It's beautiful, Tor," I told him honestly. "You're really talented."

"I know." He grinned. "But it's nice when other people say it."

On the tennis court, Z whooped his victory against August and came jogging over to us with a broad grin on his face. He wasn't as heavily built as Xavier or even August, more of a lithe, muscular tone similar to Minho's dancer body. Tattoos decorated a huge portion of his visible skin, mostly song lyrics and small illustrations relating to his music, and a primal part of me ached to study them closer. To read all the lyrics that resounded so deeply that he needed to permanently wear them on his skin.

"For me?" he asked with a toothy smile as he plucked the coffee from my numb fingers, then took a huge gulp. "Mmm, Noah blend, delish."

"Hey!" I protested weakly, trying to snatch it back, only to have him move it out of my reach *again*. "Not cool, Z."

"Don't be an ass. Noah earned that coffee," Torin said, poking Z in the ribs with his toe. "Give it back to him."

"Tor, can you please come play now?" August pleaded, swiping sweat from his tanned face. "Z cheats too much."

"Noah's here now. We can play doubles," Z suggested enthusiastically, handing my coffee back to me after stealing another sip. "I'll grab the extra racquets." Then he disappeared into the house before I could tell him not to bother.

I shook my head, taking a step backward. "Um, thanks but no thanks. Noah can't play tennis."

Torin quirked a lopsided smile my way. "Did Noah just shift to third person because he's nervous? Interesting."

Glowering, I clutched my coffee and searched for a decent excuse. "Noah isn't nervous. He just sucks at tennis."

"Aw, come on," August argued with a grin. "You can't be *that* bad. But just in case you are, I'll take Tor and you can play with Z so he gets a disadvantage. Fucker is too damn good at sports for a brooding musician."

Torin closed his sketchbook and hopped off the rock wall to put it safely on the patio table. "I like this idea. Noah, can you let me and Augie win? Z needs the ego knock."

I laughed despite myself, knowing they weren't going to accept no for an answer here. Eventually they'd convince me, and I was too weak when they ganged up on me with those sinful smiles on their lips. Damn hormones.

"Fine," I groaned. "I'll play, but I'm not letting you win. You're not streaming it, are you?" I gestured wearily to the camera tripods set up on each corner of the court.

August shook his head, sending out little droplets of sweat in a way that should have been gross but somehow he made it appealing. "Nah, not streaming, just recording raw footage. Ace and the crew will cut it all together later and remove anything we don't want shown."

That was a relief. "Can they remove me entirely? I would hate to drag you guys into my *cheating scandal* with me."

Torin scoffed, stuffing his bare feet into a pair of sneakers. "Don't dwell on it, Short Stack. The whole thing will be forgotten in no time." Then he paused and grimaced. "Or it would be if there wasn't a murder involved. But I'm sure PR will handle your involvement."

"Yep, put your trust in the stuffy suits," August agreed. "As unpleasant as they are to deal with, they only make money if we make money, so it's in their best interests to cover our asses at all times."

Z returned then with extra tennis rackets and an armful of cold water bottles, and I reluctantly dragged my feet down to the court with them all. At least I was dressed appropriately in a loose T-shirt, baggy shorts that came down to mid-calf, and sneakers. Boys clothes really were comfy as hell, I had to admit.

"You on my team, Rocky?" Z asked with a teasing grin, handing me one of the rackets.

I wrinkled my nose in question. "Rocky? Lemme guess, because I dropped off that high wire like a rock?"

Z barked a laugh, tossing his head back. "Nailed it. Come on, let's kick some ass."

Torin and August snickered, and I realized Z hadn't heard me protesting how dreadful at tennis I was. And weirdly, I didn't want to tell him, because he was so enthusiastic about winning. I just had to hope the ball would come nowhere near me and he could carry our team.

Of course, that is the opposite of what happened. Z served, a perfect overhead swing that caused his bare torso to ripple with muscle contractions as he sent the ball whizzing over the net. August intercepted before it could hit the turf, smacking it straight back and directly toward me.

Damn it! I swung my racket in a genuine attempt to hit the ball but missed by a mile. The ball bounced and I staggered as my center of gravity shifted, and both August and Torin erupted into peals of laughter.

"Good try, Noah!" August cackled.

Z just stared at me in shock, his mouth open as he scooped up the ball. "What was *that*?"

My face heated and I scuffed my toe against the turf, but August's and Torin's whoops and chuckles had me almost on the edge of laughing myself. "So I did try to explain while you were fetching the rackets that I really suck at tennis."

Z swiped his fingers through his merlot-dyed hair and groaned. "You fuckers set me up!" he accused, pointing a finger across the net to our opponents. "It's fine, just... Here." He tucked the ball in his pocket and wrapped his arms around me to adjust my grip on the racket handle. "Hold it like this, okay? Then swing back like *so*...and whack! Easy as that."

Something something swing, whack, fuck his arms feel so right *around me like this... His girlfriend is insanely lucky to have Z holding her like an actual—*

"Got it?" he asked, letting my hands go and ruffling my hair. "Don't worry, Rocky, I can still win two against one. You can just stand there and look pretty."

Christ. Time had just stopped when he held me and I had no clue what he'd said. But I certainly wasn't going to go admitting that, so I swallowed hard and nodded in what I hoped was a reassuring kind of way.

Of course Torin and August took *every* opportunity to hit the ball to me, and I missed every single fucking one of them. To my surprise, though, it wasn't the humiliating, frustrating experience I expected. Instead it was *fun*. The guys were teasing and taunting, but it was all from a good place. By the time Z and I admitted defeat, my stomach and cheeks hurt from how hard I'd laughed the whole time.

Z tossed water bottles to us all, and I took a grateful gulp.

"Uh, do you guys hear that?" Torin asked, frowning in the direction of the house. Now that he mentioned it, a sharp masculine voice yelled "*Stop!*"

Before any of us could react, a skinny guy with bright blue hair came sprinting around the side of the house *completely naked*, making a beeline for the tennis court. And us.

"Torin Mura!" the guy shrieked in elated shock. "I'm your biggest fan!"

Torin grinned and scoffed, eyeing the dude's flapping dick. "Are you, though?"

He said it quietly enough that the streaking fan wouldn't have heard him, and two of our security guards were right on the nude dude's ass so he didn't slow down, instead performing a couple of cartwheels across the tennis courts—in front of our cameras—before being tackled by a huge guy named Steve.

"Sorry, please—" the other security puffed, slowing beside us as he weakly gestured to the house. "Can you head indoors while we check the grounds?"

Z quickly took charge, wrapping his fingers around my wrist to pull me along behind him as August and Torin followed. Because despite the fact that our security had caught the streaker—who seemed to have no malicious intent other than showing his little dick on camera—we were rattled.

Or I was, for sure. The fact that I'd forgotten about last night's murder so easily sat uncomfortably in my gut. We'd all been out here laughing and having fun, while a girl no older than me was lying dead in a morgue somewhere.

She had just been doing what any of us did: live streaming, talking to her fans, garnering Cliks. And someone broke into her house and slit her throat for the whole internet to see.

My pulse thumped hard and my chest locked up tight with fear. If Cat Kay could be murdered on a live stream in her own home, what was to stop it from happening to any of us?

TWENTY-FOUR

News of the streaker reached us right as Ace was in the middle of a heated argument with one of the creative directors around what the next stage of Clik Games would be and whether Cat Kay's murder would delay—or even cancel—the games entirely.

When the text came through, I immediately put my phone under Ace's nose. He paused to read it, then shoved back from the table and gestured for me to leave with him. Not that I needed the encouragement to haul ass out of there. All the message said was, *There's been an incident at Mount Olympus, but all team members are safe.*

It wasn't until we were halfway home that we got more information, thanks to Torin in our team group chat, letting us know about the streaker's cartwheels and subsequent tackling.

Reading that and seeing all the jokes from the other guys that followed—about the streaker being Torin's *biggest* fan—helped me relax a little. Noah must have been okay or there's no way the chat would be so relaxed.

"You and Noah are close," Ace commented aloud after I replied in the group chat, joining in on giving Torin crap.

I glanced up from my phone, eyeing the side of his face while he drove. "Yeah. Is that a problem?" Because I knew he'd recently had heated words with Minho about his unsubtle *claiming* move with letting Noah wear his hat. And shit, Ace didn't even know Noah was a girl.

"No, it's not a problem," he replied quietly. "I think it's great that you two get along so well. You've got so much in common; you were always destined to be best of friends or worst of enemies. I'm glad you decided on friends."

I grinned, thinking of how hostile Noah had been when we first met. "Yeah, me too."

"How do you think he's settling in with the rest of the team?" Ace asked in a weirdly emotionless tone.

I frowned, scratching my cheek. "Uh, it's been nearly six weeks. I'd say he's settled in just fine. Wouldn't you? It feels like he was always meant to be on the team, and I think everyone seems...I dunno, maybe happier when he's around?"

It wasn't even a challenge to remember Noah's masculine

pronouns because to me, she was just as she presented. He. As *he* presented. Whatever. Noah was my best friend and that was all that mattered, regardless of genitalia.

Ace was quiet for a moment, considering what I'd said before he nodded. "Yeah, I think you're right. With the exception of Xavier. Those two *really* don't get along." He said it with a grimace, and I got the feeling it was something that'd been playing on his mind for a while. "Any ideas how we can fix that? Or maybe if you know *why* they don't get along...?"

I hadn't been joking around when I told Noah I was a vault. Nothing on this whole earth could make me tell Ace the real reason Noah was so angry. That anger was 100 percent justified with context, but the problem was that Xavier didn't *have* the context. So he was pissed that Noah was pissed, and it was a whole vicious cycle of taking cheap swipes at one another.

"I mean...Xavier did drop him off a high wire and make Noah think he was about to die." And that in itself was enough to create some ill feeling.

Ace frowned. "But Xavier knew the net was there, and that Noah would be safe."

I shrugged. "Okay, but Noah *didn't* know. Neither did the rest of us. The outcome is sort of irrelevant to how he'd have felt in the moment."

Ace didn't respond to that, instead just taking in what I'd said and thinking it over as he always did.

Arriving back, we discovered the security already doubled,

and a police cruiser on its way out. Ace parked us in the garage, then headed out to speak with Jeff, our head of security, so I decided to go in search of Noah and the guys.

I meant what I'd said to Ace. Noah had brought a much-needed dynamic to our team, and everyone was benefiting from it. Even Xavier, despite how he was acting toward her. It seemed like a dumb observation even in my own head, but Noah's addition to the team had mellowed out all the testosterone.

To my surprise, I found everyone outside in the pool.

"Uh, I don't know why I figured you'd all be inside with the doors locked," I commented as I approached where Noah sat cross-legged on a sun lounger. Of course she wasn't swimming... would be a bit hard given the whole anatomic discrepancies situation.

Noah looked up at me from behind Ace's Deity sunglasses that he'd let her keep. "There was a brief discussion about doing that," she admitted with a grin.

"But then we watched the footage of the 'intruder,'" Z said, pulling himself up out of the pool and shaking his red hair like a dog. I couldn't help glancing at Noah to clock her reaction, because she was so *obviously* attracted to him it was laughable. "And Torin laughed so hard I thought he was going to piss himself."

"Oh come on, it was *funny!*" Torin yelled from in the pool.

Noah, grinning, generously offered to explain the rest. "We decided that we weren't actually in any danger and everyone was sweaty and gross from tennis so...we ended up here."

"Yeah, except Noah refuses to come swimming with us," Z added as he flopped down on the sun lounger beside my best friend. "Skye, tell Noah that five minutes without his back brace won't kill him?"

I scoffed, kicking my sneakers off, then sitting on the edge of Noah's lounger to peel off my socks. "You a back surgeon now, Z? If he doesn't want to take it off, then we don't question him. Got it? We don't fuck around with peer pressure, bro, that's not our vibe."

"Yeah," Z mumbled with a pout, "you're right. Sorry, Noah." Then he popped back to his feet and tackled me around the waist, scooping me up off my seat and throwing me—and himself—into the pool. Fucker didn't even wait for me to take my shirt or jeans off.

The water was colder than anticipated, and shock seized my lungs for a moment before I kicked Z away and resurfaced.

"Asshole!" I yelled when he also popped his head above water, grinning broadly. "I was coming in anyway, you dick."

"So I did you a favor!" Z replied with a cackle, swimming away before I could dunk him under.

Grumbling, I swam back to the edge and peeled off my T-shirt and jeans, tossing them out onto the side of the pool while Noah laughed. "Yeah yeah," I grumbled, giving her a glower. "Very funny."

Swimming away, I made a beeline for Z to get my revenge, but he hid behind August with unhinged cackles of laughter. It hadn't escaped my notice that he was spending more time with the team since Noah joined us, too. Before, he was gone a lot of the time, sneaking out to see his girlfriend. Maybe they were *off* again? Or maybe he was also enjoying the changed dynamic in our house?

Distracted as I was horsing around with Z and August, I wasn't paying attention to Noah. Or Xavier. And it all happened *so* fast. One moment Noah was saying something about getting a drink from the kitchen, and then Xavier had appeared out of freaking nowhere to toss Noah into the pool.

"Dude!" Torin yelled in anger. "What the *fuck*? Noah said he didn't want to swim!"

Xavier, laughing, just waved Torin off. "Chill, I didn't make him take his shirt off. He looked like he needed cooling down."

Except Noah hadn't resurfaced.

Minho had clocked it faster even than I had, diving into the deep end from where he'd been sitting on the edge of the pool and hauling Noah's spluttering, thrashing body back to the surface while I frantically swam closer.

"Out!" I puffed, panic ripping through me as all the worst-case scenarios ran through my mind. Had she hit her head on the bottom? Couldn't swim? Fuck. *Fuck*. If she needed CPR, then everyone would know her secret, but right now I couldn't give two shits. I'd rather that than have her drown.

Somehow between Minho, me, and August, we got Noah out of the pool, and to my intense relief, she started coughing up water almost immediately. Minho looked just as terrified as I felt, his eyes wide and worried as he rubbed the back of Noah's neck and murmured shaking reassurances.

"Twin, what the fuck was that?" I asked in a strangled voice, swiping water from my face with a trembling hand. "Are you hurt? Did you hit the bottom?"

Noah wasn't in any state to answer, though. Her face was sheet white, and the quiver in her arms as she braced on the tiles was violent. Like a panic attack. Fuck...was that what it was?

"Hey, Twin, let's go inside and get some dry clothes on," I suggested hesitantly, meeting Minho's worried eyes with my own and giving a small shrug. "Minnie and I will help you up, okay? Tell us if anything hurts."

Noah managed a small nod, her breathing in harsh, shallow gasps. "I'm-m f-fine."

Bullshit, bro. But I wasn't going to argue the point as we got her upright and I slung my arm around her slim waist to take most of her weight as we started inside the house. Minho walked with us, holding Noah's arm protectively, but he couldn't come upstairs with us.

"I'm s-scared of w-water," Noah confessed in a harsh whisper as she started to walk a little stronger. "Of d-drowning. I panicked."

Oh, fuck. I stopped dead in my tracks and dragged her into a hug, holding her trembling body tight like I could somehow take all the shitty trauma out of her life. It wasn't fair.

"I've got this," I told Minho in an attempt to sound brave for Noah's sake. "Go kick Xavi's ass."

Minnie frowned with concern, then dropped a quick kiss on Noah's wet hair before leaving us.

"Come on, Twin, you need dry clothes," I murmured, giving her another squeeze before continuing through the house toward the stairs. We passed Ace in the foyer, who did a double take at seeing me in my boxers and Noah soaking wet and in shock.

"What the *fuck* happened?" he asked in a voice that promised violence and retribution. Ace took his role as group leader very seriously, and a part of that was protecting his members from *everything*.

My focus was on Noah, though, so I just scoffed. "Go ask Xavier," I growled and guided Noah to continue up the stairs with me. We could deal with that shit *after* she'd come back to herself.

TWENTY-FIVE

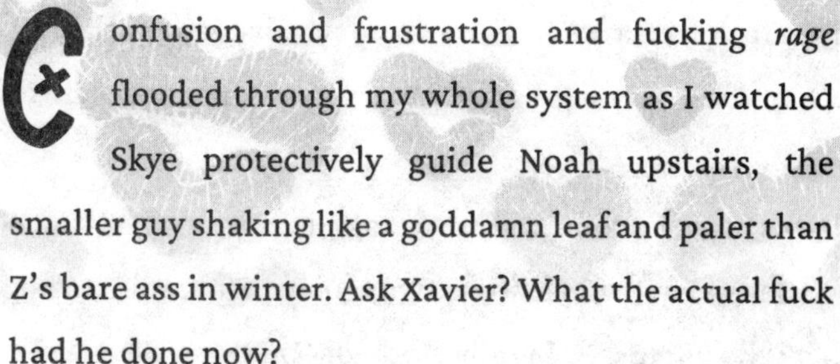

Confusion and frustration and fucking *rage* flooded through my whole system as I watched Skye protectively guide Noah upstairs, the smaller guy shaking like a goddamn leaf and paler than Z's bare ass in winter. Ask Xavier? What the actual fuck had he done now?

I stormed through the house toward the back patio just in time to witness Minho violently shove Xavier backward into the pool, then jump in after him. Fuck. It was worse than I had initially thought because Minnie was most definitely trying to drown Xavier right now.

"Let him up!" I barked, as I rushed out there to break up the fight. "Minnie! Cut it out!"

He glared absolute daggers my way, his black hair

plastered to his face and neck as he hauled Xavier back to the surface with a handful of Xavi's hair. "This isn't fucking over," he snarled at my best friend, shoving him away before swimming to the edge and hauling himself out.

"Someone start talking," I snapped, glaring at the other guys who were all watching the scuffle in various degrees of shock and anger. Minho drew a breath, and I held up my finger in his direction. "Not you. August, talk to me. Please."

August grimaced, handing Minho a towel. "Honestly, Ace, there's not much to tell. We were all messing around in the pool, and Xavi tossed Noah in."

"After Noah made it crystal clear he didn't wanna go in," Z added with a furious glance Xavier's way as the bigger guy hauled himself out of the water with guilt and frustration etched across his features.

"Yeah, because he didn't want to take his shirt off," Xavier shot back defensively, "which no one was going to force him to do, but so what if he got tossed in fully clothed? You threw Skye in!"

"Skye was coming in anyway!" Z yelled back. "Noah had said a dozen times that he didn't want to!"

Xavier threw his hands up with exasperation. "How the fuck am I supposed to know he can't swim? I didn't realize the famous NoFear was so fucking fragile."

The stress of this team was starting to give me stomach cramps. "He can swim just fine," I snapped, interjecting before their argument could escalate into more physical shoving. "Or

I assume he can. It's irrelevant. Noah said he didn't want to go in because he has a phobia of being underwater, you fucking morons. He was in an accident a few years back where he technically drowned, so I think it's perfectly fucking understandable that he's got some lingering trauma around being submerged."

Guilt panged in my chest for betraying Noah's confidence on this matter, but Xavier's ignorance could have caused some serious injuries, so in this case the safety of the team took precedence over keeping secrets.

And honestly, that revelation had the desired effect. Remorse and regret seemed to smack Xavier in the face, and his whole posture changed as he realized how badly he'd just fucked up. Then his brows drew tight with frustration and he shook his head.

"Fuck, Ace. I didn't know that! I thought he was just being fucking precious about taking his shirt off or getting his hair wet or something."

"You didn't know because you didn't *need* to know. Even if he did just want to keep his hair dry, that's *his choice*, not yours. You've been acting like a real asshole lately, and it needs to stop." I was being harsh, but it was needed. Nothing else seemed to be getting through to him, and next time I might not be around to stop Minho from drowning him. "We know he has a back issue, and throwing him in could have hurt that too. But all of that is irrelevant. He said *no,* dickhead. That should have been the end of the conversation."

Xavier's jaw dropped with an edge of outrage, as he gestured wildly. "I wasn't trying to be a dick! I thought we were... I just... I thought he just needed a push to join in, and Skye didn't have a problem getting chucked in so—"

"Bro, shut up," Torin muttered. "Just say sorry and move the fuck on."

For a moment we all just stared at Xavier, fully expecting him to dig his heels in and refuse. But a moment later his shoulders drooped with defeated slump. "I *am* sorry. You guys know I wouldn't have done anything to deliberately hurt him. I just... everything I do around Noah turns out bad, and I don't know how to fix it. The dude hates me."

I huffed a sigh. "I don't think he *hates* you. But I also don't think he likes you much."

Xavier scowled my way. "Gee, thanks. Very encouraging, Boss."

"Facts are facts, Xavi." I shifted my gaze to the other four guys and swiped a hand over my face. "Go get changed, all of you. Then I want a family dinner, so if you had other plans, cancel them."

That was mostly aimed at Z, but considering how much he'd been around the house lately, I had a feeling him and Tessa were in another rough spot. Which didn't shock me, since I really felt like he wasn't actually in love with her anymore. They were just together because they felt obligated, and that shit was *sad*.

They all dispersed, leaving me alone with Xavier.

For a long moment we just stared at each other, then he glowered. "I didn't mean to scare him."

"I know," I muttered, running my hand through my hair. "But you did. This team...it only works if we're *actually* a team. What is it about Noah that gets under your skin so badly? You guys seemed to be fine a few weeks ago. What changed?"

Xavier shrugged, grabbing a towel off one of the chairs to dry his hair. "Nothing. He just got it in his head that I deliberately sabotaged the high wire to prove a point, and he can't let it go."

I scoffed as he brushed past me. "Oh, come on. It started before that." I walked with him back up to our shared bedroom—arguably the biggest—and flopped down on my own bed while he got changed into dry clothes. "Look, I'm not going to torture you into talking about your feelings, Xavi, we both know that'd end badly. But I do need you to try harder with Noah. The other guys look up to you and—"

"Yeah, okay," he groaned, cutting me off. "I get it. No need to harp on about what a child I'm being. I'm well fucking aware. I don't—I don't know why he's getting under my skin. I'll try harder. Do you think it'd be a good idea if I cooked dinner to say sorry?"

I winced and gagged a little. The last thing we needed was for him to accidentally give Noah food poisoning or something. "I think it'd be better if you didn't. But you *could* organize a replacement coffee machine. We're all hurting from that argument, bro. All of us."

He chuckled and threw his wet towel at my face. "Literally any one of you could have bought a new coffee maker the same day it broke, and you know it. Any of the staff would have picked it up and installed it for us."

I grinned, shrugging. "I know. But it was your responsibility to replace it, so you learn not to break our precious toys."

Xavier rolled his eyes dramatically. "Oh, but sure, *I'm* the stubborn one on this team. Should I go and apologize to Noah now or..."

I hesitated, thinking about how pale and shaken he'd been tucked under Skye's protective arm. "Maybe wait until he comes down for dinner. Give him a minute to bounce back."

My phone buzzed in my pocket, and I gestured for Xavier to go ahead before answering it.

"Ace, I understand the team is all safe?" Mr. Leight asked in a guarded voice. "I've just spoken with Jeff, and he assures me that security measures are as tight as they can possibly be without relocating the team entirely."

I blew out a breath, wondering if that might be an option. "Yes, everyone is fine. It sounds like it was a fairly innocent breach but definitely a wake-up call, given what just happened to Cat Kay. Have we heard anything more about how that'll impact the Games going forward?"

Mr. Leight grunted a frustrated sound. "Yes, they made the call to cancel the live stream of the judging results and assigning the next challenge. We'll be sent both the results and next stage information via email, and it's up to each team to submit a 'reaction' video for them to use."

"Yeah, okay, we can do that. What's happening with Cat's team?" Because those girls must be an absolute wreck right now.

"They've violated contracts and withdrawn from the Games entirely," he replied in a gruff voice. "Which seems like a waste, considering the staggering increase in all their follower counts."

My mouth opened but words didn't come out. Stunned at his callousness was an understatement. "Yeah," I finally croaked out. "Right. Well...if that's all?"

"It's not. I wanted to raise the issue of the Deity Designs offer for Noah."

I frowned, rubbing the bridge of my nose. "What about it? He was quite firm that he wasn't interested."

"Yes, I'm aware. But when we passed that along to Deity, they more than doubled their initial offer. It's now on par with what they pay you as Global Ambassador."

Wow. That was huge... And for Noah's first fashion brand? Very impressive. Deity must really want him to come in so aggressively. Actually, maybe that was why I had a message to call my agent back.

But it didn't explain why Leight was telling me and not Noah or his manager. "So...you want me to tell him to take it?"

"Yes. He won't listen to me, he thinks I'm just out to make a quick buck, but you know how valuable these offers are, so I think it'd be wise if you could just guide him in the right direction, Ace."

Ah. "I'm sorry, Mr. Leight, but that's not going to happen. If Noah wants to talk to me about it, then I'm happy to share my experience. But I absolutely will not persuade or pressure anyone on the team into taking a deal they aren't comfortable with."

There was a tense pause for a moment before our team manager gave a frustrated grunt. "I figured you'd say something like that, Ace. You drive me up the fucking wall, but you're a good leader for those little shits."

I grinned at what was undoubtedly his version of a compliment. "Is there anything else?"

"No, that's it. I'll have Marcy forward the Games info when she gets it. And you need to film more content for the next episode since bubble soccer got cancelled."

"Yeah, we'll sort it out. I'll put together some concepts tonight and shoot them over for your feedback by morning." Because I generally did all my best work between midnight and five a.m. for some wild reason.

Mr. Leight sighed, his tone softening for a rare moment. "Or you could sleep, Ace. This can wait for tomorrow. If your father knew how hard you were—"

"Ah, but he doesn't, does he?" I said with a bitter laugh, cutting him off. "All he knows is that we're growing his empire beyond anything he could have imagined when he got me into show business as a toddler."

He responded with a sad laugh of his own. "You've come a long way since *Chips Ahoy*, Ace. Let's workshop some ideas in the morning. Just take the night off and get some sleep."

I didn't agree, instead giving a noncommittal response and ending the call. Then I laughed and shook my head. *Chips Ahoy* was where Leight and I first met, when he was a production assistant and I was a toddler dressed as a fucking chipmunk sailor. We'd both come a long way, thanks to Olympus Corporation and the invention of ClikByte.

A night off kind of sounded nice, though. Maybe Noah would want to watch another one of those horror flicks like *Sister Demon*...

TWENTY-SIX

Once I calmed the fuck down—which involved telling Skye my whole story about the car crash, the drowning, and the subsequent coma—I was just straight-up embarrassed. I'd completely panicked and nearly drowned myself *again* in the process.

The stupidest part was that I had no memory of the actual accident that caused my trauma. There was a whole blank spot in my memory from about four hours before the crash right through until I woke up in the hospital days later. I knew the facts, from what I'd been told. I knew that the car I'd been in had crashed off the side of a bridge and plunged into the river below. That the taxi driver had died when the car was fully submerged for an unknown amount of time before a Good Samaritan

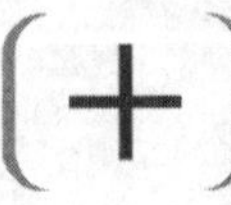

passerby pulled me out and called the ambulance. But I didn't *remember* any of it.

Unfortunately, as I discovered a few weeks after getting out of the hospital, just because I had no memory didn't mean my body had forgotten. I couldn't even take a fucking *bath* without freaking out, which was a tragedy because I used to love baths and hot tubs.

"Can we just pretend like that didn't happen?" I asked Skye when we eventually emerged from our shared room. "I'm actually horrified I acted like such a..."

Skye snickered. "Like a *girl*?" I whacked him in the stomach with the back of my hand and he groaned. "Ow, I'm kidding. And there's nothing to be embarrassed about, Twin. Xavi was way out of line."

I paused in the hallway, remembering fragments of what'd happened after they pulled me out of the water. "Wait, didn't you tell Minnie to kick his ass?"

He smirked. "Sure did. I kind of wish I'd stayed to watch that play out."

I bit my lip, not wanting to admit that I kind of wished I'd seen it too. Skye, perceptive little shit, must have read my mind, because he nudged me with his elbow while we headed downstairs.

"He likes you, you know?" he said quietly. "Minnie, I mean."

I forced a laugh, shaking my head. "Nah, he's just playing up the fan service. I literally heard him say as much to Ace when they were discussing the whole branded-hat saga."

Skye groaned. "Well, duh. Of course he's going to lie to Ace... as much as Ace looks after us all in the team, he takes our contracts super seriously. While he kind of turns a blind eye to Z's thing with Tessa, he would *not* be cool with inter-team fraternization. Like in a big way. Anyway, food for thought."

I didn't respond because we had reached the kitchen, where half of the team were all laughing and joking about the mess that Torin and August were in the middle of making.

"Short Stack!" Torin called out, offering me the kind of grin that could melt the coldest of hearts. "Come cook with us. We're making our own pasta!"

I grinned back at him, unable to stop myself. "I'm just fine watching from a safe, clean distance, thanks."

Minho gestured for me to join him where he leaned against the counter, but I sidestepped with a quick, hopefully reassuring smile and took a seat on the barstools beside Z instead.

"I hate to point out the obvious," Z said quietly, with a hint of a smirk playing on his pretty mouth. "But you sank in that pool like a..."

"Ha ha," I replied, smiling despite myself. "Very funny. I suppose Rocky is fitting after all."

Z snickered, bumping me affectionately with his shoulder. "You good?" His question was quiet and to the point, but his gaze was soft and concerned as I met his eyes. It did *things* to me, and for the hundredth time I was struck by the strangest feeling that we *knew* each other. Intimately. Or maybe that was my feral hormones acting up again.

"Yeah, just would love to pretend nothing happened," I replied with a small shrug.

"Done," he replied with a nod, taking a sip of his drink. It was a sweet pink cider, according to the label, and I loved that he didn't feel the need to drink manly beer all the time because it was manly.

Minho opened the double doors of the drinks fridge, calling out my name. "Do you want a soda?"

Undecided what I was in the mood for—since the staff had fully stocked our fridge with a million nonalcoholic options—I slid off my seat and went to take a look. Minho shifted slightly out of the way to let me browse but rested a casual hand on the small of my back as he did so.

I bit my lip, trying not to overthink it. He was a touchy guy with *everyone*. This wasn't anything new or different, but Skye's words were echoing through my head and making me read way too much into the innocent gesture.

"This looks interesting," I commented, pulling out a brown can with the letters L&P on the front. The staff had gone out of their way to accommodate me when they heard I didn't drink alcohol, making sure I had a variety of options from all around the world. According to the can, this one came from New Zealand.

I cracked it open and took an experimental sip, then hummed my approval before handing it to Minho to try. Which was, I quickly realized, a fucking terrible idea because he always somehow made the act of sampling my drink so sexy.

"Yum," he murmured, licking his full lips as he handed it back. "Lemon but a subtle lemon. I like it."

"Same," I whispered, eyes wide as I stared at his mouth. Then realized what I was doing and quickly turned away, closing the fridge doors while internally screaming at myself to *pull it the fuck together.*

Thankfully, Torin provided the perfect distraction when he threw a fresh pasta noodle at me and it landed perfectly draped across my nose. He cracked up as I laughed in shock, then retrieved the noodle off my face for me.

"Sorry, Short Stack," he chuckled, wrapping me in a warm hug. "I intended for that to hit Minnie."

I hugged him back, quietly soaking in his infectious joy as I inhaled his distinctive jasmine-and-honey scent. Torin *always* smelled incredible. Somehow he understood that I *needed* that hug, and held on longer than maybe necessary under the circumstances, until August reminded him that he was supposed to be making pasta.

"Shit, sorry." Torin gave me one more squeeze, then returned to his pasta maker, which was pushing out messy piles of fettuccini.

August shot me an amused smile, crossing over the kitchen mess to ruffle my damp hair. "I have it on really good authority that Xavier *hates* when we spill flour everywhere." Then he handed me an open bag of flour and winked before returning to the sauce he was stirring.

I looked at the packet in my hand, then glanced to Z, who watched with a wide grin on his handsome face.

"Do it," he urged. "He deserves it."

Skye scoffed, shaking his head. "You won't."

Poking my tongue into my cheek, I held my roommate's dancing eyes as I upended the flour onto the kitchen floor *right* as Xavier appeared in the doorway.

"Shit," I squeaked, trying to hide the now-empty packet behind my back. As if he hadn't *just* seen me deliberately dump it out.

"Oh *nooooo*!" August exclaimed with the heaviest sarcasm known to man. "What an unfortunate mistake. Those pesky flour bags are always so flimsy." He tsked his tongue, smoothly retrieving the packet from my hand and tearing it across the base. "You see? Faulty. No one to blame here."

Xavier just stared at the pile of flour with one eye twitching for the longest moment, and the rest of us simply *waited* to see how he was going to react. But then he shocked me by drawing a deep breath, closing his eyes, and counting to ten quietly under his breath.

Around the number four, I glanced at Z in confusion, but he just shrugged back to say he was equally puzzled.

Finally, Xavier huffed a sigh on *ten* and fixed his warm hazel eyes on me. "Noah," he said in a carefully calm voice. Minho's hand returned to rest on the small of my back, silently offering support if Xavier was going to lose his shit. But despite how tight his posture was and how tense his expression sat, he remained calm. "I'm sorry," he gritted out. "For throwing you in the pool."

That was unexpected. Xavier, as far as I'd known him, did not apologize easily. Not even when he was painfully in the wrong and aware of it. So him offering up an apology without prompting was...weird. Uncomfy.

"And..." he grumbled, looking like he was being tortured. "I'm sorry for dropping you off the high wire like I did. I'm *not* sorry for arranging the safety net, but I should have told you before letting go."

Well *fuck*. Xavier could have announced he was secretly a little green alien and I would have been less shocked. My mouth flapped a couple times before I managed to squeak out a weak response.

"Um, thanks? I guess. Um, sorry about the flour. I'll clean it up." Because now I felt like a real dickhead. He was coming in here to offer a genuine apology and here I was, inflaming the situation.

"I've got it," August said, handing me his stirring spoon. "You just keep that sauce from burning."

Largely because I was still in shock about Xavier's apology, I switched places with August and took over the sauce, keeping quiet as he started cleaning up the pile of flour. From the corner of my eye, I caught Skye glaring daggers at Xavier, but Z gave him a nod and fist bump as if to say "good work being a big boy." It was cute.

It only took a few minutes before Xavier cracked and told August he wasn't cleaning up properly, and then everything was back to normal. Comfortable and enjoyable, with the added bonus of Xavier on his hands and knees cleaning up my mess. By the time Ace joined us, everyone was in good spirits once more.

Dinner was amazing—as always when Tor and Augie cooked—but even better was when Ace took to the kitchen to make butter and brown sugar caramelized bananas with vanilla ice cream for dessert. Pool panic attacks were totally forgotten as I stuffed my face on that.

"Anyone up for a movie?" Ace asked as he and Skye cleared the empty dishes from the table. "There's a new installment of *Intrusive Thoughts* just released..."

I lit up at that suggestion, as did Skye—because the first movie had been *brutal* with jump scares and gore—but the other guys all groaned with disagreement.

"Can we play *Tekken*?" Tor asked with a hopeful smile. "Skye owes me a rematch, and I really feel like I can kick his ass this time."

Skye snort-laughed, shaking his head. "You're *dreaming*, amateur. Save your dignity and challenge Z instead. He hasn't been putting in the practice like I have."

That in turn dissolved into a lighthearted, insult-throwing match which resulted in all eight of us camped out in the living room to play video games. Somehow—unclear how—I ended up being the one to challenge Torin first, and I perched on the edge of the sofa to give it my best while Minho sprawled beside and halfway behind me. Not touching but close enough that he had my attention firmly in his grasp.

Unsurprisingly, I lost that game and tossed my controller to Z with a laugh of defeat, collapsing back against Minnie's leg. Amid the ribbing from the guys about how I couldn't beat Torin, Minho pulled me closer and interlaced our fingers.

Surely this time I wasn't reading too much into it? But we were in plain view of the whole team. Torin even glanced over at our connected hands and gave no reaction at all. Because it was normal for Minho. Right? Totally normal.

TWENTY-SEVEN

Hours of competitive *Tekken* combined with the residual crash from my panic attack saw me doze off on the couch multiple times before I stopped fighting it. I vaguely registered when the guys stopped gaming and switched to a movie, but I didn't bother opening my eyes. I was too comfortable curled up on the sofa with my feet up on Torin and my head on Minho's thigh.

At some stage, the muscles in my neck stiffened up enough that I needed to accept defeat and go to bed, so I groaned and rubbed my eyes.

"Go back to sleep, Chicken," Minho murmured softly, his long fingers stroking through my hair hypnotically. "You're fine there."

"Mmm, no, my neck hurts," I mumbled in a sleep-thickened voice, pushing myself up slightly and blinking through the darkness. The TV was still on, but the volume was turned down and subtitles were on instead. And we were alone. "What time is it?"

Minho yawned and glanced at his watch. "Uh, one thirty-ish." Last I'd checked, it was around ten fifteen.

My eyes widened in surprise. "Holy crap, I was asleep for ages! You should have woken me up; your leg must be totally dead by now." I gripped the thigh I'd been using as a pillow, and he groaned with pain.

"Ow," he admitted with a small laugh. "I was fine until you moved. Now I have pins and needles."

I bit my lip, knowing full fucking well that I needed to get up and go to my room. I needed to move away and stop touching him. And yet, I massaged his firm thigh with my fingers and tried to act like I was just helping the blood flow return faster.

"Fuck..." he uttered on a breathless exhale. It was enough to jolt some small semblance of sanity into my brain and I sat back abruptly, snatching my hand away.

"Shit, I'm sorry. I...I'm still half asleep," I said by way of excuse, giving a little shaking laugh to cover my awkwardness. "I should go."

He stared back at me, the darkness of the room casting deep shadows across half his face in a way that Torin would probably froth over and make him rush for his sketchbook. When I started to get up, though, he grabbed my wrist and pulled me back down.

"Don't," he said softly. "Don't do that, Chicken."

My breath hitched and I bit my lip as I eyed his fingers wrapped around my wrist. His grip loosened, and his thumb stroked the side of my hand, making my heart flutter. "Don't do what?" I asked, playing dumb. Because nothing on this earth could make me make the first move here. If he wanted to clear the air, then he needed to take the lead.

"Don't pretend like nothing happened. We *kissed*, and you've been avoiding me ever since. I want to know why because I know it's not that you're not into me. You *are*. So what's the problem, Chicken?" He used his grip on my wrist to pull me closer still, so one of my legs ended up hooked over one of his and our faces were close enough to kiss...

I wet my lips, and his eyes dipped to my mouth without even trying to hide the gesture.

"I think this crosses the line past fan service, Minnie," I murmured in an attempt to lighten the mood, freeing my wrist from his grip to run my fingers through my hair.

He frowned, eyeing me with confusion. "Is that what you think I'm doing? Playing it up for the cameras? No one is watching right now, Chicken. It's just us."

I swallowed to choke back the fear of rejection. We needed to have this conversation. "Isn't it? As far as I know, you're not into *guys*"—I wasn't going to fess up about my vagina right now—"and I heard you talking to Ace the other day about the hat thing..."

His brow drew tighter, and he shook his head slightly. "I lied to Ace. I wanted everyone to know you were wearing my favorite hat because you're my favorite person. And I don't need to be *into guys*. I'm into *you*, Noah, and I know you're into me, so what's the problem?"

My pulse was absolutely thundering as I gave a nervous laugh. "You seem real confident of that fact, Min."

His gorgeous lips curved in a sly grin. "I am. Because I've seen the way you melt when I play with your hair, and I've heard the little breath you draw when I touch the small of your back, and I can feel the way your pulse races when we're close..." He picked up my wrist again, and for the first time I realized his fingertips were resting right over my pulse point. "And I know you kissed me back. That wasn't just an adrenaline rush, Chicken."

Fuck. Was I that obvious?

His other hand found the nape of my neck, sliding into my hair and pulling me close, but I stiffened and pulled away.

"If I were a girl—" I started to stammer, my insides in turmoil. Minho Park had me all kinds of messed up, but I knew I couldn't do this to him. I couldn't fuck around with his head and fall any deeper into this entanglement without coming clean.

"I don't want you to be a girl, Noah," he interrupted with a small growl, underscoring those words that cut me like a knife. "I just want *you.*"

Fuck. I was putty in his hands, losing the battle with my better judgment as I softened and met his lips with my own. One of us moaned, but it was unclear who because my whole head was a rush of static and butterflies as his soft lips caressed mine, coaxing them to part and then...

Holy shit, this was all wrong. I needed to stop and get some distance and make up an excuse—literally any excuse—to push him away, because if things kept going the way they were going, he was going to find out really fucking fast that I didn't have a dick.

But at the same time, I couldn't seem to stop. Kissing Minho was the single most euphoric, erotic thing I'd ever done—which was fucking wild when I considered the shit I'd done in bed with Rich and the career that had made me millions.

That was the ice water I needed to regain some sanity, and I reluctantly pulled back from Minnie's intoxicating kiss. "I can't—" I gasped, breathless and flushed with desire. "We should, um—"

"Take it slow?" he guessed, swiping his tongue over his lower lip with a small moan. "Yeah. We should. I'll admit, this is new for me... But I *really* like kissing you, Chicken."

Well, shit, I wasn't strong enough to resist when he looked at me like *that*. Which was what I told myself as our lips crashed back together again in another heart fluttering, core clenching, breath-taking kiss.

"Whoa, what the—"

Torin's voice was like being struck by a fallen power line, and I lurched backward out of Minho's lap faster than I'd even known

I could move, clapping a hand to my mouth and snapping my eyes in the direction of the doorway.

Words utterly failed me as Torin met my panicked gaze with a conflicted mix of emotions playing out across his face. Hurt, anger, shock, panic, disbelief... Then he snatched up his phone off the coffee table, spun on his heel, and disappeared out of the room once more, leaving me in a state of anxiety and guilt.

"Shit," Minho groaned, scrubbing his hands over his face. "I need to talk to him." Then he chewed on his beautiful lower lip for a moment with his eyes on the empty doorway. "Maybe in the morning. Don't worry, Chicken. I'll fix that."

Whatever the fuck *that* even was. "Um, I should go to bed anyway." I stood and tried to make a quick escape, but he snagged my wrist in that perfectly familiar way of his, reeling me back in until my knees were on either side of one of his thighs and his free hand found the nape of my neck again.

"I meant what I said," he said softly, his dark eyes heavy as he looked up at me. "We can take it as slow as you need. Glacial pace, if that's what you want...so long as I can kiss you when no one is around."

A deep shiver of desire ran through me as I bit my lip, admiring just how utterly stunning he was. It was easy to see how attractive he was for those high-end luxury fashion houses, because who wouldn't want this gorgeous creature displaying their clothes? He'd make a garbage bag look chic.

"I'll think about it," I murmured eventually, knowing deep

down there was no way I could let this continue. I was already in too deep to come clean, and when he inevitably found out my reality, there was no way he wouldn't be furious and suspicious, wondering if I was intentionally fucking with his head. And the idea of hurting him like that made me feel physically ill, so I needed to not do this. I couldn't fall for Minho Park any harder than I already had.

His fingers stroked the back of my neck, tugging lightly on my short hair as he studied my face. "Good," he whispered, sitting up straighter to close the gap between us. "Think about this." And then those pretty lips were on mine once more, and I forgot all the reasons for hesitating. He kissed me like we had all the time in the world, releasing my wrist and moving his hand to my waist as he deepened our kiss, our tongues meeting in the most delicious tangle.

And then I remembered once more. He thought I was someone I wasn't.

With a gasp, I broke away and stood up, taking a couple steps out of his reach with wobbly legs. "I'll... Yeah. I'll definitely think about that," I admitted with full honesty. I was now just mad as hell that I shared a room with Skye and couldn't lie in bed and flick the bean while *thinking about that kiss.*

I stumbled as I left the room, and Minnie's quiet and deadly sexy chuckle followed me. Damn it, so much for coming off cool and collected. Ah, fuck it, who was I kidding? I hadn't managed cool or collected from the moment I met this fucking team.

The whole way back to my room, I flip-flopped on how the fuck I could dig myself out of the sexy but very deep hole I was suddenly in. By the time I reached my bedroom door, I had come to the conclusion that I absolutely needed to just come clean. Whatever Minho's reaction was going to be, it'd only get worse the longer I let the lie drag out.

Drawing a deep breath of fortitude, I turned around and quietly made my way back downstairs to tell him. Rip the Band-Aid off and let the pieces fall wherever they landed.

The flickering light of the TV lighting up the hallway told me he was still where I'd left him, and I paused a moment to find my backbone. To find the confidence and determination to blow up what was only just starting between us. But as I stood there mentally berating myself for being a coward, a strange noise trickled through the quiet night, weaving its way into my tangled thoughts.

Quickened, harsh breathing, and a rhythmic sort of... *Oh shit...*

Shocked and intrigued, I drifted closer and peered across the dark room to where Minho remained exactly as I'd left him, sprawled out on one end of the sofa. Except, the point of difference was how his sweatpants were pulled down to mid-thigh and his gorgeous fingers were wrapped around his impressive erection.

I froze, locked in place as I watched his fist pump up and down, his head tipped back against the sofa and the long line of his throat exposed to the air, like it was begging to be kissed. His sooty lashes fanned across his cheeks, his eyes closed as he pictured someone.

Me?

But in what way? Was he thinking about those kisses we'd just shared? Or something more?

Was he thinking about what it'd be like to fuck another guy and that was what had him so turned on? Was he fantasizing about sucking dick and getting topped by me?

Holy hell, I needed to get my head checked because I was all kinds of messed up. And that wasn't fair to Minho. But I sure as hell couldn't tell him *now*, so as painful as it was to do, I silently backed out of the room without alerting him to my voyeurism.

We could talk in the morning. We'd go out for coffee and I'd tell him everything... Then he could make an informed decision whether he was actually into guys or just, as he insisted, into *me*. I really badly hoped that was true, because now that I'd seen what he was working with, I couldn't unsee it. Minho's dick would have the starring role in my dreams for many nights to come.

TWENTY-EIGHT

Typically, I spent Wednesday nights at Tessa's place. She lived a half-hour drive from Mount Olympus, and with how busy both our schedules were, it somehow ended up being the best night for both of us to sneak away.

Except the last few weeks I'd found myself leaving after a couple hours to go home. I wanted to sleep in my own bed and be there in the morning for coffee and breakfast with the team. Since the Clik Games had started, the whole mood and vibe of our team had shifted dramatically...for the better, too.

From the minute I got there, I'd recognized I would be leaving early again. Tessa was grating on my nerves, and I was frustrated as fuck. We hadn't had sex in nearly

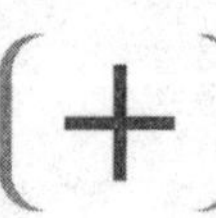

a year, because her manager decided Tess would win more Miss America votes if she was perceived as wholesome, and she was buying into it with her whole fucking bank balance.

"The girls at pageant training have been talking about your team," she told me casually as she gave me the weakest hand-job of my whole damn life. She wasn't even into it, and to be honest, neither was I. "About your new guy. Noah. He's cute."

Yeah. He was. And that weird sense of familiarity hadn't gone away. I'd stopped fixating on it because I was driving myself mad trying to figure out where we'd met before, but we'd definitely, without question, met each other before he joined our team.

"Uh-huh," I mumbled, tipping my head back and shutting my eyes. I really needed to get off, but Tessa seriously wasn't doing it for me today. Or for a long time, if I was honest. To be fair, I had tried to leave after dinner and she was the one who *insisted* on getting my dick out and just for this? Come on.

"Is there something between him and Minho, then? Everyone is saying they seem really close, like—"

"What?" I snapped my eyes open shooting her a frown. "No. Of course not. Min's affectionate with everyone, and Rocky's just easy to love, that's all."

Her hand stopped mid-stroke—if that was even what it could be called—and she gave me a bewildered look. "Rocky?"

I rolled my eyes. "Noah. They're just friends who are comfortable enough in their own skin that they're not afraid to show affection. It's not a bad thing, and the more people, like you, who try to pretend there's a sexual undertone, the weirder it gets."

She sat back, clearly offended. "People like me? What the fuck is that supposed to mean? Are you calling me stupid or shallow? Or both?"

I stifled a groan. "I didn't mean... Ugh, never mind. I should go, anyway." I started to fix my pants but Tessa batted my hands away with a little mew of protest.

"No, you didn't finish. Just let me make you feel good, Zeth." She slid off the sofa and onto her knees, dropping her hot mouth onto my already deflating erection. I *really* wasn't in the mood. She was determined, though, doubling her efforts in trying to get me hard again, and it was going to cause a whole fucking argument if I rejected her advances now...

So I pressed the heels of my hands to my eyes and tried to give her the physical response she seemed to need so badly. My mind wandered, searching for a sexy memory to revive the moment, but it wasn't Tessa that eventually filled my mind and hardened my cock. It was my own personal Cinderella... the girl I'd met at a charity gala two years ago. The girl I'd drunkenly fucked on top of some random desk at the Rainburst Springs Public Library in an attempt to soothe my own heartbreak over my own cheating girlfriend.

She used to be huge on ClikByte back then, doing the same vapid beauty shit as Tessa was into, but after that night she turned into a phantom, a figment of my imagination, and a hazy one at that, because of how much liquor I'd already consumed that night.

"Mmm, that's more like it, baby," Tessa purred as she licked my freshly hardened dick. "I knew you wanted this as much as I did."

It took everything in me not to verbally disagree. Her newfound wholesome image meant we couldn't have sex, and I couldn't get *her* off, but this was okay? It made no fucking sense but hadn't actively bothered me until now.

Shut up. I growled it inside my head, and took care of it by pushing her head down on my dick. If she stopped talking, I could picture that sexy blond from the library. My eyes squeezed shut tightly as I let my imagination wander. Blond hair and pillowy lips filled my head, and I fucked my girlfriend's throat with an edge of desperation as I chased that ghost.

When I came, it was a more intense release than I'd achieved in months, and Tessa choked dramatically, bringing me back to reality. Way to kill a euphoric high, ma'am.

I grimaced and grabbed her a box of tissues so she could clean herself up while I fixed my pants, then stood up to grab my phone and keys from the table.

"You're leaving?" she asked, blinking up at me with big brown eyes. Brown...not green. A small pang of disappointment reminded me Tessa wasn't *her*. But even so, I did love Tessa, so it wasn't fair for me to be such a dickhead. It wasn't her fault that things had cooled between us. We were just growing and changing. "But you only just got here..."

With a small sigh, I forced a smile to my lips. I'd meant to cancel entirely but ended up coming over when family gaming night wrapped up early thanks to Noah falling asleep on the couch.

"Yeah, I have to be up early for a filming segment with the team. I'm sorry." Feeling guilty, I offered her a hand to bring her to her feet, then kissed her quickly. "I'll text you."

Then I was gone, sneaking out the utility entrance to her apartment building and sliding into my car parked in the back alleyway with a sigh. I was excited to go home, and that probably meant I needed to end things with Tessa. For real this time. Sneaking around with her against my Olympus contract was no longer fun...and I definitely didn't see myself going through with the ten-year plan Tessa's mom had mapped out for her little girl's future, so why was I wasting our time?

I'd talk to her about it next time we met up. It wasn't a phone or text sort of breakup, not when I was well aware she'd already picked out her wedding dress.

Thankfully at such a late hour, the streets were deserted, and I made it home quickly, getting the luck of green traffic lights the whole way. To my surprise, the TV was still on in the living room, and I found Minho sprawled out on the sofa, watching a movie in subtitles without sound.

"Hey, how come you're still up?" I asked, dropping my ass into the armchair with a heavy sigh. It was nice to be home.

Minho yawned and shifted his gaze my way. "Too many things on my mind," he admitted in a husky voice.

I nodded my understanding. "Yeah, that shit with Noah was intense, huh?"

He inhaled sharply, sitting up suddenly more alert. "Uh..." The look he gave me was pure bewilderment, and I wondered if I had totally misjudged what he meant about things on his mind. Maybe there was something else going on?

"With Xavi and the pool," I elaborated. "That's not what was on your mind? What's up, bro? You can talk to me."

His shoulders lowered and he relaxed back into the sofa once more. "No, that's what it was. I thought for a moment something else had happened, but I'm half asleep. My mind is playing tricks on me."

"Come on, we both need sleep. Ace said we need to film the reaction segment for round-one results tomorrow." I stood and offered my roommate a hand up, which he took with a groan.

He smirked when he released my hand, moving away from the sofa to grab the remote. "I just jerked off with that hand, by the way."

I scoffed, shaking my head. "Uh-huh, sure. I can imagine that watching *Snakes on a Train* in subtitles really got you in the mood. Fucking weirdo."

He just laughed, turning off the TV and leading the way up to our shared room. We took turns showering and getting ready for bed, even though it was already two in the morning. We'd shared a room long enough now that it was a comfortable routine.

"I think I need to end shit with Tessa," I admitted into the darkness once we were both settled in our beds.

"Yeah?" he asked, not sounding all that shocked. "How come?"

I drew a long breath, thinking it over. "I can't put my finger on it. I just...lately when I'm with her, I wish I were here at home." And it was definitely wanting to be *here* and not just anywhere else. So the attraction might be dying—or maybe it was dead and buried and we just needed to have the funeral already—but I didn't think it was about someone else.

"Aw, it's because you love us so much," he teased with a sleepy chuckle. "That's cute. But maybe not a good enough reason to dump Miss America. You guys have a whole ten-year plan don't you?"

I sighed. "I don't, her mom does. But maybe it's just because of how busy we are with Clik Games. Maybe when this is over, things will go back to normal with Tessa."

But that idea made me feel even worse. I didn't want to go back to normal with Tessa. I wanted to track down my Cinderella and find out whether that spark between us was real or whiskey made. Did wanting to find some random hookup from a party count as wanting someone else? Was I "cheating"? Shit. I scrubbed a hand over my face, but the vision of her was just right there, almost laughing at me.

Fucking hell, why was I thinking about her so much all of a sudden? It'd been two years, and she'd never even tried to reach out. It hadn't bothered me then—cause I didn't exactly reach out to her—but fuck, did I screw that up? Did she get back with that douchebag boyfriend?

"Go to sleep, Z," Minho yawned. "All problems become lighter with the sun of a new day."

I folded my pillow over, tucking it under my head to get just the exact right position. It didn't make the ghost of my one-night stand go away. A fantastic fuck on a desk counted as a one-night stand, right? Maybe? *Stop thinking about her.* Grasping for anything that wasn't a soft, sexy blond who moaned beautifully, I focused on the team. On here. On now.

"Do you think Noah will be okay? He was pretty shaken up about the pool."

There was a long pause, and I almost thought he'd already fallen asleep. But then he gave a weirdly content sort of sound. "Yeah, I think he's just fine."

That was a relief. I worried about our newest member... He seemed so much more breakable than the rest of the team, which was *wild* considering his area of specialty. Maybe it was just that we all liked him so much, we just wanted to protect him. Yeah, that was probably it.

Rocky was part of this team now, and we all needed to look after each other. Stretching, I worked the pillow into another position. Better. Look after Rocky, help the team, win the games.

That was the plan. For now.

TWENTY-NINE

Whoever said that sleeping on your problems would make them go away was either a fucking liar or incredibly naive, because everything seemed *so much worse* the next morning. The stark realization of my late-night make out with Minho hit me the moment I woke up, and I buried my head under my pillow for as long as possible before Skye annoyed me into getting up.

Things did *not* get better once we headed downstairs.

Okay, that wasn't strictly true. Things briefly looked up when I sleepily realized that we had a new coffee machine, and Z generously made me one without even asking. But then I noticed Torin was avoiding me while I was avoiding Minho. It was a whole mess.

I desperately needed to talk with Minho and tell him the whole truth, but every time I worked up the nerve, I would hear his voice in my head saying *I don't want you to be a girl* and then I chickened out all over again. Not that I had a whole lot of opportunities, anyway. We barely finished our coffees when the hair and makeup team arrived, quickly followed by the production team.

"Clik Games round one results," Ace announced as I yawned into my nearly empty coffee, pushing Skye into the makeup chair ahead of me so I could buy a couple more minutes to wake up. "Live announcement show was cancelled due to the ongoing murder investigation for Cat Kay, so we have to film our reaction and submit it instead."

I gave a sleepy nod because he'd already told us about this. I just hadn't realized it'd be so damn early in the morning.

"How are you doing this morning, Eight?" Ace asked, planting one of his big hands on my shoulder and giving it a little squeeze. "Did you sleep all right?"

I blinked up at him, getting lost for a minute in his almost unnaturally pale blue eyes. "Um..."

Did he know what'd happened between me and Minnie? Had Torin told him? Had he *also* seen us and just not said anything? Or was I being paranoid and he was just referring to the incident with Xavier and the pool? "Yup. I slept."

Sort of. A little bit.

Ace cocked his head to the side, looking at me with curiosity before one corner of his lips kicked up in a half smile. "Are you sure you're not mad that I told the team about your drowning phobia? You seem not quite your usual self this morning."

He'd already apologized to me for breaking my confidence, but it was a nonissue. I didn't withhold that information because it was a secret or because I was embarrassed. It just hadn't come up so I hadn't felt any need to share with the whole team. Better that they knew, so no one else tried pressuring me into swimming with them.

"I'm not mad, Ace," I assured him, forcing a smile to my own lips. "I just slept weird."

His hand remained on my shoulder and his eyes studied mine, like he was trying to pry inside my brain and work out what I was really thinking. Thank God he couldn't, because when he locked gazes with me, all I could think about was: What kind of kisser would he be? Controlling and careful, like his personality? Or total opposite, all instinct and desire?

"About Xavier," he finally said in a quiet voice, clearly not wanting the whole team listening and offering their opinions. "I know you guys don't get along great right now, but it's starting to become a topic of concern for management."

Dread pooled in my stomach and my spine stiffened. Xavier was Ace's best friend and a core member of the team. If I couldn't convince management that we could work together, then it wouldn't be him leaving, it'd be me. And then where would that leave Miles?

"I'm not saying it's an issue or anything, Eight," Ace quickly tried to reassure me, squeezing my shoulder again like he wanted to physically ease the tension currently coiling through me. "But I want you to bear it in mind while cameras are on. And be warned that they'll be asking more from the both of you, to squash rumors that our team isn't cohesive. None of that means that you have to suddenly be best friends or even like each other much privately, but—"

"But publicly, put away our weapons and pull out an olive branch?" I guessed, grimacing through my anxiety. It was somewhat disheartening to know that Xavier's dislike of me wasn't just my overactive imagination. If Ace and management had noticed, then he must not be hiding it.

Ace nodded, still holding my shoulder and my gaze. It was hard to look away when he stared so intently. "Ideally, yeah. Can you do that for me?"

For you? Shit, when you phrase it like that... "Yeah, of course. Easy. Don't even worry about it, Boss. Xavier and I will be best of friends in no time." Then because those words tasted like a lie, I added, "At least on camera."

Somehow, despite his apology last night, I seriously doubted Xavier had undergone a personality transplant in the past twenty-four hours, so we wouldn't be braiding each other's hair and sharing secrets anytime soon.

"That's all I'm asking," Ace replied with a warm smile. "Thanks for understanding. I've already spoken to Xavi, too, so he's on the same page. Leight wants us to film new content for the episodes later, and you guys will likely be paired to work together. I just wanted you to be prepared."

He gave me another little shoulder squeeze, then released me when Skye stood from the makeup chair looking just the same as when he'd sat down except with flawless skin. I had to hand it to them; the makeup team did a good job of stage makeup without making any of the team look girly.

The production team set up to film in our living room, which was both comfortable and seriously uncomfortable at the same time. I found myself sitting between Ace and Minho, which was a position I sort of didn't hate, even if I was being a little bitch about telling Minho all my secrets.

There was a whole segment where one of the directors asked us a bunch of questions about our Byte challenge and what sort of preparation we all had to do, why we'd chosen such a public location, and pointedly asked why I'd decided to forego the safety harness.

For the most part, the rest of the team handled the answers with the grace and confidence of practice, and I just offered smiles and nods where appropriate. When Ace answered the questions about our public location *and* my lack of safety harness, he draped his arm over my shoulders to give me an affectionate side hug.

Almost immediately, Minho cracked his knuckles, then oh-so-casually rested his hand on my thigh. My pulse raced, and everything Ace was saying sort of faded to static as I tried not to react, but internally I was screaming. Was Minnie *jealous*? Why the fuck was that such a turn on?

Stop it, Noah! This isn't okay!

But at the same time, the cameras were rolling so...what the fuck did I do? Ignore it? Seemed like the safest option. Especially when Ace left his arm there and Minnie's hand slipped higher as he responded to a question, one of his fingertips finding a rip in my jeans and smoothly sliding under.

Fuck. Why the hell was such an innocent gesture making me so hot and bothered? Maybe I needed a night away from the team to blow off some steam. Maybe then I could actually think straight around my team, instead of assuming they were also feeling all the sparks flying.

At least I knew Minnie reciprocated. Any doubts remaining in my mind about him playing me for fan service were erased when I'd seen him taking care of business after he thought I'd already gone to bed. Fake feelings didn't get a guy that worked up.

It wasn't until Ace ruffled my hair that I realized a question had been specifically directed my way and I'd been sitting there like a statue as I overthought everything and everyone.

"Hmm?" I asked, internally wincing at how warm my face just became. "Sorry, I...um...I was a million miles away. What was the question?"

Minho chuckled slightly under his breath, his fingers flexing ever so subtly on my thigh, and I nearly batted him away in retaliation. That would have brought *more* attention to it, though, so

I cleared my throat and tried to pay attention while the director repeated his question about whether I knew the safety net was there to catch me.

"Ah," I said slowly, the cogs of my brain working overtime as I tried to decide how to answer. I decided on honesty. "No, I didn't."

Ace inhaled quickly beside me, and I knew he was bracing himself for a potential shitstorm.

"But Xavier and Ace take the safety of the whole team really seriously, and I'm glad they do. I feel like the underlying message of our Teamwork Challenge was not in completing the course itself but more about our leader proving that he would always take care of us, even in the face of our own stubborn god complexes." I turned my head so I could meet Ace's eyes with a smile, even as his stiff posture relaxed. "Thanks for not letting me die, Boss."

Ace gave a small shake of his head, his breath puffing out in a quick exhale. He couldn't try to shift credit to Xavier without disagreeing with everything I'd just said. But the irritated grunt I heard from Xavier perched on a barstool behind our sofa was satisfying as hell.

There were just a few more questions, then the director handed Ace a sealed envelope containing the final Clik numbers and judging scores for our first challenge. I peered over to read the paper before he announced it and gasped slightly at what I saw there.

Ace, of course, read out the relevant data, which named our team as the winners of the challenge by a huge margin on second place, and the team gave the expected cheers and smiles for the cameras. But I had to force mine, because the line *above* our team name and results was struck out. Cat Kay's team had earned enough Cliks on their Byte to win the challenge, even though our judging scores were higher. I suppose live stream murder wasn't what they were looking to showcase, though. Cat Kay's team had already formally withdrawn, so there wasn't any reason to announce the actual winner.

With a pointed look my way, Ace firmly folded the paper and put it back in the envelope, hiding it away.

I forced myself to act the part of exuberant winner until the director called "Cut!" and cameras stopped rolling, then I quickly excused myself to catch a breath.

I'd bet anything those Cliks were almost entirely generated thanks to her murder. People were kind of sick, even if they pretended they weren't. Her terrible death drove an absolute tidal wave of traffic toward the team's Clik Games entry.

A sick feeling coiled through my gut as I poured myself a glass of water with a slight tremble in my hand, and Ace approached with a worried frown.

"What are you thinking, Eight?" he asked quietly, studying me with that intense gaze of his.

I took a sip of my water, and then licked my lips. "I'm thinking..." I said carefully, keeping my volume low, "that if anyone else sees those results, they might draw parallels between the near-death content of our win and the *actual death* of Cat's live stream. And I worry that hers won't be the last of the bloodshed during these games."

I wanted Ace to disagree and tell me I was being paranoid. But he didn't. He just gave a small nod and brittle smile. "You're smarter than I initially gave you credit for, Eight," he said with a lopsided smile. "No more unnecessary risks from here out, okay?"

I nodded my agreement quickly. One brush with death was enough to remind me that I was, in fact, just human. And that I really didn't want to die. But maybe it wouldn't be due to my own negligence next time.

THIRTY

Xavier glared daggers hard enough that I actually took a step backward before remembering looks couldn't kill. And fuck him, I was standing my ground on this one.

"I'm *not* putting that on," he growled, shifting his disgusted gaze to the costume on the hanger in my left hand. "It won't even fit me. Just give me the other one."

I jerked the second costume away, thrusting the first toward him. "Not a fucking chance. We rock-paper-scissored, and you lost. Be a big boy and accept defeat, Godzilla. Look, it's got Velcro adjustments at the back, you'll be just fine. Make sure you wear some boxers just in case, though."

"Xavi, just put it on. You'll look cute and fans will go

wild." Z grinned as he said it, doing a little twirl in his own costume. "I look good, right, Rocky?"

"Adorable," I agreed with a smile, pushing the costume toward Xavier again. "Sulk all you like, but this is what you're wearing. If you have a problem with it, talk to Ace."

He glowered and snatched the hanger from my hand. Good enough, I supposed. I didn't wait for him to argue further, taking my own costume into the bathroom to get changed. Admittedly, it was loose on me and probably would have fit Xavier better, but fuck if I was going to take that option. The way I'd sweated during rock-paper-scissors was insane.

"Cute," Minho commented when I returned to the main room where the other guys were dressing. "Those suspenders suit you, Chicken." He prowled closer, and my breath caught as he ran a finger under one of the brown leather straps of my lederhosen. The shorts were *short* on Ace but thankfully reached below my knees thanks to my height. Paired with the high socks, no one would notice my *girly* legs...hopefully. Laser hair removal meant I couldn't just let my leg hair grow wild to blend in, too.

"This is fucked," Xavier grumbled, snapping me out of the dizzy little bubble I'd slipped into with Minho so close. "I look ridiculous."

I ripped my gaze away from Minnie and poorly stifled a laugh when I took in Xavier's appearance. In fairness, he wore the same costume as Z, Minho, and Skye, but somehow on Xavier it looked *extra* comical. Maybe because the short skirt barely covered his tight boxers or because of the way the bodice almost turned his muscular chest into cleavage.

"Aw, come on, Xavi, it's all in good fun," Skye laughed, somehow managing to look casually masculine even in his own milkmaid costume. "Besides, think of how breezy this dress is. Better than those leather shorts, that's for sure."

"Okay, enough bitching," Ace barked, clapping his hands with authority. "Let's get this started."

Everyone obediently followed him out of the little clubhouse where we'd been changing, making our way to the sports field where the production team had been setting up for today's episode filming. One of the AV technicians approached and quickly rigged everyone up with subtle microphones and battery packs, then ushered us over to the starting line where Ace would explain the game.

It was—in theory—a basic kind of obstacle course. Tunnel crawl, balance beam, over-under hurdles, hula-hoops, egg-and-spoon race... Fun, easy, kid stuff. Except we'd be in teams of two and would be joined together. One ankle and one hand would be tethered, turning each pair into a single unit of awkwardness.

A couple of the staff provided the tethers—wide, decorated leather handcuffs which matched our lederhosen—while Ace talked through the obstacle course, and I stifled a sigh when our turn came.

"Smile, Little Dude," Xavier muttered under his breath after carefully covering his microphone. "We're meant to be squashing rumors, not fueling them."

I swiveled my head to look up at him with my brightest, most sarcastic smile imaginable and drew a breath to tell him where to shove his rumors.

"Ah-ah, cameras are rolling," he reminded me with a click of his tongue.

Motherfucker was begging to be tripped up...except now that our ankles were cuffed together, that'd take me down too. Goddamn Ace knew what he was doing.

One of the staff gave a dramatic "Ready-Set-GO!" and Xavier all but jerked me off my feet as he rushed forward like a bull in a goddamn china shop. I fell, my knee striking the ground and dragging him down with me until we were both sprawled across the grass, red-faced and angry.

We weren't the only ones. Torin and Minho had been paired up and also tumbled into a mess of arms and legs. Z and August took it slowly, carefully shuffling toward the first obstacle while laughing and joking, but Ace and Skye were in the lead.

"What the fuck, Little Dude?" Xavier growled, pushing himself up to his knees then physically hauling me up off the grass. "Are you trying to—"

"Trying to work nicely together as a team? Sure am. Are you?" I winced as I got my feet back under me, then flicked his clipped-on microphone as a reminder that we were meant to be playing nice.

He glowered, then pasted on the most painful-looking smile I'd ever seen. "Of course. Shall we try again then?"

I rolled my eyes, unable to help myself, but I did disguise the gesture by pretending I was scratching my forehead. As calmly as I possibly could, I suggested we walk in sync with our middle—joined—legs first, then outside legs in a one-two-one-two format. Xavier then proceeded to argue the point that caution would sacrifice speed, and I *very politely* told him to shut the fuck up and do what he was told.

His face was utterly priceless until he glanced at my back pocket to discover I'd just pulled the cord out of my microphone battery pack.

"Cheater. I should expect nothing less," he scoffed after doing the same to his mic-pack.

Gritting my teeth, I refused to take the bait. "Are we going to do this or stand here arguing all day?"

Grudgingly, Xavier followed my plan, and we made it through the tire steps in last place but only by a small margin. The next stage was a net crawl, and we clashed on ideas *again*. Shocker. At some stage Xavier caught his pinky finger in the net and gave a pained yelp that actually made me pause.

"Fucking hell," I hissed, "give me your hand. This is stupid." When he ignored me, I forced the issue and turned his tethered hand over to link our fingers together and held on tight. "Now can we just *pretend* to get along for the sake of not dying in this dumb game?"

He gave an irritated growl, but his grip on my hand tightened. "Hurry up. *One...two...*"

Somehow, with minimal bickering, we made it through the next few obstacles while our other teammates carried the entertainment value, laughing and joking around the whole way. Xavier and I just barely managed to keep brittle smiles on our faces and our scathing insults muttered under our breath so other microphones wouldn't catch them.

Despite that, we actually managed to overtake Minho and Torin somewhere on the wall climb, thanks to Xavier's willingness to physically lift me over the wall. Not that I couldn't have done it myself, but he had a considerable advantage in both arm span and leg reach, which made it challenging.

"How the fuck is this one meant to work?" he muttered when we arrived at a big orange hula-hoop.

I snorted a laugh—a real one this time—and tugged him over to stand inside the hoop, face to face. "This is going to be awkward. We need to move our hips as one so...just shut your eyes and suffer through it." Then before I could lose my nerve, I planted my hands on his hips and physically demonstrated what I meant. He immediately stiffened up but then followed my lead to get his hips moving.

"Okay, you got it? Now I add the hoop in." I leaned down and scooped up the hula-hoop in my free hand and lifted it up as high as possible beneath my armpits. It was an awkward thing, trying to hula-hoop one-handed while also trying to get a guy who'd clearly never hula-hooped in his life to move his hips in wide circles. Understandably it took a few failed attempts before we achieved the five complete circles needed to move on.

Frustratingly, Minho and Torin nailed that challenge *fast* and had overtaken us, but at least it was nice to see Z and August failing miserably as they tried to do it side-by-side rather than face to face.

The balance beam went easily thanks to both of us having fantastic balance and the fact the beam was barely a foot off the ground, and then the final stage was a big plastic cow with rubber udders full of milk that one of us needed to milk into a jug, then the other needed to drink.

"I'm not milking the cow," Xavier announced when we reached our plastic animal. "It's not fucking happening. I already wore the dress; you need to milk the cow."

I shrugged, not really bothered by that task. "Fine by me. I'd probably gag drinking room-temperature milk anyway."

Xavier scoffed. "Sure you would."

I swiveled a sharp glare up at him. "What the fuck is that supposed to mean?"

"It means," he leaned down to bring his lips to my ear, "that I'd bet you don't gag on much of anything, Little Dude."

My cheeks flamed and I spluttered in outrage, my mind reminding me how he'd seen all of the Peaches content my stupid, vindictive ex had uploaded. One small mercy being that my face was never in any of the clips. The few blow-job scenes that'd been uploaded, I was wearing a blindfold that Rich had claimed was a kink thing. Turns out it was a "I'm secretly filming you" thing.

“I find it alarming how much you think about my gag reflex, Xavier. Maybe that’s something you should discuss with your therapist.”

“Everything okay over there, Twin?” Skye called out from his milking stool, looking utterly priceless in his milkmaid dress. Actually, he could really pull that off as a muscular woman, which reassured me I’d dodged a bullet in escaping that costume. If Skye looked like a passable woman, then my secret surely would have been out.

I jerked Xavier over to our cow and sat down, forcing him to kneel so I could use both my hands on the rubber cow teats. “Just fine,” I replied with forced levity. “We’ve got this.”

Frustratingly, the teats only had the tiniest of holes, and there was nearly forty ounces of milk to squeeze out, one squirt at a time. I blocked out Xavier as best I could, which was easier said than done while our wrists were cuffed together, and focused on milking the fake cow faster than the other duos.

“Done!” I announced finally, my hands cramping from all the squeezing, and Xavier grabbed the jug of milk from beneath the rubber udders.

Not hesitating even a moment, Xavier tipped the jug up to his lips and chugged the whole damn thing, spilling rivulets of white liquid down his chin and neck like some kind of dairy-kink porn clip.

I stared, somewhat dumbfounded and uncomfortably kind of aroused as his throat moved, then he slammed the empty jug down and slapped the buzzer on the plastic cow's nose to signal we were done.

And we'd won.

"What the fuck?" Z exclaimed from our other side, having only just arrived at his and August's cow. "How? You guys were dead last!"

"Turns out, Xavier doesn't have much gag reflex," I replied with a smirk.

In response, he wiped his mouth on the towel a staff member tossed over, then scratched his nose with his middle finger. He didn't try hiding his grin, though, so maybe Ace's plan had *sort of* worked out?

Nah. Unlikely. I still wanted to drown him in a shallow sink.

THIRTY-ONE

I couldn't count how many times August had expressed his concerns about my little obsession with Noah, and every damn time I'd brushed him off. Assured him that it was purely an artistic muse and nothing more. Honestly, I'd believed that too…until I walked in on him and Minho making out on the couch late at night.

That moment, I couldn't lie to myself anymore. Noah was far more than just an artistic muse. I *liked* him. Enough that seeing him kissing Minho fucking hurt, and I hadn't been prepared for that. It hit me by surprise, and then I didn't really know how to deal with that new insight so I just…avoided the issue. Both issues, really, Noah *and* Minho, even though Minnie had tried

to corner me at least a dozen times. Probably wanting to make sure I wouldn't tell Ace.

I would never do that. Because if Ace thought the team was in danger due to romantic entanglements, he'd remove one of them. And it'd almost certainly be Noah.

Thank fuck they'd mic'ed us up at the same time as cuffing our wrists and ankles together or Minnie would have 100 percent used that opportunity to corner me on the subject.

What the hell could I have said, though? That I was happy for him? I wasn't. I was devastated. But I couldn't even be mad at my friend, because not even I knew how hard I was crushing on Short Stack until that moment.

"You doing okay?" August asked as we drove back to our house after the absurd milking game. We shared a van with Ace and Xavier, but I missed simply *looking* at Noah. He had such pretty facial features. I'd never get tired of drawing him.

I nodded, refocusing on my best friend and noting his worried frown. "Yeah, why wouldn't I be?"

His eyes narrowed slightly, suspicious, then he sighed. "No reason. Ignore me, I'm just...reading too much into everything at the moment. Are you hitting the studio this afternoon? You were going to work on that new vase, right?"

"Yeah, I think so. I need to film content, anyway." And I needed a break from drawing and painting. I needed to clear my mind and work with clay for a bit, see if that helped me gain some perspective. Distance. I needed distance. "You?"

August grimaced, nodding. "Yeah, same. Content, I mean. I won't disrupt your creativity by trying my hand at pottery again. I'll probably head out to Yorba Linda and film some long-range target shooting with the camera crew." He didn't look thrilled about it, though, and it made me sad.

"You don't have to," I said softly for probably the ten thousandth time. "You could do anything you wanted. Just walk away from this life." He'd heard it all before, and the answer never changed.

"Ah, but it's the only thing I'm good at, Tor. Can't let all that natural talent go to waste now, can I?" He said it like he always did, with a smile that didn't come close to meeting his eyes.

August was a sharpshooter. A one-in-a-million kind of marksman with raw talent for hitting any target, with any projectile, whether it be guns, knives, or arrows...but he *hated* doing it. Childhood trauma would do that to a guy, but I wished he would find something that actually made him happy. So far, in the years I'd known him, he only seemed to actually relax since joining Team Olympus. It was the family environment and dumb games that made his smile touch his eyes, but now he felt double the pressure to maintain his platform as a trick shooter.

I didn't push it with him, instead trying to shift my mind onto the project I wanted to work on today. There was a huge lump of clay sitting in my art studio just begging to be transformed into something beautiful, and I was pretty sure today was the day.

The milkmaid filming had taken up the whole morning, so when I got to the studio on the top floor of the house—technically the attic—it was bathed in midafternoon sun. Stunning.

Determined as I was to change the course of my own obsession, I ignored my painting and sketching supplies and pulled out the lump of clay I'd been thinking about. Setting up my work station, I hummed a song that was stuck in my head, so I turned on the sound system to play music. I'd remove sound from the recording and overlay some trending track before uploading, so it didn't matter that I was playing Z's unreleased music.

My phone went onto the little magnetic tripod on the far side of my pottery station, and I pressed record before sitting down on my work stool. I hummed along with Z's voice on the speakers as I unwrapped my lump of material and started the laborious process of wedging the clay. It was a huge piece of clay, so it would require a whole lot more wedging than usual, but fans seemed to love that part of the process so I took my time.

Just like when I made bread—except this dough was a lot tougher to knead—my forearms took the brunt of the work as I systematically worked the clay, ensuring there were no air bubbles and it was fully blended together. Around ten minutes in, when I'd worked up a decent sweat, the studio door opened and someone slipped quietly inside.

I figured it was August, coming to tell me he was heading out, but I was startled to find Noah lurking awkwardly near the door.

"Short Stack," I said in surprise.

"Sorry, I didn't realize you were filming," he replied in a whisper, gesturing to my phone on the tripod. "I can come back later."

I shook my head quickly, my heart racing for some reason. "No, you're fine. I'll edit this footage later and remove all the sound. What's up?" Casual. Nice. Nailed it.

"Oh, um..." Noah seemed to hesitate, like he wasn't sure what he actually wanted to say, and I took pity on him.

"You wanted to talk about the other night?" I guessed, dropping my gaze back to my clay to avoid showing how weird I was being about the whole thing. "About you and Min?"

Noah cleared his throat, drifting a couple steps closer but carefully staying behind the camera view. "Yeah. I just...uh...it wasn't what it maybe seemed, and I wanted to, um, clear the air in case you thought that...uh..."

"So..." I kept my eyes lowered and focused on the clay getting smoothly amalgamated under the heel of my hand. "You weren't making out?"

Noah gave a choking sound that made me flick a quick glance in his direction. "Um, okay, yes, we were. But it was a mistake and won't be happening again so, um, if we could pretend nothing happened then I'd be super grateful."

That wasn't what I'd expected. I paused my work and frowned over the camera at Noah. "Why?"

One of his light brows lifted, and those intense blue eyes flickered with confusion. "Why do I want to pretend nothing happened? Uh, it seems—"

"No," I cut him off, now offended on behalf of Minho. "Why was it a mistake? Are you not attracted to him?" I refused to believe that; Minnie was fucking gorgeous. Literally everyone with a pulse was a little bit attracted to him.

Noah's eyes almost seemed to pop out of his head as he shook his head. "What? No, I *am*. I'm not fucking blind. But—" He broke off with a frustrated sound. "It was a mistake, so there's just no need for anyone else to know what happened."

"Because nothing happened," I murmured, playing along and noticing how Noah's shoulders seemed to lower with relief while I started kneading the clay again. "I wouldn't tell Ace, if that's your only concern."

Noah puffed a breath. "It's not. But thank you."

Interesting. If it wasn't just fear of Ace finding out, what was it that had him so certain it was a mistake? Any fool could see how close he and Minnie had become over the last few weeks; it was almost a natural progression for them to become more romantically entangled, even if Minho had never dated a guy before.

Was that it, perhaps? Was Min second-guessing his attraction toward Short Stack? I'd kick his ass if he was.

"Um...so...we're cool?" Noah asked when I said nothing back, shuffling his feet awkwardly and running a hand through his shaggy platinum hair.

I wet my lips, pretending to focus on my clay when I was really watching him from under my lashes. "Yep, nothing happened."

He nodded, seemingly reluctant to leave. "What are you listening to? I like it."

I smiled, satisfied that I'd wedged my clay as much as it was ever going to need. "It's Z's unreleased tracks. So when I said I'd remove the audio, you know I meant it."

"Ah, got it. Well, it's really good. He should think about releasing it." Another awkward pause. "Um, I should go and leave you to this. What are you making, anyway?"

"Mmmm, a vase, I think. We'll see how it goes. Maybe it'll turn into something else once I start shaping. Did you want to stay and watch?" What possessed me to make that offer, I had no clue. I usually hated people watching me work, but the way Noah's face lit up with interest had me hooked all over again.

He drifted closer still, stopping just behind my tripod to take a closer look. "You're going to make a vase out of *that*?" he asked skeptically, and I grinned.

"Yes. Grab that bean bag and get comfy. It's not a fast process."

What the fuck am I doing? This was supposed to get Noah out of my head, not deeper in.

But...he said kissing Min was a mistake, which meant maybe I hadn't totally missed my opportunity? This was such a bad idea, and I damn well knew it, but I still stood up from my stool when Noah dragged over my leather bean bag. I filled up my bowl of water from the little sink, then returned to my work station and tugged my shirt over my head, tossing it aside.

"Oh," Noah squeaked, and I couldn't fight my sly smirk at his shock. I tried to act casual, like I hadn't heard him, but part of me was waiting for him to change his mind and leave.

But he didn't. He settled into the bean bag—out of view of the camera—and watched with rapt fascination as I started to throw the clay on my potter's wheel. Usually that kind of focus would make me self-conscious, but it was strangely comfortable having my muse so close while I created art.

"Can I ask a favor, Short Stack?" I asked after a period of silence between us. It wasn't uncomfortable silence, thanks to Z's music on the speakers, but I needed to get this question off my mind.

He lifted his head slightly from where he'd rested it on his forearm. "You don't want my help on this. I promise I will ruin it."

I chuckled, shaking my head. "You touch this and I'll push you down the stairs. No, I wanted to ask if you'd be okay with me drawing your portrait sometime? You have really nice cheekbones and your little button nose is—" I cut myself off with a cough before I could get carried away.

"Oh," Noah replied, seeming puzzled, and I held my breath while waiting for his response. "Yeah, I don't mind. Do you need me to do anything?"

The relief rushed through me and I exhaled heavily. "Nope. Just wanted to ask. Some people can get a bit funny about it, that's all." Which wasn't technically *untrue*...but at least now I had his permission, so if he ever was to flip through my sketchbook, it wouldn't be weird. Well, *as* weird.

Noah shrugged, settling back down into the bean bag. "Nah, we're cool. So what shape is this vase going to end up in? What's the process?"

I relaxed even further, quietly explaining my process as I worked and basking in the undivided attention of my muse. It was glorious.

THIRTY-TWO

It ended up taking several days for Torin to finish his vase project, and he invited me to hang out with him each time he went up to the attic studio. For a whole host of reasons, the biggest one being my need to avoid hard conversations with Minho, I accepted and became a temporary fixture in Torin's studio while he worked.

In fairness, I took my laptop and worked on cutting together some of my own content from previously filmed stunts, and he spent a good amount of time working silently with music playing over the speakers, but it was a comfortable environment.

Once the vase was glazed and fired, I helped him edit all the timelapsed footage into several Bytes, which ended with a showcase of the finished piece.

"You're really talented, Tor," I told him as he packed up his supplies and cleaned his work area. "I admit I kind of thought the worst of you—of all of you—before joining the team, but I'm a big enough person to admit when I'm wrong."

He arched a brow at me, his muscles rippling as he cleaned his work station down. He'd taken his shirt off for the content and just hadn't put it back on, which really shouldn't be as distracting as it was, had I actually been a dude. But I wasn't, and Tor was sexy as hell, so I'd been fighting the urge to drool constantly.

"The worst?" he asked, tossing his cloth into the little sink at the side of the studio. "How so?"

I huffed a short sigh, feeling like an asshole. "That you all gained your followers with cheap tricks and thirst traps. That you wouldn't have had the same success without...you know..." I gestured to his gorgeous body and prayed my face wasn't blushing.

A slight smile tugged at Torin's lips, and he shook his head slowly. "I don't know. Without *what*, Short Stack?"

I rolled my eyes at his feigned ignorance. "Don't be coy, Torin, you know what I mean. Team Olympus is kind of known for the shirtless content, but you are genuinely mesmerizing to watch creating art. Even with a shirt on."

His brows both shifted up in surprise. "Mesmerizing, huh?"

Fuck, is that what I said? "Uh, in an art-appreciation kind of way," I quickly mumbled, gathering up my stuff and heading for the door. "Thanks for letting me hang out, Tor. It's been fun."

"Anytime, Noah," he replied, but I was already beating a quick escape before I could embarrass myself further. I dropped off my laptop in my room, then headed out to the backyard to spend the rest of the afternoon playing with Skye's tracking drones on the cliff-drop trampoline.

It was exactly what I needed, a healthy dose of adrenaline to balance my frazzled nerves and mixed-up emotions. Even better when Skye came out to join me and we made a game of how many funny poses we could strike in the air after rebounding on the trampoline.

At some point August and Z arrived to watch and cheer, scoring us out of ten for each bounce. They whooped and hollered for the good ones and booed dramatically for the shit ones.

Eventually Skye and I were out of breath and sweaty, collapsing on the grass at the top of the cliff beside our cheer squad.

"Sick," Skye murmured, lying on his stomach and scrolling some of the footage on the drone camera. "There's some gold here. Want me to ask Ace to edit?"

I bit my lip, unsure. I'd always edited my own clips, but that was largely due to the secret nature of my platform. Ace was good at it, though, and I could admit it wasn't my favorite job. If I didn't like what he put together, I could just do it myself, right?

"Okay, sure. Thanks," I replied after my moment of reflection.

"Ace wants to see us inside anyway," Z announced, checking his phone. "Leight's here to discuss episode content."

I groaned, burying my face in my hands. "I really hate that guy."

"You're not alone," August muttered as he pushed to his feet and offered Skye his hand to get up. "But he basically created the team, so we don't have much choice."

"He means well," Z protested, grabbing my wrists to pull me up to my feet. "He always has the team's success as his top priority."

"Yeah, because that's how he gets paid," I shot back cynically.

Z just shrugged. "Mutually beneficial arrangement. Besides, he's all bark and no bite once you get used to him."

Sweat dripped down my spine as we approached the house, and I slipped away for a lightning-fast shower, promising to meet the team in the living room. I rinsed off quickly, then dressed in fresh clothes—and a fresh binder—before exiting the bathroom and nearly jumping out of my skin when I found Minho sitting on the end of my bed.

Thank fuck I'd taken my clothes into the bathroom to dress.

"Sorry, I didn't mean to startle you, Chicken," he said with a small frown on his pretty face. His black hair was down and messy, falling softly around his face like a shadow. "Are you avoiding me?"

I wet my lips, drawing a shaking breath. "Yes," I admitted honestly.

His frown deepened. "Because of what happened the other night?"

"Yeah," I confirmed, giving a small nod.

His dark eyes locked on mine, and genuine sadness seemed to hit me like a sucker punch, then he pushed to his feet abruptly. "I see. I should go—"

"Min, wait." I darted over to grab his arm before he could leave the room, stopping him. "I didn't mean—I just can't—"

Words were failing me, and panic was rising in my chest at the thought of hurting him. But guilt damn near choked me out when I thought about how I was deceiving him.

"No, you're fine," he quickly said, forcing a tight smile. "I thought maybe we were on the same page because you definitely kissed me back...but maybe I misunderstood."

"You didn't," I said in a small voice before I could stop myself, my hand slipping from his forearm to his hand, and he interlaced our fingers together like it was an unconscious reflex. "But we can't—"

I didn't get any more words out because his other hand was at the base of my skull, tilting my head back as his lips met mine in a bruising kiss. A shocked moan slipped out of me, but my whole body reacted exactly as it had the other night, like we were magnets.

Powerless to resist, I gripped the front of his shirt in my free hand and kissed him back, parting my lips to let him in and drinking down the heady waves of euphoria that were fast becoming as addictive as adrenaline.

"Noah," he growled when I bit his lower lip like I'd been dreaming about doing for far too long. "I need—"

Shit. We couldn't do this. *I* couldn't do this. It wasn't fair. "Minnie, I need to tell you something," I blurted out in a hurry, attempting to put some distance between us and failing miserably, because somehow his lips were on my throat and holy shit it felt good as he kissed the sensitive spot just above my T-shirt collar.

"You can tell me anything, Chicken," he murmured against my skin. "It won't change how I feel about you."

But it would. There's no way it wouldn't. I'd lied and deceived them all, and now I was fucking with Minnie's heart.

"Noah! Minho!" Ace called out from somewhere down the hall, "Hurry the fuck up! We're waiting on you!"

Crap. The meeting with Leight.

"Damn it," Minho groaned, burying his face in my neck and dragging me into a tight hug. "I want to continue this later, okay?"

I gave a noncommittal hum, knowing full fucking well I'd lose my nerve again later. Maybe I needed to start drinking alcohol with the guys? Nah, that was a recipe for disaster. I'd probably end up confessing feelings to more than just Minnie and destroy the whole fucking team.

"We should go," I muttered, peeling myself out of his hold with reluctance, licking my lips and wondering how obvious it was that we'd been kissing. What would the other guys think? Torin had been weird about it...

Minho kept hold of my hand as we left the room and tightened his grip when I tried to tug free before reaching the living room. It was harmless enough, seeing as how affectionate he was in general, but when we sat down on the sofa he hooked his leg over mine in what could easily be interpreted as a possessive move.

Torin met my eyes with a curious look, his brows lifted, but I ducked my gaze away before I could blush. Fucking Minho didn't seem to care if anyone guessed what we'd been doing, and I didn't know what to make of that.

"Good of you both to join us," Mr. Leight said with a dry tone as he dragged over a dining chair to sit in. "I trust you all saw the episode that went live last night?"

I wrinkled my nose because I *hadn't* watched it yet. Considering how often Xavier and I had both disabled our microphones, I figured there wouldn't be much footage of us to cut in anyway. None of the guys had said much about it this morning, either, so maybe I wasn't the only one.

"Yeah, what about it?" Minho asked, releasing my hand and draping his arm along the back of the sofa so the tips of his fingers brushed my shoulder. It was a tiny gesture but incredibly distracting.

Ace shot us a sharp look, and my stomach turned cold. Does he suspect?

"Initial public response has come back with a surprising result," our team leader informed us in a quietly thoughtful voice. "I'm assuming you haven't looked at the comments, Eight?"

I wet my lips, suddenly nervous. Why was it me under the spotlight again? I'd done what he asked and worked with Xavier, so what was the problem *now*?

"No, I was helping Tor this morning," I murmured. "Why?"

Ace held my gaze steady with his ice-blue eyes unreadable.

"Fans have responded really well to the teamwork between you and Xavier," he said, then glanced from me to Xavier and frowned. "In fact, the response has been more positive than anticipated, since we all know you disconnected your mics so you could trade insults the whole time."

Xavier shot me a smirk and I responded with a subtle middle finger as I pretended to scratch my face.

"Why are you making out like this is a bad thing, Ace?" Xavier drawled, unbothered. "That was the point, right? Play nice and show the Acolytes that we're all one big happy family?"

"It's not a bad thing," Mr. Leight replied with a huff. "This is the highest-viewed episode we've had in a long time, and it hasn't even been twenty-four hours since it went live."

"Because it's fucking funny," Skye said with a chuckle. "You did a good job on the cut, Ace."

"Thanks," Ace murmured, "but I don't think Noah and Xavier will be quite so pleased by this turn of events."

Mr. Leight gave a dismissive hand wave. "Nonsense, it's just business. You're all playing a role. No one cares what happens when the cameras are off. Xavier, Noah, you're both trending. Or rather, you're trending together, and we need to lean into that with the upcoming fan meeting event."

I blinked slowly, not understanding what he meant even as Minho's arm shifted from the sofa to rest on my shoulders, like he wanted to pull me closer. "Huh? What do you mean?"

Ace pulled up some stats on his phone and handed it over to

me to read. "Hashtag Novier is the number one trending tag on ClikByte right now, and still climbing."

My mouth went dry as I scanned the stats for the hashtag in question. Novier. Noah and Xavier. There were already *thousands* of fan edits using that tag, and the comments were ticking over by the second. "What the fuck?" I whispered in disbelief. "How? Why? What about—"

Unable to curb my own curiosity, I clicked on the top-trending edit Byte and watched a series of way out-of-context clips of Xavier and I overlaid with a song about soulmates that was usually reserved for romance book edits. Some of the *longing glances* between us I knew perfectly well were actually death glares, or in one case the camera had caught Xavier's wide-eyed reaction to me cursing him out. My face was away from the camera, though, so without context... Fucking hell.

Over and over, the clips showed the moment on the high wire with my hand clasped in Xavier's as he yelled *trust me,* then shifted to a close-up shot of our hands clasped together during the milkmaid challenge.

"This is fucked-up," I finally said out loud. "They can't seriously have misread our dynamic *that* badly."

"They have, and we're running with it," Mr. Leight announced firmly. "Starting tomorrow, producer Sally will assist on this matter and guide the interactions with just enough to keep the Novier fans invested. I trust you're both professional enough not to fuck this up?"

Stunned, I glanced over at Xavier. Surely he wasn't okay with this? We barely tolerated one another on the best of days. He'd refuse, for sure.

But he just shrugged, giving nothing away. "Whatever Olympus wants," he drawled with a yawn. "So long as Little Dude understands it's purely for cameras and doesn't go reading anything more into it."

My jaw dropped in outrage, but Mr. Leight spoke before I could tell Xavier to go fuck himself.

"Yes, that's a very good point, Xavier. Fan service is just that—for the fans and always innocent. The idea is to feed their fantasies with subtle gestures, nothing more. I'm sure you're all smart enough to make the distinction and not blur any personal lines." The hard look he sent my way made me squirm with guilt and worry. He made a very pointed glance at Minho's arm around my shoulders and his knee hooked over mine, and dread curled though me.

Was this deliberate? Leight guessed that Minnie and I were closer than we should be, so he was driving a wedge between us?

Surely not. He couldn't manipulate the fan response, right?

"Okay, now that's sorted, Torin, your recent Bytes have also been met with higher than usual Cliks and comments. Are you willing to sell the piece you were working on? Several offers have been submitted for—"

"No, sorry," Torin cut him off without hearing the offer. "I'm keeping that one."

Mr. Leight nodded, unbothered. "Very well. Clik Games judging committee is still stalling on announcing the second challenge as Cat Kay's murder investigation continues, but Olympus Corp does still expect you all to continue as per usual while we wait. That means the fan meeting tomorrow will go ahead as planned, and I want to see at least two Lives before end of week. Got it?"

Everyone else murmured their agreement, but I was speechless. I stared at Xavier in confusion, waiting for him to say something about how insane this direction was. We barely survived the milkmaid challenge and only got away with it because the cameras couldn't capture our insults. That wouldn't work a second time.

"That's all," Mr. Leight announced, standing up. "I look forward to seeing you all at the fan meeting tomorrow."

"Can I have a word?" Minho asked, speaking for the first time since this whole Novier bullshit was dropped in our laps. For a moment I thought he was speaking to me, but no—he meant the team manager. The two of them left the room and I scrubbed my hands over my face with a groan.

"Don't stress about it too much, Eight," Ace told me with a reassuring kind of voice, making me look up at where he stood, offering a hand to pull me up. "They won't make you do anything that'd be uncomfortable. All you need to do is act like you don't hate each other, and I'll do the rest in edits."

That was comforting. I could handle that. But could Xavier? Something told me he wouldn't make this easy or pleasant. *Such* a dickhead.

The fact he was so handsome only made me hate him more because I still struggled to forget how badly I used to crush on him. I sighed. I remembered when I wasn't this idiot who lusted after every shirtless man in her vicinity.

THIRTY-THREE

"Elbow me one more time and I will stab this pen right through your hand to pin you down like a butterfly," I growled through my teeth. Outwardly, I kept my expression soft and calm. Happy. But internally I was wound so tight it hurt. Xavier seemed to be going out of his way to elbow me every three seconds, and it was tipping me over the edge.

"Sorry for being left-handed, Little Dude," he muttered back, flashing a bright smile to the fans waiting their turn to get photocards signed. "But I don't want to hear about your fantasies of pinning me down. Keep it professional, could you?"

I choked on my breath, coughing a little and cursing my own cheeks for heating. Because shit, now I had the mental image of pinning Xavier down in *that* way, and it was a disturbingly detailed picture.

"What are you guys whispering about?" a young fan asked breathlessly as she moved along the signing line from August to me and presented her photocard for signing.

I forced a smile, scribbling my NoFear tag across her photo with a silver marker. I decided to ignore her question and focus on the reason she'd come out. "Hi, what's your name?"

She blinked a couple times. "Louise. You can call me LouLou, though." Her gaze shifted to my wrist where I wore a black cord bracelet. One of the stylists had put it on me right before we started, and I'd thought nothing of it until I realized Xavier wore a matching one in white on his opposite wrist.

Sure enough, the girl then zeroed in on Xavi's bracelet, and her smile brightened even more. "You guys are really cute together," she gushed, and I handed the photocard back to her.

Neither Xavier, or I commented on that because, as Sally had lectured us all morning, we were *not* to confirm or deny any rumors. Just let them breathe and grow organically.

Xavier chatted more comfortably with the girl, directing the conversation to ask her about herself as he signed her photocard and elbowed me *again*. This time I lashed out under the table, stomping on his foot with my boot, and was rewarded by his slight grunt and flinch.

Stupidly, I didn't remove my foot fast enough and he somehow trapped my chunky men's boot between his own to prevent me doing it again. Asshole. I huffed with frustration, but refocused on the next fan while assuming he'd release me once his point was made.

"Hi, what's your name?" I asked the next person in line, extending my hand to take the photocard for signing.

"Joshua," the guy replied, eyeing me with a slight frown set on his face. He was maybe a little older than me, with bleached hair and blue contact lenses. Definitely an Ace Hart fan. "You look really familiar, Noah."

I glanced up from the photocard, my pen paused as I noted his narrowed, suspicious eyes. "Uh, from Clik Games?" Because it seemed like an odd statement for someone attending a fan meeting to make. Of course I looked familiar, I was all over the internet as a part of Team Olympus now, and he'd literally handed me a photo of myself to sign.

The fan shook his head. "No, not like that. There's something else."

My smile froze, and I quickly handed the photocard back to him. "Thanks for coming out. Have you met Xavier?" Now that I remembered, I tried to tug my foot free, but he wasn't letting up. Childish shithead.

Thankfully the fan moved along the line, and I released the breath I'd been holding. It wasn't entirely paranoia at play, because sooner or later someone *would* connect the dots. I hadn't altered my appearance with surgery, only removed the heavily feminine cosmetics and clothing of Norah Sparkle, so it was only a matter of time.

"Let go," I hissed when the Ace-lookalike fan moved along.

"Not a chance," he whispered back. "You'll just stomp on me again, and I like my toes intact, thank you."

I stifled the urge to roll my eyes. "Only if you elbow me again."

"I'm hurt that you think that's deliberate, Little Dude. We're just seated too closely together, that's all."

"Dude, quit being an asshole," Torin scolded quietly from Xavier's other side. "You have plenty of space without elbowing Noah every time you sign."

"Cut it out, all of you," one of the producers muttered from behind us. "You're here to meet fans, not bicker with each other."

Xavier and I exchanged a long look at that, and the corner of his mouth ticked up. "Agree to disagree," he whispered under his breath, referring to the producer's scolding, and I snorted a quick laugh despite myself.

Luckily, the next fan had arrived and I put my focus on her, pretending I didn't notice how warm Xavier's leg was against mine under the table. He was being an asshole, not flirting, but my body didn't seem to know the difference. So stupid.

He somehow managed to keep my foot clamped between his for the remainder of the signing, but thankfully eased up on the elbows, because I could already feel a bruise forming and I'd started flinching when he moved to sign.

Once we got to the end of the signing line, we had to take some photos, so Xavier *finally* released my foot, acting like nothing had happened when he pushed his chair back to stand for the photos. Dick.

"Are you good?" Ace asked quietly, placing his hand on my shoulder as we posed for the group picture. The gentle squeeze he gave me was comforting, and I breathed out a small sigh.

"Yep," I replied, because in the grand scheme of things, we'd been practically besties for this event. He hadn't thrown me in the pool or dropped me off a high wire, so there was nothing to complain about, right? "Am I okay to run to the restroom? I drank too much water while we were signing."

"Yeah, of course, go." Ace pointed me in the direction of the bathrooms, and I hurried away from the crowd before hesitating. I should be using the men's room, but what if they only had a urinal? How would I fake that? Shit, how the hell had I never thought of this before?

No, surely the men's room had stalls as well. How else would dudes poop? Okay, so I would just use the stall. Easy.

Decided, I bit the inside of my lip and pushed open the men's room door. Thankfully, it was empty *and* there were several stalls. What a relief. I hurried into one and locked the door, peeing as fast as humanly possible in an effort to get out without running into anyone.

Frustratingly, though, someone else came in right as I was finishing up and I quickly fixed my jeans, flushed, and exited the stall, only to stop dead in my tracks when I spotted Z standing at the urinal.

"Rocky, do not tell me you just took a shit in public at a fan event," he teased, looking at me over his shoulder when I hurried to the basin to wash my hands, determined not to look anywhere else. "That's bold, dude."

My face flamed hot. "I didn't. I just wanted privacy."

Z chuckled, zipping his pants back up. "Sure, whatever you say. Your secret is safe with me, public-pooper."

"I didn't!" I protested, grabbing some paper towel to dry my hands. "Some people just prefer privacy."

"Uh-huh, I believe you," he laughed, clearly *not* believing me as he dried his own hands. "Come on, let's finish these photos so we can go home."

He left the restroom ahead of me, leaving me glaring at his cocky swagger while I followed, almost running into Minho when we rounded the corner.

"Hey, dude," Z said, smacking Minho on the ass as he passed by, not glancing back and therefore not seeing the way Minnie grabbed my arm and dragged me back around the corner with him.

I drew a breath to ask what was wrong, but his mouth was on mine before I could get the words out. For a moment, time seemed to stop. Everything around us faded away, and all that mattered was the perfect curve of his full lips caressing mine and the desperate way his fingers dug into the back of my neck.

"I've never hated Xavi more than I do today," he told me in a husky whisper, then as fast as he'd grabbed me, he disappeared into the bathroom and left me standing there with my pulse racing and my lips tingling.

I really, *really* needed to come clean with him...but selfishly, I didn't want to lose what we now had. I was *so screwed.* Drawing a steadying breath, I returned to the group—and fans—and pasted on my best happy-to-be-here smile.

Torin seemed to see right through me, grabbing my hand and pulling me over to his side as we headed back to the interview area where we'd do five back-to-back question sessions with various magazines and online publications.

"You okay, Short Stack?" he asked quietly, draping his arm over my shoulders in an affectionate gesture. I appreciated that move, because the more other guys did it, the less suspicious it was when Minnie did it.

I mustered up a genuine smile for him. "Of course. I'm not fragile, you know? You're all acting like I can't handle Xavier's mood swings and snide remarks, but I'm more than capable. I've dealt with a lot worse."

Torin frowned. "That makes me sad, Short Stack." But before we could dive any further into that, our producers arranged everyone into seats where they wanted us, landing me right beside Xavier again. *Kill me now.*

Thankfully a lot of the interview questions were aimed at Ace and Xavier, with just the occasional one tossed to the rest of us, meaning for the most part we could just nod and smile. There was only one really uncomfortable moment when Minho—who was sitting on a taller seat behind me—had casually rested his hands on my shoulders, and Sally frantically gestured from behind the camera to take them off me.

Minnie *must* have seen her, she was basically flapping directly in front of us, but he took his sweet fucking time before letting go. Even then, he trailed a finger down the back of my neck out of view of the camera, and I shivered with arousal. Not cool at all. Especially when Sally then made forceful gestures toward Xavier and he dropped a hand onto my knee.

Super uncomfortable, but at the same time I sort of didn't hate having his hand on my leg. Like my seventeen-year-old self was getting to play out her dreams of dating Xavier Stone and nothing could convince her it wasn't real. Probably should have smothered seventeen-year-old me with a pillow.

The rest of the interviews went smoothly, and once the cameras turned off, Xavier snatched his hand away like I'd just bitten him. So fucking dramatic.

Torin immediately grabbed me in a side hug when we got up from our seats, muttering a creative insult about Xavier under his breath and making me snicker before Ace shot us a warning glance. Torin sighed and dropped his arm off my shoulders before we reached the main signing room again, as there would likely still be fans out there.

"You know," Xavier muttered, falling into step with me as August and Skye waved to the lingering fans ahead of us, "this bullshit Leight wants us to insinuate only helps your Clik rates. It wouldn't hurt for you to participate so it's not entirely on me."

I scoffed, shaking my head. "Are you fucking serious?" I kept my voice low, barely a whisper. "I've done everything Sally asked: sat beside you, wore the dumb matching bracelets, smiled sweetly even when you're being an asshole. What more do you want me to do, drop to my knees and suck your dick in front of the fans?"

Xavier flinched like I'd slapped him, a twist of confusion crossing his gorgeous face as he looked down at me from his stupidly tall height. Somehow he managed not to scowl, but the daggers in his eyes were unmistakable. "Don't get carried away, Little Dude. This is for Cliks and nothing else. I'd hate for you to catch feelings because you can't separate fiction from reality."

This time I couldn't stifle my laugh of contempt, tossing my head back. "Calm your tits, Godzilla. We're in no danger of that happening. I'd rather sit naked in a fire-ant nest than let you touch me off camera." Then, because I was anxious, stressed, nervous, embarrassed, and honestly far too aroused for my own good, I gave in to my childish, petty desire. I put my foot out right as he took a step and tripped him.

That saying about the bigger they are, the harder they fall came to mind as Xavier came crashing down to his knees, and my reactive gasp wasn't even faked. I'd thought he'd just stumble and continue on, not topple like a felled tree, and yet—

"Look out!" someone screamed, and I glanced up just in time to see one of the temporary media walls toppling over toward us. They weren't crazy heavy, but they also weren't made of tissue paper, so if they fell on a person, it'd hurt.

Luckily, the falling wall stopped just inches away from smacking me in the head while I stood there frozen in shock.

"Are you okay, Eight?" Ace asked in a rush, adjusting his hand placement on the wall which he'd just caught before it could knock me out. "What happened?"

"Um..." I looked down at Xavier, who was still on his knees, and offered him my hand up. "Xavi tripped and must have knocked one of the supports?"

Ace shot us both a suspicious look, like he knew we'd been bickering. "Don't forget, there are still a lot of eyes on us right now."

With that warning, he turned to the venue staff, who were frantically trying to stabilize the wall, and Xavier reluctantly took my offered hand. He then refused to let it go, going so far as intertwining our fingers like how Minho usually did...except Xavier used it to squeeze my hand to the point I squeaked in pain before he eased up.

Such a dickhead! He actually seemed to be enjoying himself as we posed for a few final pictures before staff ushered us out to the waiting cars.

THIRTY-FOUR

The fallout of the fan-signing footage was so ridiculous I couldn't do anything *but* laugh about it. Skye and I had stayed up way too damn late scrolling ClikByte and a few other social media sites to read comments and get a general feel for how the Olympus fans were responding to our new dynamic.

Clik Games were still stalling on announcing the second challenge, using the ongoing murder investigation as their reasoning. It made sense, and I was kind of glad for it, but at the same time that meant there was a *lot* of focus on our other content.

Leight hadn't been exaggerating about how much fans were going feral for Novier, unfortunately. Stupidly, we hadn't realized the tablecloths at the fan signing

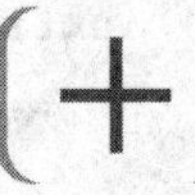

were not completely floor length, so there were images all over the damn internet of Xavier and I "playing footsies" during the event.

Best of all, though, were the reactions and edits of Ace saving us from the falling wall. Skye and I had laughed so hard we were crying before calling it a night, but judging by the raised voices that woke me the next morning, Xavier wasn't pleased.

"Noah," Ace sighed when I sleepily wandered into the kitchen in search of coffee and gossip. "Did you seriously heart react to an edit of Xavier last night?"

I froze, my hand on the cupboard door. Crap. "Technically, no. Skye did. But it was an accident, and he unclicked it really fast."

"Not fast enough!" Xavier barked like he was ready to break another coffeepot. Just in case, I moved over to the brand-new appliance and put my body between it and Godzilla. "And why that one? Did you not hear anything we said about implying, not confirming, and—"

"I said it was an accident!" I yelled back, too sleepy to tolerate his temper. "And it wasn't even me!"

He rolled his eyes dramatically, like I was lying. "It was *your* account, and it got screenshot within a split second of it happening, so no, you didn't unclick it fast enough."

I threw up my hands, shrugging. "Okay? What exactly do you want me to do about it now?"

"Sorry, bro," Skye offered, joining us with a yawn and cheeky grin. "That was my bad."

"Okay, everyone needs to take a breath," Ace urged in a calming, reasonable tone. "Noah's right, there's nothing he can do about it now. Skye, come on, you know better."

My roomie just shrugged. "Sorry, Boss. We were laughing really hard and my thumb slipped."

Shockingly, Xavier didn't appreciate that extra information. His left eye narrowed into a twitch and his face darkened with fury while Ace gave a long-suffering sigh.

"Thank you for adding that information, Skye. Really helping to diffuse the situation, aren't you?" Ace shot Skye a frustrated glance, but my roomie just nudged me out of the way to make a fresh pot of coffee, seemingly oblivious to the enraged monster behind him.

"Why that edit?" Xavier asked again with an edge of a whine. It made me give him a closer look, and I frowned my confusion.

"Uh, I honestly don't remember which one it was," I admitted with a shrug. "I mean...none of the ones we found funny were particularly flattering, in all fairness, but I thought it was one of Ace that Skye heart-reacted."

Ace shook his head, looking severely unimpressed. He pulled up the clip in question and turned his phone my way, jogging my memory.

"Oh." I said, fighting my grin as I watched the edit again. "That one. Yeah, that checks out. Um, sorry?"

Xavier threw his hands in the air, like he was fighting the urge to throw punches. Crap, I really should be careful of that, since boys were not adverse to roughhousing, and they all thought I was one of them.

Skye glanced at the clip and snickered. "Oh yeah, I remember now. It's a great edit. Very creative."

"The caption is literally 'Noah's Babygirl'," Xavier growled in a voice like thunder. "They're making it seem like I'm some sort of..." He flapped his hands around, apparently at a loss for words. Rarified air, indeed.

"Baby*girl*?" Skye finished when he trailed off, enjoying himself way too much. We'd laughed a whole lot about this turn of events, seeing as I—as an actual girl—apparently gave off bigger dick energy than Xavier Stone himself. In fairness, the edit had compiled a bunch of out-of-context clips that really painted him as submissive and breedable—the fans' words, not mine—which wasn't helped by his milkmaid costume or the image of him on his hands and knees at my feet.

Xavier glowered absolute death at my best friend. "I swear to fuck, Skye, if you—"

"Hey, don't threaten him!" I interjected. "It's not his fault you give off bottom energy. I don't see Ace flipping out about *his* edits this morning." Then again, the rumors of Ace being a Daddy were a whole lot more complimentary and, frankly, accurate.

"Okay, come on, that's enough." Ace clapped his hand down on his roommate's shoulder with clear warning to cut it the fuck out. "Xavi, you can't be mad about fan edits, and you can't blame Noah for the way it's playing out. You know how this shit works; this isn't new to you. Skye...stop antagonizing him. Noah—"

"I didn't do anything!" I protested, desperately not wanting to be scolded by Ace before coffee.

Ace gave me a deadpan stare right back, not buying my innocent act. Damn it. "Noah, for fuck's sake, use a burner account when you're doom scrolling, so accidents like this don't happen again. As it is, the Acolytes are in a frenzy, thinking your reaction is confirmation that Xavier is...you know..."

"Noah's babygirl," Skye helpfully clarified with eyes that burned with mirth. "Don't stress about it, Xavi, it's not your fault. Some people just don't have masculine energy online and that's okay. In this case, Noah just vibes a bigger dick than you. It's nothing to be ashamed of. And Ace is obviously a Daddy, but we already knew that."

"I'm not," Ace grumbled, folding his arms. "I'm barely six months older than Xavi."

Skye shrugged. "Daddy is a state of mind, Ace."

I snorted then coughed in a lame attempt to cover my laughter as I turned away from Ace. If I made eye contact with him now, I'd turn bright red. Because after the unhinged thirst comments some fans had made about him saving me from that falling wall, he'd definitely appeared in my dreams last night.

"You know what? I need a change of scenery," I announced in a somewhat strangled voice, slipping past Ace and Xavier to head for the front door. "I'm going to Boba-Kitty instead."

Not waiting for their response, I stuffed my feet into my sneakers in the foyer and made it all the way out onto the porch before remembering that I needed to actually call for one of the drivers to pick me up. Damn it again.

"I'll drive," Ace said, exiting the house behind me, keys in hand. "So long as you refrain from calling me Daddy."

I pursed my lips, fighting a laugh. "I dunno... That's a tall order. I could just call for a car." At his loaded glare, I grinned wide. "Okay, fine. Deal. Can we get pastries from the café across from Boba-Kitty, too?"

"That's basically the only reason I offered, Eight," he said with a smirk. Ace, I was coming to realize, had a wicked sweet tooth. He unlocked his BMW sitting in the driveway, and I slid into the passenger seat, a little surprised that Skye hadn't tagged along.

For several minutes, we drove in silence, and I started panicking that I was actually in trouble. Was Ace pissed about the accidental react on that post? Or annoyed that I couldn't seem to get along with Xavier despite his request that we be civil? Or...shit, did he know about Minho? *Or me? Did he know about me?* Crap.

"What's on your mind, Eight?" he asked right in the middle of a panic spiral, and I nearly jumped out of my seat. "You look like your thoughts are going a million miles an hour over there."

I wet my lips and wiped my palms on my jeans. "Um...are you mad?" Keep it vague. Let Ace direct the topic of conversation.

He glanced over at me, his ice-blue eyes oddly warm and concerned. "No. Should I be?"

"No?" I replied with uncertainty. "I just thought that after... uh...I know you asked me and Xavier to try harder, and that's, um, not quite what we've done..."

Ace let out a long sigh, his focus on the road ahead while his thumb tapped the steering wheel thoughtfully. "You have for public appearances, and that's all I would ever ask of you. I'm not going to force you two to play nice when the cameras are off, because what happens behind the scenes is nobody's business."

I nodded slowly. "Oh. Okay."

"But I saw you trip him yesterday at the fan meet. You're lucky *that* didn't get captured by any of the fan footage or the narrative today would be very different." He cast me a warning glance, and I squirmed in my seat.

"Noted," I murmured, suitably chastised. It had been a stupid thing to do, with all those cameras around, but sometimes Xavier pushed me to do stupid things.

Ace pulled into a parking spot right outside Boba-Kitty, then frowned at me thoughtfully. "You didn't bring a hat or anything, did you?"

I shook my head. "No. Should I have?"

His lips curled in the kind of smile that said I was being cute. What the shit, why did that smile make my insides go all weak and fluttery? "Yeah, Eight, you should have. I don't know if you've noticed, but you're *very* recognizable. Here, use these." He pulled out a pair of Deity sunglasses from his car's holder and handed them over.

"What about you?" I asked as I put the sunglasses on and glanced in the mirror. I'd already stolen one pair from him, but I kind of liked this shape better.

Ace just shrugged. "I'm used to it. Besides, they'll still know it's you, but at least you can hide your expressive reactions a little more. I don't know that the internet needs any more content to edit out of context today."

Ah. Very good point. I hopped out of the car and flipped up my hoodie's hood to hide my hair as we entered the bubble tea shop. We'd been there a handful of times already, so I knew what my safe order was—brown sugar fresh milk with brown sugar pearls and brown sugar milk foam. There was no actual tea involved in that, but it was absolutely delicious.

Ace ordered a grapefruit green tea with mango popping pearls and made relaxed small talk with the staff while we waited. One of the girls working behind the counter nervously asked him for his autograph, and he even offered to take a selfie with her after signing her metal water bottle.

"Would you mind?" the girl then asked, extending her cup and sharpie my way.

Startled, I took it and scribbled my awfully childish tag beside Ace's elegant signature.

"Girls, could you do us a favor and wait ten minutes before posting those photos?" Ace asked in his seductively charming voice. "Noah and I want to grab some pastries from across the street before anyone knows we're here."

The girls gushed their promises to hold off on posting, and Ace handed me my brown sugary goodness. I tipped it up and down to mix the syrup while we crossed the road to the bakery and let Ace choose a huge array of pastries to take home.

"Damn it," I grumbled when I messed up the straw pierce of my bubble tea and the stupid paper straw folded. "Now it's going to go soggy faster."

Ace shot me a puzzled look, like he wasn't following my train of thought, so I gestured with the bent straw. "I get it, save the turtles. But soggy straws are a fucking crime, Ace, and you know I'm right."

"And it goes soggy faster because you bent it?" He shook his head and swapped straws with me, popping his through the seal of my drink with one smooth motion. "There. Problem solved."

Not *really,* but at the same time I wasn't complaining. He'd already used his, so it tasted vaguely of grapefruit on that first sip...which I didn't hate.

"How are you feeling about everything at the moment, Noah?" he asked once we were back in the privacy of his car, pastries safe on my lap. "I know this level of fan scrutiny is new to you. You never really had such personal interactions on your platform before, right?"

I gave a vague hum in response because that wasn't strictly true. As NoFear, sure. I was totally anonymous, and although there were a lot of unhinged comments, none of it was personal. Because they had no idea who I was, what I looked like, how I behaved...so yeah, it was different now.

But I wasn't exactly a stranger to it, since I'd had my fair share of comments as Norah Sparkle. The difference now was that boy Noah had a majority female fan base, and while they were *wild,* they were also largely fucking funny. Like Noah's Babygirl content—funny as hell.

"I'm fine," I finally responded after several sips of my drink. "Itching to get into the next challenge, though. Do you know when they're going to announce it?"

"No clue," he said with a frustrated sigh. "It was supposed to be at the same time as the reveal of challenge one results, but with Cat Kay's murder..."

"Have they found the guy who did that?" I asked, hopeful. Because although we'd been assured multiple times that it was a targeted attack on *her* specifically, the worry was always in the back of my mind that any of us could be targets. Maybe not by the same guy, but there were lots of disturbed people on the internet just waiting for a push to cross the line.

Ace shook his head. "No, not yet. I'm heading into Olympus's office later today, though. I'll ask for more information. But back to you—are you really okay with the Xavier crap? I know you were a lot more comfortable feeding rumors about Minho, but—"

"I'm fine." I quickly cut him off before he could think any deeper on the authenticity of me and Minho. "Xavier just seems to be struggling with the idea that the world doesn't revolve around his inflated ego."

Ace chuckled, nodding. "True. Xavi and I have been friends for a really long time, but I'm not ignorant to his flaws. If he ever takes things too far or you become uncomfortable with what producers are asking, you tell me. Got it?"

I smiled, my insides all warm and fuzzy by the level of support he was offering. I'd never had someone like him to lean on in this crazy career, and it felt *nice*.

"Thanks, Daddy," I teased, and snickered at his sharp glare.

"Shut the fuck up, Eight, or I'll swap around room assignments to put you with Xavier."

I made my eyes wide and pantomimed locking my lips shut and throwing away the key. That was a threat I took seriously.

THIRTY-FIVE

I'd officially found my new happy place. A new core memory to lock away, thanks to Team Olympus. Lying on the floor of the dance studio, sweaty and exhausted, with my head in Minho's lap while Torin drew cherry blossoms on my hand and wrist with colorful markers.

August was still on his feet, humming under his breath as he practiced the choreography Minnie had just come up with to support his former K-pop bandmate's solo release. We'd filmed our best take, and he'd sent it to his friend for feedback, so we were just waiting to hear back.

"Do you miss it?" I asked, looking up at Minho from my comfy position. "Being in a group, I mean?"

"I am in a group," he replied with a teasing smile, his fingers combing through my hair lazily.

I rolled my eyes. "Not the same thing. You still seem like you're on good terms with your old group. Would you ever get back together?"

He shook his head, a sad sort of smile playing across his lips. "No, what happened was deliberate. I miss some parts of being in 1-4-3, but there are so many aspects I'm incredibly lucky to have gotten away from."

"Deliberate?" I repeated, frowning my confusion as I remembered the rumors of Minho being fired due to a scandal with his boss's daughter. "What do you mean?"

Minnie sighed, raking his fingers through his own hair before leaning back on his hands. "Uh, it was a setup. We were all really young when we signed the contracts with our record label—like, I was sixteen when we debuted and nowhere near mature enough to understand what I was agreeing to. I'm sure you're not shocked to hear it was a really bad contract."

Torin huffed a sound of agreement, clearly already having heard this story. "Always read the fine print, bro."

Minnie extended his middle finger toward Torin before shifting his focus back to me. "Yeah, well, by the time we realized, we were already in too deep. For a while we made it work and focused on the benefits, focused on the art, but we eventually hit a breaking point. Two of my group members had started dating in secret, and when production found out, it was not pretty. Idols are meant to always maintain the illusion of availability to sell the boyfriend concept, so literally any relationship is forbidden. Long story short, they were miserable, it was impacting everyone's mental health, and we knew we needed to break contracts by whatever means necessary."

"You couldn't just walk away?" I asked, despite the fact I knew full fucking well these things were never that easy.

"Not if we didn't want to spend the rest of our lives in debt to the company, we couldn't," Minho replied with a grimace. "The only way to get out was for them to end the contract. So..." He shrugged.

"So you live streamed while fucking your company CEO's daughter?" I finished for him, trying not to sound judgmental, but at the same time, given what I'd just gone through with Rich, it was ick.

Minnie let out a long sigh. "Yep. But to be perfectly clear, it was *her* idea. She wanted to launch her CB:AO account and thought it would be a great publicity hook...not to mention it'd piss off her dad, who was majorly absent for most of her life."

"And it got you fired," I murmured, understanding their plan and relieved to hear the girl had been a willing participant.

Minho nodded. "Morality clause. Which in turn triggered a disbandment clause, allowing the rest of the group to cancel their contracts with no financial repercussions."

I was quiet for a moment, turning that information over in my mind and finding a new respect for what, on the surface, had seemed like a shallow act from an arrogant celebrity. "Things must have been really bad, to go to those lengths," I finally said out loud, looking up at him as his fingers returned to my hair.

He shrugged again. "It worked out in the end."

"What about your friends?" I asked with curiosity, wondering if it was the group members I suspected but not wanting to pry. "Did they stay together?"

A warm smile curved his lips and he nodded. "Yes. Still technically a secret—for publicity purposes they're just living together as friends—but they got married last year and have adopted three cats."

"It's sad they have to hide it," I commented, glancing down to where Torin was extending the cherry blossoms up my forearm. "Even though you broke your contracts?"

"It's a business decision," Minho replied with a shrug. "And at least they're together."

"Meanwhile, Minnie is still paying off the consequences for the whole group," Torin muttered under his breath, keeping his eyes lowered to the drawing on my arm.

Minho just scoffed and poked Torin in the arm. "Good thing you fuckers and Olympus Corp took me in to help pay the debt off, huh?"

Before I could ask what that all meant, the door opened and my least favorite team member came strolling in with his phone in hand.

"What's your secret, Little Dude?" Xavier asked with a suspicious look.

Alarm shot through me and I sat up, making Torin growl as his marker slipped. "What do you mean? What secret?"

"You tell me," he shot back, eyes narrowed. "Someone is spam-commenting on every one of our team Bytes saying they 'know your secret.' So, what is it?"

Ice formed along my spine, and my stomach twisted. Was it just a troll or did someone actually know? Had someone connected the dots and was ready to out me as a fraud? Fuck. Where was my phone?

August took a smooth step closer, like he was presenting a physical barrier between Xavier and the rest of us, putting his hand out. "Dude, is that why you came up here? To poke at Noah about some spam commenter? Surely you have better things to do."

Xavier shrugged, drawing far too much attention to his smoothly toned shoulders in the black tank top he wore. "This seems fairly important. So what are you hiding from us, Little Dude?"

"Nothing you need to know, Godzilla," I drawled in my most unaffected voice possible, considering the utter panic filling my chest. "Don't you get tired constantly thinking about me?"

Xavier's eyes widened a moment before he sneered back at me. "Don't flatter yourself. I'm simply worried that whatever bullshit you're mixed up in will eventually hurt this team. So what is it, huh? Gambling debt? Murder? Porn?"

I flinched because that last guess hit way too hard to home, and damn if his eyes didn't narrow further with the sharp recognition that he'd hit a sore point.

"Xavier, that's enough." Minho pushed up off the floor and offered me his hand up. "Don't we all need to be somewhere that's not here?"

"Literally anywhere else," Torin agreed with an eye roll and scathing glance Xavier's way.

That only seemed to push his buttons, though, and he glowered pure venom my way. "Fuck off, you guys. I'm not being an asshole just for fun; I'm looking out for our team. Little Dude has been shady since day fucking one, and you're all going to pretend it doesn't bother you? Like you don't notice how secretive he is with that supposed back injury that doesn't actually seem to hinder any activity?"

"It's none of our business," Minho growled, stepping slightly between Xavier and I, as though he thought this was going to turn physical. Was it? Fucking hell, that'd be a first for me and really not likely to end well given my lack of fighting ability...or strength in comparison to *actual* men.

"Back off, Xavi," August warned, folding his arms and shooting Xavier with a hard glare. "Or do you want us to start digging through your closet for skeletons? We all have our fair share, and you're no exception."

Xavier cast a long look in August's direction, and I thought for sure he would ignore the warning, but instead he shrugged.

"Whatever, this isn't worth my time. I'm sure your secret will come out sooner or later, Little Dude. This commenter seems determined enough to out you, so maybe you need to think about damage control while you still can."

Ace appeared in the doorway a moment later, casting a worried look between the lot of us. "Everything okay in here?" he asked with concern.

"Xavier just came to remind us about the photoshoot this afternoon," Torin replied with a glare in Xavier's direction. "Right, Xavi?"

"Right," he agreed with a brittle smile. "The underwear campaign. This will be interesting." He gave me a long look, and I jerked my gaze to Ace in confusion.

"Not you," Ace replied with a reassuring head shake. "You get the night to yourself, Eight."

Xavier whirled around in outrage. "Why? It's a team campaign, isn't it?"

Ace arched a brow as if to tell Xavier to reassess his attitude *fast*. "Yes, but the contract was signed prior to Noah's joining, and his personal contract excludes him from any preexisting brand deals and sponsorships. *Not* that it's any of your business. Min, Tor, Aug, you all need to shower before we go. Let's move, please. I don't want to be late."

He stepped to the side, gesturing for the boys to all leave the dance studio and making it real clear he wouldn't be leaving us to continue arguing while his back was turned. When it was just me and him left, his expression softened.

"Are you okay?" he asked quietly, his gaze scanning over me ever so quickly. "Do I need to speak with him?"

I shook my head, tucking my hands into the pockets of my sweatpants. "Nah, he's just the same old Xavier. Getting bent out of shape about a troll commenter."

"Ah, that one. He should know better."

I shrugged. "It's whatever. So...underwear shoot? What's that all about?"

Ace grimaced, running a hand over the back of his neck. "It's a brand collaboration thing, but on the upside, we will get a shit-load of free underwear out of it. I'll bring some back for you, if you want. Boxers or briefs?"

He gave me a thoughtful look, pursing his lips. "Briefs."

I gave an outraged gasp. "Boxers, thank you." Which was extra funny, seeing as I used to be a micro G-string kind of girl.

Ace laughed, shaking his head as we exited the dance room together. "Yeah, sure, if you say so. If you go out, make sure you take a security guard with you, all right? I've got a weird feeling about how intense some of our fans have been getting with this extended silence from Clik Games."

"Valid, but I have no plans. Probably hang out here and doom scroll while planning my next content batch." At least I was honest about it.

Ace laughed, ruffling my hair. "I'm jealous. Enjoy the quiet, Eight. We'll probably be gone most of the night with the shoot starting so late."

A whole night alone in Mount Olympus? Definitely unexpected, but at the same time I wouldn't be letting my guard—or binder—down for a minute. It'd be just like Xavier to show up unannounced and find me strutting around naked with full tits and vagina on display. Nope, not risking it. My willpower was stronger than that.

THIRTY-SIX

Somehow I managed to pretend like my curiosity and fear weren't getting the better of me while the guys got ready to leave, acting like I'd already forgotten Xavier's outburst about the comment troll. Somehow, I pulled it off, and no one mentioned anything more about it. But the moment the company-driven vans exited our driveway, I logged into my new CB burner account faster than my phone knew how to handle.

AceHartsHeart was the username of the viral commenter, and Xavier hadn't been exaggerating when he said they'd spam commented under every single one of the group Bytes. On my own page it looked like he—or she—had hit every single Byte with at least a handful of comments, but the newer ones were flooded.

I know your secret.

I know your secret.

I know your secret.

I know your secret.

I know your secret.

I know your secret.

I know your secret.

Dread pooled in my stomach as I scrolled through the Bytes quickly. No one seemed to have taken the bait to respond to any comments, seeing them for the troll commenter they clearly were. But the concerning part was that they'd taken to commenting on the boys' individual accounts, too.

I know Noah's secret.

Most of the team would ignore it, but would Xavier? When he got nothing out of me directly, would he engage with the troll?

Fucking hell! what if *AceHartsHeart* really did know my secret? What if they exposed me to Xavier of all fucking people? Disaster.

Maybe I needed to get ahead of it all and come clean to Ace myself. At least if Ace knew the truth, then he could make his own decisions about how to handle the information. He was a good leader, and I did think I could trust he wouldn't kick me to the curb for lying. Especially when *technically* I never lied, I just allowed them to assume and never corrected anyone as to my lack of Y chromosome.

Somehow I doubt the distinction would make a difference.

I misled them, and my gut told me that Ace wouldn't take the breach of trust with a shrug and smile.

Chewing on the edge of my thumb, I exited out of ClikByte and searched for my manager's number. If anyone could point me in the right direction, it was Jared.

"Oh, hi, stranger," he said with warmth on answering my call. "I was starting to think you'd fired me."

I smiled, my phone to my ear as I turned on the patio and pool lights and headed out to sit on the edge of the pool. Not *in* the pool, just near it.

"Nah, just respecting your paternity leave time. How is mini-Jared doing, anyway?"

He barked a laugh. "You mean mini-Noah? How the hell my daughter looks more like *you* than either of her parents, I don't understand."

Warmth rushed through me as I grinned up at the ceiling. He'd been sending me photos, and realistically, it was just his baby's bright blue eyes that made her resemble me. Other than that, she just looked like a baby. All babies looked like babies. Well, her eyes and the fact that she started rolling over at three weeks old, nearly giving Jared a heart attack while changing her diaper.

"Aw, here's hoping she doesn't start crawling early, too," I teased. "Or you'll really have your work cut out for you."

Jared groaned, and from the background I heard his baby let out a cry. "Give me a second, Noah. I'll just check if Kelly needs anything." I waited patiently as he put the phone down and checked on his wife and baby, then came back a minute later with an exhausted sigh. "Okay, I'm back. What's up, kiddo? Are we safe to chat or...?"

"We're safe," I confirmed. "The team all left a few minutes ago to do a photoshoot for some underwear line."

He gave a surprised grunt. "How'd you get out of that one?"

"Ace excused me, citing my contract restrictions. Good thing he did or that would have become really uncomfy, really fast." Speaking of uncomfy, it probably wouldn't hurt to take my binder off so long as I was wearing an oversized hoodie, surely. I reached under my shirt to undo the Velcro and swallowed back a groan of relief as it came loose. "Anyway, I wanted to get your advice about...everything."

"Everything?" he repeated as I rolled up my binder and secured it with its own straps. "That sounds ominous. Is this about your comment troll?"

"Yessss," I hissed on a heavy exhale. "Good to know you also noticed."

"How could I not? I've got Olympus PR team working on reporting the comments and getting the profile deactivated from ClikByte, but—"

"But what if they *know*?" I finished for him, my anxiety damn near choking me. "What if this isn't just an annoyance?"

Jared didn't answer for a moment, clearly considering what I was saying before blowing out a sigh. "And hence the reason for your call. You think you need to get ahead of this?"

I chewed the edge of my thumb nail again. Did I? "Yeah, kind of. Except dickhead Leight will lose his shit, won't he?"

"I don't know. I'd have to review the exact wording of your contract before you made any moves, but I'd really want you to consider the bigger picture consequences of revealing that you're actually a girl. The blowback from Olympus fans, the media storm, not to mention—"

"The team will be *pissed*," I groaned, rubbing my eyes.

Jared gave a short laugh. "I was going to say not to mention the possibility of being linked to Peaches, but yeah, your team won't be happy about this. Unless they would be? Gossip mill seems to suggest you've formed a few *close friendships* despite your disguise?" His tone was teasing and inquisitive, and I rolled my eyes.

"Stop it, you know that shit is all for Cliks." But...would Minho hate me or would it maybe be a good thing? What about Torin? I got the feeling he was into me, but he'd never made any kind of move, so maybe he wasn't as attracted to guys as Minnie was?

Fucking hell. What would Xavier say?

"Look, I'm just saying not to do anything too hastily," Jared continued, oblivious to my inner turmoil. "I need to make sure we aren't opening ourselves up to any nasty repercussions or...I dunno. Just give me a couple days to run it past legal and our own

PR consultants, all right? But you'll likely find this troll will get banned from CB and it'll all dry up with no harm done."

I nodded despite the fact he couldn't see me. "Yeah. Maybe. But sooner or later this is going to come out, and I would feel a hell of a lot better if it came from me rather than some random obsessed fan who's run my face through an AI filter."

"I agree," Jared said with a grim voice. "Let me work out a strategy that minimizes risk and I'll get back to you. In the meantime, are you okay there at the house? Is the shared room situation becoming a problem or are things still running smoothly?"

A pang of guilt vibrated through my chest, because I hadn't told him that Skye knew all about my secret identity already and had done since basically day one. "Yeah it's all fine. Skye's the perfect roommate. Very into privacy and respectful of boundaries."

"Good, that's good to hear. You two have gained a *lot* of Cliks on your recent collabs too. That's a great partnership to hold on to even after these games are over. Actually, on that topic...talk to me about Xavier Stone."

I winced, because he'd just put on his recently acquired dad voice, and I already knew he wasn't fooled by the illusion Xavier and I were even remotely friends, let alone anything more. "There's nothing to tell, Jared. Apparently we get good interaction from fans, but I could quite comfortably push him off a cliff with no wingsuit and never give it another thought."

Jared barked a laugh. "Good to hear. I remember how you used to feel about—"

"Ancient history, Jared!" I quickly cut him off. "Ancient fucking history. Teenage girls are fucking stupid, didn't you know?"

Right as I made that very firm statement, a shadow filled the doorframe from the house, and I gasped so hard I nearly choked on my own breath.

"Noah, you okay? What happened?" Jared's voice was full of concern, so I forced myself to laugh despite how hard my heart was thumping in my chest.

Shaking my head at how badly I'd just panicked, I lifted my hand in a weak wave. "Yeah, sorry. Ace just scared the hell out of me. I thought..." *I thought I was about to be murdered like Cat Kay.* "Nothing. All good. I should go, but you'll get back to me and, uh, tell me what the fuck to do?"

"Of course. In the meantime just block the troll and ignore, all right?"

"Got it," I murmured. "Thanks for chatting. Give my love to Kelly and Isla."

"Will do. Call Miles when you can, too. He's worried about you." His dad voice was back, and I didn't like it. Still, I quickly mumbled that I would, and ended my call as Ace sat on the sun lounger beside me with a yawn.

I gave him a curious look, taking in the fact he was still dressed exactly as he was when the team left the house. No makeup, hair still exactly as it had been. "Aren't you supposed to be modelling underwear right now, Boss?"

His lips kicked up in a half smile. "They were running way

behind schedule, so Z and I dipped out. We'll do ours tomorrow instead."

I glanced toward the house. "And Z is...?"

"Gone to visit his girlfriend," Ace replied with a small grimace.

It made me curious about this girl that they all seemed to know about, despite the strict Olympus contracts forbidding "unapproved" relationships. It made me think of what Minho had said about always appearing available.

"You don't like his girlfriend?" I asked, shifting to sit cross-legged and hoping my sweatshirt was baggy enough to maintain my disguise.

Ace shrugged, lying back on the sun lounger with an arm under his head. "It's not that... She's nice enough. It's complicated." It was a clear implication of *not my story to tell*, so I let it drop.

"What about you?" I prodded with a smirk. "No secret girlfriend lurking in the shadows?"

He laughed, shaking his head. "Nope."

My brows rose. "Boyfriend?"

Ace's grin widened. "Smooth one, Eight. If you wanted to fish for information, you can just ask. But no...no one lurking in the shadows for me because when the fuck would I even have the time? I'd be the worst boyfriend on earth, always putting my work and my team first."

He had a good point. Aside from being Team Olympus leader and having a heavy hand in the editing and content planning, he was still somewhat active as an actor. It'd been a year or so since his last movie release, and as far as I'd seen, he wasn't working on anything new right now, but that could change. I couldn't imagine how busy he'd be if he was also juggling an acting role.

"How about you, Eight? I feel like you don't share much about your life, so none of us really know you all that well. Do you have someone waiting for you when the Clik Games are over, or was that what you were talking to your manager about?" He sat up, leaning closer with a curious glint in his eyes. "About teenage girls being stupid."

Huh? Oh. Ah, he must have heard that and assumed... Good thing he didn't realize I was referring to myself and my dumb teenage crush on Xavier.

I gave a short laugh, shaking my head. "No, that was...something else." Then because I actually didn't like that he felt like he didn't *know* me, I answered his actual question. "Also, no, I don't have *someone.* I actually just ended an insanely toxic relationship before joining the team, and it's pretty much scared me off m—uh, relationships in general." I almost slipped up and said *men* but caught it. Not that it'd have been the end of the world; he'd have assumed I was gay before guessing I was a girl.

Ace nodded thoughtfully. "I remember management mentioned you were dealing with some personal legal issues which delayed you joining us. Was that connected?"

I grimaced, rubbing my forehead. "Yeah. My ex..." It was too hard to explain in general terms without airing the whole mess, and I *never* wanted Ace to know about Peaches. "It wasn't pretty."

"But you're okay now? Legally, I mean. You sorted it out?" He seemed genuinely concerned, and I tried to lighten the mood with a laugh.

"Don't worry. I won't drag the team into the scorched earth of my bad decisions." I really hoped I never would. If Rich respected the contracts he'd signed and kept his mouth shut, no one need ever know.

Ace frowned, giving a short sigh. "That wasn't my worry, Eight. I was asking if *you* were okay now. If you need our lawyers to look over anything—"

"No, it's done." I cut him off quickly because the level of caring in his tone was starting to make my chest tight and my eyes hot. "Thank you, though."

He held my gaze for a long, tense moment before nodding his acceptance of my answer. "So what are we doing out here tonight? I didn't expect to find you beside the pool, of all places, considering your fear."

I wet my lips, glancing at the serene water all lit up and glowing with soft blue light. "Exposure therapy, I guess? I was on the phone to Jared, who is one of the only people I really trust, so I thought maybe I could look at the pool while talking to him..." I shrugged, feeling silly now that I said it out loud. "I'm fully aware I need therapy."

Ace offered a warm, lopsided smile, standing up from his seat. "It makes sense. But I think you need to do more than just *look* at the water, Eight." He put his hand out to me, palm up, and I stared at it like he was offering me a mouse trap.

"What?" I asked suspiciously.

He gave a huff of frustration. "Let me help."

Biting my lip with nervousness, I cautiously took his hand and let him pull me up to my feet. His small, satisfied smile was almost worth the risk, but then he tugged me closer to the pool and released my hand to sit on the edge, pulling his shoes and socks off.

"Come on, Eight, just trust me." Ace patted the tiles beside him as he dipped his legs into the water. "Sit with me. I promise I won't let anything bad happen."

Did I trust him? Like *really* trust him?

Chewing on my lip, I kicked off my own shoes and gingerly sat on the edge of the pool beside Ace, my heels on the lip and my arm wrapped around my knees. "Happy?"

He rolled his eyes, a soft smile playing across his lips. "No. Put your feet in the water. Just your feet, that's all I'm asking."

I released my pent-up breath in a drawn-out sigh, eyeing the water with a tangle of emotions inside me. Logically I knew there was no harm in putting my feet in the water. The terror only ever set in when I was *fully* submerged. But there was always the possibility that I might fall in and then panic and—

"Hey, I'm right here." Ace's calm voice cut through my

spiraling thoughts as he offered his hand, palm up, once more. "It's just us. You're safe with me, Noah."

Truer words had never been spoken. Ace was everything I could have hoped for in a leader *and* a friend. Sucking in a breath, I placed my shaking hand in his, gripping tight as my feet descended into the pool water.

"Okay?" Ace asked in a low voice once both my feet were underwater. His fingers interlaced with mine, and he held on to me just as tightly as I was holding on to him. Maybe. My knuckles were definitely white, and I couldn't let up even if I tried.

I forced a jerking nod. "Uh-huh. Now what?"

His lips curved up again, his ice-blue eyes catching mine in a hypnotic gaze. "Now nothing. We just hang out here. Tell me something I don't know about you, Eight. Where did you go to school?"

Huh? He wanted to *chat*?

"Um, I was homeschooled," I replied, confused and a little flustered as he continued holding eye contact while his thumb stroked reassuring circles on the back of my hand. "I wasn't—"

All of a sudden, darkness smothered us as the power cut out, leaving the only light coming from the moon.

"Huh," Ace muttered, turning his face toward the dark house. "That's odd."

Odd wasn't good.

"Probably just a blown fuse," he said with thoughtful confidence, standing up before offering his hand to pull me up out of the water. "I'll go check the fuse box and check with security."

Panic flashed through me, and I grabbed his arm as he started to head toward the house. "Wait, I'll come with you."

Ace gave a short laugh, looking over his shoulder at me despite the heavy shadows. "You scared of the dark, Eight?"

I swallowed hard. "Not usually...but remember how the power cut out right before Cat got her throat slit?"

"Good point," he murmured, his tone grim as he grasped my hand in his once more. "Come on, then. Let's stick together."

Relief calmed my nerves slightly that he wasn't insisting I sit there in the dark waiting for him to fix the power. Ace wasn't the kind of guy to make anyone feel silly or dumb for being scared, but under the current circumstances, I probably would have thought less of him if he wasn't at least a little anxious.

"Holy crap, it's dark in here," he commented, pulling out his phone to use the flashlight and navigate through the living room, then grunting when he walked into something. "Watch your leg on the table, Eight."

"Thanks," I murmured, pulling out my own phone to light the way. "Where's the fuse box?"

"Just inside the garage," he replied, heading in that direction. "Can you see if there are any alerts from the power company? Maybe it's a grid outage or something."

I nodded my agreement—despite the fact he couldn't see me—and unlocked my phone screen. "Yeah, good thinking. Except...no reception."

Ace gave a short groan, letting go of my hand as we

approached the internal door to the garage. "Because without power, our Wi-Fi won't work, and the mobile coverage here sucks." He opened the door as I refreshed my mobile settings, hoping it might pick up a bar of reception. As he stepped into the pitch-black garage, he seemed to trip on something and drop his phone, the light skittering across the floor as he grunted and disappeared in the dark.

"You okay, Boss?" I asked with a forced laugh, trying not to let the stress get to me. "I hope that didn't break your screen."

His phone had ended up under the front of his BMW so I went to pick it up for him...but never made it that far.

THIRTY-SEVEN

My head hurt. A lot. Pain radiated through the back of my skull, making my eyeballs throb, and my stomach churned like I was on a boat. *What the fuck happened?*

Had something fallen on my head in the garage? I remember leaning down to pick up Ace's phone and... that was it. Did I smack my head on the car or something?

Fuck, I could taste blood and my tongue ached like I'd bitten it when—had someone hit me?

"Ahh, there she is. Wakey wakey now," an unfamiliar voice crooned, and I cracked my eyelids open with monumental effort. Light stabbed through my eyes, making me wince, and I squinted up at Ace.

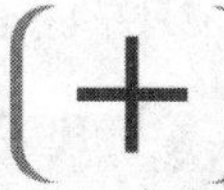

Wait. Not Ace. Ace's eyes weren't that close together,

and his jaw was stronger, and this version wore colored contacts that screamed Temu.

"Who the fuck...?" I mumbled, my tongue heavy with how badly my head pounded. Was I seeing things? "What—?"

"Ah, good, I thought for a minute maybe I hit you too hard and then all the fun would be ruined," the creepy Ace lookalike said, making me wince as I frowned. Why did he seem vaguely familiar?

Wait. Where was Ace? The real one, not this budget knockoff version.

I tried to look around, trying to get my bearings and work out what'd happened to Ace, but it quickly became apparent that I was tied to a chair. As was Ace, who also had blood dripping down his face and a gag between his teeth. The power was back on, apparently, with the pool lights glowing blue and music playing through the outdoor speakers in a mockery of the situation we'd woken up in.

"Ace!" I exclaimed, gasping at the sight of him. Stupid fucking us, we'd walked straight into a trap while attempting to fix the power outage. "You son of a bitch! Let him go!"

"Ah-ah-ah, none of that language, Noah," our attacker scolded, clicking his tongue and moving away a couple of steps. "ClikByte is a family platform, after all."

That was when I noticed the tripod and ring light with a phone in the holder. The stranger moved behind the setup to presumably check the angles, and I met Ace's gaze with panic. Why were we still alive? Why was Ace gagged and I wasn't? Who the fuck even was this psychopath?

"Now then, Noah, you refused to heed my warning and reveal your secret yourself, so I feel the need to force the issue. It's unfortunate that Ace had to get hurt, but you were meant to be here alone tonight. Why aren't you alone?"

"You're the troll," I murmured, my brain sluggish with how much pain I was in. "You were at the fan signing, too." That's where I knew him from. I'd been so distracted by Xavier I nearly didn't remember, but it was those awful contacts that jogged my memory.

"Ding ding ding, give the girl a prize!" the crazy guy crowed exuberantly. It was only then that I clicked. *Girl.* Yeah, shit, he really did know my secret.

"Okay, you got me," I said slowly, my heart pounding a million miles an hour in my chest. "Now what?"

He scowled, shaking his head. "No, no, no—you're going to admit to all your lies, Noah. You're going to come clean to *him*," he gestured wildly to Ace, whose eyes were a flood of confusion and worry, "and to all the fans out there. No more secrets."

I scoffed, frantically trying to think of a way out of this mess. Where was our security?

"To all twelve of your followers, you mean?" I taunted, unable to help myself. "I'm sure that will have a huge impact. Have you never heard of coercive confessions? People *lie* under pressure."

The stranger just grinned, way too confident. "My followers? No, don't be silly. This will be live streamed to *your* followers, Noah. All one hundred and twenty-three million of them. You definitely have the reach to make this confession hit hard, coerced or not." He moved back to the phone on the tripod, and I groaned when I recognized it was *my* phone. He must have used my fingerprint to unlock it while I was unconscious. "And action!"

I tightened my lips, refusing to play along. If he wanted to expose my secret, he could do it himself and then PR would discredit it all later.

If we survived, that was.

"Noah, tell your fans your secret," he ordered, glaring at me in absolute hatred. "Tell them what you've been hiding for the last seven weeks of Clik Games. Since your sensationalized face reveal. Tell them!"

From the corner of my eye, Ace shook his head like he was urging me to keep quiet. I couldn't look at him, though, or I'd panic so hard I was likely to black out. The only way I was keeping a clear head was by blocking him out. By not focusing on the dark blood dripping down his handsome face, staining his pale hair.

"Eat a dick," I snapped instead. "And let Ace go. He has nothing to do with this, and you're hurting him. You don't want to hurt him, do you? Your username and your appearance suggests you're a big fan. AceHartsHeart, right?"

The Temu-Ace frowned, uncertainty passing across his face for a moment as his gaze flicked to my team leader. "No, I'm not hurting him," he argued, swinging his glare back to me. "This is your fault. You hurt him, Noah. You're hurting all of them with your lies and deceit. That ends now. Tell Ace your secret. Tell *everyone* your secret. Or you'll kill him."

He pulled out a shockingly long hunting knife from the back of his threadbare pants, bringing the blade to Ace's throat.

Fuck.

My only plan had been to keep him talking long enough that help would arrive. He was live streaming, which meant that surely police had already been notified. If I could just stall him for five freaking minutes, that would be enough. Wouldn't it?

But with a knife at Ace's throat... Well, that changed things.

"Okay," I gasped, shaking my head and frantically tugging at my bound hands. My wrists screamed in pain, and I suspected we were zip-tied. There was a technique for breaking zip-ties, wasn't there? I'd seen a series of viral Bytes about it a couple years ago, teaching girls how to free themselves, but now that I needed it, the information was like smoke.

"Okay?" the knife-wielding man repeated. "Okay, *what*, Noah?"

"Okay, I'll do whatever you want. I'll say whatever you want. I'll quit the team, okay? That's what you wanted, right? You want me to quit Olympus so you can keep the team safe, right? Done. I quit." I wet my lips, my gaze locked on the knife across Ace's throat. It was pressed hard enough that his skin was dented but not broken.

At my words, my promise to quit Team Olympus, the man eased up his blade pressure and moved away from Ace slightly. "No, that's not good enough. You need to *tell him*—"

Right as he started to speak, the music on our outdoor speakers changed to a track with increased volume, Seventeen Daggers's hottest new hit pumping through the pool area in a mockery of our dire situation.

"*Tell him your secret!*" the crazy guy bellowed, his voice booming over the music. "Tell Ace and your fans who you actually are. Noah Fearly. Norah Sparkle. Peaches."

He spat the names at me like bullets, and I flinched with each direct hit.

I couldn't look at Ace. I simply wasn't strong enough to see how that bomb was hitting for the team leader, finally discovering the depth of my deception.

"You think that stripping away the cosmetics and girly outfits is enough to hide? To make a mockery of this team and all the loyal fans?" our attacker spat. "It's not. And now everyone knows who you truly are. A liar. A temptress. A Trojan horse sent to destroy this team from the inside out."

It was foolish of Olympus Corp, of the management teams, and of *me* to think this would never come out. It was utterly stupid of us all to think the reaction wouldn't become steadily worse with every passing day and that the feeling of betrayal for both the team *and* the fans wouldn't end my career.

And here it was. Judgment day.

I had *so many regrets.*

As if pulled by a magnet, my eyes rose from the tiles to lock on Ace's gaze. The shock and betrayal I found staring back at me was even more of a sucker-punch than I'd ever anticipated. When this whole idea was formed, I'd never imagined forming such close bonds with this team. I never in a million years thought I would care if I hurt them or that I'd feel such soul-deep shame for betraying Ace's trust.

It made me want to vomit.

"I'm so sorry, Ace," I whispered, my guts twisted up so hard it physically hurt to speak. "Olympus Corp blackmailed me, and—"

When the music changed to a quieter track, the distant scream of sirens reached us, and I sucked in a breath of anticipation and relief. Help was coming. Could they get here before this asshole killed us, though? Or at least fast enough to save Ace?

"Shit!" the guy exclaimed, stiffening in fear. "That was so fast. Why was that so fast? I should have had longer! This is—argh! Doesn't matter. It's done now, everyone knows who you really are, Noah. Norah. Peaches. Whatever the fuck your name really is. And no amount of crisis management can change that fact."

"Was it worth it?" I sneered. "Was exposing me as a girl really worth spending the rest of your life in jail for attempted murder? Because that's what will happen to you now, you fucking dumbass. There's no scenario in which you actually get away with this crime. You've live streamed your face to my audience and the cops will be here in no time."

Except...would he try to kill us both to make it worth the prison time? Fuck. Maybe poking at him was a bad idea, but I challenge anyone else to make better decisions under this amount of pressure and fear.

"Minutes? That's plenty of time to get away," the Ace-obsessed stalker muttered, glancing around him frantically like he hadn't actually thought out his exit strategy. That one fact made me suspect this *wasn't* the same guy that killed Cat Kay. This asshole wasn't a killer; he was just crazy.

Hope surged in my chest, and I drew a sharp breath. "There's a path down the back of the garden," I told him. "It takes you down to the beach. You could still run if you're fast..."

Crazy guy glanced from me to Ace to the camera—still streaming, I assumed—and back again. Then he nodded quickly as the sirens grew louder. He turned around in several circles like he'd totally lost his bearings on which way to go, and the hope of our survival bloomed stronger within me. He wanted to run, which meant we could be rescued rather than end up in a hostage situation. Or worse.

"That way!" I snapped, jerking my head in the direction of the cliffs. "Fast!"

Our attacker took a confused step, then as if playing out a scene from the worst kind of horror movie, he stumbled and tripped over the corner of a sun lounger. He crashed down hard on his hip, crying out in pain and dropping his knife. But then as I watched, helpless and horrified, he lurched to the side as he tried to regain his footing and knocked straight into Ace, still gagged and bound to a chair.

"Ace!" I screamed as his chair fell and his head smacked against the edge of the pool with a sickening crunch.

"Oh fuck!" the clumsy villain exclaimed, scrambling to his feet as Ace's chair toppled over the edge and disappeared into the pool with a gagged, bound, and unconscious Ace bleeding from two head wounds.

I screamed again, wordless in my terror as he sank beneath the surface.

The sirens were louder but not loud enough. Our attacker was gone, and I didn't even care if he was caught or fell off the cliff and died. All that mattered was that Ace would be dead in minutes—or less. And no one was here to save him...except me.

His expression from just moments ago flashed through my head. That *hurt* he'd displayed to find I'd played him, and the utter disappointment. I couldn't just sit by and let him die. I couldn't live with myself if he didn't make it out alive...

Sobbing and screaming for help—on the off chance someone might hear—I yanked against my wrist bonds with *all* my strength. To my shock, they loosened. I did it again, and they loosened further, enough to let me squeeze my hands out.

Gasping relief but still choking on terror, I threw my weight forward to knock my chair over and reached out to snag the hunting knife that the crazy guy had dropped. I sliced through my ankle bonds with zero regard for my own skin, cutting deeply through my left ankle and barely registering the pain as I kicked free of the chair and pushed my knees under myself.

Ace was still underwater.

How long had it been? Seconds? Minutes? Was he already dead?

I had to try. Ace Hart deserved to live. He had too much love, support, and encouragement to give to the world.

Pushing all my fear aside, I tried to focus on the only emotion—or hormone—that'd ever served me well. Pure adrenaline flooded through me, and I cast aside my own sense of survival, drawing a huge breath, and diving headfirst into the pool to rescue Ace.

The moment water engulfed me, I realized I may have made a mistake.

Some emotions, some traumas, were simply too strong for even adrenaline to drown out.

TO BE CONTINUED IN BUBBLES - CLIKBYTE BOOK #2

EXPLORE MORE TATE JAMES WITH HER DARK ACADEMIA DEVIL'S BACKBONE SOCIETY SERIES. READ ON FOR A LOOK AT

Dear Reader, if you've found this diary, then I must be dead. That's the only way I'd have let anyone find this account of what's been happening to me. What they've put me through. What they're <u>still</u> putting me through.

If you're reading this...then I'm dead and the Devil's Backbone Society is responsible. You, whoever you are, will probably be next.

I should probably start at the beginning, so you have context for what I record next, so you can understand how they fooled me for so long and how I ended up where I am now. Probably dead. Definitely dead, because you, dear reader, have found my journal. I swore that if they let me live, I'd destroy any evidence against them...

Because of where I plan to hide this book, you must be a student at Nevaeh University. I was too. When I got awarded the Mariah Greenberg Scholarship, I thought I'd won the lottery. All my dreams were going to come true at Nevaeh. How utterly wrong I was.

The first time I heard about the Devil's Backbone Society was a month after the school year started. I was at a party with my friends, beside Lake Prosper, and overheard some girls whispering about "initiation" and speculating on who would be chosen. The criteria for selection seemed to be obvious. Wealthy, influential, beautiful—only the best were invited to join. But then apparently, each year a few extras were chosen at random. Cannon-fodder, the girls called them.

Someone died. No one will talk about it, and when I tried to ask my TA what had happened, she shushed me very abruptly. All I know is that a girl named Sarah Black supposedly jumped off Cat's Peak at midnight. But if it was unrelated to the DB Society, why is everyone pretending it never happened? Or worse than that, they're pretending she never existed at all. It's creepy, and knowing now what I know of their initiation...I'm 100 percent convinced she was pushed.

You've probably already guessed by now, the DB Society selected me as one of their supposedly "random" initiates this year. Just a week after Sarah Black's so-called suicide on Cat's Peak, they grabbed me on my way to the dining hall for dinner. Someone put a bag over my head, and I was manhandled into a van. For far too long, I genuinely thought I was going to die. I didn't...obviously. Otherwise, I wouldn't be writing this account now. But that first initiation made me realize I needed to start writing things down...just in case I ended up like Sarah. Like I probably have, if you're reading this now.

Shit. If you're reading this...please don't end up like me. Be smarter than I was and <u>don't trust anyone</u>.

ABOUT THE AUTHOR

Tate James is a *USA Today* bestselling author of contemporary romance and romantic suspense, with occasional forays into fantasy, paranormal romance, and urban fantasy. She was born and raised in Aotearoa (New Zealand) but now lives in Australia with her husband and their adorable crotchfruit.

She is a lover of books, booze, cats, and coffee, and is most definitely not a morning person. Tate is a bit too sarcastic, swears far too much for polite society, and definitely tells too many dirty jokes.

Website: tatejamesauthor.com
Facebook: tatejamesauthor
Instagram: @tatejamesauthor
TikTok: @tatejamesauthor
Pinterest: @tatejamesauthor
Mailing list: eepurl.com/dfFR5v